The Vanishing Point

Paul Theroux is the author of many highly acclaimed books. His novels include *Burma Sahib*, *The Bad Angel Brothers*, *The Lower River*, *Jungle Lovers* and *The Mosquito Coast*, and his renowned travel books include *Ghost Train to the Eastern Star*, *On the Plain of Snakes* and *Dark Star Safari*. He lives in Hawaii and on Cape Cod.

ALSO BY PAUL THEROUX

PAUL THEROUX

The Vanishing Point

STORIES

HAMISH HAMILTON
an imprint of
PENGUIN BOOKS

HAMISH HAMILTON

UK I USA I Canada I Ireland I Australia
India I New Zealand I South Africa

Hamish Hamilton is part of the Penguin Random House group of companies
whose addresses can be found at global.penguinrandomhouse.com

Penguin Random House UK,
One Embassy Gardens, 8 Viaduct Gardens, London sw11 7bw

penguin.co.uk

First published in the United States of America by Mariner Books,
an imprint of HarperCollins Publishers LLC 2025
First published in Great Britain by Hamish Hamilton 2025

001

Printed and bound in Great Britain by Clays Ltd, Elcograf S.p.A.

The authorized representative in the eea is Penguin Random House Ireland,
Morrison Chambers, 32 Nassau Street, Dublin d02 yh68

A cip catalogue record for this book is available from the British Library

HARDBACK ISBN: 978–0–241–56775–3
TRADE PAPERBACK ISBN: 978–0–241–56776–0

Penguin Random House is committed to a sustainable future
for our business, our readers and our planet. This book is made from
Forest Stewardship Council® certified paper.

A great calm stole over him. Great calm is an exaggeration. He felt better. The end of a life is always vivifying.

    —Samuel Beckett, *Malone Dies*

Contents

Aide-Mémoires

THE VANISHING POINT

In the bewilderment of being an only child on his parents' failing chicken farm in Maine, his face fixed in a scowl for being nagged at, Guy Petit experienced the day of his greatest happiness. He was nine.

"We have to drive to Waldoboro for Sarah Strunk's funeral," his mother said. "You'll be okay on your own."

Then they were gone, the house was still, its odors stronger in its emptiness. He sat as though bathed in light, serene in the stillness, smiling at his luck, in the rapture of solitude. It was as though he had been swallowed whole.

He did not want anything more than to be contained by that bliss, spared the disruption of the human voice. You couldn't see the future, so there was no point looking. For some years he waited for a return to such happiness. After high school, other boys got jobs as sternmen on lobster boats, or in the paper mills or other farms; and the girls got married or worked the cash registers at Osier's. Guy joined the navy, to be far from home.

His father died in the barn with a hayfork in his hand while Guy was on maneuvers at Subic Bay. The man was a smoker and asthmatic and had always coughed in choking and suffocating fits; coughed his life out was how Guy imagined it.

In the navy Guy learned pipe fitting, and later deep-sea diving—underwater repairs on ships' hulls. His ready "Aye, sir," his willingness to take on deep dives, several with faulty gear, led to a ruptured eardrum, a diagnosis of serious hearing loss, and an early discharge. Disability payments allowed him to earn a degree in history in Orono; but preferring to work with his hands, he opted for a job as a carpenter and a welder. He kept his mind active by reading, mostly biography and military history. During the day he wore a hearing aid in the damaged ear.

When his mother moved with Bud Strunk to a trailer park in Bradenton, Florida, Guy relocated to Water Street in Ellsworth, where he lived as a lodger with a woman called Mrs. Semple and her three children. He traveled each day to work full-time in the Bar Harbor studio of the artist Elliott Stanger.

Stanger had hired him as a carpenter. Guy made frames, stretched canvases, built crates for shipping pictures to galleries, and now and then manned the paint sprayer, drenching the canvases with color, Stanger looking on, usually squinting through his own cigarette smoke at the images he had planned now soaking and swelling on the cloth.

"This is my handyman," Stanger told visitors who came to see his work. The studio's interior, as big as a barn, was once the Elks Lodge and had been renovated by Guy under Stanger's direction. It was now a great, warm, yellow-painted space, with a cathedral ceiling and skylights, Stanger's latest finished paintings hanging along two walls, drying.

The area occupying one corner some visitors mistook for a partitioned parlor, or den, because of the old sofa, and easy chair, and a one-armed bandit, with a slot for nickels, that rang when its arm was yanked, sometimes delivering a clatter of coins into the cup in front. But just out of sight, beyond a smeared and spattered curtain, a steel frame, the shelves of paint cans, the sprayer, the spools of masking tape, and on another rack, the thick roll of pale raw canvas.

"So this is where you work your magic," visitors said, when Stanger suggested his method of painting, adding that it was too emotional a process for him to go into any detail.

Stanger's thick hair was tousled as though in defiance. He usually wore a spotless, untucked shirt, blue jeans and espadrilles, while Guy would be standing by with Mack Spinney, the other assistant, and it was they who were spattered, their aprons stiff with paint, streaks on the toes of their shoes.

The only secret to carpentry, Guy said, was having the right tool. "That's a five-sixteenth," he'd say of a nut, selecting a socket wrench. He was proud of his assortment of tools, which he kept in trays and steel chests and on hooks in Mrs. Semple's garage. If he found a broken object, he could always devise a way to fix it.

What he knew of modern art was what Stanger had told him, that figurative painting was obsolete, Picasso was a con man. Only pure color mattered, Stanger offering his own work as an example, his horizontal stripes and perfect circles—ribbons and targets.

Guy told the facts of his life and his work—family, navy, diving, deafness, college, carpentry—to Tony Semple, who was sixteen and full of questions, because Tony was wondering what his own life might be. And Guy, though still only twenty-nine, was like an uncle to Tony and the younger children, too, Adreth and Small Bob, less a lodger than an affectionate friend to the family.

Guy paid rent and had his own room upstairs in the Water Street house, his window facing the river. Six months into his renting, Mrs. Semple knocked on his door. He was in bed, a biography of Joshua Chamberlain propped on his chest. Mrs. Semple grasped the book and said, "You'll ruin your eyes."

Surrendering the book, Guy said, "What time is it?"

Mrs. Semple latched the door. "The kids are in bed. Tony's with his father. It's raining. The tide's up." With these pronouncements she seemed to put herself in charge, but Guy (his hearing aid on the bedside table) had not understood a word. His deaf, questioning look was always a smile.

She sat on the edge of Guy's bed, her hands in her lap, and shimmied closer, slightly crushing him. Then she reached for the lamp and switched it off. She was naked when she slipped under the covers.

"Hold me, Guy. Just a cuddle."

He was soothed by the sight of the rain on the window, diamond-like in the light of the streetlamps, and—though it had been years since the navy—he remembered the young woman with fragrant hair in the hotel bedroom in Olongapo, kneeling to help him untie his shoes. With Mrs. Semple he was reminded that a woman's buttocks, no matter how smooth, are always unexpectedly cool to the touch, a different temperature from her lips.

The pleasure, the relief, the satisfaction that he was useful helped Guy overcome his nervousness with Mrs. Semple that first time. She was out of bed as he lay gasping and gone before he found the nerve to speak. The next day, stammering to thank her, she shushed him and turned her back. But there were more times, always late at night, sudden, brief. She clapped herself to him, and he returned the embrace with gusto, as though saving her from a bad fall.

"I'm getting fat," Mrs. Semple said, one morning in the kitchen, seeing him off. The children were at school, but even so Guy approached her cautiously as though they were being observed.

Guy said, "I'll love you as long as I can get both my arms around you."

Instead of replying, Mrs. Semple made a pushing motion with one hand, indicating that he should go, and covered her face with her other hand, tears seeping from between her fingers.

He was privately strengthened in ways that shocked him. In one dream he stood, his feet apart, his hands on his hips, and wore a pistol, saying to a reporter, *That man believed that he could break into my house, terrorize my wife, and intimidate me, and still leave my house alive.*

"I don't do op art," Stanger said in a scolding way one day when Mack Spinney used the term.

And Guy, relieved that he had not said it, listened carefully, because he had wondered what you'd call what they were making.

"It's color-field painting," Stanger said. Seeing Mack Spinney squint at the words, he added, "It's flat. It's meditative."

When Spinney murmured later, confiding to Guy, "Everything's got a name. Even this flat stuff we do," Guy went hot with guilt, as though he'd been disloyal.

Earlier that day, Stanger had said, "This one's no good. Get rid of it," which had provoked Spinney saying, "I guess you'd call this op art."

Wearing masks against the fumes, they toiled in the big studio, spraying between the templates on the stretched canvas that lay tightened on the upright rack, Stanger issuing orders. They used wide paint rollers, too, pushing color between measured lengths of tape, saturating the cloth.

Linear painting, bands of color, some thick, some narrow, some pencil-thin, none intersecting, none overlapping, sprayed over an off-white background.

Target paintings, concentric circles, different combinations of color, separated by the pale background, always with a bull's-eye, a round clot of color.

Chevrons another year, slanted stripes meeting at sharp angles, different colors, some of the stripes with a hairline margin of gold as a highlight. These Guy loved to make, because they reminded him of navy badges he knew, a petty officer's red chevrons, master chief's gold ones. Chevrons were like rafters, too, the carpentry in ceilings, like slanted planks in the eaves of the cathedral ceiling in Stanger's own studio. These chevrons, more than the others, seemed to contain a meaning, but an obscure one; and Guy was glum when they went back to circles.

"Circles sell better," Mack said, another murmur, and Guy, flustered, wished he hadn't heard. But who bought them? What did they cost? What did people do with them?

"I see spatter," Stanger said. He demanded hard lines. "Get rid of it."

Guy, who never threw anything away that he thought might come in handy, rolled the rejected canvases into tubes and took them home.

"What's it supposed to be?" Small Bob would ask, and Tony, too, would wait for the answer.

"A painting," Guy said. "It's a Stanger."

"More like a drop cloth," Tony said. These days he was an apprentice in construction down the coast.

"A work of art," Guy said.

"Why are you laughing?" Small Bob said.

"Because I did it. Or most of it."

An illustration on an oil-company calendar in the studio depicted a young man in a suit and tie waiting for a train on a railway platform. Guy had often stared at the picture, trying to imagine from his posture, the mood of the man. Going home? Going away? He was alone, his duffel bag at his feet, the sort of bag Guy had used when he'd joined the navy.

Mack drew Guy's attention to the railway tracks, the way they narrowed in the distance.

"That's your vanishing point," Mack said, putting his blue-paint-splashed finger on the uppermost part of the tweezed-together tracks. "Gives you some idea of depth and perspective, which the boss"—he glanced behind him—"don't approve of."

"It's a point," Guy said, reassured that Stanger had left the studio. "It doesn't really vanish. It's just that you can't see what's beyond it. It's not invisible. It's unreadable. A mystery."

"Anyway it's a real picture," Mack said later, when they were stretching one of Stanger's canvases. These canvases they stacked against the wall, in various stages of saturation.

"Could be a mystery to this one," Guy said of some chevrons. "Something coming that we can't see."

They worked longer hours these days in the studio, to keep up, because Stanger was away more often, in New York, and left instructions for Guy and Mack to prepare canvases for his arrival.

"The assembly line," Mack said.

As always, Guy glanced around, fearing they might be overheard in their mockery, though it was always Mack who was the mocker.

On one of his arrivals back in the studio, Stanger had Guy and Mack gift wrap a big painting in sparkly paper and a red ribbon. "This is a first," Mack said. They crated it, sending it to an address in New York City of a catalog company.

"Boss is going to be in a catalog," Guy said.

"You don't read too good," Mack said. "It's going to Babe Brickman."

"Brickman Catalog it says."

"She's the catalog. See? 'President and CEO.' Stanger's on the hunt."

Stanger began shaving, though he kept his hair tousled. He was sixty-seven, an old man to Guy, but that he might be wooing a woman made Guy hopeful and happy. Stanger's wardrobe improved, silk shirts, a cravat, a Panama hat on warmer days.

One Friday in late spring Stanger arrived in Bar Harbor in the driver's seat of a sports car, a convertible, a woman beside him. She was small, child-size almost, and wore a large blue hat the blossom shape of a lampshade, and goggle-like sunglasses. When Stanger pulled up in front of the studio, Guy hurried out to help. He saw the woman struggling with the door handle, hitching herself forward in her effort.

Guy extended his hand.

"Don't touch me," the woman said from under her hat.

"Grab the bags," Stanger said.

"They're in the boot," the woman said.

"Like—all of them—in a boot?" Mack asked. He laughed at the image in his mind.

But by then Guy had lifted the trunk lid to find the bags crammed into the small space.

Now the woman had managed to jiggle the door open and, stepping out, she tipped her head back to survey the building, piercing it with a possessive gaze. "Those curtains have to go," she said. Her scrutiny of the building revealed the uplifted face beneath her hat brim. It was a girl's face, but crumpled, a painted-on mouth fixed in a frown, severe in concentration, and when the woman tugged down her sunglasses to see better she widened her deep blue eyes and Guy thought, *Lovely.*

"This is Babe," Stanger said in his friendly drawl.

"But you can call me Miss Brickman." She turned her back and hurried into the building.

Stanger lingered to say, "Like the car? Babe gave it to me for my birthday."

"Wicked nice," Mack said.

Stanger and Miss Brickman spent the weekend at his house overlooking the harbor. Although Sunday was his day off, Guy agreed to drive over from Ellsworth to the studio, to slide finished paintings out of the storage racks for Miss Brickman to see. The larger ones he propped against the wall, the smaller ones he put on easels.

Miss Brickman sat on a sling chair, murmuring in approval, nibbling an earpiece of her sunglasses.

"This is one of my personal favorites," Guy said. "Chevrons."

He wanted to say more—what chevrons meant to him, the navy, rafters, the bones of a house. He also wanted to convey to Stanger and the woman newly in his life that he had not minded leaving Mrs. Semple and the children on a Sunday to drive over to Bar Harbor.

"You might have one of these in your future," Stanger said.

Before Stanger had finished speaking, Miss Brickman stamped her foot and sighed, folding her arms in impatience.

Guy smiled, thinking, *I've already got thirty, the ones I was told to get rid of.*

That was the first Brickman visit. On the second weekend visit a month later, to show his goodwill, Guy indicated the broken strap on Miss Brickman's handbag and said, "I could fix that for you. I've got just the right size awl. A five-ten, fine point. I use it on bridles."

Miss Brickman clutched the bag and held it to her chest, as you would from a thief. The leather was like soft rich cloth in her anxious fingers, with the pebble-grain of orange peel. The bag was a remarkable color, lime green, and the broken strap its only flaw.

"This bag is probably worth more than you make in a year."

Elliott Stanger and Babe Brickman were married that September, four months after "Don't touch me." The service was held on Stanger's lawn, the reception at the studio, which was converted to a Stanger show, the walls covered with his paintings. Mack tended bar, Guy was a waiter in a suit borrowed from Tony, one with shiny lapels he'd bought for the Ellsworth Prom's Grand March. Guy offered trays of hors d'oeuvres, tidied tables, emptied bins, and assisted the caterers who said they were shorthanded. He said nothing; he listened to "hottest restaurant" and "Her third—possibly her fourth. She's buried two of them."

The people widened their eyes as they chewed, showing their hunger, like monkey hunger in a cage at feeding time. Watching them killed Guy's appetite.

"You'll be all right," Mack said to Guy after they arrived back from their honeymoon. "I heard the boss saying how much he depends on you."

"Who was he talking to, exactly?"

"The little woman."

Probably, Guy reasoned, because they were preparing for a show in New

York, at a new gallery: a lot of paintings to stretch and frame, crates to be made, late nights, making Guy eager for news of the show. But when Stanger returned, the two men met on the front stairs. Without any preamble, Stanger said, "I'm going to have to let you go."

Guy thought he'd misheard—often the crackle in his hearing aid misled him. So he smiled, hoping for clarification.

Stanger was tearful. He snatched at his hair and in an anguished voice said, "I don't know how I'm going to manage without you."

"After all you've done for him," Mrs. Semple said.

She held him in her arms. But her caresses went no further.

"And it's come at kind of an inconvenient time," Mrs. Semple said, still holding him, seeming to prop him up.

Guy leaned back and smiled at her, looking sadder in his smile.

"I've met someone," she said. "Adreth and Small Bob are going with me to Waterville. Tony's moving in with his girlfriend. Says he wants to start a business. Renovations."

"That's great you met someone," Guy said. "You'll be happy. And the kids will be happy, Adreth's at that age."

Adreth was sixteen now and sulky and often stayed out late with her friends. She was a beauty, with piercings—eyebrow, nostril—and a tattoo she'd gotten at a party, a bird on the back of her neck, usually hidden by her green-tinted hair. She sprawled when she sat, and she yawned constantly.

"You could get a place of your own, Guy," Mrs. Semple said. "It's time, you being—what?—thirty-six."

"Eight."

"Find somewhere for your books, and those tools and drop cloths. Maybe bunk with Lane Frater."

Lane Frater was a quilter, a friend of Mrs. Semple from the garden club. At Mrs. Semple's suggestion, Guy had sometimes repaired his loom. Lane was black and flamboyant. He made most of his own clothes, colorful ones, red trousers, a fitted purple vest, and sometimes on chilly days a poncho of his own weaving.

Lane's art—quilted and sometimes woven hangings—looked to Guy like hall carpets or area rugs, rectangles with stark patterns stitched into them, wide stripes or cubes picked out in contrasting wool. Lane said that as an African American, quilting was part of his heritage.

"Stanger would be interested in these," Guy said once on a repair visit. "He's color mad, like you."

"He's a bubble reputation, if you ask me."

"He got married not all that long ago," Guy said, to deflect the mockery.

"I pity her," Lane said. "I used to see his first wife at AA meetings. Golly, she had a tale to tell. My lips are sealed!"

"I've always meant to drop in to one of those meetings sometime. Not that I have an issue. Just for the experience."

"I have an issue. More than one. I say it straight out. 'I'm Lane. I'm black. I'm gay. I'm an alcoholic. I'm sixty years old. Plus, I smoke too much.'"

Guy tried not to show surprise. He was working on the loom all this time they were talking. A crack in the upright, Lane explained, affected the head roller, and in response to Lane's outburst, Guy said, "Making a spline here."

Seeing Guy step away from his work, Lane tramped on the treadles and the roller held, the threads meeting and lacing.

"Perfect," Lane said, pushing with the heel of his hand. He was wearing fingerless wool gloves. Then he turned to Guy and said, "May Semple says you adore chocolate."

"Can't get enough of it," Guy said.

"This is for you," Lane said. He brought his hands from behind his back and gave Guy a candy bar.

After that, whenever Lane needed a tree cut down, or branches trimmed, or the lawnmower repaired, he called Guy, who did the work while Lane talked, often stories of recklessness related to his having been a waiter in Key West. And when the work was complete, Lane said, "I know what you want," presenting a candy bar with the same ceremonial gesture. Two candy bars on the day of the snowstorm, when Guy shoveled Lane's driveway, an all-day job.

Nevertheless, Guy felt that he had a friend, and after Mrs. Semple told him that she was moving to Waterville, he visited Lane and asked whether he had any work for him.

"I'm dusting and rearranging. I need help moving the wing chair."

With the chair in his arms, Guy said, "I need a place to stay. Mrs. Ess found a fella."

"There's my attic," Lane said. "You'd have to do some renovation. Bring it up to code."

Guy fashioned a new stairway, building it against the wall like a ship's vertical ladder. He roughed out a room, the slanted roof giving it the sloping walls of a pup tent; insulated it, lined it with drywall. The window in the eave looked onto the cove. Though the room was smaller than the one at Mrs. Semple's there was space for some of his books, and Lane's shed held most of his tools.

"This is for you," Lane said, each day offering Guy a candy bar. And when Guy had finished and moved in, Lane said, "I hope you'll forgive me for being a wicked, greedy old beast."

Guy smiled at Lane's extravagant words, thinking: *He is flamboyant. He is not afraid.*

"It's a little question of rent. See, I never had to heat the attic before, but now that it's a proper room, and you're in it, I have to crank up the oil burner. That means more oil."

"I didn't expect to live here free," Guy said.

They agreed on an amount, Guy inhabited the cubbyhole, and to raise money for rent he advertised in the *Uncle Henry's Weekly*, offering himself as an odd-job man ("Old High School Kid," his ad was titled) for tree cutting and disposal, carpentry and—as he had a gas-powered wood splitter—splitting logs for winter woodstoves.

"High school kids used to do these jobs. They don't anymore. I'm the high school kid."

And at night, in bed reading, that was how he felt, but much happier than he had felt as a high school student, and he always had work.

He saw Mack Spinney at the Depot Grille now and then. Mack said, "The boss misses you. Says his work has suffered."

"How's the wife?"

"She's a dragon, but she's selling his stuff."

Seeing how well Guy went about the odd jobs, the person who had hired him would think of three more jobs to be done—a broken hinge, a wobbly table, a cracked pane of glass, a loose downspout, an errand to run—and would then recommend him to others.

"Some sort of leak in my chimney," a woman said.

"Loose flashing." Guy was calling down from a ladder. "Plates need to be replaced and soldered. I've got a rivet gun and a soldering iron."

Fall wood splitting became winter shoveling, then spring-cleaning, and summer mowing. Guy kept to his upper corner of Lane's house, in the nest he had made in the attic, which was always warmer than the rest of the house, being small and high.

"You're the only person who's warm here," Lane said, his bobble hat showing above the ship's ladder. "It's toasty here."

Back when Guy was only lending a hand, Lane had seemed cheery, bright and confident, always quick with a smart remark as he presented Guy with a candy bar, grateful for Guy's help in fixing something, or when he was seated at his loom. But as a tenant, Guy saw that Lane had many down days, when he stayed in bed, lying on his side; that his smile was a mask; that he was often resentful in the left-behind mood of melancholic people.

Guy's burden—which he saw as his duty—was to encourage Lane in believing he was a wit, and a tease, never mentioning the days in bed, maintaining the illusion that Lane was strong, even when Lane lay like a dead man.

"You're an artist," Guy said. "You're creative. You can make things."

"But you're handy," Lane said, without force.

"I can't make much. I mainly fix things."

Lane said, "True. That's a crucial distinction."

Lane was weak, he was helpless, he was lonely. "Let's talk—you're not going to read all night, are you?" Lane didn't read. He said that smoking had killed his sex drive. "But I'm glad to be without it. I'm not a dog anymore. And I know I have a lot to offer."

Insisting he was happy sometimes drove him to spells of uncontrollable sobbing, his gray face shining with tears, his chin dripping.

"I get these crying jags, Guy."

"It's because you're the sensitive type."

"My mother used to tell me that," Lane would say, touching his wet face in wonderment and renewed pride. "'Just be fabulous' she said."

"Fabulous doesn't always work in Maine," Guy said. "Me, I guess I just have a tougher skin."

Guy knew he wasn't tough. "You'll get no argument from me," he'd say, or the useful, "You might well be right!"

Paid in candy bars! But he reasoned, Lane is mean with money. He can't help it. His incessant calculation made him miserable. Guy wondered: How do you become like that? He did not know, so would not judge him.

Guy had never thought of happiness as a goal but only of the contentment of having enough. As a child he'd thought of his future as unknown and imponderable. "Let's see what happens." He had never reflected on what would become of him; and as an adult he did not look ahead to the secrets that lay in the vanishing point. He was grateful for every moment of calm, and at the end of each day considered it a victory to have lived through a day without disturbance, safely back in his narrow bed, with a book on the go.

He did not think about the next morning, and most nights he did not dream. He was grateful to wake in sunlight and the warmth of the attic room. He earned just enough to pay the rent to Lane, to fuel his pickup truck, to buy food—simple meals in Lane's kitchen—eggs, noodles, mac and cheese, beans, soup; and in return for using the kitchen he tidied it, did Lane's dishes, scrubbed the sink, mopped the floor.

"You're so good to me," Lane said.

"It's only fair."

Mrs. Gerwig, a widow, was one of Guy's regular customers. He mowed her lawn, trimmed her trees, reshingled her shed, ran errands, cleared the sink trap: simple jobs. She was not old, she went for brisk walks, she was sinewy and strong, but Guy saw impatience in her treadmill-like stride.

"What do you do with yourself?" she asked him. "When you're on your own?"

"I guess a lot of reading."

Mrs. Gerwig tried not to smile, as though he'd confessed a weakness.

Sensing her discomfort, Guy added, "History and biography mostly."

"What are you reading now?"

"The life of Alexander von Humboldt."

Mrs. Gerwig winced a little at the words.

"Met Thomas Jefferson. Tangled with electric eels. He was all over South America. Stopped in Acapulco, too. He named ten species of animals, and lots of flowers. Kind of lonely, though. Never married." He paused, because Mrs. Gerwig had only breathed and not said anything. "German."

Bewildered by the information, but impressed as a consequence of her bewilderment, Mrs. Gerwig invited Guy for a meal the following Sunday at the East Wind.

"I've never been here before."

"But you were born here."

"Oh, yes, I've passed by this place many a time."

She talked, glancing around the room at the other diners, and with his bad ear to her he had trouble following. He missed whatever had led up to her saying, "People here always complain about his philandering. Yet I have considered having an affair with the president. Out of respect for the First Lady I would have to turn him down, though."

Guy was never more silent than when someone talked a lot, and he nursed a hope that the person would become self-conscious and stop. But it seldom happened, silence seemed to make them garrulous. Once she asked him an odd question.

"Does it seem strange to you that we're eating together and yet you work for me in a menial capacity?"

"I was in the navy almost six years," Guy said. "Based in San Diego, then Subic Bay. Then a supply ship off Danang. After all that nothing seems strange to me."

She clapped her hands at his certainty.

Guy smiled. He said, "Or Idries Shah."

"In English, please."

"He said that when you realize the difference between the container and the content you will have knowledge."

She screwed up one eye as though questioning him and then smiled and said, "I'm going to call you 'Ghee' in the French way."

"It's butter in India. Ghee."

Mrs. Gerwig had raised a fork full of fish to her mouth, but she put it back on her plate and stared at him.

"Mentioned by Gandhi in *My Experiments with Truth*."

"What were they, the experiments?"

"I suppose you could say his marrying his wife, Kasturba, when they were both thirteen was an experiment." He saw that Mrs. Gerwig was still staring. "It was a marriage in every sense of the word."

On a day when he was retiling Mrs. Gerwig's downstairs bathroom, she suggested going out for pizza for lunch. "My treat," Guy said. All through the meal he was uncomfortable, wondering whether he'd have enough money to pay for it; he excused himself and in the men's room counted the money in his wallet, but he continued to worry.

"What happened to Von Humboldt?" Mrs. Gerwig asked when he returned.

"I've done with him. I'm reading *Andersonville*."

Cocking her head, and eyeing him carefully, as though he'd lapsed into another language, Mrs. Gerwig seemed to be asking for more.

"It was squalor, it was mayhem. One of the many disgraces of the war."

"Which war was that?"

Guy was embarrassed for her that she did not know. To spare her, he said, "I'll tell you all about it sometime," and when the bill came and he realized he had the money to pay it, he became jaunty. Mrs. Gerwig said, "You've got a lot of pep!'

That week, Lane said in his teasing singsong, "You've been seeing that Betty Gerwig woman."

"Just a friend."

"She's a widow, you know. One of the hungry ones. She'll eat you alive."

Another time, also at the pizza restaurant—perhaps she chose this place because Guy could afford it—she tapped his sleeve and said, "That stitching is so intricate."

"Tore it on a ratchet. Just simple sewing," Guy said. "If you have a darning egg and the right needle, it's easy. Shirt's too good to use for rags." Mrs. Gerwig said nothing, so he continued. "I like patching an inner tube—I love the smell of glue. Changing my own oil, mending things."

"I usually throw things away when they're broken. It's so cheap to replace them."

He suspected she despised him for his frugality, but he felt that in small ways like this, keepings things, fixing them, you could help change the world.

On the weekend of the Lobster Festival, Mrs. Gerwig and Guy strolled among the stalls. Guy spent his last twenty dollars on two orders of lobster, corn, and steamers.

They took their plates to a picnic table by the harbor, away from the shouts of children and the jazz band, and ate looking at the moored sailboats, all facing the same way, big and small, their backs to the noise of the festival.

The way Mrs. Gerwig held her ear of corn in both hands, turning it against her teeth and chewing, brought to mind, *She'll eat you alive*. Putting the bitten cob down, Mrs. Gerwig dabbed her lips with the back of her hand. She said, "Where exactly is this going?"

Guy tapped his hearing aid, as he sometimes did to give himself time to think of a reply, pressing the earpiece as though to clarify what he had just heard.

"I like being your friend," he said finally.

Mrs. Gerwig found a seagull to stare at and followed its alighting near a trash barrel to stab at a stained pizza box with its beak. She folded her plate, enclosing the last of the lobster, and dropped it into the barrel—the seagull taking flight.

At her house, she said, "I need to be alone for a while," and slid out, leaving the door ajar.

Guy walked to her side of the truck and, as he closed the door, saw her mounting her new front steps. He had built the steps and painted them. He had used glue on each tread just before driving in the screws, so that they would never squeak or loosen. He was pleased to see that they were solid under her departing feet.

Where exactly is this going? was the big question. But Guy had no answer. Losing Mrs. Gerwig as a customer was bearable, but it pained him to lose her as a friend, especially as he'd felt he'd hurt her. Running into her at the post office or Hannaford's would now be awkward.

The following Saturday, as he feared, he saw her exiting the post office. He hurried to hold the door open for her. She walked past him without speaking, her confusion giving her a lopsided gait.

The jobs were fewer when the summer people departed, leaving a shoreline of empty houses and dock floats dragged onto lawns. Within a month Guy was behind on his rent.

Lane said, "I hate to say this, Guy . . ."

He stood at his loom, wearing his fingerless mittens and a woolen skullcap and his Peruvian waistcoat, and he reminded Guy of the cost of heating oil.

Guy said, "I've got an idea."

The idea, which had come to him in the night, had to do with his trove of books. What was the point of keeping books he had no intention of rereading? Books on a shelf in a room were meaningless trophies, gathering dust. But they had value.

He filled three large boxes of books—a third of his collection—and took them to a bookstore in Bar Harbor. But when he carried the first box into the store the owner looked alarmed.

"Don't unpack it," he said. "I'll have a look."

Guy wanted to say—as a greeting, as a boast—that many of the books were ones he'd bought in the used section of that same store. But the man was digging into the box, frowning in distaste, pushing the books aside.

"They're really no good to me at all," the man said, going deeper into the box. "Most of these you can buy for a penny on the internet, if you pay the postage."

"Mainly biography," Guy said, as if he had not heard. "Churchill. Roosevelt. Lord Salisbury. Some war history. Fall of Singapore."

"What's that?" the man said, plucking out a glossy pamphlet.

"Elliott Stanger catalog. One of the New York shows. It's signed."

"Twenty dollars," the man said. "Any other signed material?"

"Plenty, by former owners."

"I'd advise you to donate these to the library. They'll give you a printed receipt to use for a tax write-off."

Guy chuckled, thinking he had no income to report, no taxes to pay. He took the books to the prison in Thomaston and left them just inside the

door, where, without speaking, a duty officer indicated, pointing his trun-
cheon. Back at his attic room Guy heard a knock on the ladder and saw
Lane's head. But Lane held on, just his head above the level of the attic floor.

"Guy—you're a friend, you've been very good to me, you've been perfect,
really . . ."

Such praise always came before a "but." To forestall it, and to save Lane
from embarrassment, Guy said, "I have another idea."

It was to sell some of his tools. They had more value than books, yet to contemplate selling them was like facing an amputation. The wood splitter was
worth a lot, and he knew a possible buyer, a man who had complimented him
on the machine when he had split a cord of wood for him.

"Alvin's not home," the man's wife said.

Driving back to Lane's, Guy was relieved. And perhaps it was a sign, because when he arrived at Lane's he had a message.

Tony, now a contractor, had left a number for Guy to call.

"I need a roofer," Tony said.

I'm a carpenter, Guy had always said with pride, because woodworking was
a trade of precise measurements and visible symmetries, and sometimes it was
an art form. Cutting and fitting wood required both skill and an aesthetic
sense. Wood had a lovely odor, certain woods smelled edible, the tang of pine,
the resinous aroma of oak, apple and pear trees—fruitwood; and the complex
grain, the variety of hues. All other materials were inartistic—canvas, metal,
plastic, asphalt shingles, composites without pith or sap or veins.

"I'm your man," Guy said.

"Maybe better not tell the crew that we used to know each other," Tony said,
when Guy showed up at the house in progress down the coast in Camden.

Guy nodded and thought, *Yes, it will give Tony more authority*.

The job down the coast in Camden was renovating a bulky square-
shouldered oceanfront house with gables and a wide porch, white cedar shingles on the sides of the house and, to Guy's delight, red cedar shingles on the
roof. Red cedar was another fleshlike wood that gave off a spicy smack when
it was sawed.

"How much exposure does he want?" Guy asked.

But Tony, who knew little of roofing, didn't understand the question until Guy laid out a sequence of shingles on the tailgate of his pickup truck and showed him the varying depths of overlap.

"This inch-and-a-half exposure can take more weather," Guy said. "Lasts longer. And you want to install battens to help them breathe."

On the roof later that day Guy heard Tony explaining to the owner, "It's an inch-and-a-half exposure. I've designed it so that it can take more weather," and Guy was proud of him for his poise. Tony always was a quick study, he thought.

Guy supervised the roofers but he used the nail gun, too, and worked until dark most days, until the job was done. The work expanded, as construction always seemed to—the owner seeing greater possibilities or having second thoughts, and Tony making suggestions. When the roof was finished, Guy worked inside on drywall, flooring, cabinets. They found rot in some floor joists. "Rip it all out," the owner said, and he complimented Guy on the new joists he fashioned, the way they slotted together.

In his second month of working for Tony, Guy realized that he was so frugal with his salary he was able to bank more than half of it. What had seemed a high rent at Lane's when he was paid for odd jobs was now a modest amount compared to what he was earning. He never bought new clothes—Goodwill was his clothing store—so his expenses were rent, food, used books, and the upkeep of his truck. He had a radio but no TV: he read, he listened to ball games, he went to bed early.

Guy set a goal for himself of saving five thousand dollars. And when he had achieved that amount he decided on ten thousand. With that he felt he could do anything—go anywhere, buy whatever he needed, a trailer, a mobile home, an RV. Ten thousand was freedom.

"Seeing as he's like a son to you, is he kicking some extra money your way?" Lane asked.

"The owner's happy—that's the main thing," Guy said, knowing it was not the answer Lane was looking for.

Guy's reticence on the subject of money aroused Lane's curiosity, as though Lane suspected that his frugality might be an indication of Guy's growing wealth, rather than his indigence.

"Heating oil is going up this year," Lane said. "And so are my property taxes."

He raised the rent by twenty dollars and the speed with which Guy agreed made Lane glum, as though regretting that he had not asked for more.

"My gallery claims they're having trouble selling my work."

"Stanger used to say that."

"I'm not surprised. I look at his paintings and I think, 'What's it all about?'"

"Because there's no perspective in it? No vanishing point?"

Lane said, "You're teasing me!"

But the mention of Stanger's work reminded Guy that among the crates of his possessions in Lane's shed was a roll of the canvases Stanger had rejected, saying of each one, *Get rid of it*. Guy had added new canvases to the roll, so that by the time he'd left Stanger's studio—was fired, rather—the roll was the thickness and the shape of a bolster.

Using some fine, flower-patterned brocade discarded by Lane, Guy sewed a sausage-shaped sack for the roll of canvases, and used it as a bolster on his bed.

"Now that is a very attractive accessory," Lane said on one of his visits, clinging to the ladder, peeping above the attic floor.

Lane's admiration for Guy's small achievements was always tinged with resentment—but why?

One evening when he got home from work, Guy found Lane lying on the sofa crying, sobbing into a pillow. Hearing the door shut, Lane raised himself. His face was wet, twisted with grief.

"People think there are answers to the world's problems," he said, his lower lip thrust out. "But there aren't any answers because the world's fundamental problem is that most people are stupid. Never mind that they don't buy art and don't read books and don't think for themselves—that's a given." He snorted and gasped and wiped his nose with the back of his hand like a small boy. "It's another kind of stupidity—animal stupidity. Dumb instinct. People make the same fatal mistakes every generation—in war, in politics, in business. The history of the world is the history of human folly. Nothing will change. Everything gets worse."

Guy said, "Einstein mentioned something along those lines."

The next day Lane sat at his loom, plucking at the wool strands as though nothing had happened; however, he seemed to have a dullness, a hangover, a result of his weeping.

"You claimed you'd like to go to an AA meeting," Lane said one evening. "If you want, you can come with me to my Wednesday meeting."

Guy said, "Just for the experience."

On that dark late afternoon, Guy driving, Lane remarked on how well-kept the truck was.

"A clean vehicle always runs best," Guy said.

The meeting was held in the annex of the community center in Ellsworth, fourteen men and woman on folding chairs, a bearded man in a baseball cap presiding at a table. Lane was the only black person present. One by one they introduced themselves, some offering a story—of temptation, of success in their number of days sober. Each person who stood up was applauded at the end of the testimonial. Lane spoke about the abuses he'd suffered as a waiter in Key West.

Guy admired them for their truthfulness and humility, for their valiant stories. He saw bravery in adversity, the old clothes and raw faces and trembling hands. Most of all he sensed an air of acceptance in the room, a comradeship he'd known in the navy. Dressed in uniform, they could have been mariners on the quarterdeck, a cluster of swabbies.

"I've got your back," was the most reassuring assertion Guy knew. It helped make the world whole. They seemed to be repeating that here at the AA meeting in different words.

Afterward, Lane introduced Guy to a woman, one of those who had told her story of struggle. "I'm Nicky. Sober for twenty-two months. I lost my daughter due to my drinking," she had said, and when the applause died down she added, "I don't want to lose myself."

"Nicky, this is my tenant, Guy. He's a genius at fixing things."

Her thin face gave her startled owl's eyes, her hair was lank and long, and her hands reddened either from the cold or work. Like Lane, she had stepped outside to smoke a cigarette.

"Know anything about leaky pipes?"

• • •

Nicky's house trailer sat on a foundation of railway ties in a clearing surrounded by towering spruce trees that had dropped a mat of needles on the roof. Neglect showed in the rusted window frames and the loose door handle, but seeing the window boxes—empty on this winter day—Guy was sure they would be full of flowers in the summer. The narrow interior smelled of cats and mildew and burned toast and syrupy perfume.

Guy lay on his back to work under the sink, first using a wrench, then a hacksaw, to detach the leaky joint from the pipe to the faucet. Nicky watched with interest, standing over him as he fitted a new pipe and then cleared the mess of wet rags and sodden paper under it.

"It's rotted out the floorboards under your sink."

With a little moan, Nicky became a small girl, her hands dabbing at her face and tugging her hair.

"Easy fix," Guy said. "New floorboards."

"Lane was right"—she touched his hand—"you're a genius."

"Simple carpentry." The pressure of her fingertip on the back of his hand still glowed. "But at the moment I'm a roofer."

Nicky said, "In this weather."

"It's tough some days. But the boss says, 'If you're cold it means you're not working hard enough.'"

"I'd tell him what he could do with his Christless roof."

"It's my son, Tony. Stepson, sort of. I helped raise him. But he pays me well."

Nicky did not say, as Guy feared, *You mean your stepson is bossing you around?* She softened and touched his hand again; then she made another cup of coffee for him and urged him to sit with her at her kitchen table. Holding a cat on her lap she talked about her drinking, about the Higher Power, and taking one step at a time, stroking the cat as she spoke, and sometimes purring to it.

"I'm Abenaki," she said. "Black Wildcat clan. My father grew up in Stillwater."

"I was at U Maine in Orono," Guy said.

"So you know Indian Island."

"I have great respect for those people."

"We are the people of the dawn," Nicky said, still fondling the cat. She worked in accounting at the creamery, she said. "You could pick me up on your way home. That way we could go to meetings together."

Guy had not intended to return to the meetings—his curiosity was satisfied by that first visit with Lane. But he said, "There's a good atmosphere in there, something spiritual," and agreed to take her the following week; and then every week for a month.

In arriving back at her trailer, she always invited Guy in for coffee. He hesitated until she mentioned a repair she needed—a loose tread on the front steps, a faulty light switch, a bad circuit breaker. Guy readily agreed to the repairs. Nicky asked him what he meant by "spiritual."

"Different from my usual outlook," he said. "Like the fellow said, a humorous skepticism towards everything."

"Which fellow?"

"Montaigne—not one essay, but the tone of most," Guy said, and as they were eating at the time—the routine of meetings and repairs often ended in a meal—he added, "Montaigne tells us he ate with his hands."

"Cute," Nicky said.

After one of these meals, Nicky said, "It's raining real hard. Why don't you stay the night?"

The thought had not occurred to Guy. From habit he resisted, then said, "Good idea."

"The spare room is at the back end, as you know."

Where he had caulked the gap in the window frame.

Within a week, at Nicky's urging, Guy moved in—emptied Lane's shed of his tools and transferred them to Nicky's shed. "Who will dry my tears?" Lane said; but he seemed relieved that Guy was going.

Guy's room in the trailer had been used for storage. He built shelves, sorted the cartons ("It's my idiot daughter's junk," Nicky said), and slept on a camp cot. Each morning, Nicky made coffee and toast and Guy drove to Tony's jobs, more far-flung now, in Rockland and farther south, like the modular homes in Falmouth Foreside.

One of the roofers on a modular home was a tall black man they called

Ollie, who though slender had no difficulty climbing the ladder with a fifty-pound slab of asphalt shingles on his shoulder. Guy complimented him on his balance and asked him where he was from, thinking that he could mention that he had a black friend, Lane, who made brilliant quilts.

Lowering his head, and in a soft confiding voice, the man said, "Somalia. I am Allah Rakha."

Guy, who had expected him to say Boston, was excited by the revelation. "Where in Somalia?"

They were kneeling on the roof now, side by side, with Dennis Colcord, who was fast at nailing but too old now to haul bundles of shingles.

The man brightened and said, "Not Mogadishu. You have never heard of it."

"Maybe I have," Guy said. "Is it Berbera?"

The man lost his smile and stared in alarm at Guy, as though frightened of what he might say next.

"Because Richard Burton was attacked there," Guy said. "A Somali warrior jabbed a spear through his cheek. That's the scar you always see in his portrait."

Before Guy had finished speaking, the man turned away, and though Guy admired him for his hard work, the man avoided him, always placing himself at the far side of the roof.

When Guy remarked on this to Dennis, Dennis said, "Why didn't you tell him about Elizabeth Taylor? That's the real Burton story."

Nicky welcomed Guy home, always with soup, which he praised. She had made no mention of rent at the outset. Guy broached the subject and asked if he could pay her what he had paid Lane. She replied, "Why don't we become partners?" and led him to her bedroom. As they made love, Guy reflected with pride, *I am fifty-six years old, the great lover*, and smiled in the darkness.

He did not return to his camp cot at the far end of the trailer, but he amused himself by thinking that Nicky's bedroom was narrower than the attic room at Lane's. In good weather, on weekends, Guy fashioned a projecting roof for the trailer, and built a deck out front, and lined it with benches.

Buying and planting flowers with Nicky in the late spring was to him an affirmation of hope. He blessed his luck and said, "This is a little slice of heaven."

"I only wish I could pay off my loan," Nicky said.

By then, through monthly deposits at the First National, Guy had almost achieved his goal of five figures. It seemed like a sign.

"We're partners," Guy said. "I might be able to help. I've got about ten thousand."

They were married in a small ceremony attended by most of the folks from the AA meeting as well as Lane and Mack Spinney, Tony Semple and Tony's wife, Beth-Ann. At the reception on the porch of The Anchor in Bar Harbor, they sat at long tables and had lobster and corn and the pub's signature moon pies; no alcohol was served.

Nicky worked nine to five at the creamery. Guy's jobs were seldom nearby. Their lives were parallel; they rose at six and after breakfast went their separate ways, meeting again in the evening, these days too exhausted to cook, so Guy brought takeout from the Dairy or Moody's and because of his hours he was never able to drive Nicky to the AA meetings.

A full year of this, Guy reflected, because dates were significant to him for being milestones. But marrying was the great change he'd hoped for without ever discerning beforehand what it might be. He had not imagined having a wife, and sometimes wondered how it had come about. In this first year he understood that Nicky was easily hurt, that she hated to cook and drove too fast, and that she often craved to be alone. "You snore," she told Guy, and many nights he returned to the camp cot in the spare room. Her furious telephone conversations with her daughter made him anxious; nor would she speak about her ex-husband. "Those people in AA are my family," she said. But she was lonelier than she admitted. Guy told her he loved her, and he was lonely too.

In the winter of their fourth year of marriage Guy tripped on a newly poured foundation slab and injured his back. After two weeks in the hospital he was weaker, with a high temperature, not caused by his back but a bronchial condition that would not respond to drugs.

Nicky visited but seemed aggrieved. She said, "Addiction is an illness too. I guess you don't know that."

"You might have caught a bug in here," a nurse said in a whisper. "Hospitals are full of germs."

But when Guy mentioned this to his doctor, the man said, "That is just not possible. We take great precautions to keep this a sterile environment."

At last he was discharged. Nicky said, "That's what I need—three weeks in bed, all my meals brought to me on a nice tray, and plenty of television."

"I read a lot of books there."

"You would."

Guy eventually returned to work, still suffering a tug of obscure back pain behind his chest, and he was often short of breath.

"Is it like an elephant is sitting on your chest?" the doctor asked.

Guy said, "Elephant? Honestly, I wouldn't know."

After tests, being hooked to monitors, tabs taped to his body, a spell on a treadmill, Guy got a verdict from the doctor. "You need a stent. That's not a back problem. It's your heart."

The stent was inserted, a simple procedure, and Guy was sent home with an array of pills. But the pain grew worse: Guy walked with difficulty. He saw another doctor, who said, "It's your back—it might respond to physical therapy."

Nicky said, "I know all about hypochondria from AA."

"Someone once said every hypochondriac is his own prophet," Guy replied.

But sessions with a physical therapist, and mornings at the gym, followed by massages, relieved the pain. Guy took up yoga and felt better.

"Massages," Nicky said. "I know about them too."

Guy joined Tony again, who said there was money specializing in kitchens—he needed Guy's cabinetry—and Guy was earning again, after the months of hospitals and the wrong diagnosis and therapy. The pills tired him, he worked long hours, and came home after dark, often forgetting to bring food.

"You're turning into such a drag," Nicky said, one night. Guy had just stepped into the trailer, exhausted from work, blinking and pale. "All you do is work. Or get sick. You have no time for me."

Approaching her, to hold her, as she had once held him, he said, "How can we fix it?"

"You make me want to drink," she said.

Instead of going home the next day, Guy searched the cards tacked to the corkboard at the general store and found one offering a room for a single man in a house on the Otis road. Guy called and visited that same night. He smiled to think that it was even smaller than Nicky's bedroom in the trailer, that each room in his life was growing narrower.

Through her lawyer, Nicky disputed that Guy had loaned her ten thousand dollars. "Where's the paper that proves it?" But Guy—the saver—had kept the canceled check. He handed it to his lawyer, and around that time had another dream, in which Nicky figured.

Up front, I want you to know I've killed a man, Guy said in the dream, his feet planted apart, facing a stranger. *So what deal are you offering?*

After months of negotiation he got half the money back, but not enough for a down payment on a house or even a trailer. He was sixty-one and feeling— not defeated, but low. Meeting Mack Spinney in town one Saturday he asked about Elliott Stanger. "Dead," Mack said. "And the wife's in Florida. No one's happy."

"But she's settled, and so are you," Guy said. "I don't know about me."

For the first time in a life of trusting fate and happy accidents, Guy began to think about the future. He was peering at the vanishing point but seeing only a small dot that he hoped was not a period, the full stop of oblivion. He wasn't sad, yet he looked back and subjected his past to an interrogation and saw that what he had taken to be his choices had actually been the demands and urgencies of other people saying, *Go away, Get out, You're fired, I don't love you anymore*. He wondered how his life might have been different if he hadn't always responded to those demands, and he asked himself, without pride but as a simple bemused inquiry, *Why aren't I sadder?*

Then Guy knew the answer, from two episodes that followed one after the other.

Working in a house that a family inhabited always gave him a window into the way other people lived, and sometimes through an actual window he was installing.

This was the house of a wealthy couple on the granite cliff overlooking Rockport Harbor. The house was full of exotic artifacts, statues, carvings, bronzes, pots, porcelains—trophies of travel. On the staircase wall of this Rockport house Guy saw a Stanger painting—chevrons—and winked as though to an old friend.

The couple's son, a young man—midtwenties, baggy sweater, spiky hair, sleepless-looking—sometimes spent part of the week there, filling the house with music that cheered Guy in his work. The couple complained about the dumpster in the driveway, the size of it, its ugliness. "Is it going to be there forever?" the man asked. "We thought you'd be finished by Christmas," the wife remarked.

Much as he enjoyed the son's music, Guy began to dread going to work, fearing he would have to think of a reply to the couple's complaints. Tony was no help, having put Guy in charge of the job.

"I'm doing the best I can," Guy said to the owner.

"Maybe your best is not good enough."

Guy said, "You might well be right!"

One whole week the house was empty. In that week the job neared completion. Guy thought, *They will be so relieved when they come back and see it done.* They returned the afternoon of the tidying up, walking past the dumpster without a complaint.

"Their son passed away," Tony said in a whisper. Tony had come to make the final inspection. "The one that used to play the piano. I think it was suicide."

Gathering his tools, Guy saw only one room lit in the big house, the yellow window solitary in the winter darkness.

Not long after that—the second episode—a fretful call from Nicky. "It's the driveway."

She did not have money to pay anyone to plow it, so Guy agreed to clear it—she was stuck—though he had not been near the trailer for years. Glancing up from his shoveling Guy was proud of his handiwork on the front stairs, and the way the deck and roof had withstood the weather.

"Do you ever hear from Lane?" Nicky asked. "He stopped coming to AA ages ago."

She looked much older, wearier, uncared for, and was still smoking.

"I've been meaning to get in touch."

"I should email him," Nicky said. "I could do it right now."

Guy did not have a computer. Email was a mystery. "You might find what you're looking for online" was a tease. *I'm a dinosaur*, Guy sometimes said, but secretly he was pleased he was not burdened by technology he could not fix, and information he did not need.

He shoveled the last of the driveway. Then Nicky was at the door, holding a small phone with a glowing message on its screen. *This is it. I'm checking out. I'm in a hospice.*

Lane died a week later, before Guy could visit.

"Lane Frater was colorful in every way—in his life and in his work and his clothes," Guy said at the memorial service held at the AA hall, all the other AA members attending. Guy recognized many of them as the wedding guests from long ago. And he remembered with fondness how, after Guy had finished a job, repairing the loom or cutting branches or changing a tire, Lane would present him with a candy bar, looking pleased, eager to be thanked.

In his truck, about to drive away, Guy saw a young black man running toward him holding a paper parcel.

"I'm Lane's nephew," the man said, handing over the parcel. "He would have wanted you to have this. Lane was very fond of you."

It was one of Lane's wall hangings, vivid patterns on a red background, a gold medallion like a sun, glowing between two vibrant black bars aslant, intersecting at a distant point in a corner. Guy hung it on the wall of his room. It was the smallest room he had yet lived in. *Fits me like a snail shell*, he thought.

The message in Lane's quilt was like the revealed secret of art, that at the farthest end of the vanishing point, at that seemingly unreadable dot in the buzz of color, a life was being lived. His hope was restored, and of Lane of the crying jags and the candy bars, Guy thought, *Poor dear suffering black man.*

Medical expenses had drained Guy's savings, yet he still had a few thousand as a cushion. Each year he had less, but the dwindling was inevitable: you got older, worked less, saved less, got deeper into a hole that was harder to climb out of and might end up being your grave. He could no longer balance on a steep roof, nor was he able these days to sling a bundle of shingles off a truck.

Hoisting the air compressor was a two-man job. One of the young crew guys, Dale or Aiden, had to lend a hand. Reading was still his satisfaction. Library books now, because even used books were expensive and once a book was finished it was no more than a brick of dead weight.

The crew was kinder, taking pains to speak loudly so he could hear. Tony, too, was patient, a wealthy man now because of his reputation, and the demand for custom homes. He and Beth-Ann had three children and a boat and a mooring at the Municipal Pier in Bar Harbor. Tony sometimes mentioned his mother, who had remarried and lived with her husband in a retirement home. Guy resisted asking for further details. Guy was seventy-one, so she was probably in her late eighties.

A flare-up of his back pain and—for the first time—an attack of gout kept him from work for two months. That, with the breakdown and repair of his truck (ball joints, cracked engine block), depleted his savings. Contemplating a move to a smaller place—it would have to be a closet, with a pocket door—he laughed out loud. But he knew he needed some money to get him past this spell of bad luck.

Yet as Guy lay in his small room watching the Christmas snow come down, the light blowing snow of small flakes on a cold day, the beauty of them whirling past his window, transforming his usual view, making it new and softer, purifying it with the bluish white of fresh snow, dusting the tree branches, leaving dunce caps on fence posts, *I am lucky*, he thought—*lucky to be alive in this cozy room, lucky still to be able to work, lucky in my tools, and luck will make me well.*

The landlord, Finn Rooney, inquired after him, and brought him soup that his wife had made, fish stew with buttery potatoes, that warmed him and helped him sleep. Yet the illness persisted, and a week later when it seemed to abate, Guy was unsteady and dared not drive.

The whole time he'd been bedridden he'd studied Lane's multicolored quilt on the wall, the quilt the nephew had given him in gratitude. He'd ceased to meditate on the two dark bars, but rather on the way they converged in a vanishing point. Ingenious Lane had made the point ambiguous and indistinct in a frizz of wool. Geometry proved that such lines never met; life wove ever onward.

You managed best in growing older when you learned how to lighten the load. All you needed was enough. And a painting or a quilt was never the equal of a window giving onto sculptural snow-bandaged trees and the tracks of jittery sparrows.

Guy called an auction house in Bangor and said he had one of Lane Frater's hangings and wished to consign it in an upcoming sale.

"One of the bigger ones?" the man asked.

"A wall hanging. Almost as tall as me and a little wider," Guy said. "Dark stripes not quite converging, and a sort of golden sun, red background. Very nice."

The man said, "I'll send our appraiser over."

The appraiser was a ruddy-faced man named Fraser Aitken—Canadian, he said, and familiar with Lane's work. "Never got the recognition he deserved. Probably racial."

Aitken was thin, with a full head of white hair, streaked with yellow, and a reflective manner—Guy was glad for his silence. His gaze went through the room, registering each object—the ladder-back chair with the seat Guy had recaned, the brass barometer, the fruitwood bowl Guy had himself turned on a lathe, with thin sides and a lovely grain. Aitken stroked each one, evaluating them with meaningful blinks.

He teasingly tapped the roll encased in silk brocade. "Looks like what we'd call a Dutch wife."

Guy coughed, and he was seized by gagging and could not answer, but he finally managed in a gasping voice, "Helps me sleep."

"As it's been newly recovered with material that's not vintage, you wouldn't get much for it," Aitken said, poking it again with his finger. "Hard, too."

"Reason being . . ." Guy said, and he felt awkward, stifled in his small room with the tall stranger filling it, nowhere to sit except the ladder-back chair or the edge of the bed.

Guy did not finish the sentence. It was too odd to explain the scraps of what the bolster contained—and he had not stopped smiling at the expression "Dutch wife." Instead of speaking he tugged on the laces that held the end gathered like the neck of a flour sack, and undoing the knot, in that motion, the loose end fell open releasing dust.

Fraser Aitken bent his knees and peered inside. Looking down at the man's head Guy saw through the yellow-white hair to the scalp growing pink with exertion. When the man straightened, his face was flushed from the effort, making his face impressive, almost angelic.

"Canvases," Guy said, choking on the dust. "Stangers."

"Let's have a look." Stepping back to give Guy room, the man bumped his head on the edge of the dormer and cursed.

"Barely able to swing a cat in this place. Fortunately I don't have a cat." Guy pulled the wrapper free of the roll of canvases.

As he did so, he recalled Stanger saying *Get rid of it*, and Small Bob asking, "What's it supposed to be?" But he had found something to like in canvases, the evidence of work—the solid color, the crisp lines, the concentric circles of the targets, the chevrons that had always reminded him of navy badges and the eaves of well-made houses.

Aitken had lowered his head again to see more clearly, as Guy stepped back, still coughing from the release of dust in the bolster bag; then apologizing, and coughing some more; and turning away, because he could not control his cough that also seemed to be tearing at his heart. Soon he was bent double, choking in misery; nor could he speak.

Fraser Aitken, intent on the canvases, was turned away, hunched, softly touching the edges of the canvases with reverence as though palpating human flesh, and then he turned to Guy, nodding, with the ghost of a smile.

At auction that spring, the Stanger canvases, after commission and the deduction of the consigner's premium—brought in one million, eight hundred and twenty-seven thousand dollars, and seventy-four cents.

In his tiny room, Guy put the check on his bedside table, which no longer wobbled—he smiled at the leg he'd repaired with a shim he'd whittled. He was a small boy again, revived in a buzz of color, swallowed whole, rejoicing in what he saw out the window, trees in bud.

Hawaii Nei

DIETROLOGIA

L isten, in the debris field otherwise known as my life, I recall one funny thing—but when I say funny I don't mean it was funny chuckle-chuckle. It was horrible and obvious, yet I didn't have the capacity to see it then—the gift I developed later. At the time it was like when you're staring at something floating in the water at the beach, say, and your back is turned, and you don't realize that a monster wave is going to wash over you. Maybe a little pink slipper, like yours, in the shore break, that someone lost, is distracting you, while the monster wave is coming up behind you— *Mannaggia!* Except it wasn't a wave. I was in my car. It was after work, and I was tired from a long day. And here's the funny—not very funny—thing. Instead of going straight home, I drove around, not near my house but on back roads and through the woods until it got dark. And even then I didn't go home. Look, I didn't want to go home. I kept on driving, not in a hurry, keeping to the speed limit, on and on, into the darkness. I did this for weeks—got out of work, set off in my car, and drove around, noticing things I hadn't seen before. People sitting on the porch chatting away. Kids on bikes. Man going into a house—'Hi, honey!' Old man and old lady, scuffing along the sidewalk, holding hands—beautiful. And after a month of this riding around, it came to me—the not very funny thing. That the monster wave in the background was my marriage situation. I was killing time, driving longer and longer, staying behind the wheel, in my car. My wife was the reason, I was putting it off. See, I didn't want to go straight home, because she was there. That was my first wife."

"Uncle," the small girl said.

"Yes?"

"Can I have another cookie?"

"Sure," Sal Frezzolini said, but he remained seated in his rocker. "Now you see that it was home—the idea of home that I was resisting."

"Can I have a cookie, too?" the boy said.

"And me, I want a cookie!" said the smallest one, a little girl, in a demanding screech, batting the air with one hand.

As Sal led them indoors, the boy said, "Other people's houses smell funny."

"True—and that's also part of the ambiguity I feel now," Sal said. "By that I mean my state of mind. I'm confused."

"Why are you confused?" the bigger girl asked, but Sal pretended he didn't hear, and made a business of removing the lid from the ceramic cookie jar, and presenting each child with a cookie. Then they padded out to the porch again, and he was back in his rocker, and they were crouched at his feet, chewing.

"Home," he said, "the notion of home, like the condition of marriage, requires the illusion of being indispensable to someone. And I didn't have that illusion anymore. I can't honestly say I have it now."

He fell silent, squinting past them, while they watched him, as though waiting for more. But he was calm—spent and satisfied, benign again, relieved, liking the careless crunch and the catlike way they licked the crumbs from their lips. He wanted to confess to them, *Usually I hate to see people eat, especially old people, the way they chew their food, and swallow hard, looking disgusted. Imagine having to look at that every day in the cafeteria of an assisted-living facility. But your eating is beautiful.* He said nothing; he watched the children with pleasure.

"Uncle," the boy said. "Want to see me do wheelies?"

"Yes. But tell me your name again. I forgot it."

"Kamana."

"And you?"

"Bella," the bigger girl said. "And she's Nanu."

"Cookie!" the child howled.

"It means 'wave,'" Bella said.

They jumped to their feet and ran to the driveway and mounted their bikes—the small girl on a tricycle—and wobbled on the gravel, skidding back and forth. Kamana pulled his handlebars back and reared, balancing for seconds on one wheel and whooping. Then they made for the gate and were gone.

"They were back again today," Sal said. "When I keep the gate closed, I don't see them—they stay away. But when it's open—even a crack—they take it as an invitation, and come right in, running on the stones, barefoot." His face was lit with admiration. "It gives me hope that they'll succeed, with an attitude like that. Curious—maybe a bit *temerario*. Nice."

He was faced away from his wife, smiling at the driveway, in the direction from which they'd come, across the gravel, the fixed expression of welcome on his face, as though still seeing them.

"My glasses," Bailey said, opening and closing drawers, slamming them and sighing. "Have you seen them?"

He turned his smile upon her, thinking of the children, but she went on with her clattering search, the noise she was making meant to remind him of her effort and her mood—these days more frenzied. He knew why: he saw behind the noise.

"On the counter, near the cookie jar," Sal said. He was in his easy chair, under the lamp, a book on his lap, a drink in his hand, his usual place in the evening, waiting for Bailey to arrive. She was still opening drawers and clawing their contents. "The cookie jar," he said, and raising his voice, "Behind it."

In the silence that followed, he looked up and saw that she was wearing her glasses.

"You found them."

"Obviously," she said without looking up. She was staring at something in her hand—her phone, he saw, but regarding it with pained concentration. "I thought we agreed that the cookie jar was going, along with all that other stuff."

Sal clucked, to indicate he'd heard her, but instead of replying to that, he said, "Those kids—they reminded me of that time when I was in Malabotta, that forest—my first year in Sicily, trying to be a poet. I was on a path and heard it coming, the rain, the way it announced itself, as it swept through the trees, the sound of it hitting the leaves high up in the canopy, the edge of the storm approaching. No water, just darkness and that smacking sound, like running feet, foot soles hitting pavement—a big mob on the move. And then the rain itself, the hard splash and the hiss of it, beating on the leaves, a deafening racket, the sky collapsing on me, with thunder and lightning. In one sudden flash I saw a shed—open-sided, just a thatched roof on poles. I ran under it and sheltered there and marveled at how the bright afternoon had become *crepuscolo*, and a tumbling creek of mud where the path had been. And as I stood away from the dripping eaves, a small boy ran into the shed. He held a big floppy philodendron leaf over his head like a parasol. He was wearing a yellow shirt, a sort of smock. Thick black curls, and his wet face gleamed. Nine or ten years old, skinny legs, barefoot, peering out of the shed at the water rushing down the path. About the same age as our neighbor boy. He'd found refuge. Then another lightning flash, he dropped his big leaf, and he carefully stuck a finger in each ear. And as the thunder rumbled over us he stumbled in alarm, stepping back, seeing me smiling at him. I said something, and that was worse. More lightning, more thunder. But he was more startled by me than by the thunder. Again he put his fingers in his ears and rushed into the storm, his yellow shirt jumping, terrified."

Sal paused, seeing the rain, hearing the thunder, and in the distortion of the lightning his last glimpse of the yellow shirt twisting into the forest.

"Maybe his first *straniero*."

Bailey made a sound in her sinuses that Sal could not translate into words, nor could he read anything in her eyes. She had a way of snatching with her fingers when she was agitated, and she was doing that now, her arms to her sides, one hand grasping air, the other wagging her phone.

"I don't think I've ever told you."

"That those neighbor children come by? Yes, many times."

"Not that," he said.

But she hadn't heard. "I've had an awful day. The agent said she'd have an offer by this afternoon—but where is it? And I need to sign off on the unit."

"God, I hate that word," he said.

Bailey was walking away, the phone pressed against her ear, conspiring, he knew. "And we've got to do something about all those books. You promised."

"I need them."

"You never read them."

"I've read all of them, some more than once."

"The unit is twelve hundred square feet," Bailey said, perhaps to him, perhaps into the phone.

"It's not enough," he said.

"How do you know?"

But she didn't wait for an answer. *I know*, he thought, *dietrologia*.

The next day he left the gates open.

He saw them, heads bowed in the peculiar way they listened, taking slow steps, pressing forward, their arms out, as though moving through deep grass and parting it, the boy in front, the bigger girl just behind him, the small girl dawdling at the rear. They were halfway toward him when he went to the porch rail and greeted them. But even so they walked slowly, perhaps with caution, or was it because they were barefoot on the stony driveway?

"Uncle," the boy said, announcing himself.

"Come on up," Sal said.

They brightened and hurried to the stairs, jostling, and as they mounted them Sal moved back to his chair, as though to encourage them, too, to sit.

"Let me guess your names," he said, and pointed. "Kamana."

The boy was dark, with short spiky hair and the face of a dusky cherub, his faded T-shirt lettered TOON TIME over a mass of big-eyed kittens.

"And this is Bella."

The girl turned her red baseball cap back to front. Her T-shirt, KEIKI GREAT ALOHA RUN, showed the stenciled image of a winged foot. Her jeans were torn at the knees, the cuffs turned up.

"You're Nanu," Sal said. "And your tongue is blue."

"Lollipop," she said, licking her upper lip.

When Sal laughed out loud at this, they looked alarmed and drew back a little.

"What did you learn at school today?"

Kamana began to speak, stammering badly, but Sal realized the boy was mimicking his teacher, who'd reprimanded them for talking—imitating a scolding tone, peremptory but wordless nagging.

"I had a teacher like that," Sal said. "Miss Sharkey. And you, Miss Bella, what did you learn?"

"Nothing," the girl said, twisting her face as though to show futility.

"Nothing!" the small girl, Nanu, said.

"She doesn't go to school," Kamana said.

"Uncle," Bella said. "Can I have a cookie?"

"I don't have any cookies for you just now," he said and saw they looked defeated. "But I have a story. You like stories, don't you?"

"Miss Oshiro tells us stories," Kamana said.

"This one is true," Sal said. "Listen, I was in Italy a long time ago . . ."

He told the story of the sudden storm in the Sicilian forest, the way the raindrops smacked the leaves, sounding like running feet, the open-sided shed and the child in the yellow shirt holding a big leaf over his head. Then the flashes of lightning, the thunder, the shock of the boy seeing him. Rising from his chair, Sal stood up and put a finger in each ear and showed how the child had darted away, into the thunder and rain.

The children sat before him, their faces fixed in concentration, as though hearing music—unfamiliar music but a melody they could follow, seeming to track its syncopation, nodding softly. And their attention encouraged him to tell the story in greater detail, more slowly, with pauses—because he was able to observe their absorption in the drama. Their listening was visible, he could see it in their faces, the progress of the story shining in their eyes, their lips moving with his.

"Ha!" Bella said. "He was afraid."

"Maybe he never seen a big haole before," Kamana said.

"That's what I thought then," Sal said. "Afterward, I had to conclude that he was employing a sort of inbuilt *dietrologia*—that he knew he had to separate himself from me. But it was a long time ago."

"How long?" Bella asked.

"More than fifty years," Sal said.

The children jeered at the number, Kamana shouting, "That's silly—fifty years!"

Sal stared at their wonderment, thinking: *They have just arrived on earth.*

Time, which is everything to me, is nothing to them. It reassured him to think that for them big numbers were impossible.

"Now can we have a cookie?" Bella said.

The possibility of cookies stilled them, encouraged them to linger, seemed to tame them, made them more attentive, like the simplest sort of magic, or a drug.

"Did Miss Oshiro tell you a story today?"

Bella said, "Poem."

"What kind of poem?"

"Itsy-bitsy spider."

"Here's a real poem," Sal said, and he recited,

> *If you're senselessly unhappy*
> *On a cloudy afternoon*
> *And regard the hand that feeds you without wonder,*
> *And say everything is crappy*
> *As you blow it off the spoon—*
> *May I please call your attention to the thunder?*

Kamana frowned. "Are you afraid of thunder?"

"Yes," Sal said. "Like that little Italian boy."

"You said crappy," Bella said.

"Because it's in the poem. And it's my poem. I wrote it with this old hand."

"How old are you?" Nanu asked, her fingers in her mouth.

"Guess."

"Twenty-five?"

"No."

"Eighty-five?"

"No."

"If we guess the right number, can we have cookies?"

"Yes."

Kamana said, "Fifty—a hundred—thirty."

"All good guesses," Sal said and led them into the house for cookies, which he dispensed in the usual way, tipping the jar, framing each cookie with his fingers, presenting them as though awarding a medal.

Kamana began to dance on the polished wooden floor, skidding and jumping, and was joined by Bella, while the small girl, Nanu, squatted and watched. Sliding sideways, Kamana bumped a table and upset a large glazed plate that had been resting on a display stand. Its smash silenced them, then Kamana began to shout at Bella.

"You made me do it! It's all your fault!"

"It's okay," Sal said. "I never liked that plate. I'm glad you broke it."

The boy laughed as Sal swept up the glittering shards and wrapped them in newspaper, making a parcel of them, placing it in the trash bin.

Outside, Sal said, "I wish I could tap-dance. I wish I could play the piano. I wish I could fly. Though I often fly in my dreams. There's so many things I want to do before I get too old."

"I can fly," Bella said, and she ran from the porch to her bike. She mounted it and rode in circles, crunching the gravel.

"Look at me, uncle," Kamana called out, and he too skidded and howled, chased by Nanu, and soon they were gone.

That evening, Bailey said, "What happened to the majolica plate?"

"I'm having it valued," Sal said.

"It was a wedding present," Bailey said. She surveyed the room. She sighed and said, "God!"

He knew what she meant: all this furniture, all these books, the pictures, the vases, the house itself—dispose of it all. Then proceed to the unit.

In the succeeding days, Sal left the gate open but the children did not visit, nor were they playing in the neighborhood or on the road where he often saw them. He missed them, and wondered where they'd gone, and envied them for not needing him, and was shamed because he so badly wanted to see them. He admired them as important little vessels, and in the hope that they'd return, he began saving up stories, and thoughts that were a burden to him, to tell them.

When at last they came back, unannounced, as though materializing from the emptiness beyond the gate—creeping softly down the gravel and noiselessly on the stairs to the porch, tentative in their movements, as though stalking him—he greeted them fondly, almost tearful in his gratitude.

He surprised himself saying, "I used to be so afraid of strangers. Come to think of it, I'm still afraid. But you're not!"

They took their usual places before him and crouched in their listening postures, watchful and compact.

"I've been meaning to tell you that I've spent my whole life on the periphery. But I always knew what was going on. I just didn't know how to avoid the consequences." When they did not react to this, he asked, "Where have you been?"

"Father's house," Bella said.

"He lives in town," Kamana said. "He doesn't live with us."

"What about school?"

"Rudy laughed at my shirt," Kamana said.

"Why did he do that?"

"Because it had a hole in it. He said he could see my belly button."

"That's terrible. I know. Lots of people used to laugh at me," Sal said. The children looked at his shirt, as though to see whether it had a hole in it. He said, "It was because I said words wrong. I could read them. I knew what they meant. But I couldn't say them right."

Bella wrinkled her nose, looking doubtful. "What words?"

In a chanting, tone Sal said, "Posthumous. Elegiac. Incunabula. Oregon. Phthisic."

The children nodded at each word and laughed when he was done, Bella saying, "Again!"

Grateful for her shout, to be able utter the words, to cast a spell that would rid him at last of his humiliation, Sal spoke the words to the children, watching their bright eyes.

"Phthisic," Kamana said.

Bella said, "Posthumous."

Sal wanted to weep for their saying them correctly. "Don't let anyone laugh at you," he said. "It hurt me that Jane Godfrey laughed at me when I said 'post-hewmous.'"

"When did she do that?"

"Sixty-two years ago," Sal said.

"It's bad to laugh at people," Bella said.

"I feel better now." He was astonished that he had carried the memory all those years and only now disposed of it in expiation.

"Can we have a cookie?" Kamana asked, on all fours, tipping himself upright.

"One more thing," Sal said, and he indicated with his hand that the children should listen. "When people asked me what I did for a living, I never told them, 'I'm a poet.' But that's what I wanted to be. The truth was that I was a claims adjuster for Territorial. At a desk where I wrote poems in secret."

"Cookie," the small girl, Nanu, said, in a beckoning tone, as if calling to a cat.

"Even Bailey doesn't know." *Poetry is my secret*, he thought, *but poetry is also my embarrassment.* "By the way, Bailey insisted on keeping her maiden name. She hates my name." He saw their solemn faces and said, "Frezzolini."

They seemed startled by the word, but they followed Sal into the house, and emboldened—because they'd been inside before—they ran around the chairs and slid in a skating motion on the polished floor.

"You have a lot of books," Bella said and ran to the shelves and slapped the spines of the books. Seeing her, Kamana joined her and punched them with his fist. Their glee, their fury, caused Nanu to shriek.

Sal said, "Why are you hitting the books?"

"Because they're bad!" Bella said, slapping at them.

"Did you read them all?" Kamana asked.

"No," Sal said, and again, "No."

"Then why do you have them?"

"Because I'm a silly old man," Sal said. "And you're right. A lot of them are bad." Seeing that slapping at the books had somehow calmed them, he said, "Does your father have books in his house?"

"Fred," Kamana said. "Got a flat-screen TV."

"Is he nice?"

His question silenced them, and when he asked again, Kamana said, "He hit my mom in in the kitchen."

"What did you do?"

"Watched TV."

"What did your mom do?"

"Cried," Bella said.

"Does he hit you?"

"When we're bad," Bella said.

"He gives us lickings," Kamana added, in clarification.

They spoke glumly but without rancor, as though they were to blame.

Bella said, "Tell us a poem."

"The 'crappy' one," Kamana said, giggling on the word.

"Let's go outside," Sal said, wearied and saddened by the talk of their being hit.

"Can we have another cookie?"

Feeling sorrowful he gave each of them three cookies, formally presenting them, and felt sadder when they shrieked, surprised by the number, bobbling them, Nanu barely able to hold them in her tiny hands, bringing them to her face and gnawing.

On the porch, he said, "A different poem," and recited

"I'm glad you're back," I lied,
You hugged me, then you cried,
"At last you're home—we're one!"
I feel I want to run.
With you I'm more alone
Than when I'm on my own.

They chewed, they wanted more, they insisted on hearing the other poem, for the pleasure of hearing the word *crappy*. So he said, "If you're senselessly unhappy, on a cloudy afternoon," and they screeched when he spoke the word.

"Here's another," he said, "from long ago," and began,

"Anyone can skin a gatto when it's morte."
So the Siciliano told her.
"Ma, il più forte
A scorticare é la coda."

But not just taxidermy, also other arts,
In love and work, and things essential;
Bottom line—even the fate of hearts—
Beware, or you will surely fail;
Remember that the hardest part's
The skinning of the tail.

"That's silly," Kamana said.

"*Dietrologia* often seems silly," Sal said.

"What's that?"

Sal said, "You visit me and I'm happy. You're near and mysterious. But *dietrologia* tells me it's cookies."

Bella asked, "I know what happens when you die."

"I wish I knew," Sal said. "I'd put it in a poem."

"When you die they put you in a hole and you go to heaven," Kamana said.

"Uncle," Bella said. "What's going to happen to you?"

Sal clutched at his knees and thought hard and said, "I sometimes think it's already happened." He squinted and savored the silence. He said, "I don't like what I see."

He was glad when they seemed to brush the statement aside, and Kamana said, "Tell us the story of driving around in your car, when you didn't want to go home."

So he told the story, slowly, now and then interrupted by the children who insisted on the same words, delighted when they corrected him when he missed a line or used a different word.

"It's not my story anymore," he said. "It's yours. And obviously driving around in the dark was a big mistake. I should have thought of something else."

He was relieved to be rid of it, but when the children left, Kamana churning the gravel with his bicycle tires, Sal finished his thought, *Something reckless and decisive.*

The children did not appear for another week, and he came to understand the pattern, that they spent the longer periods of time with their mother, who lived up the road in a house obscured by a monkeypod tree and a mounded mass of bougainvillea, and the rest of the time they lived with their father, somewhere in town.

Sal longed for them to visit, especially on those days when Bailey was describing the progress of the move. Listening to the details he found unbearable, and to prevent her from saying them—often she read from a list she'd made, holding a notepad and speechifying—he pretended a weird enthusiasm, agreeing with whatever she said. This worked better than—as in the past—begging her to stop talking, which had not worked at all, but only infuriated her into a more detailed monologue. But it was all like thunder. He wanted to put his fingers into his ears and run.

"The idea," she told him one day, "is that we can initially stop for lunch at Ocean View—the cafeteria—and get acquainted with the other residents, and maybe spend a night or two in the unit."

"Good idea," he said, stiffening, convulsed with terror at the words *cafeteria* and *unit*.

"Until the sale of the house goes through."

"Perfect." His throat burned with the lie.

"Acclimate to the new environment, while at the same time arrange an estate sale."

Sal looked wildly around the room at books, lamps, cushions, carpets, the cookie jar, and his rocker on the porch.

"What we don't sell we can put into one of those units."

"Our unit," he stammered saying the shocking word.

"No, no, not Ocean View," Bailey said. "Storage unit. And we'll have to do something about the car."

"Yes, yes," he said, in a panic, wanting her to stop.

"Because we won't need it—we'll be near all the shops. We'll have our meals in the cafeteria. We . . ."

"I'm glad you're handling it," he said, interrupting, and using his hands, too, to make her stop.

His smothering voice, his pushing hands, provoked her to say, "I don't think you realize how much effort I'm putting into this."

"Just take your time," he said. But what he intended to calm her only angered her more.

"Time is the one thing we don't have," she said. "We're on a strict schedule. Contracts. Deposits. Deadlines."

"Yes," he said, a shriek in his voice, and when Bailey began to speak again, he said, "Absolutely!"

She lowered her head, tugging down her glasses and looking over the top of the frames, a doubting gaze, she said, "I sometimes think you're resisting this."

"It's such a big move."

"Downsizing," she said. "It's part of growing old."

"We're not that old," he said.

Turning away from him and adjusting her glasses, she laughed—a loud knowing shout that made her seem strong, and even the way she walked was like marching, leaving him behind with the echo of her laugh.

He yearned for the children, and when a few days later they returned, he gave them cookies without their asking, and they sat in the afternoon sunshine, eating them in silence.

"When I was a boy I was always hungry," he said. "I didn't realize it until I had a meal at a friend's house. His mother would pile my plate with food, and when I ate it all, and sometimes had seconds, she'd say, 'You're really hungry!'" He looked for a reaction, but the children were absorbed in their eating. "I thought it was a compliment 'You're a good eater!' But they understood what was behind my hunger. Only it came to me much later—that I didn't have enough to eat at home. A terrible thing that they knew."

The word roused the children, they looked up, staring at him. Bella said, "What was terrible?"

"That we were poor. But it didn't occur to me until thirty or forty years had passed."

They laughed, as they always did at large numbers, finding them absurd, and he joined them, seeing that the numbers were indeed absurd, and grateful that he had these children near him, like finely calibrated instruments that only he could read.

He said, "What did you do with your father?"

"Watched cartoons."

"Does your mother let you watch cartoons?"

"No," Kamana said.

"What do you do with her?"

"Church," Bella said.

Sal said, "Soul butter."

Kamana hooted at the word, Bella said, "Butter!" and their shouts excited Nanu, who wagged her head.

"Tell us a story, uncle," Bella said.

"Wait, what happened to your arm?"

She drew back when he went to touch the bluish patch, the bruise like a botched tattoo, making the girl seem older.

"I was bad."

Sal involuntarily stood up, hurting for the small girl, but feeling futile. He controlled himself enough to ask, "Fred?"

She blinked a yes.

"You need a cookie. We all need cookies."

On the lanai he said, "Fred what?" and Bella told him her father's last name. "He's a policeman."

"Ah."

He told them his driving-around-after-work story, giving it a happy ending, which Kamana objected to, because it was different, but Bella said, "Cool." After they had gone, Sal sat for a long while in the rocker, murmuring his declaration, and measuring how much he would need to say to rouse the policeman to action.

When at last he picked up his cell phone and was connected, he replied to the gruff hello, saying, "I know what you've been doing to your children."

Sal wondered in the silence that followed if he'd been heard. But then came the confident blaming voice he'd expected, "I know who you are." Then the voice went gummy. "Cookies."

At that, Sal put the phone down and, still sitting, interrogated the shadow of the obvious. Seeing behind it, he knew just how it would play out, and he drummed his fingers on the arm of his chair as though tapping a fast-forward button, to speed the ensuing drama.

The future jerked before him, accelerating in sequence—the vindictive response from the man, the misapplied accusations, the unfortunate fretting of the children's mother, the certain involvement of the police, and their intimidating visit, the howl from Bailey when she read the conditions of the restraining order. Finally, as her plans fell apart and she found that Ocean View would not admit him, another howl: *This will follow you, Sal!*

She did not see behind, what he saw clearly. That she'd be fine, and better off without him. Anyway, he was not thinking of himself, the certainty of his living alone, somewhere to be determined, among his old things; but only of the children, whom he knew he'd never see again.

THE FALL

As lovers and fellow students, Stan and Marge lived on the beach in a shack near Kahuku on the North Shore of Oahu and had begun their married life as Mr. and Mrs. Sidway in a fixer-upper cottage on the windward side, later moving to a condo in downtown Honolulu to be near Stan's law office, not far from where Marge worked in real estate. In time, they found a teardown in Manoa Valley and replaced it with a bungalow, the wide lanai supported by pillars of lava rock. A year before Stan's retirement they bought a two-story house that needed renovation, with an ocean view a block from Kahala Avenue, the most stylish street on the island—"Millionaire's Row," Marge called it. Trading up, nest building, no offspring; but they had each other. They were now both retired, and for the first time since Kahuku, wondering how to get used to being together all day.

This would be their last house, they told themselves. But a month into the remodeling, examining work in progress on the second floor, Stan fell into the stairwell, down a flight of splintery unfinished steps, and for the minutes he lay twisted, unable to move on the plywood subfloor, he believed he was about to die.

A week later, when the pain had subsided somewhat and he could think more clearly, he was able to tell Marge how it had happened. At the top of the roughed-out stairway, he had stepped backward onto an unsecured plank and had tripped, falling forward into the opening, clawing air, bumping down the sharp edges of the treads until at last he had struck bottom, contorted, terrified, unable to draw a breath and choking. Then rising from his chest came a labored honk, an agonized cry of animal fear, futile and deranged. The sound scared him further, as he lay on his back in the sawdust on the floor. A gecko he'd startled remained on a dusty board at eye level, then unstuck and lifted one foot—Stan could see its thick toes—and darted away, so alive, almost insolent in its agility.

Stan's body was immobilized as though by a leaden slab of pain. He thought he might have snapped his neck or broken some bones. But with effort he was able to move his head, and he tried his arms and legs, feebly kicked his feet, and was relieved to think that he was banged up but whole.

"Marge," he called in a weak voice. Then louder, "Marge."

She was probably in the garden where he'd left her, saying, *Let's see if those guys have made any progress.* Marge was a gardener. She'd remarked on the mango tree and how Kahala was perfect for fruit trees, and the garden, too, for the house in which they'd told their friends they'd end their days.

Hearing no reply, Stan lay, silently grateful that he wasn't dead, yet he was unable to get to his feet. Each time he tried to angle himself to a sitting position his body lit up with pain—hot knives stabbed his legs and arms, his back was aflame. He was frightened and called Marge again.

He was convinced that he might have internal injuries, he felt his body swelling, blobbing with blood, and he was resentful that Marge didn't respond to him. He cried out, in a strained, weepy voice.

His cry had the desperate note of a child's terror in it—this tremulous voice was who he was now, and still no reply. He imagined that Marge was tramping away, wagging a bunch of flowers in her hand, her big healthy shoulders turned against him.

He scrabbled at the floor and with difficulty dragged himself across the planks on his bruised knees, on aching arms and legs, to the wall opening where the new sliders were to be installed. He called again, into the open air, under jeering bird squawks and the papery rattle of the fanlike fronds of loulu palms.

This time he heard a screech from the guesthouse, "Oh god, what happened?" and coming closer, "Stan!"

Her sudden panic frightened him—something about hearing his name screamed—and made him think that he might be in greater danger than he feared.

"Fell down the stairs," he said, but so softly the words scarcely left his mouth.

"Don't move!"

Yet he had moved, and he still snatched and pulled with bruised fingers through the door to the guesthouse while she watched, chewing her lips in horror. He hitched himself partway onto the sofa and groaned, feeling his joints jammed and swollen.

"Darling," she said and swept a pillow under his head, gently tipping his legs onto the cushions.

He loved her for that; he felt grateful and small, like a man released from a trap, soothed by her presence. In his relief was all the love he'd felt for his wife in almost forty years of marriage. He thought he might cry, she saw his face crumple, and in a reflex of compassion she embraced him—too hard—and he howled in a low moan. Her embrace reassured him yet the pressure hurt, but he was too badly injured to remind her that her overeager hug was painful.

"You should drink something," she said.

He pawed the air, his way of saying no.

Marge then did an odd, unexpected, and unwelcome thing. She called her best friend on her cell phone.

"Laurie, an awful thing just happened. It's Stan. I don't think anything's broken. He's in shock—talk to him." She then handed him the phone.

"How you doing, handsome?"

"Not good," he said, in a whisper.

"It's a leading cause of death among seniors," Laurie said. "Falling. Sometimes tripping on a crack in the sidewalk."

He couldn't speak. When he dropped the phone, Marge picked it up and said, "He's a wreck," in a tormented voice.

Marge was saying "Hospital," as he went limp. The effort of crawling to the sofa, the shock of the fall had exhausted him. He mumbled, he drowsed, he drooled, and he was soon asleep. When he woke in the dark, Marge was sitting in a chair before him, her knees against his legs, canted forward in a posture of concern. He could feel heat, like worry, radiating from her body, penetrating his skin, making him feverish.

"We've got to get you to the hospital."

"In the morning," he said, in a suffering groan.

"What are you thinking?"

"Thirsty," he said. When she'd given him a drink of water, he begged her to let him sleep again, and he lay clutching himself, smaller and more compact, in a clump, like a wounded animal, until dawn, the sunlight scorching Kahala, blazing in the palms.

So this is what old age is like, he thought. Enfeebled by the fall, he felt a hundred years old, uncertain, weak, and humiliated, needing Marge's help in getting up, in washing and dressing. She was sturdy, insistent that he lean on her, as she led him to the car, seating him, folding his legs into the vehicle.

In the emergency room of Queen's Hospital, Stan lay on a gurney, and was visited by a succession of nurses, each performing a specific function, first his insurance forms, his temperature, blood pressure, and then a chatty one with a clipboard, "Stanton, the doctor, will be with you in a little while."

I'm Attorney Sidway, he wanted to say. *The trial lawyer.*

Being injured meant you were in someone else's hands, a new experience for him, as the dependent submissive one, seeking help, unable to manage on his own.

"You're all right," the chatty nurse said. "If you'd really injured yourself, you'd never be able to move. You'd be in traction." She brushed at the hem of her white smock. "New knees. I wiped out on a black run at Whistler two years ago. I was in leg braces for three months." She lifted and tapped her knee. "Ceramic."

"This is all indistinct," the doctor said, examining the x-rays, hardly looking at Stan, who was told to wait. In the early afternoon he was slid into a cylinder and given a noisy MRI. The doctor reappeared, this time with new photos. He tapped them with a chrome device. "Chips and trauma to four thoracic vertebrae."

"Guess you did hurt yourself after all," the chatty nurse said, still seeming to jeer at him. She gave him a paper cup of water and two white tablets.

Marge drove him home, all the while in an anxious voice urging him to be calm. At the guesthouse, struggling to lower himself into the bathtub, he heard the workers hammering in the main house, the sound of a buzz saw, and a loud radio.

"Tell them to stop," he said, rattled by the noise.

"They have to finish," Marge said. "You need a place to rest."

"This is fine for now," he said, but when she went out to send the work-men away for the day, Stan found that he could not raise himself from the tub. He called to Marge, shamed by his weakness. She helped hoist him and guided him to the bedroom, where he sat on the bed, while she swung his legs up and into the sheets, all the time sighing—he took it to be a blaming noise, capped with a forgiving cluck. Marge seemed energized—the bounce of the caregiver in the presence of an invalid, the way such injury makes a bystander oddly hearty and grateful and insincere. Her high spirits made him feel older.

Thereafter, he lay in bed and often heard Marge on the phone to her friends, "A whole flight of stairs. He didn't miss a step, top to bottom." She did not say that it was she who had insisted on building the open-plan stairway. And often, "Chips and trauma to four thoracic vertebrae."

She who had been a real estate agent, away from him all day, was now in charge of him and central to his life. She was not an inspired cook, and the guesthouse kitchen was limited, but she toiled at the stove and insisted he eat.

"Soup," she said. "You need strength. Eat up, my darling. What are you thinking?"

Stan was thinking that he felt no better, but because he didn't want to dis-appoint her he said, "I'm on the mend." He felt an obligation to heal for her. The white tablets helped, but when they wore off he ached, with that same encrusted feeling of infirmity and old age. He began to fear the painkiller tablets. He wondered if he should stop taking them because they masked the pain. He was afraid that he might overdo it and injure himself.

Marge lay next to him in the narrow bed, stroking him. She said in a sleepy voice, "I've never loved you more. I've got your back."

Her touch, what she meant as a caress, was an unwelcome pawing of his hot hypersensitive skin, and far from easing his pain the pressure of her fin-gers, slight as it was, kept him from relaxing, as though she were prodding him awake; and her insistent voice grated.

Her attention exhausted him, her talk put him to sleep, and when he woke she was there, leaning at him, her face seeming to fill the room. He could not see past her cheeks and ears and wild hair.

Stan hugged himself and gathered himself into a ball. He wanted only to go on sleeping, to repair his body. It was a misery, like sin, to be so wounded in this the loveliest neighborhood of the sunny island.

Marge did the driving now. She did not drive well. Her nervousness at the wheel intensified his feeling of frailty. Because of the fall, he knew in advance what a car crash would be like and he whinnied a little as she snatched at the steering wheel.

She said, "You're making me nervous," and swerved and braked, as though to prove it.

Another week went by, a week of feeble old age. Stan lay inert, while Marge urged him to eat her food. And then a wonderful thing happened. He woke one morning and felt dull but improved; the blaze of pain had abated. That was a later thought. At the time he did not think immediately of his back or his legs and being oblivious of his body was like a sign of health. When before he could not sit comfortably, now he could sit upright without bracing himself. His back pain had diminished. He knew this, because—against her orders—he had stopped taking the tablets the previous night.

Still, that day and the next, he needed Marge to put him to bed. She lifted and swung his legs with exaggerated care. She plumped his pillows. She brought him soup.

"I need rest," he said, refusing the soup.

One of his law partners had once said, "Men need sex, women need security. I'm oversimplifying of course. 'I will protect you in your nakedness, the way a gander stands sentry duty near a brooding goose on a clutch of eggs.'" Stan had smiled, and the man added, "It is necessary to know that fundamentally we are animals."

That was not wrong but there was more. In his fragile state, a few days after the first hospital visit, in his first week of pain, Stan concluded, This is what love means—two people mutually supportive, not the tingle of desire, the greedy insistent *I want you* leer of the early stages of romance—not romance at all; but the profound assurance that, no matter what, you could absolutely count on each other, prop each other up. *I've got your back*, Marge had said.

She woke him. In a mothering singsong she said, "Time for your medicine."

"I've stopped taking it," he said. "I don't need it."

"You do need it. It kills the pain."

"I don't like the way it does that," he said, enunciating each word.

"Doctor's orders," she said, severely but with a twitch of panic. "Read the label. It's for your own good."

She was afraid, and to calm her he swallowed the tablets.

The medicine took away his pain so completely he began to believe he was much better, and he walked more confidently, upright with the approximation of a stride. His mood was lighter too. But it was a delusion. When the medicine wore off, he was reminded by the pain of his injury. Beneath the sinister chemistry of the tablets and the illusion of relief was tortured muscle and chipped vertebrae. He was walking on cracked bone and bruised tissue. The medicine might make him worse—and the pamphlet that came with the tablets mentioned possible side effects—dizziness, nausea, seizures, and more, including the absurd notion that he was better because he had so little pain. Pain is a warning, he told himself; pain is a guide, pain is wise. The wisdom of pain would make him better.

"Try getting up—I'll help," Marge said.

"The pain in my legs says, 'Don't get up.'"

"You're not taking your medicine, are you?" she said, "You think you know more than the doctor."

Then she was holding a glass of water and two tablets.

"I want to see him," he said.

She reminded him of what the doctor had prescribed, but he insisted, and he believed he had won her over until, in the car, she said in a mollifying tone, "I understand. Sick people can be very unreasonable."

He wanted to scream. He said quietly, "I'm not sick. I don't have an illness. I'm injured, and I know I'm improving."

In the doctor's waiting room he saw a Chinese couple, the man about his age, slumped in a chair, and the man's wife, sitting upright next to him, flicking the pages of a magazine.

"Wipe," she said, lowering the magazine. "Darwin."

Spittle-froth had formed in the corners of the man's mouth. He nodded and dabbed at it with a crumpled tissue.

"You didn't get it all," the woman said. "Dar."

The man tried again, his fist against his face.

"Better," she said and returned to her magazine.

When the receptionist called him—"Stanton?" she said, in a querying familiar tone—and they were out of earshot, Marge said, "Poor thing. He's lucky to have her."

Stan said, "Yes," because disagreeing might cause an argument for which he didn't have the strength. Yet he hated himself for giving in. And when the nurse signaled for Marge to go back to the waiting room, Marge insisted, saying, "My husband wants me there."

"How are we doing?" the doctor asked, after the nurse's formalities with blood pressure and temperature.

"The medicine is worrying me," Stan said, and he explained.

"Side effects," the doctor said, smiling. "Everything has side effects. Coffee has side effects."

With a new awareness of her body that was almost uncanny, Stan could sense Marge swelling in triumph behind him.

"I'd rather have the pain than risk further injury," he said.

"Some people feel this dosage helps them relax."

Now he felt he was facing the doctor and Marge.

"I have no trouble relaxing. I'm doing what animals do, rolling up in a ball and keeping still."

"If that works for you, by all means discontinue the medicine. How's your appetite?"

"He won't eat," Marge said. "He's off his feed."

That rankled, the way she put it. "I needed to lose a little weight. Not eating seems to have helped."

And now as Marge crossed her arms he noticed that she was heavier—had gotten so since his fall; and when they walked to the outer office he saw that she walked slowly and unsteadily, as though she was carrying something— and she was, the added pounds.

"I'm improving," Stan said when the receptionist saw them out, feeling obliged to declare it.

"You've got a good nurse."

"I sure do."

Stan was feeling better and in a strange new way, as though the center of gravity in his body had shifted. He still had pain in his back and legs, but the pain was half of what it had been, and it guided him and helped his posture. He was reminded of how the fall had made him feel ancient and frail; but each day he was younger. This improvement boosted his morale. He could now dress himself, he could put one foot, then the other into his trouser legs while balancing; he could sit for longer periods.

"I'll drive," he said to Marge one morning.

"Not on your life, mister," she said. "You're not up to it."

"I want to try."

"And what if you crash the car?" she said. "I love you too much to let you."

He relented. They went to Makapuu and when Stan said he'd prefer simply to stay in the car and look at the surf, Marge said, "See?"

Another week went by, a lessening of his pain—he needed to poke himself, or to flex hard, to feel anything. When he said so to Marge she smiled a little, and in a fluttering motion with her hand seemed to suggest that he was imagining the improvement, or trying to fool her. That night getting out of the tub he asked for her help.

"Just as I thought," she said.

He said, "It's hard for anyone to get out of a bathtub. And dangerous. I've seen the injury statistics. Two percent getting into a tub, ten percent getting out."

Then he sat at the edge of the bed, summoning the strength to slide under the covers. He held his left leg, but Marge was quicker, more efficient and adept. She clasped his ankles and swung his legs up and into the bed.

"I wanted to try," he said.

"My love," she said. But she was breathing hard—the effort of helping him had winded her. "These things take time."

She lay beside him. She was plumper, her body was big and hot, and it bulked against him. He could sense the rhythm of her troubled breathing, the rise and fall of her flesh, like a motor overheating beneath her damp dress.

Hot and uncomfortable, Stan lay in an awkward posture. She stroked his skin and moved his arm to make room for herself, as though he was a big doll, or perhaps the child they had long ago decided not to have.

"You're going to be fine."

"I am fine," he said.

Flesh to flesh, he felt the convulsion of her doubt, the angle of her body, refuting what he'd said.

Now he was with Marge every day, all day, as at the beginning of their love affair, when being together had represented to him joy and completeness. She wouldn't leave him, she sat across the room and watched him read, and—observed, with anxious scrutiny—he struggled with sentences, losing his place. If he groaned or made a sound, she sat forward and said, "Stan?" and made him hate his name.

She cooked, and that was another thing. Until his fall, he had been the cook—he said it calmed him and he had a good repertoire of simple meals. She had always been the one who washed the dishes, tidied the table, put the pans away, sorted the silverware. No longer; but he had not realized how little she knew of cooking. She was inattentive, she hurried the chopping. Her onions were either too thick, or ended up burnt or undercooked. Her soup was watery, or too salty, the meat untrimmed, the hastily cooked eggs inedible. He couldn't blame her—she had never been the cook. And so, feeling resentful, he compensated by overpraising her cooking, and her gratitude made him sad.

In the meantime, there was nothing he could do but sit or lie down and regard his injury as a postponement. He was too weak to resist her, but he vowed to become well.

Marge discouraged him from walking, saying that he needed visitors. She called her friends over to visit. Olive came, so did Laurie and Gwen. They talked about their husbands. They teased him, seeming to believe it was affectionate. "Jurassic vertebrae!" "You done a *huli*!" What was this sisterhood of fellow sufferers? Did Marge need witnesses? When she showed him off—he was her triumph—they marveled at Marge and hugged her.

"You're a lucky guy," they said and gaped at him until he agreed.

Feebleness isn't interesting, he thought. But he said, "I'm really much better."

The women exchanged exasperated looks they attempted to mask with murmurs of agreement, and what made it worse was that he was sitting like a stubborn child, and they were standing, smiling past his head.

After they left he urged Marge to see them for lunch at the Outrigger, or go with them to a movie, or maybe some shopping?

Sounding valiant, she said, "I will not leave you alone."

But Stan longed to be alone; he believed he could only recover completely if he were on his own, like the wounded animal he imagined himself to be, a slowly healing ball of fur. Sometimes, just the sound of her voice reawakened his pain, put his nerves on edge. He felt trapped in the small guesthouse, watching the workmen on the main house, and though their noise rattled his nerves and made them seem efficient, their progress was slow in fitting the doors and windows, and the house was still unpainted.

Marge said that she would take him to Kailua, their first real residence as a married couple, so that they could sit on the beach. Walking from the parking lot, Stan saw that Marge was lagging behind, panting a little, seeming to struggle as though laboring uphill, burdened by the folding chair she insisted on carrying. He had been striding under the drooping ironwoods, his own chair flung across his shoulder—he waited for her and felt sad again at how slow she had become.

Then they sat, side by side, gazing out to sea, Marge smiling, Stan solemn. The ocean looked large and bleak in the sunshine, under a sky with only two rags of cloud—the sunshine wasted in that vast emptiness was so melancholy, it filled him with foreboding. And the ocean, though blue, was a desert of water, the wrinkled surface of something dark and deep and unvisited. The waves flung ribs of low surf at the frothy shore from the brooding slab of blue.

He was reminded of a table from which everything had been cleared, a floor swept clean of all human remnants, a vision of abandonment. The end of the world will look like this, the drowned earth, submerged hope, the last man treading water, kicking his legs in useless effort. Once, people had believed that horizon to be the edge of the world—and it will be again, he thought. This view of the sea was the look of death.

A few weeks more of this idleness and severe reflection passed, and then one morning Marge found him in the driveway. Stan had risen early. He was looking beyond the almost finished house, past the hibiscus hedge, preparing to take a walk.

"And where do you think you're going, mister?"

He stared at her, annoyed by the superior tone she had used ever since his fall, a stern mother speaking to a wayward son, a caretaker to an oldie. She waved his cane at him and he thought for a moment she was going to whack him.

"Get over here this minute. You're in no condition to be out on your own."

Marge moved toward him, swinging the cane like a threat, but she was gasping as she hobbled, heavier than ever, and as he watched her struggle, he felt an overwhelming sadness, which kept him still, almost tearful.

For the fact was that he was himself again, able to climb stairs, to sit at his desk, to stretch, even to walk briskly, as he had at the Kailua beach. His back hurt—a spasm in his lower spine—only when he lay flat next to her in bed. In a chair alone he was comfortable; alone in the bed, able to thrash, he slept soundly.

Without the painkillers, he had recovered his strength, his old mobility, and he marveled, thinking: *I couldn't do this before—lift my leg, sit this long, hoist myself.* He was being reborn, a stronger man, a different man, one who had been broken and who might have died, but who lived again. And the world looked new, too; the view from Kahala was gorgeous, a long set of waves breaking on the reef, the sort of sight that said to him, *Arise, follow, meet the day and rejoice.*

Stan surrendered this morning, though. He accepted the cane she jammed into his hand and retreated to the house to brood. The next time they went out for a short walk she insisted he was walking too fast, he'd injure himself; he realized that she wanted him to slow down because she was slow, but he was happy, stepping past a shimmying gecko.

Seven weeks after the fall Stan was able to walk normally, perhaps with a hint of hesitation at times, yet that was not fragility but caution. The pain was gone, and what astonished him was not its disappearance but that in its place was renewed strength. Having overcome the fall and that damage he was more powerful than he ever imagined—younger than before the fall, healthier for having fallen. The fall had made him a new man. You fell, you cracked, you healed, and were stronger, rising with strength you never knew you had.

He was alarmed to see that the house was almost finished, a new kitchen, a new stairway where he had fallen, the painters at work with their radio jangling. Marge had seen to it all. She sat these days in an odd fixed regal posture of repose, like a vain elderly queen inviting compliments—and while he was confident in his walking, she walked less, she sat more, in a thronelike armchair she had claimed as her own.

"What are you thinking?" she asked. Her usual question.

He stood and watched her for a little while, not listening to her but to the painters' radio, trying to tune out the awful music that made him sadder. He shook his head, but she asked again.

"You're not going to like it," he said. And then he told her.

Her howl shocked him, because it was so similar to his own agonized animal cry, when he had fallen.

ADOBO

From the lanai at my house on the slopes above the old cane fields near Waialua late that night, I looked for the wild pigs that often gathered after sunset. When there was moonlight, their dark hairy bodies were like tarnished silver. They were fat bulky things propped up on dainty trotters, but they moved without a sound, and in the semidarkness seemed to glide, spiriting themselves across the grass, hardly touching the earth. Feral pigs, people called them; but I thought of them as friendly familiar shadows, keeping me company. Where were they tonight?

I sat there reflecting on the send-off for me in town that had just ended. I had taken early retirement from my job in the welding division at Pearl Harbor naval shipyard—I had risen to supervisor—and my men decided to celebrate my leaving at a Korean bar—beer and karaoke. The mama-san pushed a skinny girl at me, saying, "You go with her—she very nice!" I knew what that meant.

"No thanks," I said. "I'm good."

Some of the men mocked me, but my buddy Rick said, "Harry, I'm impressed. You're a real decent guy. You should find yourself a decent woman."

He knew I'd been divorced for years, that I'd have plenty of free time as a retiree, living alone in a plantation house on an acre of trees on the North Shore, and that I was not yet sixty.

"Someone like Bing," Rick said.

Bing was his Filipina wife, much younger, hardworking, good gardener, great cook, and tough: for their first year in Hawaii they'd lived in a shipping container Rick had welded into a simple habitation, but on a hot day like an oven. No complaints from Bing.

"Pass," I said.

"She has lots of friends back home."

"I'm good, Rick."

But on my lanai later that night I considered my situation. For the first time since high school I would not have to go to work the next day, which was a Monday. I wondered what I'd do—some errands, I supposed, and then? The nights I could manage—beer, sleep, dreams—but the days ahead looked empty.

And that's when I saw the shadows on the moonlit grass. A stranger would take them for wandering dogs, but they were too fat for dogs and didn't sniff and mutter like dogs; except for the occasional snort, they were utterly silent, shifting on the large sloping lawn, six or eight of them. Usually they headed for the tallest tree. It was a Java plum. The pigs ate the ripe fruit that plopped onto the ground.

But this was not the Java plum season—the small plums were just swelling and would not drop for a month or more. It was as though the pigs knew I was lonely and was harmless and needed consolation. Noted for their intelligence and resourcefulness, they seemed to smell loneliness. I pitied myself for feeling grateful for their companionship, the way I'd once felt for my ex-wife's occasional calls to ask how I was doing.

They were dark silhouettes, tame and two-dimensional at night. But in daylight they looked much bigger and mean, lumpy and feral and usually mud-caked, with stiff black hair, a spiky ridge of it rising like a wiry comb down their spine, and a way of standing still and watchful, the big boar always up front, the others gathered behind him, the sows, the smaller ones, sometimes a clutch of hairy frisking piglets.

I said out loud, "I know why you're here."

My voice did not spook them, but when I got to my feet, slightly drunk, to repeat it I heard a snore-like piggy honk from the big boar. He looked up, narrowing his eyes at me. They did not run; they melted away into the darkness.

That was my future, the company of wild pigs, the brotherhood of the boar.

The next day I called Rick. He told me what I knew already, that he'd fixed up other guys from our welding unit, and he mentioned that they were very happy. It is not unusual to find older haoles married to young Filipinas. And the men know what they sign up for: a kind of dowry at the outset, regular payments to the family back home, money for educating a brother, or to support a relative. That prospect did not deter me—its implications made me feel less lonely.

Within a few weeks I was in Manila, interviewing candidates—all of them Bing's friends—to be Mrs. Harry Lappin. They were young, friendly, eager to please. One was a nurse—a plus for an older man. Another a sales clerk in a department store—cosmetics counter, very prettily made up, lip gloss and long lashes. A third was chaperoned ("my uncle and auntie") and said she was a trained masseuse. If I gave her uncle and aunt some money for a taxi, she said, winking, she would massage me.

It seemed they took me to be an easy mark for being a predictable male, not hard to find the right buttons to push, simple to switch on, getting me to say "Yes, dear." But I wasn't looking for sex. I wanted a good companion—a female buddy—which is a more difficult assignment.

The last candidate was Josie, from Bing's distant hometown. At once, I knew she was the one. She was older than the others, midthirties, but was still way younger than me. The kicker was, "I live in the village." No big city manners, no makeup, no ploys; a plain speaker, and practical. She'd taken a twelve-hour bus trip to Manila from Badoc in Ilocos Norte, where she worked on the family farm with her widowed mother. They raised pigs, they harvested bamboo, they had fruit trees. She was sturdy, unlike the others, a farm girl who did not yearn for expensive shoes and manicures—her hands were toughened from hard work. She had the shoulders of a welder, and that same squat stance, too, someone I would have hired on the spot.

In the course of our talking about work, she said, "You know why Filipino people work hard?"

"No. What's the secret?"

"Because we so poor."

I said, "I want to take you to Hawaii."

She agreed, with conditions, to marry me. I knew the conditions: dowry, presents, payments, airfare for her mother to visit, the ticket bought in advance. Her mother came to the wedding, planned by Josie's uncle and some

of Bing's friends, a priest officiating. It was held at a hotel function room—
hastily arranged, the priest, the food, the flowers; simply a matter of money.

Just before the ceremony began, sitting in the front row of folding chairs,
with her mother beside me, the old woman turned to me, I thought to con-
gratulate me, welcome me to the family, saying "Good luck, Harry!" But she
looked fierce, her lips parted, her bony teeth clamped together.

"You not beat my daughter!" she hissed through her teeth.

I was startled, but I managed to say, "She's safe with me."

The reception afterward was a buffet, a table of platters and pots, the biggest a bubbling stew in a tureen.

"Adobo!" one of the guests said, a woman poking her fingers at her smiling
mouth, indicating "Tasty!"

I looked in and saw meat and bones, the sort of density that retained the
look of the carcass it was made from, a still recognizable remnant of the live
thing it had been, except that the aroma was of soy sauce and vinegar.

"You eat! Adobo is tradition!"

But I couldn't. It looked more like a hacked-apart animal—probably a
pig—than a pot of food. My sour expression was noticed. It's natural for people to judge you by your reaction to their food. Afterward, I thought, *Next
time I'll say yes to adobo.*

We flew to Honolulu together. Josie got a temporary visa, and I applied for
her residency, which would lead to a Green Card and—after the usual proba-
tionary period—citizenship.

Having a young wife in Hawaii—a woman raised in poverty from a far-off
place—was a thrill. The simplest pleasures delighted Josie—a movie, an ice
cream in Waikiki, a picnic on the beach, a drive around the island in my car,
listening to music on the radio. Meeting Rick's wife, Bing, after so long was
a relief for her, talking excitedly in their own language. She had a supportive
friend.

Rick said, "What did I tell you?"

And one night coming back late from a movie, sitting on the lanai, we
saw the pigs. They were less obvious—not much moon—but Josie saw them
clearly. She said she was used to such sights in her village. The creatures

prowled without a sound, and because we were so quiet ourselves they lay on the grass, flopped sideways, six of them tonight, the biggest one who usually stood guard gazing upward, his head cocked at an inquiring angle, looking at me and then at Josie, as though I'd spurned him for her.

Josie touched my leg and leaned, her whisper hot in my ear: "Adobo."

She spoke softly but in the juicy salivating way of someone very hungry. Yet before I could say anything—I was about to say, *They're kind of my friends*— she pressed my thigh again, letting her hand warm me, a fond gesture, the more loving for being spontaneous and casual, as though that's where her hand was happiest.

As she led me into the house I glanced back and saw the pigs on the lawn, ranged together upright, the dim moonglow lighting their eyes, staring at Josie and me—or was I imagining it? That night, and the nights that followed, were bliss—Josie in my arms—I blessed my luck.

She was, to my delight, frugal and old-fashioned. It was her farming background. She did not use the dishwasher—she washed the dishes in the sink, then dried them and put them away. She fashioned a clothesline at the edge of the lawn, from the Java plum tree to the monkeypod, and hung the laundry, instead of using the dryer.

"My mother used to do that," I said.

And she ironed the clothes, as my mother had once done, on a creaking ironing board.

She found guava and lilikoi in the woods, and one day said, "*Longboi*"— indicating the swelling fruit on the Java plum tree—and promised to make jam with the fruit when it was ripe.

I said, "Not if the pigs get there first!"

The pigs were more frequent, always seeming to appear when we were together on the lanai, looking out at the sunset and the sea beyond the treetops. I'd be smiling at the last of the light and my eye would be drawn to the shadows on the grass; and I'd see them, the big boar, the fat sows, the four smaller ones, all of them standing still, silent and watchful.

Whenever Josie saw the pigs she said, "Adobo."

And I laughed, thinking how I'd scowled at the meat and the bones in the tureen at my wedding reception in Manila, and walked away, while the guests clucked disapprovingly.

One evening, Rick called me and after inquiring about how I was getting along—"Never better," I said—he asked, "Josie told Bing you want to use my rifle—is that so?"

"I don't know anything about it."

"Something about your pigs."

"The wild pigs? They've been around so long they're like part of the family."

"Anyway, if you want to dust one of those pigs, let me know."

Something I have not mentioned so far. Josie could not read, her English was passable, yet she always seemed to know what was going on—what I was saying, even what I was thinking. It would be silly to call it animal cunning. I saw it as her having developed keen observation, as a compensation for her poor English. She must have been listening in another part of the house, because she hurried into the room where I'd been talking to Rick and she raised both arms as though aiming a weapon and said—like a kid with a toy gun—"Pah! Pah!"

She knew we'd been talking about Rick's rifle.

Still in the gun firing posture, she smiled and said, "Adobo."

"Not me," I said.

"Me. I do it," she said, smacking her chest with the flat of her hand.

I hate guns, I think they're magnets for violence, but I saw her eagerness. This was Josie's element, probably the reason she was so happy—the wild pigs, the Java plums, a gun: a little bit of Ilocos Norte here on the North Shore of Oahu.

It was a black 9 mm carbine, wickedly sleek and quite new. Rick handed it over saying, "Regular ammo won't do the job, so I'm giving you a box of hollow point shells. They sort of swell and mushroom on impact. Go for the heart, just behind the shoulder."

Josie took the rifle from me and fiddled with it. What a strange experience to see someone I loved, but did not know well, expertly work the safety lever, click the sights into position, and use her thumb to push bullets between the steel lips of the magazine, all the while seated with the weapon on her lap.

I say "strange," but I mean like a different person, dangerously so, well armed with this black rifle: a hunter, her finger tickling the trigger. She looked alert—more than alert, wired, poised to shoot, a potential sniper.

Disturbed, unsettled by the new demeanor of my wife, I went inside, leaving her on the lanai. After a long while, an hour or more, I called out.

"See anything?"

She shushed me furiously, a scolding reaction that I hated. And so I avoided her, that night and for some nights thereafter, whenever she was holding the rifle and watching the lawn for the pigs.

This business seemed to cast a shadow over us, as she reverted from being the placid picture bride to the gun-savvy farm girl, awaiting her prey.

And so I joined her, and that very day, late afternoon, as we sat together on the lanai, the pigs appeared from beyond the Java plum tree and the clothesline flapping with laundry. It was as though they were reassured by my presence, but questioning it too. The piglets as usual wandered near the flower garden in front of the house, while the big boar watched, and the plump-bellied sows dug beneath the flowers, unearthing roots and allowing the smaller pigs access to them. I was fascinated, because I recognized the habit of a hen scratching the soil so that her chicks can peck at ants. It was mothering—the fattest pigs were sows.

I was studying this when I heard the bang, a noise that almost toppled me from my chair, that rang in my ears. And then I saw a big-bellied sow knocked flat, her hind legs kicking slowly, but the creature remained silent in its suffering. Another bang and blood gushed from beneath her chest, not red in the bad light, but black, like motor oil flowing among the flowers.

Josie put the rifle down, she laughed a little, she said, "Adobo."

With gestures she indicated she'd skin and gut the pig in the morning. Her mother had taught her, she said. Her mother had a good knife and was expert with the knife—Josie slashed, as though demonstrating the gutting and disemboweling of a pig, looking murderous as she did so.

But in the morning I called my Hawaiian neighbors, the Kailana family, and told them what had happened—they had heard the gunshots, they said.

They sent over twelve-year-old Brenda and ten-year-old Kanoa with a wheelbarrow. They hosed the dirt and blood off the dead pig and wheeled it up the road. Old man Kailana set up a table outside his house and gutted the pig and smoked it. He gave us a plastic bag full of slabs of meat a few days later, saying, "Back strap—tenderloin! Taste *ono*!"

Josie shrugged in a superior way. "My mother have a better knife."

She used the smoked pig meat for adobo, cooking it in a cast-iron stewpot, and insisted I help her—I passed her the onions, the garlic, the vinegar, the soy sauce. And when she was done I looked in and was reminded of the tureen in Manila at our wedding reception, the still recognizable portions of the carcass—sinewy meat and slivers of bone.

She made so much of it I took a container of it to the Kailana family. Brenda was at the door, wide-eyed, looking offended. She took the container from me and whispered sorrowfully, "She had babies—was pregnant!"

"Was a sow," old man Kailana said. "Plenny keiki."

The boy, Kanoa, said, "You never see those pigs again. They real smart. They get scared away."

But that very night, after delivering the adobo, walking back to my house I saw the shadows, lurking near the Java plum—not eating, not rooting in the flower bed, but watching in a way that unnerved me, silently, with a stubborn look—because all they were doing was staring, the big boar rigid, severe in his gaze.

I mentioned this to Josie. She said quickly, "Where the gun?"

"I gave it back to Rick."

"Adobo," she said in a tone of complaint, as though I was denying her this meal.

"We've got enough." I did not add that I found adobo gamy and repellent, not just for the sharp taste of the soy sauce and vinegar, but for the look of it, the meat and bones.

"Gun," Josie said, insisting.

Rick said he'd been surprised that Josie had succeeded with one shot in taking down the big sow. He also cautioned me. The police would not make a fuss about one dead pig, but it was a different matter with the Department of Land and Natural Resources. For them you needed a hunting license to shoot an animal, even a wild pig or a mongoose on your property. Rick didn't want to get into trouble by loaning his gun, perhaps losing his firearms permit.

I told this to Josie. She didn't like hearing it. And when I said she'd have to be careful after dark hanging clothes on the line, or walking around the property at any hour, she scoffed.

"Wild pigs," I said.

"Adobo," she replied.

This was another side of my wife I had not seen before: defiant, willful, mocking what she took to be my softheartedness. It was annoying, but I reminded myself that these were the qualities that had made her self-sufficient on the farm. And still the pigs appeared most evenings, not eating, but watching—vigilant shadows, staring upward at me. I thought of Brenda's sorrowful, *She had babies*.

Rick called. He had become a sort of interpreter. His wife's English was better than Josie's, so he reported on what was on Josie's mind.

"Bing says that Josie wants you to get a hunting license, so that you can bag a few more pigs, legally. She's pretty keen on more adobo. Reminds her of home. But I can't let you use my gun unless you get a license."

"I looked online. It takes ages—a long application, red tape, a waiting period."

"It's in a good cause. And it seems you still have a pig problem."

"I never saw the pigs as a problem," I said. "And Rick, don't tell Bing, but I hate adobo."

He laughed. He said, "You want a happy wife?"

It was forty miles into Honolulu to the office of the DLNR, to start the process of applying for the hunting license I did not really want. On the long drive I reflected on the four months of my marriage, the little pleasures of ice cream and movies, the occasional evenings of passion. I realized that in those four months Josie and I had not been apart—we'd always been together, in the house, in the car, on the beach, on the lawn. So this drive into town was odd for the freedom I felt, my old self, the silence, the empty seat beside me. It was the mood of my facing the friendly family of pigs that first night of my retirement party.

I found the office at Punchbowl Street and took a number, and when my number was called I went to the window and submitted my application, showed my ID, and paid the fee.

"How long before I get the license?" I spoke into the hole in the glass.

"Try wait," the smiling man said in the Hawaiian way.

On my return home I called out, "Josie!" There was no reply. It was late afternoon, failing light, the distortion of shadows on the grass—and that was when I saw her. But it was not Josie, it was the rags of her torn clothes, my poor dear wife twisted and mauled on the grass, almost unrecognizable, just meat and bones.

Frantic, I called the police, I called Rick, and I asked Bing to break the news to her family, saying that I would have her cremated and take her remains back as soon as I could.

A week later—a week of misery—the coroner at the morgue asked me to sit, and his expression was of a great sadness that matched mine, which somewhat consoled me. Then he said, "Did you know your wife was pregnant?"

At home, grieving, I was sitting on the lanai and saw the shadow—just one, the big boar, Josie's killer, staring upward at me, and there was just enough light for me to see Josie's blood caked on the stiff bristles of his snout. The telephone rang, and yet the pig was undisturbed by the ringing, but only kept staring.

"Hello?"

"Me Josie mother."

"I'm so sorry," I said. "I'm planning to fly to Manila, maybe next week. Where are you?"

"Me here."

LOVE DOLL

Like most night-school classrooms it smelled of anxiety and misfortune, and in the Honolulu heat it was saturated with the industrial odor of floor polish, the sourness of mildewed ceiling tiles, the stale whiff of chalk dust, and the hum of noodles in grease-stained oyster pails. Throughout the class, the yawns of the students, the creak of their desks, the clank of their chairs as they shifted to get comfortable. All of them had done a day's work and were glassy-eyed with fatigue.

But new to Hawaii and now sleep-deprived himself with a small baby and a weary wife—accidental baby, accidental wife—Ray Blanton had asked to teach this extra subject, "Business English," because he needed the money. He realized how resentful he was when the students, all of them immigrants—hungry, working at menial jobs, wishing for better—in the course of a lesson jeered at the people in Hawaii. Their contempt diverted him and relieved the tedium of the hated ninety minutes.

It had started with Balsamo, the Brazilian in the front row, patches of his wild hair tinted blond, who said, "I am go to the museo—"

"I went to the Honolulu museum," Blanton corrected, gesturing for him to continue.

"I waynt to the Honolulu museum and I see all the feengs they are robbed from odder countries, even my country. These people are feefs!"

The students laughed—all but one, Miss Van, the Vietnamese woman at the back, who sat with her hands folded on her notebook, her silence like a reproach, as though sitting in judgment. She made Blanton self-conscious, her beauty and her gaze and her upright posture giving her an aura of power.

"And the museo not clean," Balsamo said. "I know, because I am clean the airport."

"And we cleaning, too," said Wesley Hauk, tapping the shoulder of the man next to him, John Wia, who nodded. They described themselves as "Micros"—from Chuuk. "Hawaii people they no want this work."

"Too much lazy these people," Marivick Fargas said. She was the one Fili-pina, an older woman, who washed dishes in a nursing home. "Too much they throw paper and stuffs in the street."

The Thai boy Sah chipped in with, "They play music all the day," and the severe Chinese man, Mr. Bai, said, "Dey makes nothing here. Dis bad para-dise."

Speaking slowly, Blanton wrote the words on the blackboard, "These peo-ple are very lazy. They tend to leave rubbish by the roadside. This is a bad paradise."

And they chanted this, while he led them, even Miss Van, who had not volunteered to speak. She was always the holdout.

"What do you think, Miss Van?"

"Some people good, some not good. It is the world."

Enunciating slowly in his correcting voice, Blanton said, "Many people are good. Some are not. That's the way things are."

As Miss Van repeated this, Blanton said. "Look at the time—see you next week. Leave your essays on the table."

Irritable and sleepless, because the baby was so wakeful, Blanton took a reckless pleasure in hearing the students complain. They were new Ameri-cans struggling for a foothold, anxious to learn, and, as though to justify their presence, disapproving of Hawaii work habits. Blanton was disapproving, too—feeling he'd made a mistake coming to teach on this expensive island, where he lived in a small apartment and still had not paid off his student loan.

Faye, who'd been a librarian in Seattle, was fully occupied with the baby. When Blanton returned home after work and saw her cradling Lily, he was struck by how contained, how remote, Faye seemed, staring at the baby, pre-occupied, like a Madonna. She often held a small plastic doll in front of the baby's face. It was a hula girl in a grass skirt, a lei of red flowers covering her breasts, arms behind her head in a provocative pose, a big bloom tucked in her ear—a piece of island kitsch that was also a bank. A coin pressed into its base activated a spring inside, and the hula girl shimmied mechanically, her grass skirt twitched, and Lily gurgled. Faye had discovered it in a souvenir shop and seemed to find it satisfying, its shimmying on command, with the insertion of a coin. The baby on her lap, Faye herself was like a girl with a doll.

An accidental doll. A year ago in Seattle, Faye said she wanted to move out, and Blanton had been relieved that she'd at last understood what he had seen for months, that they had no future. She was practical, but her need for order made her impatient, and sometimes repetitious. His unfinished dissertation was always on his mind; he carried its incompleteness around with him, and he was in debt—a student loan weighing him down. He became like her negligent son, and so when she said, *This is not working*, he said, *I think you're right. We need to reboot—with someone else, somewhere else.*

They had what they called their breakup dinner, and drank, and made love one last time, and separated. They were briefly happy, they still talked. But four months after the dinner, Faye came to him and said, "Guess what?"

They became partners again, for convenience. Faye was granted maternity leave and said she would not be a burden to him but that they needed this arrangement for now, in the way accidents always forced obligations on you. And in another unexpected turn, Blanton casually applied for a job in Hawaii and was hired. He disliked it at once, the suburban sprawl of the city, their tiny apartment, the uncertainty of the provisional. Lily was born, and Faye was fully occupied. His misery was always, *How will this end?*

He was overworked, he felt old, he felt poor. The mockery of the night class helped his mood: he was among other malcontents, but they were worse off than he. His daytime classes were routine, monologues on literature; but teaching English language required dialogue, a tiring back and forth, and constant correction. Yet these night class students were motivated. They had paid for these weekly sessions. They did their homework. The stack of essays before him was proof of that. He always read Miss Van's essay first, wishing for—what? Perhaps a clue as to what was in her heart.

To provoke her, the previous week he had chalked the words *LOVE* and

LIKE and *ADMIRE* on the blackboard and explained the distinctions and tried to initiate a conversation.

"*Love*—you know what love is," he said, and they had nodded. "A great feeling, like a dream." He faced the weary students, their eyes glazed with fatigue. "I love you. I love my children. I love my mother. Balsamo?"

"I love my mudda."

"Good. Do I love to drink beer? No, I *like* to drink beer. I *like* my friends. The word is less powerful. What do you like, Mr. Hauk?"

"I am like drink beer." And the others laughed.

"What do you like, Miss Van?"

She stiffened, she did not smile. She said, "I like some things. Other things not like."

"Then there is *admire*." Blanton tapped the word, whitening his fingertip with chalk dust, and took a step back. "You look up to this person. You might love them, but really the person is bigger than you—maybe better, someone special."

Now they were apprehensive—he recognized the vibration, the fear that he was going to pick one with a question. He smiled at Balsamo, who smiled back and said, "I am admire Pele. Footballer. *Grande homem*."

At the end of class Blanton had assigned an essay, just a paragraph, he said, slashing at the blackboard with his stick of chalk, so that they could copy: "A person I love—or like—or admire."

It had been a hard week, not just teaching his usual courses (Stevenson, Twain, Jack London, Somerset Maugham, and others who'd visited and written about Hawaii), but dealing with Faye and the baby, the night feedings, the shopping. He thought, *If I sit down, I will go to sleep.*

Now he was reading, *I admire Auntie Ong. She is a mother to me, because my mother died from the Agent Orange cancer. Auntie Ong had a hard life, first absconding from the country by a small vessel. In the ocean water for more than a month period, she saw the weak ones die. But she making a business in America and know how to control the inebriation ones who do not admire her.*

Miss Van, with a dictionary. The following week, handing her the paper with his *Good job* written at the top, and the grammatical mistakes corrected, he said, "Aunt Ong sounds amazing."

Miss Van folded the paper without reading it and slipped it into her note-book. She seemed to hesitate; she had a habit he'd noticed of saying, "What?" She mouthed that word now.

"Which country did Aunt Ong escape from?"

"My country, Vietnam, but long ago."

"I've read about that. She watched people die. What sort of work does she do?"

But Miss Van bowed her head, and clasped her notebook, and for a moment looked fragile, her skin feverish-seeming in its pallor, her hair in a bun, wisps of it and ringlets trailing on her skinny neck. She was the size of a schoolgirl, in her mid- or late twenties, but her aura was majestic.

"Business," Miss Van said, expelling the word like a breath.

Blanton said, "You're very pretty."

Miss Van stiffened and backed away and averted her eyes—as she lowered them Blanton saw her lovely lashes—and he thought, *I'm a fool.*

He'd promised Faye he'd bring some food home. And so he bought two cartons of won-ton saimin and fought the traffic to the small apartment, and the laughter of his neighbor's TV, the odor of teriyaki sauce wafting from up-stairs, a fugitive salty hint of sea water in the air. And Faye with the baby on her lap, tapping a coin into the hula doll to make it twitch.

He'd accepted the job, to prop himself up in the period of "We'll figure something out"—the accidental pregnancy, the accidental marriage—and they'd come promptly, knowing there'd be a time when Faye would be too far along to fly. The small apartment and the new job had been a strain, but the weather was better than Seattle where he'd gotten his doctorate. Hawaii sunshine made his life bearable.

Faye reminded him to look for a baby carriage, and he kept saying, "I'm on it," by which he meant to ask if any of his colleagues had one to spare. The problem was money—paying off his student loan, making ends meet here, car payments, rent and food; the extra cost of the baby. Thus, night school, the language class.

Teaching language involved hectoring students to open up and talk. But they were tired too. Balsamo the Brazilian was the only animated one, the

Chinese were tense, the Micronesians smiled in ways that suggested they did not understand much. Miss Van at the back was watchful but did her silence mean she was confident? She replied when spoken to, but volunteered nothing. Blanton loved the contours of her angelic face, her pretty lips, her thin, bird-bone fingers.

"Language learning is an activity like play," he said. They did not react. Perhaps they knew little of play. He taught the expressions, "This is mine" and "This belongs to me" and "I would like this for myself." These statements made them smile. All they knew was deprivation.

He placed a banana on the table and invited each student to grasp it, repeating "This is mine" and "This belongs to me." Balsamo clowned with it, Mr. Bai merely tapped it, Miss Van plucked it with her pretty fingers, saying with seriousness, "This belongs to me. I would like this for myself."

"Let's go through some responses," he said, writing on the blackboard, *Would you like to join me?* and under it a list of choices: *I'm not sure*, and *I'm not comfortable*, and *Perhaps later*, and *That's what I want.*

They recited in turn, choosing from the list, stammering at times, while he corrected their pronunciation; and then, "Miss Van? 'Yes, I'd enjoy that.'"

"Yes," she said—and Blanton held his breath—"I'd enjoy that."

"Homework," he said. "One paragraph. 'What I Enjoy.'"

And he was out of the room while they were still gathering their papers. He had parked near the library, and so by the time he found his car it was ten to nine. Passing the bus stop on University Avenue, he saw Miss Van standing on the curb and peering anxiously at the oncoming traffic; she was looking straight at him.

She stepped back when he drew next to her and called through the window, "Need a lift?"

Miss Van crossed her arms against her upper body, as though in defense, but the gesture also made her seem demure.

"It's okay. Come on, get in." Leaning across the seat, he pushed the door open.

Only then did she seem to recognize him. She slipped in and was silent.

"I can take you as far as Kalakaua. I'm picking up something at Holiday Mart."

"Yes," she said.

"You're going near there?"

"Yes," she said, the same hiss.

"Would you like to join me?" he said and laughed. When he saw that she did not react, he said, with emphasis, "The lesson."

He could think of nothing else to say and remembered that she was the one student who did not offer any criticism of Hawaii, but sat and stared, which reminded him that he was wrong to encourage the others in their banter. Her silence gave him a greater awareness of her physical presence, and for the first time her perfume, an aroma of flowers that seemed like an entreaty to him, more eloquent than words.

Turning the corner into Kalakaua, approaching Holiday Mart, she stirred and said, "Here."

"You live here?"

"Thank you."

He could see only shops, a grocery, a computer store, a bar, a pawnshop. Once out of the car she had darted away. He looked to see where she had gone, but she had vanished. After he'd bought the diapers at Holiday Mart and was driving back, past the spot where he'd dropped Miss Van, he looked again and saw that it was not a residential area. A short distance away he saw a looming structure, steel and glass, *Pacific Park Tower* lettered over its entrance, clearly an office building.

The succeeding days, after classes, making his routine trips to Holiday Mart for groceries, for diapers, allowed Blanton to size up the area. It seemed even less inhabited in daylight—the dry cleaners, the liquor store, the shop selling curtains, and that large commercial building, Pacific Park Tower.

Was Miss Van trying to fool him by asking him to drop her at this empty soulless junction so he would not know where she lived? He could not rid his mind of the pale, slim woman, so serious in class, in a jacket and blue jeans, disappearing into the shadows, slipping away from him.

"You're a darling," Faye said each time he returned from Holiday Mart. And though the acknowledgment he knew was unspoken, she was grateful he was not pestering her for sex. It had been months, but she was fatigued with the baby. The presence of the baby in the bedroom killed his desire, and her breastfeeding the baby, so sweet, was another form of exclusion. The baby had taken possession of her body, of the vitality of their marriage, filled the apartment that had become a dollhouse.

And there was something about Faye's ignoring him to amuse Lily with the hula doll that annoyed him, her fiddling with the coin, the whisper and scratch of the spring, the doll's predictable shimmy, the twitching of the grass skirt.

Blanton looked for Miss Van at the bus stop the following week, and again saw her facing the traffic, awaiting a bus; but she stepped back when he slowed down before her. She shrank and said, "I rather not," as in the lesson.

"I'd rather not," he corrected.

The insistence of her refusal made him reflective. The blunt rebuff stung him. He had hoped to make her a friend, perhaps more than a friend, and the grim thought that he was lonely made him angry. He was mulling this over when his office mate (Blanton was too junior to have his own office), Ray Kellogg, walked in and said, "Union meeting."

"I hate those things."

Kellogg said, "Your absence will be duly noted."

"So you think I should go?"

"We're voting for a salary increase—cost-of-living supplement."

"I'm in," Blanton said, and then, "By the way, you know this big building on Kalakaua, Pacific Park Tower?"

"Four floors of whores," Kellogg said.

And hearing this, Blanton sensed a glow rising up the back of his neck and settling on his scalp, and a warmth around his eyes that made him blink as, tasting the dryness on his tongue, he steadied himself for a breath, grateful that Kellogg was still talking.

Another week, another class, and at the end of this one Blanton parked near the bus stop; when Miss Van boarded, he followed the bus to Kalakaua and the Pacific Park Tower. Seeing Miss Van crossing the street, he double-parked, leaving his blinkers on, and watched her enter the lobby. He did not follow her until the elevator doors closed, but then he hurried in, to watch the illuminated numbers in the panel over the door stop at four. The elevator was empty when it descended, its doors grinding open.

A board on the lobby wall listed the businesses on the fourth floor. There were three—an insurance agency, Aloha Pest Solutions, and Love Doll Spa.

That night, although he was exhausted, Blanton lay in bed, awake, Faye slumbering beside him, the baby in the crib emitting a soft bubbling snore; he smiled at his sleuthing, and he considered the bewitching words, *Love Doll*.

In the week that led to his night class, a period of time he had once dreaded, he became impatient, eager to see Miss Van again. And when she took her usual seat apart from the others, at the back of the room, as the class began, he spoke directly to her and studied her features, the words *Love Doll* revolving in his mind.

That was his name for her now. He saw that her pallor was strange and waxen in a place that was bathed in sunlight, her thin face made her seem tense, she wore her jet-black hair straight now and it fell to her shoulders. Her lips were set, pursed in doubt, and her stare, her distinct cheekbones, her stillness, gave her a mask of concentration. She kept her hands clasped, holding a pen, and now and then she disentangled her fingers and made a note, then clasped them again. Her smock-like jacket was loose and revealed her body as slight. Her face was angelic.

Blanton devoted the class to questions asking for help, variations of *Would you mind telling me*, and *May I ask the way to*, and *I wonder if you could help me find the way to*, and other similar expressions of helplessness. As always he encouraged the students to address each other.

"Would you mind telling me the way to the post office?" Mr. Bai asked.

"May I ask the way to the beach?" Mr. Hauk asked.

"Miss Van?" Blanton said. "Ask me a question."

"Please," she said, straightening, fixing him with her gaze, "help me find my way home."

Blanton tried to reply but only stammered, staring at her; the plaintive appeal, almost anguished, touched his heart, and in that moment, with the simplicity of her appeal, he desired her more. This was something greater than lust—a glimpse of the future, the recognition that he would never tire of her. This reverie eased the tedium of the night class, the burden of fretful fatigue and Faye, remote, purposeful, head bowed, feeding the baby in the small apartment, his disenchantment with Hawaii and the debt that had nagged at him. It seemed childish, but he saw Miss Van as a potential ally, someone to dally with, to lighten the monotony of his routine, to lift his spirits.

The trouble now was that a whole week separated the night school classes, the times when he could see her.

One evening, crouching by the crib, Faye, said, "Things must be improving."

"Why do you say that?"

"I heard you whistling." She seemed hopeful, as though his whistling meant they had a future.

Had he whistled, and if so, what was the tune? Blanton laughed as he said, "Actually I'm more hard-pressed than ever. I need to spend some time at the library tonight."

Faye's new habit was not to turn away from the baby, but to maintain her maternal watchfulness, staring fixedly at the sleeping child, the shimmying hula girl in her hand, as she spoke to Blanton.

"Don't wake me when you get back. I need to sleep."

All he wanted was to visit Pacific Park Tower, find Love Doll Spa, and see whether Miss Van worked there.

"You need anything at Holiday Mart? I could swing by."

"Diapers," she said, gazing at the child.

Buying the diapers at Holiday Mart made him feel less furtive, gave him a reason to be in that neighborhood, and allowed him a place to park. He threw the bag into the back seat and walked to Pacific Park Tower, entering the lobby and taking the elevator to the fourth floor, where he saw a sign, LOVE DOLL SPA, on the wall with an arrow pointing right. At the far end of the corridor, its door was slightly ajar. Using the back of his hand he pushed the door open and recognized the odor—the sugary perfume and disinfectant from Miss Van's homework paper, and the one he had not been able to identify until now, the clotted smell of incense. A taper burned before a small gilt shrine on the floor against one wall, a fierce deity, a gleaming orange in a dish with some coins, and the stick of smoldering incense, upright in a jar of sand.

"Yes?" A woman approached through a parted curtain. She was elderly, and though she was shapeless and calm, her mouth was crooked, tugged down, her lower lip torn, disfigured by an old scar, which gave her a slushy way of speaking, as she said, "I can help you?"

"Just looking for someone," Blanton said. He glanced around, glad that no other man was there. But it was early.

"You want massage?" the old woman said, with the same slushiness, and this time the words seemed vicious.

Blanton could not suppress a giggle. He said, "Maybe," and then "Miss Van."

"No Miss Van," the woman said, pronouncing it *Vang*. She picked up what looked like a restaurant menu from a table—it was an oversize folder, plastic covered, sticky to the touch—and she opened it to a page of photographs. "But these girls working tonight." The women wore bathing suits, their names below their picture: Leilani and Sukumi and Minh. "More girls coming later."

She was Leilani, in a red bikini, but wearing makeup, her mouth reddened and full-lipped, the lank hair upswept, a blossom tucked over her ear, one of her slender fingers pressed to her cheek, smiling. Blanton had never seen her smile.

"This one," he said, dry-mouthed again. "Leilani."

"Cash or credit card?"

"How much for the, um," he began, but could not finish.

"Fifty dollar for house. You pay girl separate. One hour, very nice." And seeing him slapping his pockets, she added, "We have ATM machine."

He knew because he had just been to Holiday Mart that he had two twenties and some ones in his wallet. Faye would see the credit card statement, so that was out of the question. The ATM would generate a line item on his bank statement. He took out his wallet and, pinching it, weighed it before the old woman as though casting a spell.

"Thirty dollars—cash," he said. "Half hour."

"You want to cheat me," the old woman said, chewing her damaged lip. Blanton was mortified by the directness of her accusation. "Leilani very good. She worth more."

"Okay, forty. Can I just see her—talk to her?"

"Sorry, mister."

As she was moving toward Blanton, to evict him, the door opened. A stout older man began to enter, then he hesitated, straightened, and cleared his throat. When he saw Blanton, he crept to the shrine, smiled at the fierce deity, and fled to an armchair. As he lowered himself he snatched up a tattered magazine and held it before his face, humming softly, plucking at the pages, avoiding eye contact, like a man in a doctor's waiting room. He wore a baseball cap, an aloha shirt that was tightened by his paunch, and flip-flops on his dirty feet.

"Thanks," Blanton murmured, turning away from the man and keeping his head down. In his car it occurred to him that the piggy man might have chosen Miss Van—Leilani—from the album, and the thought disgusted and angered him with a stab of indignation.

"You're early," Faye said. "Did you find what you wanted in the library?"

In the house all day, attending to the baby, she was buffered in her bliss by her motherly warmth from all the wrongs of Honolulu, existing in a glow of innocence that radiated from her child.

"I'll have to make another visit tomorrow," Blanton said, with a shallow cough.

"Doesn't anyone in your department have a baby carriage they don't need? The cheapest one I've seen cost two hundred bucks."

And when, the following evening, he punched $200 into the keypad of the ATM machine at Holiday Mart, Blanton became grim, thinking of the baby carriage; then excited, thinking of Miss Van. He tried to imagine a plausible lie for Faye when she saw the credit card statement and questioned the withdrawal.

The old woman with the torn lip greeted him at the door, and this time she seemed like a sorceress.

"Auntie Ong," he said, to dispel her aura of power.

"How you know my name?" she said, accusingly, drawing away from him.

"Everyone knows you," he said. "I want to see Leilani."

"Fifty dollar for the house."

"Here you are."

"Pay girl separate," she said, palming the money, scuffing out of the lobby, gesturing for him to follow.

In the dim pinkish light of the corridor, he passed doors opened to small empty rooms with beds, like a dorm or a dollhouse, he thought, until he saw that each room had an oversize wall mirror, each mirror reflecting a fretful, hurrying man he recognized as himself.

At the last room, Auntie Ong said, "You wait inside," and when Blanton slipped in she pulled the door shut.

He turned away from the mirror. A double bed filled the room, and on it a big beach towel—lettered *Aloha*—had been spread over the sheet. Apart from the chair on which he was sitting there was no other furniture. No window, a mirror above the headboard, a clock.

When the door opened, he stood abruptly and swayed, dizzy from the suddenness of being upright. Miss Van in the doorway, half in, half out, leaning and then partly withdrawing. Her expression did not change, yet Blanton thought he heard a subtle ticktock, as faint as the click of a ballpoint; but he knew, her little tongue.

"Cannot," she finally said.

"I paid," Blanton said.

"I not comfortable," she said, and stepped away, closing the door.

He sat, then got up, scowled at the mirror, then went to the door, which was vibrant with murmurs. He snatched it open and saw Auntie Ong holding Miss Van by the wrist.

"What's going on?"

"You wait," the old woman said.

"I paid," Blanton said.

"Go inside. She coming now."

He stepped back and shut the door and, facing it—and the murmurs—he considered leaving. Yet he had come so far. He thought to himself, *If she joins me—fine. If she refuses, I will go home to my wife and baby. But I need to wait and see. I will accept whatever happens,* and he remembered to add, *as my fate.*

The door opened in his face. Miss Van stepped in. She was paler than he'd ever seen her, but maybe this was the effect of reddened lips and her black dress, which was loose and short, and perhaps not a dress at all but a sort of lingerie. She stared at him in a way he could not read, though he noticed an almost imperceptible shake of the ringlets beside her face—her hair was up-swept and lovely—as though in disbelief.

"What now?" he said.

"Hundred dollar." With this a beckoning, a twitching of her fingers.

"For what?"

"Special."

"God," he said, and reaching to claw his head, he realized that he was still wearing a baseball cap. He pulled it off and sat on the edge of the bed, sighing.

"Okay, I go. I rather not."

"Miss Van," he said.

But she interrupted, "I not Miss Van. I Leilani."

"All I have is a hundred."

"That what I want."

He counted the money into her hand, wishing that he could see her expression. But she was facing down, counting, too. Then he slipped off his clothes and lay back on the bed, centering himself on the towel, while Miss Van pushed the money into a purse.

Seeing her approaching, Blanton said, "Aren't you going to take your clothes off?"

"Twenty dollar extra."

He extracted the bill from his pocket—the last of his money—saying, "Take them off slowly."

She did so, stroking them against herself, teasing him. When she was naked, he leaned toward her, propping himself on one elbow. What he took to be a green belt at her waist was a green speckled snake tattooed on her body, encircling her, rising up her spine, the wedge-like head of the snake resting between her shoulder blades, its forked tongue extended toward the nape of her neck.

"No kiss," Miss Van said, framing her lips in disgust.

And then as Blanton lay on the bed, glancing past the pale spidery form of Miss Van, he got a glimpse in the mirror and was appalled by what he saw, his white misshapen body, his purplish face and crazy hair; he had to look away, keeping his face averted, as he did when a doctor was drawing blood from his stinging arm.

"This is mine," she said, her voice an insistent whisper, taking hold of him, and she began to chant it. Breathing hard, she was transformed, working herself into an amorous panting that was something like frenzied prayer, and she straddled him, facing away, her buttocks chafing against his face, still massaging him. Then she turned aside, facing him, and leered and tugged, murmuring, "Mine."

"Yes," burned in his throat.

"Watch Leilani," she said eagerly, working her tongue across her lips. "This belong to me."

As he began to whimper, "Yes, yes," he became breathless himself, and her whispering, as of someone starved, stopped with a gasp, as she took him into her mouth. It was ecstasy, for seconds.

"You like it?" he asked, as she slid off the bed, reaching for her clothes.

"It work."

"Don't go, baby," he said, because she was dressing.

"Finish," she said and was out of the room before he could think of anything to say.

To his surprise and pleasure Miss Van was in her usual seat at the back in the next night class. Blanton was encouraged by the sight of her, and he smiled at her, though she did not smile back.

"This product is interesting," he said and wrote the words on the blackboard. "This product is more interesting," he said, still writing. "This product is the most interesting of all." And when he finished, he got the students to recite these phrases.

"Football is interesting," he said, speaking to Balsamo. "Is baseball more interesting?"

"Football is more interesting product forever," Balsamo said.

"What do you think, Miss Van?"

"Football is interesting," she said.

"What is more interesting than football?"

"Business is most interesting of all," she said.

"What business?"

"Noodle shop," she said, and, hesitating, she added, "I want to make."

"Excellent," he said and turned to the others. At the end of the class he beckoned to Miss Van as she was leaving.

She approached him, hugging her backpack to her chest, shielding herself.

"Nice to see you," he said. "I thought you might not come tonight."

"I pay for class." She tossed her head, flinging a lock of hair to the side. "I come to class."

Blanton considered this. He said, "Are you hungry? We could go for noodles?"

Miss Van frowned, that sneer of disgust, as when she'd said, *No kiss*, a slight convulsion in her body that was more emphatic than no.

"A date?"

A slight twitch of her head, the lock of hair falling across her face, a sniff, another no.

"I could give you a ride," and he heard a flutelike beseeching in the words.

"I go now," she said.

Blanton struggled to say "Work?" and only managed it with a catch in his throat, for never had such a simple word held so much anguish for him.

When she was gone he felt abandoned—worse, that she was leaving him for an assignation with another man; and then he remembered, *other men*. In this mood, he stopped at Holiday Mart to use the ATM and saw on the screen *We are unable to process your request at this time*; and he knew his account was overdrawn.

I am possessed, he told himself, *and there is no remedy for it except to see her*. He hungered for her, and having no money until his next paycheck, he longed for the night class to see her. That was something but it was not enough. He taught his literature classes to the reluctant readers, and he sulked in his office, with Kellogg.

"We're looking for someone to collect union dues in the department," Kellogg said one day.

In the past Blanton had sometimes reflected on friends who were drunks or stoners, who lamented their addiction but said they could not help it. He'd said, *Just stop doing it, it'll make life easier*, and he had been surprised that they had continued drinking or drugging, bringing more misery upon themselves.

Now he understood: they were in the grip of a force and could not break free. Perhaps it was not misery, but triumph, an act of rebellion, objecting to the servitude of the everyday. The force was not sinister, not grim, it invited him on a quest—not reckless but taking control of pleasure, like churning the cosmic ocean to find the nectar of immortality. He was possessed that way now, and it excited him and promised euphoria.

In the office, with the tin box of union dues, he thought of Miss Van. Sitting at home, across from Faye holding the hula doll at the baby's face, he was happy, Miss Van on his lap. In Holiday Mart, at the beach, in traffic, Miss Van was with him, a comforting wisp, easing his mind.

After being paid for teaching a few more classes, and with stolen union dues in his pocket, Blanton returned to Love Doll Spa, to Auntie Ong, the payment of the fifty-dollar entry, and the bedroom with Miss Van.

"I want to be your lover," he said.

She stared, she sniffed a little. She said, "Hundred dollar."

When he attempted to kiss her, she ducked, and twisted out of his embrace. Then he paid her. "For your noodle shop."

She softened and smiled beautifully, and sighing with desire, she raised her arms to welcome him, then reached and drew him to the bed. He sprawled like a chieftain as, naked, she hovered over him, stroking him. "This belong to me." He groaned with pleasure, aroused most of all by the words he had taught her—her talk made her sexier. And pressing against her in the heat of his lust, he whispered his desires to her, and she repeated the wicked words exactly as he'd spoken them, with the same crazed emphasis, her hot mouth against his ear. The act was one thing, but it was a blur; her reckless words, those mad perversions, breathed back at him, thrilled him like nothing he had ever known.

Then it was over and he was alone, naked on the bed, Miss Van putting on her clothes. She scowled, she smoothed her skirt, she clicked the catch on her purse, and was gone.

A week later, in the sour-smelling heat on the nighttime sidewalk, Blanton stood across the street from Pacific Park Plaza. He hesitated. The facts were pitiless—his obsession was like a criminal instinct. If he continued this way he risked losing everything—Faye, discovering the overdraft, would scream, backing away, clutching the baby, and would leave him. Disgraced for the theft of the union dues, he would become a pariah in the department and would be fired, and probably prosecuted for embezzlement. He would never pay off his student loan. Miss Van, with all his money, would start the noodle shop, at which he'd be a customer, perhaps ignored, possibly refused service for pestering her. They were not possibilities; they were certainties, the wild froth of an insane wave about to break over his head and destroy him. Everything pointed to disaster.

He walked quickly, turning his back on the rising darkness, and—excited, eager, hungry, certain—hurried toward Miss Van and the light, the thickness of bills in his pockets like flesh between his fingers.

HAWAII SUGAR

Five women at the table sat with their heads bowed, not speaking, as though in the expectant "summoning" phase of a séance. Their prayerful stillness, and the one woman weeping, was so unusual on the Koa Lanai of the Outrigger Canoe Club, a waitress hurried over and asked, "You guys all right?"

"We're fine," Marion Pickering said—she was the sixth woman, but sitting up straight—she could have been the medium in the séance. Her story had caused the others to fall silent.

But the silence had come upon them slowly, like day fading into twilight, dimming the blaze of afternoon sun that had dazzled on the ocean and lit their faces and their flowers. And their straw hats, trimmed with ribbon and blossoms, at first made them picturesque in the failing light. Dusk continued as an awkwardness, the way shadows sometimes crept around a group of listeners and simplified them. And now the plumeria centerpiece on the table, near the sauce bottles and the sugar bowl, and the leis they were wearing all became absurd in the solemnity. The women, overdressed in the darkness, seemed faintly ridiculous, too; the only sound was low waves plopping against the seawall beyond their table, more eeriness.

The five women were still looking stunned, their faces mimicking intense thought—but they were unsure of what to say, and several were trying to smile. Throat-clearing seemed too obvious and stagy and might single them out. They could not curb their uneasiness by resorting to their phones because of the Outrigger rule, no electronic devices in the dining area.

"That news about the sugar plantation closing for good made me remember it all," Marion said. She waved the waitress away, but the waitress came back with two low candles that flickered, creating an even greater atmosphere of a séance: firelit faces like masks.

It had begun simply, as a late lunch, and over dessert, Marion looking around the table and saying, "I didn't start out a Pickering. I grew up Marion Bywater."

And the other women became attentive and stared, because this was something entirely new, sounding confessional.

"Bywater," Freeny Amaral said. "My uncle Tony worked for him. Was a *luna* on the plantation."

And both women said together in singsong, "North Shore Sugar!"

"Closed long time ago," Emma Kalani said to Milly Ah Sam.

But Milly was quietly watching Marion, reading her features, as though through thinning smoke, looking for more.

"Maui Sugar just now closing—Alexander and Baldwin," Marion said. "That's what made me think of it. End of an era. No more Hawaii sugar."

"The last plantation in Hawaii Nei," Freeny said. "Then *pau*. Hawaii sugar come bitter."

"Everybody know everybody on the plantation. Was like a *ohana*."

Marion winked, a big obvious wink lubricated by a mai tai, like a spasm, canting her head. "*Ohana* whether you like it or not."

But as she spoke, Baby Ganal had drawn attention from her by saying, "My father worked in the fields in Waialua, cutting and doing *hoe-hana*"—which surprised the others, the revelation, a canecutter's daughter on the Koa Lanai, wearing black pearls and a straw hat with a feather band around the crown. "But he worked up to milling superintendent."

Freeny Amaral said, "Maybe my uncle Tony give him lickings"—a bad joke for its implications, Portagee overseer beating a Filipino canecutter, but Baby just shrugged.

"Where your father stay?"

"Kahuku," Marion said, looking queenly before a candle, also in a straw hat but one more finely woven than Baby's. "We lived half the time in town and half on the plantation."

"Must be confusing living in two places," Emma Kalani said to Milly Ah Sam.

But Milly, staring hard at Marion, was not listening. She had lifted her lei to her face and was sniffing the sweetness of the blossoms as though for relief.

"Being in town meant I could walk to school. We had a house in Makiki—up the street from Punahou."

"You was Marion Pickering then, or Bywater?"

"Bywater, like Bywater Sugar, before it was called North Shore."

Freeny said, "What year you graduate, Milly?"

Milly had come to the lunch with Emma, who knew Freeny but not Marion. Asking about her high school was a Hawaii form of welcome.

"Should have been seventy-five," Milly said, lowering her lei to her chin to speak.

"She's a kid," Freeny said. "You one *keiki*!"

"From where?" Betty DeMent asked.

"Would have been Kahuku," Milly said. "But I never graduate. We move, too."

"So maybe you got something in common," Baby said.

"When we move to town, I was a little girl."

"Kahuku was where we stayed when we weren't in town," Marion said. "We were there, because of Dad, for the sugar. But you wouldn't have remembered the sugar."

"I remember some of it."

"You remember the rainouts?" Freeny asked.

"A little."

"A little! You don't remember the rainouts."

"I remember the plantation whistle, early morning. The big overloaded trucks piled high with cane stalks. The smoke from the tall sugar mill chimney blowing over our house on the days of Kona wind. The smell of it, half sweet, half burnt."

"Sexy smell, my dad used to say," Marion said, but Milly was still talking.

"The chugging of the roller mill, and the shredders. The molasses smell of the piles of wet bagasse."

"That's all *pau* in Maui now," Baby said.

"I remember moving one night, real sudden. The big hurry of the taxi, us kids and my mom all jammed in the back seat."

"What's a rainout?" Betty DeMent asked. She was new to the island, new to the club, where she'd met Marion—"New *haole*, meet *kama'aina*," Emma had remarked when they were introduced.

"A day when no can harvest," Marion said, lapsing into pidgin, as though speaking from the canecutter's perspective.

"A day off," Freeny said.

"Kind of," Marion said. "The reason they're memorable is that before sugar got unionized all the houses were free. Which was nice. But on rainout days the workers weren't paid. Then they formed the union, much to my father's"—here she made a face—"plenny *huhu*."

Some laughed at Marion's pidgin, but as Betty DeMent asked for a translation and Milly clutched at her lei again, Freeny interrupted.

"With the union they got paid for rainout days. On the other hand, the sugar workers had to pay rent for the house. So it kind of balanced out."

"How you know that?"

"Tony, my uncle, the overseer. He talk story about it."

"They plenny tough," Emma said. "The *lunas*. They never let you talk on the job."

"My father tell a good story," Baby Ganal said. "His *luna* say, 'You Filipinos eat dogs. That is so disgusting.'"

"I hope the *luna* not my uncle," Freeny said. "Or maybe he your father, Milly."

"My father pass away," Milly said so softly only Freeny heard. "My mother alone."

"This was Waialua, not Kahuku," Baby said. "The *luna* give them a real hard time. But they need their work, so they say nothing, just cut the cane. 'Is just a story,' they say to the *luna*. 'About the dogs.' The *luna* say, 'Whatever.' Then, one day, they invite him to a birthday party. They have adobo and all kine Philippine food. They offer him some. *Luna* say, 'Is dog?' No, they say, is a cow. He eat it and like it a lot. 'Taste *ono*. I want some more.' They give him more."

"I think I know how this story going to end," Freeny said.

Shushing her, Baby said, "When the *luna* he finish they say, 'Woof-woof.'"

Betty DeMent said to Baby, "My grandpa was in the US Army, stationed in the Philippines somewhere. He taught us a song,

> *The monkeys have no tails in Zamboanga*
> *The monkeys have no tails*
> *They were bitten off by whales.*

No one spoke, and the only sound was the slosh of small waves at the seawall.

Baby cleared her throat for attention. She said, "Stupid song."

"On rainout days all the workers stayed home," Marion said to fill the silence that followed. "No cane get cut. So my father was kind of restricted."

Reshtricted she said, in the island way, as though to imply a greater local inconvenience.

"In what way?"

"He couldn't move around like he wanted to," Marion said. Then, straightening, she added, "A divorce isn't that awful, when you think about it."

That was unexpected, no one spoke, but then she leaned forward and put her elbows on the table to steady herself and told the story that seemed to bring on the twilight.

"Sometimes a divorce is worse for others—not the husband and wife, but people near to them. More upsetting, because they haven't got the facts. My mother knew my father was unfaithful. She knew, as women know, that he'd been fooling around, and probably on the plantation. His false laugh, his lame explanations for being late—a flat tire, 'I ran out of gas'—the unexplained absences, the way other women talked to her in a kind of pitying or cheering up tone. Being a friend, being overly generous, as though she was wounded or humiliated."

In a tone of recognition, Milly said, "I used to talk to my mother like that when she seemed hurt. She didn't say anything but I knew from the way she sat with her hands in her lap, looking useless. I was little but I knew. I crawled into her lap to take the place of her hands."

"Maybe I did too," Marion said. "So when my father told her to stay in town, because"—now she spoke in a gruff man's voice—"it might be better for all concerned to separate for a while . . ." She paused and continued in a small, reasonable voice, "my mother didn't say much. She might even have been a little relieved."

"Get rid of the stress," Freeny said.

"We were relieved, too. She had always been easier to live with than my father, because she was such a good listener. When we tried to talk to him we had the sense that his mind was somewhere else, hearing another voice in his head, that other woman, his other life, maybe the only one he cared about, his big secret."

Here, Marion took a sip of her mai tai and smiled because the five women had become so attentive, wondering what would come next. None of them had known about the divorce, or Bywater. She had always been Marion Pickering from Nuuanu to them. Her father, the one they knew, Bert Pickering, owned a car dealership in town, and she had never married.

"The funny part just came to me today, because Maui sugar is closing and plantation life on the islands is coming to an end for good. I was thinking about those plantation cottages, and the people in them, my father's workers."

"Like my uncle Tony," Freeny said.

Baby said, "My father, in them fields. He knew what work was."

"My mother . . ." Marion said. "She was so sad most of the time. My father had a lover—maybe a mistress, a girlfriend, in one of those little flat-roof cottages. Her husband had run off, maybe died. But my father let her stay on—he had power. He was Kahuku Sugar—then North Shore Sugar. This woman was like a junior wife, devoted to him. But he was only interested in one thing from her. He paid visits to her—maybe in her cottage, maybe somewhere else, except on rainout days, when no one was working, just sitting on the lanai drinking that homemade gin, and he couldn't sneak around. I suppose he told her he loved her and gave her some money. She worked in the office some days, to be near him. She was pretty, I guess—I only saw her one time. *Hapa*, I think, Hawaiian Chinese."

"Japanese never marry Hawaiians back then. Chinese often did. It was a money thing," Freeny Amaral said, and because the word *hapa* made Milly squirm, Freeny added, "Get some real pretty wahine with that combination."

"But that's not the point," Marion said. "The point is that my parents split up because he fell in love."

"With the *hapa* one. In the little hut," Baby said. "Romantic."

"No. With a new one—Winnie. She was real young. Danced hula. No kids, from town. She paid a few visits, then she moved in with Dad. Was free and easy, plantation style—not like now. By that time we were living in Makiki."

"And they get married?" Emma asked.

"They get hassled, big-time, by Sugar—that's what he called her—she sweet like sugar, he said, before the big bust-up. He told my mother all about it in the end, when the trouble started with this *hapa* lady. See, my mother is official. She gets the house in town, the dog, us kids, the car, some money for child support. But the *hapa* is the mistress, she's not official. She gets passed over. She thinks my father going to leave my mother for her. But, lo and behold, my father falls in love with someone else altogether."

When she laughed at this, not loud but with a note of triumph, her laughter left the other women exposed, in the way they had gone quiet, the shadows slipping over them.

"The wife can take being rejected. But the mistress, she's in a bad position. She's real angry and all alone. She's left with nothing. So never mind the wife—and anyway my mother found Bert Pickering. It's the mistress who loses everything when the guy falls in love with someone else."

In the silence, in a small voice, Emma said, "I never think of that."

"A married man can't be unfaithful to his mistress," Marion said. "Can fool around on the wife, but not his girlfriend."

Betty DeMent asked, "Who was she?"

"He called her Kopa'a—Sugar. I don't know her real name. Maybe that was her real name. Just a young plantation wife or widow. I think she had kids. They would have been younger than me. Maybe one of them was his."

That was when the five women bowed their heads and went quiet.

"End of an era. No more sugar," Marion said, to fill the silence.

The table seemed to levitate in the candlelight, the flames in the little glass tumblers reflected upside down on the shiny wood surface; the scattered grains of sugar where they had spilled from the sugar bowl were black in the dim light of the candles. And the women were subdued, as though quieted by the light dimming. The ocean became more visible, starker as night fell, striped by breaking waves, the ribs and rows of tumbled foam, the waves whitening and pooling in the shore break, falling and withdrawing, slowly, almost sorrowfully, muted splashes like sobbing. The sound soothed them until they saw it was Milly with her face in her hands, tears running between her fingers.

That was when the waitress hurried over and asked, "You guys all right?"

A CHARMED LIFE

I.

The young know almost nothing, which is why the best of them take risks, while the others go off to work. Hard work yields a sort of knowledge through experience, but risks can make you wise—crisis as enlightenment. I had plenty of crises. What follows is my account of them.

From boyhood, with nothing to lose, I escaped to a different dimension and looked like a daredevil. The risks I took would have been regarded as dangerous and to be avoided to someone better off and privileged. Yet I never hesitated. My parents had limited means, so risk was necessary for me in making my own life.

"We wish we could help you," my father said, meaning they couldn't.

Mother added, "You're on your own, Felix."

So I would look in the mirror and try to conjure up the image of the man I wished to be—not a hero, but a boy's idea of manhood, a sturdy version of contentment. I was young, my notions were primitive, and when I played at casting a spell I gathered all the simple elements you'd find in a Waziri tribal ritual in a Tarzan novel. I was ignorant of the world but I was willing to venture into it. In this secret ceremony I made faces, I crooked my fingers, I danced, I chanted—it was a game. I suppose I was ten.

My parents shrugging and telling me that I was on my own did not make me feel powerless. Their indifference liberated me and provoked me to toy with magic, gazing at myself in the mirror, praying for the power to be transformed. I became adept at this mirror-magic. And I also read books—I lived in books. I realized that to find the life I wished for I would need to spirit my-self away and separate myself from my family. In some distant place I would become the person I wished to be.

I was a mediocre student but a dedicated reader. The good grades went to the students who drudged at their homework. I was a bookworm—perhaps an early risk, ignoring my homework to read for pleasure and inspiration. I was poor at algebra but I knew a great deal about exploration in Africa, and tribal rites in New Guinea, and mountaineering. Mount Everest had not been summited by anyone when I was a boy, parts of Brazil remained unexplored, the Gold Coast was a British colony, the Congo was Belgian, the four-minute mile was still a dream for runners, only one man had sailed single-handedly around the world, and I knew his name: Joshua Slocum. No one had traveled to the moon. The world was brimming with darkness.

Money being scarce at home, my parents urged me to get a job. I worked at a supermarket on school weekends, and in the summer at a public swimming pool and a drive-in theater. Such part-time jobs did not interfere with my reading—I always had a book in my lap in the upraised lifeguard chair, and one on coffee breaks at the supermarket, not a schoolbook, but perhaps Paul Du Chaillu's *Explorations and Adventures in Equatorial Africa* (jungle, gorillas, cannibals).

At the pool, as a lifeguard I longed to save someone. I wished for a near drowning. And so it happened. I rescued a boy and got my name in the paper: *At the Metropolitan Pool in Wellington on Monday, lifeguard Felix Jardin, 16, see-ing a boy in distress, dived in and brought him to safety. "He saved my life," Angelo DePrima (12) said*—and readers sent me money because of my heroism. At the supermarket I imagined kissing Hazel, who worked at the checkout counter, and I succeeded one evening after work, as I walked her home, tasting her bubble gum. I admired her, for her mastery of the cash register, while I was still only a bagger.

Harry Browning was the manager at the Twin Drive-In in nearby River-side, where I manned the soda fountain, calling out "Twin-tastic special!" One day, Mr. Browning asked me to help him cut some long grass at his house—a big house that fronted on one of the Mystic Lakes. As I began, thrashing the grass with a sickle, Mr. Browning standing near, supervising, his wife appeared at an upper window of the house and called out, "Wouldn't that be easier with the mower?"

"Shut up!" Harry shouted.

"I was just saying . . ."

But he didn't let her finish. Red-faced, he screamed, "Shut up—go inside! Stupid bitch!"

I was turning seventeen. I had never heard any man speak that way to his wife. It was dramatic—another crisis. He was still facing the window when I locked my eyes on the back of his head (he was wearing a tweed golf cap) and thought, *You will be punished for speaking that way—you will be harmed.* It was a game I'd practiced in the mirror, blazing eyes, crooked fingers, casting a spell.

Harry Browning had a stroke very soon after that, and later, at the drive-in, he was pushed in a wheelchair by his wife. He could not speak and had lost the use of one arm. I put it down to an amazing coincidence.

I kept after Hazel, the pretty cashier at the supermarket, and after a year I succeeded with her sexually—not easy, as both of us were virgins. Some weeks later, she sent me a note saying she didn't dare tell me in person—"I'd just end up crying"—that she had missed her period and was probably pregnant. The next day at the register she said, "I can't talk now."

Walking her home after work I asked her what she wanted to do.

"I don't want to marry you, but if you help me get through this, I'll never ask another thing of you." She began to cry. "I can't tell my parents."

I was then eighteen. I had no idea how I could help. And yet she was my ideal for being such a hard worker, tapping the keys on the cash register, always smiling, and I had imagined us rubbing along together through life as equal partners. I now thought, *Our lives are over—this is our future, Hazel and me and our child, heading into a dead end.*

"I'll think of something," I said, but there was nothing in my mind.

"We could go somewhere. I'll have the baby and then give it away."

That was brave and decisive, yet "go somewhere" bewildered me. Where would we go? I went home and wished for this torment to disappear. When I woke the next morning I remembered what she had said and I was so oppressed I wished again, but this time in an oddly formal way. I summoned up

Hazel's naked body, elevating it before me. In my vision, she lay on her back, as though on an altar, her hands folded in prayer. I did not curse her, I praised her, and watched her glow, as I performed my ceremony of purification.

She was not at work the next day, or the day after, and I was too nervous to call her. She sent me another note, which I tore open: *I woke up bleeding*, she wrote of her miscarriage, and added that she hoped she'd see me again. I did see her, not in a sexual way, only to comfort her, and told her how I admired her. But she went off to college and I never saw her again.

That crisis gave me willpower and concentration when I got to college. I avoided romantic entanglements, I studied hard, and when I graduated I decided to become a teacher in the places I had read about and fantasized living in, Africa, India, South East Asia. At that time—the early 1960s—foreign teachers were in such great demand that none of us was required to have an advanced degree. Being an expatriate was the different dimension I referred to earlier.

And I married—twice. Marriage seemed asymmetrical to me, with a lopsidedness that so impeded its fulfillment it became a version of hostage-taking. My wives were decent but so different from me, as I found out after a year or so, I felt they were out of their depth, or perhaps it was I who was in too deep. We seemed forever out of focus to each other.

Dilma was an ardent shopper. This was not obvious when I was courting her—why would it be? We had no money; we had yet to live together. Along with shopping she struggled with her weight, both traits possibly related: she was a consumer. Whenever we disagreed on something she said, "Why are you shouting?" We were in Africa; I was on the staff of a rural teachers' college in Uganda. Africans and other expats asked us if we had children. Dilma always defiantly replied, "We have a fabulous cat." I associated cat dander with her unproductive cough. She was homesick; there was no scope for shopping in Mubende, half a day's drive from Kampala. "I didn't ask for this," she said. Mubende was known for its Witch Tree, a thick and twisted thorn tree cluttered with offerings, such as baskets of fruit or ribbons. I often visited and meditated upon it, contemplating my future. Dilma at last left me.

Fiona Upton, from California, refused to change her name: she hated my name, Jardin. We met in India, my next teaching job, in Jaipur, where she was buying fabrics for her boutique in Carmel. Our marriage was an interruption of her life, she often said. She smoked. She dressed well, as you'd expect of a woman who owned a boutique. She was given to sudden silences. I had to guess what she was thinking, but I was seldom right. Her mother visited us, and disapproved of me, which was a plus in Fiona's mind and made her forgiving of my lapses, of which drinking at the staff club after classes was the worst. Fiona was a reader and generally content but addicted to unbreakable routines and inflexible judgments such as, "See? You let yourself down again." Her repeating that was especially infuriating because she was often correct. She had a frightening smile when she was angry. She was saddest on holidays, desolate at Christmas, aching to be back in Carmel, at her boutique.

I seldom wanted to be in the US. I always said, to Dilma and then Fiona, *But this is our home*—meaning the house that the school provided to its teachers, wherever we happened to be, pleasant houses, simply furnished, bathed in sunshine. I always had a garden, and a gardener.

There was no rancor; my wives were joggled into loneliness by being so distant. I was affectionate, but in other respects not enough for them. I wished them away, I mentally moved them out. They ended up happy. Divorce and half of what I had—money, souvenirs, the odd carpet or vase—was a liberation.

In each case, though my wives were different in most ways, their sex drive diminished and their need for security increased as time passed. I didn't fully understand them until long afterward, when they remarried—dull rather submissive men who never traveled and were good listeners, men unlike me.

I was deficient in reassuring them. They needed friends, they liked parties—I had no need of either friends or socializing. They were insecure in foreign badly governed places, where I thrived in the disorder, a kind of controlled chaos in which I was floating and unpindownable.

Messy divorces, people say—not in my case, though painful. My first one with Dilma left me doubled over, as though I'd been punched in the gut, my hopes dashed, the future bleak. I felt naked and fragile. Sobbing helped, yet I managed, I married Fiona, and after that divorce I knew I'd be fine: I was cured of marriage.

Early on in Africa when I was single, before Dilma, I was robbed of every-thing I had, all my valuables, in a break-in. But I got through it. I missed what I once had but these things were irreplaceable. So the second robbery in India left me peculiarly indifferent; all the thief got were cheap electronics, easily replaced. I saw that being devastated was a process of life, and not the end, just another crisis diminishing in importance.

I enjoyed quitting a job, wishing for a different one, and finding a happier one in a new country. That was the nature of being an expatriate teacher, not as common today as it once was—these countries are better educated now and have their own teachers, though they're poorly paid.

As the sort of expat I was, essentially an escapee, I saw my life as nonlinear, improvisational. My wives required certainty, something I could not provide. Not a lack of love but a lack of direction. Clearly I was not going to amount to much, but I was content in my work in these foreign parts and traveled on my holidays, never back to the States or to Europe, but locally, sightseeing, and memorably to China.

What do you want? Fiona once asked, exasperated.

Just to stay happy.

I couldn't explain how the ideal partner I imagined to be a woman ex-actly like me, like Hazel long ago, how we would resemble two brothers, on the march, like-minded, symmetrical. She would have a job, we'd meet after work, to talk about our day, have a drink and cuddle, no children to distract us from each other.

I had chosen to live and work in those places because of my boyhood belief in finding freedom far away. I was not wrong. I loved my remoteness, but I never again found anyone to share it with completely. It seemed that I was destined always to be the sympathetic onlooker. When my wives had raised objections, claiming they were homesick, I said, *I won't stand in your way*, and gave them everything they asked for. Thus, we remained friends. I never said that I had inspired their disaffection, that I had charmed them away.

What I looked for in a lover, what I valued in a wife, what I'd never found was a woman who would accompany me into the jungle—a metaphorical jungle of exoticism, as well as the actual one I aspired to explore. It was not glamor I sought, but courage, strength, willingness, someone as hardy as I was, who would share the burden, relish the adventure; someone unafraid, not a delicate creature, though I saw beauty in physical strength and an unassertive sensuality in courage.

The lioness I looked for I'd never found. I wondered whether such a woman existed. I resisted conventional sexiness, the sylphlike frailty of the coquette for whom I would be a protector and a patron, the daddy figure to whom she'd cling. I wanted an equal partner, someone as eager for risk and adventure as I was, a fellow teacher who was also a bushwhacker. I'd read of women mountaineers, hikers, explorers, vagabonds—but I'd never met one. As I'd grown older, great beauty seemed much less important than kindness and self-sufficiency. Lust was a distraction, it clouded my judgment, it made me a monkey. Though I must add that my ideal woman combined both boldness and good health. I always imagined her holding a weapon—an axe, a machete, a glittering sword—and marching beside me.

I loved my work as a teacher, I admired my students, their eagerness to succeed, and as for companionship, I was always in places where bar girls made themselves available. You hear this and think, *How could you?* But the bar girl is the secret consolation of the male expatriate—or was when I was in those chaotic countries. Casual sex may have seemed risky or sordid, but it made me happy and forgiving. I visited women and paid for sex in the same spirit that I visited a doctor or practical nurse, to relieve me of my urgent need—not lust but an itch. The money made it an uncomplicated encounter except that, unlike seeing a doctor, I paid in advance.

After my marriages ended, there was never a time when I did not have someone I was seeing for my itch. Romancing a student or wooing someone marriage-minded was out of the question, though. It was always a woman I paid, there was never an expectation of marriage, it was someone to brighten my weekends. I was discreet, and so were they—discretion was a fine art to them and part of their business plan. It was a transaction that suited us both, an old and tolerated transgression that was a tradition in these male-dominated cultures where I'd found myself.

The rest of the time I was alone and content, living what I thought of as my charmed life, not wanting more than I had, glad to be an expatriate in the years when expats had special status, before students like mine went abroad to universities in great numbers and came back with advanced degrees and put expat teachers out of business.

And there was the weird singularity of being an expat. To an outsider it might have seemed risky to be a teacher in Africa or Asia. But I thrived as an expat, and in spite of all the insecurity there was often power in being a foreigner—a strange man, unknown, perhaps unknowable. I also liked the simplicity of the situation, the undemanding job, the available excuses, the women, the food, the free housing. I was treated well. I saved money.

I sometimes entertained the thought of writing about my life as a teacher in these hot, half-made countries. But what was so special? Lots of men and women I knew had chosen to teach abroad and forgo advancement in the US. And anything I wrote would be a sort of summing up. Writing about yourself forces you to reach conclusions, some of them unwelcome and unflattering, and since I had never been a reflective sort I never wrote a word.

Being away was a form of concealment; I wanted to distance myself from my unhelpful parents. I had an expat cast of mind; I enjoyed the distractions and disorder, the English teaching was useful to my students, the hot weather suited me. It was a life of improvisation, and loose ends that made me a procrastinator—perhaps not surprising that my two marriages ended in divorce.

My students, desperate to lift themselves from poverty, were more hardworking than any I had known in the US—and many of them ended up in the US. They wished to escape from the constraints of their folk societies, yet I was fascinated by being immersed in them, constantly in the presence of the uncanny and the inexplicable, of ghosts and enchantments. In my whole career as an expatriate I never knew anyone who didn't believe in ghosts. Why question such bewitchments, when they occurred—which was quite often—a death, an illness, a curse? Any misfortune was always someone else's fault: you fell ill because someone caused it. The Africans I knew believed wholeheartedly in witchcraft, Indians prayed to Shani (mounted on a crow) the Hindu god of karma, the Chinese in modern high-rise Singapore covertly burned incense before demon gods and made bonfires of paper notes of gold-printed symbolic money for luck, to invite prosperity, and sometimes they were rewarded.

My last job was at a school in the Philippines, among pious churchgoing people who also believed in imps and witches inhabiting anthills and trees. In my small town I routinely announced myself at a house by calling out "*Tao po!*"—"Knock, knock!"—I'm a person, not a ghost. Like many other places where I lived and taught, I was comforted in the Philippines by the floating world of bar girls, the expedient of many another male expat, in my case, as I've said, a weekly treatment.

When I turned sixty-eight, I retired, but I had become so accustomed to tropical weather, instead of returning to New England I moved to the mild weather and palmy shores of Hawaii. At last after decades of travel and staff housing, I owned my own house. I furnished it with curios I'd bought on my travels, and with the help of some local stone masons I re-created on a terrace of my sloping property a Zen garden I had seen in China, with an enigmatic name, the Pavilion of the Accumulated Void. It being my garden was appropriate to my name, Jardin.

I stumbled upon this garden just after Fiona and I split up, another crisis during which I searched for a meaning. I was in Shanghai and took the short train trip to Suzhou, looking to be soothed by the gardens and canals mentioned by Marco Polo.

Strolling through a moon gate to one particular garden, I saw a small weathered signboard in Chinese and English, PAVILION OF THE ACCUMULATED VOID.

"What does this mean?" I asked an English-speaking Chinese student.

"One moment." He hurried to a nearby teahouse where some old men were conferring over cups of tea. I saw them speaking, and then the student returned to me.

"They say you can only know what it means if you sit there alone."

I stepped along the ramp to it, a terrace where there was a marble bench, and just off-center two massive boulders that were lumpy and pitted, spectacular surface features that suggested age and experience, like the eroded surface of an ancient landscape. The garden was at once calming and inspirational, those boulders known as "scholar's stones," the twisted black pine, the raked gravel, the marble bench, the stone lantern.

Breathing deeply, I experienced a sense of arrival, of an uplifting blankness of being, like a happy death, and I remained in this state of suspended animation, with no notion of time passing. I must have sat for an hour or more, and it was only when I left that I understood the meaning of "accumulated void." It was a vanishing, a form of levitation in clear air, an utter emptying of the mind, an ending that was also a point of departure—in my case I was healed from my recent split with Fiona.

Years passed in Hawaii, my nights of roistering were over. I was happier alone and settled comfortably into the supreme solitude of growing old, relishing my garden. The Pavilion of the Accumulated Void was my anchor, my retreat, my solace, my sanctuary, where I sat many afternoons to calm myself. The notion of it had been in my mind since my visit to Suzhou, all those years ago, where I'd experienced the bliss of an awakening that I hoped to re-create. I suppose I built it in the same spirit that motivated religious folks of another age to build a chapel on the grounds of their manor houses, praying that in time it would inspire veneration and invite the odor of sanctity. My garden gave me hope.

Then one day I had a message from my ex-wife Fiona saying that she had also moved to Hawaii and lived in retirement with her husband, Walter, in a condo in Honolulu. Since my house was in a rural area on the North Shore, I didn't see much of her, but now and then she and Walter paid me a visit, stayed for coffee, and we talked. Walter was friendly if a little dull, but listened, suppressing his yawns, when Fiona and I reminisced about our time in India, all our disputes forgotten in the glow of pink princely Jaipur and its marvels.

It was Fiona who reminded me I was about to turn seventy-five.

"It's a milestone, Felix."

"A millstone," I said.

"Walter and I are throwing you a party."

I have always disliked birthday parties. I feel self-conscious, all the attention on me, my needing to reassure people that I'm having a marvelous time, and most of all I feel excessively obligated by the presents I'm given—never anything I want. I'd been so private and unforthcoming, no one ever knew me well enough to give me anything that mattered to me, and never anything of value. I might have responded to a pair of pearl-handled dueling pistols, or cowboy boots, or a new bike. I was usually given a raffia basket, a brass tray, a comic T-shirt, a picture frame—encumbrances that proved no one cared very much. Birthday parties just made me feel old.

But seventy-five was such a large number that I could not avoid marking the day with a celebration—and Fiona promised to do all the work. She made a plan, she had invitations printed, and wishing to fill the room she invited people I hardly knew. I agreed, thinking: *It's only one evening, it will be over soon and then I'll be left alone*.

I dreaded the toasts, the speeches, the platitudes, the commiseration, the lame jokes, and on the day—in the Dolphin Room of the Turtle Bay Hotel—it began just as awkwardly as I'd expected.

"At your age, every day is a gift," one of the first speakers said—a man younger than me, who knew nothing of my life, simply basing his speech on the fact that he saw me as a geezer. I had not truly felt old until he began to speak.

There were more speakers; it was misery and like a grim send-off, where everyone who spoke commented on my age, and that was maddening, as though it was a marvel that I'd attained it, astonishing that I was still above-ground.

What no one seemed to notice was that I was in good health, that I exercised regularly, ate sensibly, and was in better shape than most of the partygoers, who were younger than me. It offended me that I was treated as a fossil, lucky to be alive. The speakers talked about themselves, of their parents and grand-parents, of people they knew who were old, of lessons learned.

None of this was news to me. Their talk merely emphasized that they didn't know me. To be polite I smiled and thanked them—these sententious strangers—and hoped that the event would be over soon. I imagined that I could use what they said as my excuse. "I'll need to go home soon—at my age these late nights disturb my sleep"—or something like that.

I was practicing this excuse when Fiona tapped a spoon against her glass for attention and rose to speak. She picked up a flute of champagne and faced me.

"Felix . . ." she began and paused for effect. "You are a calm and contented man. In all the time I've known you I've only seen you worked up once—not angry but crusty. You've never been an angry man. When we were married, it bothered me a little that you could sit at your desk so serene, or in a chair quietly reading—in your own world of contemplation. What is more annoying than someone sitting and smiling for hours on end, needing nothing, needing no one. It looks snooty and selfish."

I heard a chuckle from Walter. He lifted his glass, seeming to take what Fiona said as disparagement. Then he tipped his head back and drank and gasped.

"I was happy," I said, hoping my interruption would stop her, because of course she was exaggerating, another birthday tribute mischaracterizing me.

"But that one time," she said.

I had no idea what she was driving at. We'd been married for seven years, a few years in India, the rest in southern Malaysia, which she hated for its being Muslim and puritanical. All I remembered was her saying, *You dragged me all this way*, and how she cried at Christmas, wishing she was back in the US, where it might be snowing.

What she seemed to be hinting at in my contentment as an English teacher in Ayer Hitam in Johor state was my carrying on an affair with a bar girl named Yasmina. Was she going to mention this indiscretion now?

Walter had refilled his glass and was sipping it, looking fascinated at the thought of something disgraceful about to be revealed about me.

"We lived on the edge of Ayer Hitam," Fiona went on. "We had very few neighbors. The nearest one was behind a bamboo fence about fifty feet away in the kampong."

"But he had a hut on our side of the fence," I said to the partygoers, and hearing Walter chuckle again I turned to face him. He winked at me wickedly but was obviously conflicted.

Because of the robberies in Africa and India most of my valuables were gone, yet owing to my willingness in the settlement of the divorce—more than half of everything I had, money rather than things—my relationship with

Fiona was without rancor. But Walter posed a problem—the confusion of the second husband hating to hear all that history. And Fiona had once told me he was irked that she kept her maiden name.

Walter was usually good-humored in a smug and superior way, repetitious in his drollery. He didn't dare criticize me—Fiona would not have stood for it—but I knew he was, deep down, envious and competitive. It must have annoyed him to hear Fiona's stories about our travels—Walter had never been anywhere—and how, when we'd divorced, I'd given her everything she'd asked for, money to buy her own house, the few remaining artifacts and pictures I had, most of my books. I did that so that I would have no possessions to drag me back into regretful melancholy—a chair we'd bought together with such hope that would make me feel miserable whenever I sat in it. I wanted to start all over again, with no distractions.

As Fiona went on speaking I saw Walter raising his glass again, drinking eagerly. He downed it and when he reached for the bottle of vodka I set my eyes on him, letting them blaze a bit, and willed him to pour, to keep pouring, and when the glass was full I willed him to drink, to keep drinking. I loved seeing him gulping it down, lapping the rim of the glass, tipping it again and filling it as my eyes commanded, *Keep drinking, Wally*.

He was glassy-eyed, his head wobbling, wearing an idiotic smile, as Fiona said, "You've got to hear this."

Walter still had a glass in his hand. He held it to his mouth, he sipped, he smiled, he drooled through his smile, looking drunk and deaf. *Drink, Wally.*

"What about the hut?" he said.

"I was coming to that," Fiona said, and people laughed. "It was an illegal structure. The family played music in it, probably their radio. They didn't respond when I complained. I did so on Felix's behalf because he's nonconfrontational. But nothing came of it. The noisy hut was there to stay."

I saw it now, the horrible hut, and said, "I remember."

But Fiona was still talking, facing me, saying, "We were going away one weekend—driving down to Johor Bahru and across the causeway to Singapore. Before we left I saw you standing on the veranda. You weren't angry, you were determined, you were cursing them in a very measured way with an intensity that seemed demonic. It frightened me a bit because I'd never seen you in that mood before. You weren't doing it for my benefit though. You took no notice of me. Your whole being was concentrated on that obnoxious structure—the noisy hut."

I clearly recalled the day, my cursing the house, and driving off, exasperated. I nodded, gesturing for her to continue.

"When we got back from the weekend, we smelled stale smoke, we saw scorched and browned leaves on our trees, and in the distance where the hut had been there was a patch of ground blackened by ashes."

Though Walter wore a deaf and bewildered expression of extreme drunkenness, the other guests erupted in laughter and a sort of enthusiastic chattering, which gladdened me, because it seemed no one saw anything sinister in it. Just a crazy coincidence!

Fiona proposed the toast, they all drank to my health, I cut the cake, and at last to my relief my birthday party was over.

It could have been another coincidence, though the incident had taken place so long ago it hardly mattered. What I remembered was that Fiona left me soon after, and because the smell of the burned hut lingered in the trees I associated the end of our marriage with the stink of ashes.

It was a good thing Fiona was unaware of what happened later, when I was arrested by the Malaysian Morality Police for kissing a girl—it was Yasmina—in public, both of us fined for the offense. When this was reported to Ahmed Bazari, the headmaster of my school in Ayer Hitam, he reprimanded me, as I sat in his office, wishing him ill.

Retirement age in Malaysia is sixty, and I muddled along for a year—oppressed by Ahmed Bazari, telling myself I didn't want to retire. I wasn't ready to go home, but I'd been singled out and fined for kissing Yasmina—and, as she was a Muslim, and a woman, her fine was greater than mine.

My colleagues, mostly local Chinese, had drawn away from me, not wishing to be associated with a degenerate. I could not explain to them my theory of sex as equivalent to a treatment for an itch. I knew that retirement was not my decision but rather something being forced upon me. Being ignored, ceasing to matter, reminded me that I was just another expat, easily replaceable, not disliked but isolated, disposable, superfluous. And Yasmina had moved on. She saw that she had no future with me, though I'd paid her well.

In my last week at the school, I said to Headmaster Bazari, "I'm not taking this personally. I know my time will be up soon."

"It is up now," he said.

I wasn't sixty. Inside I was furious and humiliated and found as I was uttering this banal farewell that I was staring at him with utter hatred—the sort of anger that was rare in my experience because I resisted it. It exhausted me, shamed me, and left me in a sort of delirium, my fury darkening my soul.

Not long afterward I received an invitation to the staff celebration of Eid, the end of Ramadan—a period of feasting and gorging—and I supposed it as a thank-you for my years at the school. And I was headed to my last job, in the Philippines.

"Someone's missing," I said at the gathering in the staff room, the tables piled with food and soft drinks.

Headmaster Bazari wasn't there. I was glad, because he had forced retirement on me and I had nothing to say to him.

"Not really in a fit state," Miss Koh Tai Ann, the games mistress said.

"Had a stroke," Ray Tung said. "He's housebound, lost the use of one side of his body—hemiplegia. He's in a wheelchair. His brain gone, too, lah."

I said I was sorry, but was I sorry? I had cursed him, I had wished him ill. Yet I took no responsibility. I told myself that wish fulfillment is an inexact process: as a believer in coincidences, I did not want to acknowledge that I'd had a hand in these events—the burned-down hut, the stroke victim that resembled long-ago Harry Browning, my boss at the drive-in theater who'd screamed at his wife. I'd always gotten my own way, but to think that I'd been responsible for someone's misfortune was not something I wished to remember.

Though I am not a reflective person, the aftermath of my seventy-fifth birthday party concentrated my mind. I went quiet, I was alone in my house, disturbed by what Fiona had said about the burned-down hut. People had laughed at my curse: no one knew what had happened to me in my past, but this occasion caused me to be reminded of many curious incidents, my role in them, always getting what I wanted. I'd been so engrossed, so grateful, I accepted my good fortune, without examining it.

It was modest luck, and so it was hard for me to imagine much blame attached to my having my wishes granted. I had limited ambitions—to travel but to pay for it by working abroad, to live out my harmless fantasies of exoticism, to teach willing and diligent students, to make enough money to support myself in my old age and not be dependent on others. At some point I'd downsize, I'd sell my house, I'd move into one of those assisted-living facilities that I thought of as Death Row.

Up to the time of my birthday party I'd felt I'd lived a charmed life. I'd selfishly assumed I'd been lucky, having everything I'd ever wanted. Looking back I saw that in all those years there had been another element in it, but I could not say whether it was a blessing or a curse.

At my advanced age, I saw a pattern—not random instances of luck, not amazing coincidences, but a succession of wishes I'd made over many years that were granted: answered prayers.

2.

Imagine this cruel paradox, that near the vanishing point of your life, everything becomes illuminated—a lightning flash granting you a glorious clarifying power just before the thunderclap of your extinction. You gasp and see the truth, that you've been possessed all along by true magic, a key to happiness, with the prospect of more. But that gasp is your last breath—a moment later you're dead. Time's up!

It happened to me. But I did not die. I knew I was guaranteed some more good years before old age closed in and immobilized me. And I've lived long enough to write this, my testament, my confession, the witness of an old man, still pondering the revelation of this power.

For most people, time passes, the habit of living takes over, the rut deepens, becomes a grave, and then they drop into it and are gone. For some—like me—in the half-light of old age the unexpected happens, one's head is bursting with insights from having lived a full fortunate life. There is no single guiding truth; it has all been, you now see, an unfolding over the years and at the end you're granted the gift of clairvoyance—anyway, because of my birthday epiphany I was granted it: the ability to see my whole life in a new way.

I'd been pretending to play at it, calling it a game. I never dwelled on it, but I'd had it all along. I saw that since childhood I'd had a gift, a sort of psychic energy that allowed me to order my life as I'd wished—something that could pass for magic, giving me everything I'd wanted. And I was still alive—old, but alive and able to wish for more.

Perhaps—it was possible—I was not alone, that other people looked back on their lives and realized this phenomenon in old age. In some cases, they might have died soon after, taking their revelation to the grave. Or they might have lived a bit longer, and may have mentioned it, but to no purpose, since after you reach a certain age no one listens to you. Time has whittled you small, you're practically invisible, dead before you die, indistinguishable from a ghost.

Because no one listens, what most old folks do, out of self-respect, is deny they have any gift, pretend they're powerless, and surrender to indifference. The aged apparently placid face is unrevealing, yet it's often possible to discern the bleak disappointment in the sad insulted eyes of the elderly. They know they're running out of time and that no one will understand their hurt feelings.

In my case I was vivified and motivated to exploit my gift. Yet it seemed so uncanny I had to think of it as an ambiguous attribute, knowing that it was perhaps less a gift than a psychic power that could be misused. My sense of possessing this power changed my view of myself and my past. It strengthened me, it shone a light on my life, it made me want to live longer, to verify it.

That was unexpected. Take my uncle Gilbert. In the year before he died, while he was still in an old folks home, Uncle Gilbert used to smile at me and say, *I'm coasting*. I guessed what he meant, his sliding along toward the end. He was like many other older people. At a certain age they surrender to what they see as the inevitable, the last grains of sand sifting into the bottom of the hourglass. They stop making plans, they drift downward, dying. They have not been granted the revelation.

The aging person's thought *It might never happen* is provoked by physical weakness and debt, a narrowing of choices, a smothering twilight in which the worst becomes obvious: that the only certainty, coming soon, is death. Nothing new will happen to you—not love, or wealth, or vitality. No laughter. And not only are you deprived of pleasant surprises, you have nothing to offer.

Who has succeeded? you wonder. Brutes, bullies, cheats, trimmers, weasels, money-grubbers, attention sluts, the power hungry, the pushy, the well-connected, the greedy, the crooked. It's no consolation as a failure to know that they, too, will ultimately fail and be more miserable than you have ever been in a world they've corrupted, because by then you'll be dead.

In the meantime, friends drop away or die, strangers show no interest in you, and you begin to understand that for years you've been shunned or ignored. You do not exist as a serious figure in anyone's mind. A few years of shrinkage ensue—you're almost as small as you were as a child, but far less significant, a sort of orphan. "I'm old" is a euphemism meaning death is near, and no one cares, nor will anyone mourn or remember you. If you have children you weep for them, knowing that will be their fate.

With all this comes the paralyzing certainty that nothing matters anymore, that the life you've lived has been mostly an illusion, chasing trivialities; that now you're treading water, that you'll soon sink and leave no trace.

Not me! I was free of this morbidity—I was exuberant. I was not condemned to coast like Uncle Gilbert, or to stew in regret like most of the oldies I knew. I now saw that all along there was a pattern that I had imposed upon my life, a distinct plot, as a result of my wishes granted—romance, jobs, travel, money, and marriage—great while they'd lasted. I had never asked for the lottery winner's windfall of a fat fortune, but had only—I suppose wisely—prayed for problems solved, and serenity, and sunshine. Modest wishes for soft landings. And so I always knew comfort but never great wealth; I knew love but never grand passion, I had respect but never celebrity or fame. I always got what I asked for—not a dramatic life but a life of satisfactions, sorcery on a small scale, magic I'd never truly believed I possessed.

And here was the greatest satisfaction: my life was far from over, I had years more. The good fortune that had eased me into old age had given me excellent health. I'd never had a serious ailment, never a night in the hospital, never broken a bone or suffered a fever—and I'd spent my working life in tropical countries, an itinerant expat English teacher, traveling from one sunny place to another.

My good health was not an accident, not luck, but was a consequence of my having had what I'd wanted. I'd been relieved of any anxiety. A life lived without worry had granted me vitality. I didn't feel old, I still swam most days, I slept well, and as for my blood pressure—"like a teenager," my doctor quipped.

This epiphany, my seeing that I'd determined for the better the entire course of my existence, that all my prayers had been answered, was like the discovery of a deposit of hidden wealth—a chest of pure gold in the attic. I'd looked back over my long life and seen how year after year, in small ways, I'd cast spells and gotten what I wanted. I'd realized a secret I'd never known I had. Now I was certain. I was rich, I had power, and I was still alive and strong.

I was humbled by the revelation. And aware that I might have years more with this power, I thought, *How shall I use it? What shall I wish for?*

There ensued a period—torture for me—of indecision, leading to paralysis. What had seemed a liberation, my secret now revealed, was a burden. I had never deliberated much about what I'd wanted, I'd merely acted on impulse, except in that rare example Fiona had mentioned on my birthday, how I had uttered an elaborate curse against the neighbors' hut in Ayer Hitam, and it had burned down. In other cases I had whispered a solemn prayer and it had been answered.

I hadn't expected to be brought down by the epiphany, but my puzzlement soon turned to paralysis. Perhaps I was not powerful after all, that what seemed a revelation was a delusion—that I was imagining the whole business; that what had seemed to be a power I possessed was merely a conceit, based on an accumulation of random coincidences. That I had no power. I was simply a deluded old man who'd managed to muddle through life, blessed with dumb luck that had left him content.

Maybe—and this thought also tormented me—I was senile. It was not unusual for someone my age to imagine all sorts of fanciful distractions. For some oldies it was persecution mania. I had another uncle—Uncle Arthur—who, in his late seventies, began to speak of malevolent nuns gathering at the gate of his house, looking like creatures you might see in a Bosch painting, with beaks and protuberant eyes and white billowing bonnets and webbed feet. My uncle feared these freakish demons and refused to leave the house.

Or senility might take a different turn, and instead of feeling like a victim, fearful of such creatures and suffering night terrors, the opposite might occur—an exalted sense of having special powers, a folie de grandeur, in which one was granted the ability to make dreams come true. In this case, the old man was Prospero, a character I knew well from my years of teaching, *The Tempest* being an assigned text in the schools of former colonies. I'd always regarded Prospero as selfishly manipulative and a dubious sorcerer, Ariel helplessly beholden to him, and his control over Caliban a bitter master-slave relationship. I used to suggest to my students that the pairing of Prospero and Caliban was a metaphor for colonialism, the white interloper on the enchanted island dominating the natives, holding them in thrall, refusing to let go. I sometimes joked that I was like Prospero—the expat who'd taken charge. My students laughed, but in my old age, had I come to believe there was some truth in this, because of my birthday epiphany? That I had power, that I was an old coot who'd convinced himself that he'd led a charmed life and that he still had the ability to have his prayers answered?

I didn't know if this was true, and to my intense frustration, for the first time in my life, I became seriously depressed, thinking that I'd gone mad. I was not Prospero, or a fortunate soul who'd ordered his life as he wished, but an old fool.

There was only one way to answer this question of my supposed power and resolve it once and for all—and by the way, release me from the gloom that had taken hold of me to the point of utter paralysis. I had never been so lonely, so mournful. I had never minded being alone. I had relished my solitude. Now I was pathetic, feeling like an abandoned child.

I approached my garden, the Pavilion of the Accumulated Void, I peered at it beseechingly, yet I lacked the willpower to act. I tried to force myself to sit on my usual bench and be uplifted by the vibrations from the two dramatic rocks and the black pine. But something was wrong. Instead of seeing its symmetry, I saw disorder, how I'd neglected it, the scattered twigs and leaves, the unraked gravel, and I suffered.

It was more than mental torment, it was physical, a pain I felt in my whole body, an agony that kept me from eating, that induced insomnia, that weakened me. I was a miserable wraith. And why? It was the notion that I felt myself to be a fraud, a crazy old man who'd believed he had special powers and a garden that could transport him to serenity.

I simply didn't know who I was, and it dawned on me that this was the condition of many melancholic people, suffering from a crisis of self-knowledge, a darkness, an intimation of worthlessness, where there ought to have been insight. I had so slight a sense of self-esteem, combined with such pain, that it was easy for me to imagine my taking the next step and putting an end to it all, seeing suicide as a blessed release—killing myself as a cure.

After a life of satisfactions it had come to this desperate impasse, and it was now fueled by the obsession that, as an old man, I was deluded in thinking I was hearty, that in fact I had few years left to live. In most respects my time was up.

I'd begun conscientiously saving pills. I took a morbid satisfaction in counting them, with the expectation that pretty soon I'd have enough to swallow and send myself to oblivion. This prospect eased my mind, for the final solution it offered.

I was in pain but I was not stupid. I was still sentient. I had not yet surrendered, though I was fairly sure that killing myself was the only answer.

The telephone rang around eleven one night as I was counting my pills—counting them was a reassurance that I had power, the dish of pills seemed like wealth. I resisted answering the phone; I was enjoying my suicide fantasy and my pill counting. When it stopped ringing, I went on counting. I was smiling at my dish of pills. Sometime later the phone began ringing again.

"Yes?"

A howl came from the receiver—Fiona, tearful, gulping, grateful that I'd answered the phone, thanking me over and over, then unburdening herself.

"It's Wally, he's off his head. I've never seen him like this. His drinking is out of control. He says he wants to kill himself. Felix, are you there?"

"I'm listening."

"I'm sorry to call so late. I didn't know what to do. I was afraid to call the police. Are you busy?"

I almost laughed; it was now almost midnight, and before me the dish I filled with pills gave me the ghoulish pleasure of being in possession of a fatal dose.

"I'm so sorry," Fiona was saying.

"I'll be right over."

This meant driving thirty miles to her condo in a small community in a valley adjacent to Honolulu, but at that time of night no traffic, a quick trip.

"He locked himself in the bathroom," Fiona said when she answered the door. He'd stopped responding to her pleas and she thought he might be dead, but she'd heard him weeping just before I showed up.

She led me to the bathroom door. I called out, "Walter?" but there was no reply.

"Can you break down the door? I've seen it done in movies. Please, Felix, do something."

"Get me a screwdriver."

She was gone for a moment, I heard a drawer yanked open and pushed shut, and she was back with a screwdriver.

I knelt and unscrewed the metal plate on the door and dismantled the doorknob, a simple procedure, but when some small parts tumbled out and I still could not open it, I shoved the head of the screwdriver past the steel plate on the jamb and pushed the tongue back into the throat of the lock.

As I was doing this, Fiona said, "Ever since your birthday party he's been drinking."

As the door swung open I saw Walter sitting on the hopper, his fist against his chin, in the posture of Rodin's *Thinker*.

Though dazed, he gave me a wan smile and seemed relieved to see me; he looked limp as Fiona hugged him, and he was clearly still drunk. He began to cry, which seemed to me a good sign. But the kitchen knife in the sink was ominous.

"I'm so embarrassed," he said, slurring his words.

"Relax, it's fine," I said, as we helped him out of the bathroom and into the parlor. "Fiona—please make him a cup of coffee. We'll just sit here for a bit."

"Don't lecture me," he said. "I couldn't stand that."

"I'm here to listen."

He looked surprised. He groaned and said, "I'm evil." He put his face in his hands. "It's the drink."

Provoked by my silence he told me how in recent months he'd drunk more and more, to the point where he couldn't function without it, a bottle of vodka in the morning, another in the afternoon. But drinking had made him moody, he'd gotten physical with Fiona, slapped her, bruised her arm, and seeing what he'd done he experienced such remorse he'd felt the only solution was to kill himself. He was planning to use that knife in the bathroom to slit his wrists.

He lifted his tearstained face. "You're not saying anything."

"I'm listening."

"What do you think?"

"Never mind what I think. What do you think?"

He hung his head, he clasped his knees, and by this time the coffee was on the table beside him. He took the cup in two trembling hands and sipped it, looking miserable.

He was wearing an old brown robe over his pajamas, the robe hanging open, his pajamas sweat-stained and rumpled, his face pale and unshaven, his eyes still glassy from drink and shame. It struck me that he looked like me, at my lowest moments recently at home, disheveled and reckless.

"I've got a problem," he said finally. He sipped more coffee and put the cup down.

I knelt before him and hugged him, and he began to cry again, but this time with relief. I said, "That's what I want to hear—you have a problem. That's the first step to recovery in AA."

He gave me another weak, tentative smile. It was as though he'd confessed a sin that had been haunting him, and that confessing was a show of strength that had cleared his mind, offering him the hope of sobriety. Admitting he was an alcoholic meant he was aware he needed to change.

What he did not know was that when Fiona had called me I'd been in a worse state than him, not drunk and disheveled but coldly suicidal, gloating over my hoard of pills.

"You saved me," he said.

I didn't want to burden him by telling him how low I'd been, or, *No, you've saved me*. I'd had a helpful rational glimpse of the awful finality of suicide, especially of my dead body being found, another enlightening crisis.

As Fiona embraced him, holding him in her arms like a child, I said, "You're going to be fine."

And then I remembered.

3.

Driving home on the empty road, it occurred to me that it was at my birthday party, when Fiona was telling her story about my cursing the hut, that I'd willed Walter to drink—wishing him another and another, watching him drool and become helpless. I'd resented him savoring what he hoped for, a second husband's dream, the possible revelation of my disgrace. I'd decided to neutralize him. He'd become so drunk as a result he'd missed the end of the story, which was my successful curse—hilarious to the listeners, ominous to me.

Yet from what Fiona had told me he'd continued to drink for weeks afterward, and in the period when I'd lapsed into doubt and confusion, becoming so low as to be suicidal, he'd also fallen badly, to the point where he'd abused Fiona and seemed dangerous to her and himself. So she'd called me. I'd sprung him from the bathroom and helped him by listening, sharing his pain. As a consequence I'd experienced a reprieve. I was bewildered but no longer suicidal. Yet it was my willing him to drink in the first place that had sent him into his muddle. I'd turned him into a drunk, and his drunkenness had saved me from suicide. By attending to him I'd rescued myself.

Or so it seemed—that he'd become an alcoholic through the power of my suggestion. But might this be explained as another amazing coincidence?

I went to my garden, the Pavilion of the Accumulated Void, and as before I was dismayed that it looked so neglected, so littered, unraked, untended. Yet I sat on my marble bench, making a vow to restore the garden, giving it the power that strict order bestows, and with this vow I was able to meditate until I'd emptied my mind. In this clarity I knew what I had to do. I needed to test my ability to make something happen—deliberately to work a miracle of my own volition. Not an impulsive grunt of glee or playful resentment, but the formal uttering of a command—as in the story Fiona had told of the event long ago, which seemed to me so dramatic and convincing.

Again, I reassessed my life, tallying up the number of times over the years that I'd gotten what I wanted, as a boy, as an expatriate employee, as a husband. I remembered many incidents of answered prayers, the ones I have mentioned earlier. Yet I'd lived by instinct, by pure whim—never by a preconceived plan. I'd been prompted by circumstances and acted impulsively. I'd never schemed in advance. All the wishes I'd made, like *Keep drinking, Wally*, had been improvisational, and all had resulted in benefiting me somehow.

Still, I wondered whether I'd deluded myself. Maybe I was one of those rare individuals who experienced one coincidence after another, the annoying person who said, *I guess I've been kinda lucky—hey, God's been awful good to me.* I'd always depended on intuition, so this awareness of a possible power—an extraordinary gift I might possess—made me self-conscious and tentative and timid. I found myself hesitating. Did I really want to know the answer?

If I was gifted in this way—not lucky, but a truly powerful Prospero—a critical question loomed: How would I use this power in the years to come?

I was no longer suicidal—the experience with Walter had shown me the folly of that—but I was deeply lonely, oppressed by my solitude. In the past I'd never been lonely; I'd loved to be on my own, probably because it left me free, without responsibilities, unrestrained, in the selfish way I'd always lived, moving from country to country as an expat teacher. And when my wives had objected to this sort of nomadism, I'd mentally moved them out and wished them well—*I won't stand in your way, darling*—and later they'd thanked me for my generosity.

But my indecision over whether I wished to know the truth left me with a sense that I needed encouragement, some sort of companionship, a person to help guide me, someone to appeal to, a witness, a friend.

I'd never known this need before, enduring the sort of bleak loneliness that could only be relieved by a true friend. I was never a friend of a bar girl; I was a client, paying for a treatment. In the past I'd found intimate friends a burden. What I'd learned throughout my life was that other people made me lonely, they intruded upon my contented—or selfish—solitude. I'd known a degree of loneliness when I'd been married. As a single man I'd enjoyed eating alone; as a married man it was misery. Was there a greater sadness than sitting over a meal, well aware that your spouse was elsewhere in the house? Telling me *I'm not hungry* day after day I took to mean *I can't bear you*.

I could hardly swallow such a meal. I felt a sense of confinement, my wife like a jailer, hostile, the enemy upstairs. And the only hope I had was that in this frame of mind, dissatisfied, she was planning to end the marriage, leaving me blissfully alone.

I'd always assumed I'd spend my last years in such solitude. I no longer felt that way—I wished for a friend, nothing more than that. I didn't dare risk any greater wish. In my loneliness I pondered my next move.

I went to my garden but—still unraked, littered, weedy—the obvious neglect seemed a reflection of my disordered mental state. In the past I'd counted on the garden to soothe and guide me. Creating it, duplicating the garden I'd seen in Suzhou, the Pavilion of the Accumulated Void, had been the first project I planned after I'd bought this house in the woods on the North Shore of Oahu. Because my property was on a high steep-sided bluff, I hired a man with a backhoe to grade one edge of the western slope and create a sort of shelf, a level terrace. I paid some Tongan stonemasons to build the perimeter of a garden of lava rocks, installed two massive boulders, a stone lantern, and one dwarf pine—its only greenery. Last was the gravel, which I spent each day raking, smoothing it and scoring it.

The garden was a spiritual meeting place. It was where I went in expectation of soothing my innermost thoughts. I walked there eagerly, knowing that I would sit and meditate and become whole again—that my ego would dissolve and leave me lighter and levitating in a timeless void. I was not happier but I was deeply comforted, stronger and serene, uplifted, emptied of desire. I guessed this to be the meaning of "accumulated void."

I had not been to the garden for weeks and was the worse for it. My period of confusion kept me from the garden and when I entered it I saw that it was disordered. I'd neglected it again and allowed it to go weedy and become littered with dead twigs and flaky lance-shaped leaves from the nearby bamboo clumps.

It was not possible to meditate faced with all that clutter—I'd just sit fretting about how to tidy it. The seat of the marble bench was damp, a stinging centipede scuttled through the debris. It was an unsettling sight, reflecting the muddle in my mind.

I didn't have time to tidy it. What took my mind off my disorderly garden was a domestic inconvenience that many a houseowner in rural Hawaii is forced to endure. Those of us with septic tanks on our property are reminded of their fallibility when out of the blue they become blocked—roots growing into a crack in the sewer pipe, or the tank filled to capacity, rendering the bathroom unusable, the house owner agitated.

This was one of those days. The plumber was prompt—not the usual man, Wendell, but his younger partner in the business, Makua—huge, Hawaiian— well-equipped and eager to please. He snaked a camera into the sewer pipe on a cable and, like a proctologist in a colonoscopy, showed me the progress of the camera down the murky passage to—fifty feet away—the blockage, a mass of trailing tentacles.

"Roots, in your pipe."

"You can ream them out though."

"Sure, but that won't solve the problem. You need to seal the pipe at the joint where the roots are entering. There's some sort of *puka*, maybe a crack, maybe a bad joint. They'll grow back."

"How do you fix it?"

"We'll first unblock the pipe—cut those roots, I've got a snake with teeth for that. Then we'll have to dig. Find the *puka* and seal it."

I liked a workman who had a solution; it was tedious when they shook their head and described the effort to fix it—I always suspected such talk to be a ploy for more money. Makua was as good as his word. He went to work, he had the right equipment—a cable with whirring blades—and got the pipe flowing, the toilet flushing, the sinks gurgling. A simple matter, but it made me think how one blocked pipe made my whole house uninhabitable. I compared it to my muddle, how the dilemma of my possible gift, a question left unanswered—this one thing—nagged at me and made my life a misery.

Makua returned with a digger—a sort of jackhammer—and a young woman carrying a shovel. She raised the shovel in greeting.

"We'll rough out the hole with this," Makua said, his hands on the jackhammer, "and then we'll dig by hand, carefully, or else we'll risk crushing your pipe."

He gestured to the portion of my yard where he was intending to dig, and he was still explaining the procedure, dragging the jackhammer into position—but I was looking at the young woman.

I was accustomed to seeing lovely surfer girls in bikinis, a board under their arm, deeply tanned from days in the ocean, strolling barefoot along the road to the beach, anticipating the waves, studying them and smiling—water sprites, practically naked, bursting with health and confidence, preparing to walk on water.

This woman with the shovel did not in the least resemble those gleaming surf bunnies. She wore faded work clothes, a T-shirt and blue jeans and heavy yellow boots, her black hair was drawn back in a ponytail, she was slim. She was not tanned, she was naturally dark, thin-faced, with Asian features that gave her hooded eyes a kind of severity, and the power of penetration. She was not pretty in a conventional sense; her looks were unusual, her face sculptural, like a mask, with a calmness that gave her intelligence and beauty. She had the seemingly slight but intense rigidity of an insect, the same watchful gaze, the same skeletal stance, a kind of poise, seeming to hover.

I could not take my eyes off her, and she continued to stare, as Makua talked about what he was planning to do—the digging—and finally I realized I was too flustered to be so near to her and said, "I'll leave you to it." Just as I turned away I saw she'd begun to jam her shovel into the red earth, and Makua was positioning the blade of his jackhammer.

I was a bit breathless, I was not used to being stared at in this way, as though she was seeing into me—as though she knew me. She was dressed for a day's hard work—shirt, jeans, boots—yet it seemed like a disguise. Never mind her plain clothes, her face had the dignity—verging on hauteur—of a princess.

Too self-conscious—too intimidated to watch her at work—I lingered in my upper garden, trimming the rosebushes I kept in large terra-cotta pots, cutting them back, deadheading them, but still feeling dazed and uneasy, a kind of thrill of sudden hunger from my glimpse of the woman.

Around noon, I saw Makua walking up the drive from where he was digging.

"Are you done?"

"No way. Maya's still digging."

Maya. I said, "Is Maya married?"

He laughed, a sharp cackle of recognition. Walking toward his pickup truck, he said, "The wahine asked me the same question! 'Is he married?'"

I watched him leave, and when the sound of Makua's truck died away, I crept down the path to look at Maya working. She was not a girl, she was a woman; she braced herself, feet apart, over the pit and was digging steadily, unearthing my pipe, which was about two feet down. Makua had jackhammered open a long, shallow trench and she was digging deeper, exposing the pipe, a thick tube of pale plastic, its upper surface gleaming in the clay of red volcanic earth.

Maya worked with concentration, chunking and chipping away to clear the soil from around the pipe, and was so intent in her digging she didn't notice me watching her. I was impressed by the way she stroked the soil without disturbing the pipe, or even striking it, seeming like a kind of invasive surgery, clearing the tissue from around a major organ. And just as impressive as her skillful way of freeing the pipe was her neatness—she worked without visible effort, with poise, her shirt crisp, her jeans clean, her black ponytail bobbing beautifully.

You think of a ditchdigger as a brute, but this wasn't grunt work. To see it as artistry was not fanciful. Given her care and her concentration, what Maya was doing was also like a subtle sort of disinterment, and in that mass of red dirt and crumbled lava rock it seemed she was unearthing something of great value, the venerable pipe that needed repair, a smooth thick tube that had lain buried underground and had somehow become cracked and blocked, as it had aged. I had never seen the pipe, I had not known it was there, and the length and thickness of it as she revealed it amazed me.

"Sorry!" she said, glancing up. "I didn't realize you were there."

I'd been so still, transfixed by her. She'd spoken in a natural way, she wasn't winded from her work. She had a soft sweet smile.

"You're making progress. Hard work, though."

"I love doing this."

"Digging."

"Being outdoors. Your house is so lovely—this garden. I see you've put a lot of thought into it, the choice of bushes, the plants in the understory of those trees, the symmetry. I had a good feeling the minute I got here. A kind of uplift."

"Let me show you something," I said, walking away.

She stabbed her shovel into the earth she'd piled, leaving the handle upright, as though she'd planted a sword, claiming that mound for herself, and clapping the dust from her hands she followed me.

Behind the row of bamboo clumps that formed a green wall was the terrace I'd made for my garden—messy and littered now but still recognizable as a Zen garden: the pale unraked gravel, the two jagged scholar's rocks, the twisted dwarf pine.

"I made it after I moved in—what? Six or seven years ago."

"*Karesansui*," she said.

"What's that?"

"Dry landscape garden. It's the technical term."

"I used to rake it." I hesitated and then told her what I guessed that she already knew of me. "I've had a bad month. I've neglected it."

"Needs a little work, but it's got all the right elements." She rubbed her arms pleasurably. "I can feel it. What a great thing to do."

"You know about these gardens?"

"I was raised in Japan. My father's English, my mother's Japanese. I know I look local here in Hawaii, but I'm really not." She was staring at the garden as she talked. "This garden speaks to me."

She stood for a long while, utterly silent, scarcely moving, pondering the garden, inhaling it, possessing it, becoming part of it, and I thought how there was a keen intelligence in her silence, a kind of majesty in her gaze, and on her face this meditation became luminous, acquiring a kind of wisdom in its intensity. One aspect of beauty is that the slightest movement—an eyeblink, a breath—enhances and intensifies it.

Finally she said, "It can be fixed. You know the monks in those amazing *karesansui* in Kyoto and Nara rake the gravel every day, as a sort of meditation. We can put it right."

Her saying *we* made me gleeful. I said, "I did that, until recently."

"I love this."

She touched a rusty nail on the weathered board that held the sign I'd fixed to it, PAVILION OF THE ACCUMULATED VOID.

"I saw that name at a garden in Suzhou long ago, my first visit to China. I asked about it. An old man told me, 'Sit in the garden and you'll see.'"

"It's a Buddhist concept," Maya said. "It relates to one of the sutras that says, 'Matter is emptiness, emptiness is matter.' Not that life is meaningless, but that it's brief. Nonattachment is the goal."

"Embrace the void," I said, trying to understand. "Celebrate the emptiness."

"The word *emptiness* in Japanese is 'sora.' But it's not a bad thing. It's the same character as 'sky.' The sutra teaches that appreciation of emptiness saves us from suffering. You sit until the spirit stops struggling."

"That's exactly how I felt in that garden in Suzhou."

"When you're in that void you're sort of launching yourself into bliss."

"Exactly. I wanted to experience it again, so I had some guys make this garden. The trouble is, I haven't maintained it."

Maya did not seem to be listening but instead stood before it, her eyes shut, inhaling the garden, breathing its essence. Then she opened her eyes and said, "I love that nail."

"That rusty nail?"

"See how the rust bleeds into the weathered board, the wood itself smoothed and changed by rain and sun. Meditate on that rusty nail and its stain and you'll understand the nature of existence."

"That it's imperfect?"

"And incomplete. But there's beauty in its imperfection. The flaw is part of its loveliness," she said. "It's like the meaning of the garden—life doesn't last long, and it's mainly emptiness—illusion."

Standing just behind her, staring at her glossy hair, her slender neck as she beheld the garden, my thought was *She belongs here*. She understood it, her presence added an essential element to the garden, she was part of it.

"Excuse me," I said, because I was overwhelmed, and I didn't want Makua to show up and see me talking to her. I was so moved by our conversation, by being near to her, I needed to be alone, to ponder what I saw as a revelation. I had never been so certain that this was the woman who was meant for me—she was the one. It was not romantic, it was something much more powerful—more than love, because love is dreamlike and delusional. This feeling was urgent, as though I'd at last located a missing part of myself, that I was incomplete without her, that I'd awakened an old longing: that she was my future.

I watched from my upstairs window as Makua returned with food, and I stayed away until, at four, they drove away. *They haven't finished*, I thought. *Good, she'll be back tomorrow.*

It was no accident, I saw that now. It was another answered prayer. I'd mildly wished for a friend; I'd been lonely, smothered in solitude, hating to be alone. Then the blockage of my sewer pipe, and she'd come with Makua to uncover my pipe and fix it. The pipe itself, needing repair, I saw as symbolic. She was the friend I'd wished for.

But more than that, she was the ideal I'd always dreamed of, the companion, the fellow bushwhacker, the woman with the machete, traveling beside me.

That night I reviewed the events leading up to this revelation. I'd been in a quandary, wondering whether I really had a gift, imagining that it had all been an illusion. My bafflement had paralyzed me, and I'd been suicidal until I'd been summoned to help Walter. And of course Walter had been drunk ever since my birthday, when I'd mentally urged him to drink, and it seemed I'd turned him into a depressed alcoholic. So his plight and my being summoned were part of a large psychic scheme that I'd devised: I'd made him a desperate drunk, and by rescuing him I'd saved myself.

But I'd ended up lonely. I had not made a formal command, but only wished in an idle way—a yearning—for a companion. Almost immediately my sewer pipe became blocked, and instead of my usual plumber I was visited by Makua and his assistant, Maya.

The girl of my dreams. It was another wish granted, all that I'd desired. I lay awake, longing to see her again. I was glad they hadn't finished the job of repairing the crack in the pipe. She'd be back!

It was not my intention to romance her; I was too old for that, and there was something faintly ridiculous in my wooing her. The age difference didn't matter, though, because after all I was not looking for a wife, nor intending to start a family. I simply wanted her beside me, I imagined a passionate friendship, living together, traveling as partners, sharing what remained of my life, perhaps—what?—six or eight great years, a life that neither of us had imagined possible.

Our restoring the garden, the Pavilion of the Accumulated Void, was the perfect metaphor for it. She was a spiritual being, she understood the nature of the void—she would become part of my life, what was left of it; she'd complete it and I could live my last years in contentment with a companion, and I'd die happy, knowing someone would mourn me, that she'd inherit and preserve this garden.

I seem impulsive and credulous as I recount this, but in fact I'd been fantasizing about this my whole life, ever since I'd imagined an ideal woman. I had longed for someone just like her, and at last she had appeared—it seemed in my loneliness I had summoned her. It only remained for me to get to know her better, to assure her that I could be trusted. Though I was convinced, when we'd been at the garden, we'd stood in perfect harmony, and I'd had the sense that she felt what I was feeling.

Hearing the clang of my front gate the next morning at seven I looked out to see Makua at the wheel of his pickup truck, Maya in the bed of the truck, sitting cross-legged in a lotus posture, her hands clasped. I was glad that she was not sitting next to Makua in the cab. Was it because she was his employee, and employees usually sat in the back?

No, there was another reason: a dog was in the passenger seat, obviously Makua's dog, who'd be in danger, jostled, untethered, in the back. I watched the pickup truck descend the driveway and come to a rest near the worksite— the open trench, where the pipe lay exposed. The dog leaped out and frolicked in the yard, as Maya jumped from the bed of the truck, with a sack, presumably material for the repair of the pipe.

I closed my eyes and willed a delay, wished for the work to last the whole day, and it seemed that my wish would be granted.

Around noon, Makua drove up the hill to my house and, seeing me snipping my roses—I was lingering, for another glimpse of Maya—he said, "We patched it, put on a new joint, and sealed it. But the epoxy needs time to set. Better not run any water or use the bathroom for about four hours."

"Then what happens?"

"We'll fill in the hole and you'll be good to go. I'm heading out to pick up something for lunch."

When he was gone, I walked down the hill to find Maya.

I didn't see her at first, but then I crept through the clumps of bamboo to the garden—the pavilion—and saw her. She was seated cross-legged at its edge, smiling serenely.

"Sorry."

"Oh, hi," she said, but remained in that classical posture, straight-backed, her hands resting on her knees, her palms upturned, receiving vibrations.

"You like it here?"

"I couldn't wait to come to work."

Then I noticed that the garden had been tidied, the leaves swept away, the gravel raked.

"You cleaned it up."

"A little bit—it needs a lot more attention."

While she remained seated I was able to study her more closely. She was probably in her forties but she had the face of someone who had lived a good life. Our past shows in our faces—surfaces reveal inner states: I saw a kind of purity in hers, more than decency, deeper than contentment. She showed no sign of turmoil; I saw what I thought of as kindness in her features, and I was able to discern her English father in her pretty nose, her Japanese mother in her lidded eyes, and great health in her unmarked face. She was a manual worker, a ditchdigger, and yet her clothes were clean, her shirt crisp, her jeans looking just washed, and she was barefoot—she'd taken off her boots to sit at the garden. Her feet were pale and smooth and very small, and there was something madly attractive about her pretty toes that roused a fetishism in me that was like hunger.

I said, "When you finish with the pipe—hey, my new pipe—maybe you could help me with the garden."

"I'd love that."

It was an unequivocal promise, her smile was an assurance. I needed nothing else to sustain me. But not wishing to be seen by Makua—I heard his truck in the upper driveway—I excused myself and hurried back to my house.

Following Makua's suggestion, I didn't run any water or use the bathroom. I left the house and drove to town to buy groceries, then sat on the beach, blessing my luck. By the time I returned home they had gone. Tucked in my door was Makua's invoice for his unblocking the pipe and repairing it. It was a bit more than I expected, but I reminded myself of what I'd been granted—the possibility of friendship with this marvelous woman, perhaps more than friendship, a partner, a lover.

The next day I called Makua on his cell phone: "It's me—Felix. Thanks for fixing my pipe—it works great. I've got a check for you."

"Great, I'll swing by later today."

He came around four o'clock. She was not with him, though his dog was next to him, crouched on the passenger seat, panting. Makua wanted me to admire the dog, which I did, while at the same time wondering aloud about Maya.

"Your assistant is a really good worker," I said as I handed him my check.

"Maya's fantastic. Supertough. She can do the work of any man."

As casually as I could, without showing the urgency I felt—urgency bordering on desperation—I said, "She mentioned doing something about my garden. I said I'd get back to her."

Still I was scratching the dog's neck, not looking at Makua, grinning at the mutt, and wondering why Makua hadn't responded to what I'd said.

"You got a number for her?" I asked, provoked by his silence.

He hesitated, shrugging slightly, fingering my check. "I don't know." He seemed suspicious, frowning, squinting, lost for an answer. Finally he said, "The thing is," and he took a deep breath, "I don't like to share people's personal information."

This from a middle-aged Hawaiian guy in a beat-up pickup truck with a panting dog next to him seemed a bit pompous and evasive.

"I understand," I said. "That's fine. By all means, get her permission."

But I had a distinct vibration, something in his discomfort, that he was withholding her number for another reason—that he wasn't protecting Maya's privacy, he was rebuffing me. Early on, he'd told me he was married, and had children, so it could not have been that he was sexually possessive. I guessed he suspected me of intruding, of poaching one of his workers.

Instead of pressuring him, I thanked him for his work and said, "At least I have your number."

"Cool." He slipped my folded check into his shirt pocket and drove away.

My house had never seemed emptier. At first I was bewildered, then I felt abandoned, and at last—after a few days—I was not sure what I should do. Maya had vanished—well, I told myself, she didn't know how passionately I needed her. I suffered for a week, then texted Makua: *About that number—any news?*

He did not reply. After another week I began to experience a familiar feeling of melancholy, my mood of pill-counting. I was sunk in depression. It occurred to me that although Makua had told me he was married, he might have been having an affair with Maya—or wished to have one—and resented my interest. Perhaps I had not disguised my desperation, and he wanted her for himself.

One evening, restless, in despair, I gathered my wits and went down the hill to my Pavilion of the Accumulated Void. It was just at nightfall, a faint glow in the western sky. I sat where I had seen her sitting and concentrated on her and was strengthened in my vision of her, remembered how she'd remarked on my garden—its name, its likeness to other gardens she'd seen, how we'd restore the garden together. She would be part of the garden, part of my life. I saw the years ahead, years of providing for her, but encouraging her in her work—whatever work she chose—being an equal partner, completing my life. I did not see the end of my life, I saw sunshine, the two of us together, not needing anyone else, the sort of symmetry that was reflected in the pair of great boulders in the garden. I saw love.

Then I sighed and spoke one word. "Damn."

Uplifted by this vision of the two of us, strengthened by my memory of answered prayers and something truly to wish for, I overcame all my doubts and felt able to pronounce a formal curse on Makua. I damned him for withholding Maya's phone number, for intruding in Maya's life, for dismissing me. It would be another test of wish fulfillment. If it failed to work I'd know I was deluded, that everything I'd begun to believe of my possible gift was purely coincidental.

Fine, I thought. If I happened to be wrong, if Makua remained an obstacle, I'd find Maya somehow and woo her in my own way. If Makua objected, I'd deal with him, remind him he was a married man and that Maya was free to make her own decisions. I entertained all these conversations in my head. Either way I had a chance.

I was happy, I was a small boy again, with nothing to lose. Yet, when had I had anything to lose? I'd lived a charmed life. I had never asked for much, only for obstacles to be removed. I'd wished for justice. Perhaps this—cursing Makua, longing for Maya—was the most I'd ever wished for.

In a delirium of desire, I shut my eyes and begged the darkness for the worst to befall Makua.

I was startled to find on opening my eyes that I was briefly tearful, but I went to bed content, having exhausted myself in the fury of my curse. I'd done all I could and consoled myself with the thought that I'd lived a remarkable life; I'd been supremely lucky.

I woke the next morning feeling the numbness of suspense; and the day after, too, and each successive day the same. I had no inkling of anything unusual. At last, I texted Makua but got no reply. That was not odd—he hadn't answered any of my previous texts.

In my numbed state, I slept later and later, as though not wanting to wake and face the day. In that solitude, my loneliness and uncertainty returned. I realized that I'd expended enormous psychic energy in my effort to curse Makua. I was utterly deflated. It was not my imagination—I was shattered, and yet even in my fatigue I was rational enough to smile at the thought that I'd actually believed in my power to pronounce a curse and be granted a last wish. And now of course it seemed to me purely frivolous, an act of self-deception by an old fool.

With this in mind, I stopped sleeping late, my life resumed, the narrow existence of low expectations: friendless, solitary, but relieved by my old routine of sitting on the beach, swimming, going to bed early, often thinking of what might have been. And of course, in hopeful moments, trying to devise ways of tracking down Maya and initiating a friendship, starting with *Remember me?*

A week of this, one of those weeks when I was reminded that I knew nothing of social media or the ways that younger people easily found each other on the internet and exchanged messages, while all I had was an old plastic telephone.

There was Wendell, my usual plumber, who had recommended Makua to me. He might know how I could reach Maya. If Makua knew her, Wendell might also know her.

"Felix," Wendell said, when I called him. "You got a problem?"

"No—Makua fixed it. He's a clever guy."

After a silence, Wendell's tone changed, whispering, wounded, saying, "You haven't heard? About Makua?"

Before I could respond—I was still murmuring, considering how to respond—Wendell's voice cracked, not a word but a strangled sound, a sob.

"Terrible accident," he finally said. "He was hit head-on."

I felt a tremor of exaltation, a dark thrill, and almost howled—so I had it after all, the gift.

"That's terrible," I said. "But I was calling about the woman, his helper—Maya."

"She was in the bed of the truck. She was ejected. It was instant. Somehow his dog survived."

Solitude these days is no different from darkness. I still visit my stark, vivid garden and examine the rusty nail on the sign, how it decays in the November rain, bleeding into the grain of the weathered wood that looks crepey, like an old man's flesh. I feel I am part of the garden, like another feature of it, as essential as the mute brutal boulders and the twisted black pine. Now I know its ultimate meaning, the one I was promised long ago: that I had to experience the void to understand. I had now achieved the void. But there is no consolation in that.

I know exactly what is coming for me. This is not clairvoyance. It is the bleak certainty of a private promise, that this would be the last November of my life.

Elsewhere

HEADMASTER

Most of the American teachers in the Southern Region of the country knew about Larry DeMond, his bizarre arrangement with his housemate. DeMond had asked to be sent off the map, to a remote school in the bush, *Where no one can find me*. His ambition was to make a poor school great, by himself. He was assigned to Kapeni, two classrooms and a scrubby sports ground in a clearing at the limit of a dead-end road, one way in and out. The road was little more than a cycle track in most places—but that suited him because DeMond's only transport was a bicycle, eight miles to the nearest town, a small one, Kanyama: a main street, a market, a club, a trading company, a noisy bar.

At its most pinched, the red clay road passed Chinasala Village, where starved-looking dogs leaped from behind the thornbush perimeter and barked and slavered, forcing DeMond off his bike. He rattled the bike at the dogs and used it to shield himself, his heart pounding until he got away. Yet he was happy, living on his own, as he pleased, teaching at Kapeni, living in a bungalow near the school compound.

My house, my school. He had just what he wanted, and so he objected when, after two months of solitude at Kapeni, he was assigned a housemate, Cully Williams. Williams was black, but race was not an issue—Williams's expectations caused the problems. Within days, he hired a houseboy, Mahmoud, whom he sometimes called Mah. DeMond had seen Mahmoud near the bungalow when he'd first arrived, looking hopeful and hungry, but with an air, almost of defiance, of belonging to this bush place that made him seem immovable; and that made his cringing seem absurd. DeMond said, "I don't need you." But Williams had hired him.

Mahmoud was child-size but sinewy. DeMond said he didn't like the word *houseboy* to describe a middle-aged man, in a khaki uniform, gray haired when he removed his skullcap; nor did he want a servant in the house. But Williams insisted—"Half this place is mine"—and Mahmoud stayed on, living in a shed at the back, next to the outdoor kitchen, taking orders from Williams, who supplied him with "boy's meat," as the hawkers called the slab of goat meat, from the market in town, while he had chicken for himself. DeMond watched in disgust as Mahmoud clapped a rag on his head, or his skullcap, and slit the frantic chicken's throat and hoisted him to bleed into the dust of the courtyard. Mahmoud popped the caps off Fanta bottles with his teeth and could hold a hot frying pan in his heavily calloused hands—"Awesome!" said Williams and got him to repeat it in the dull hours in their shared house. De-Mond said, "You're demeaning him," and asked him to stop. But Mahmoud snorted with pleasure in the power of his party trick.

Though Williams was newer to the area than DeMond, he confronted him with opinions and warnings, which DeMond suspected he'd heard from the tea planters at the Gymkhana Club in town.

"This Kapeni road can be dangerous," Williams said. "Chinasala Village on the narrow section after the big bend below the forest? If you kill one of those goats wandering in the road, the villagers will hold you hostage until you pay them for it. They have no work, no money, nothing but their faith— they're outsiders here. If you knock over one of their children, you should drive to the police station in town or they'll kill you."

DeMond said it was tea planter talk. And then, "How are we going to kill anything with our bikes?"

Williams shrugged. It was true, all they had were bicycles—clumsy, single speed, and slow—for trips to Kanyama town. But he told DeMond several stories of violent incidents on the road.

"The village seems okay me," DeMond said. "Except for those dogs."

"They don't bark at me and Mah," Williams said—he often rode into town, his small houseboy seated like a child on the rear luggage rack, legs out, feet wide apart.

Within a few weeks of his arrival, Cully Williams, who was coach of the girls' netball team, seemed to take an interest in one of the players. Djamila Malinki was taller than the other girls, even barefoot in her school uniform— black pleated skirt, plain white blouse; and well-developed, bosomy, her smooth skin with the gloss of a new chestnut, the sort they roasted in the schoolyard along with corncobs. She was fifteen but looked older, a Form Three schoolgirl, yet in village terms ready for marriage.

"We don't romance the students," DeMond said.

"Do I tell you what to do?" Williams said. He'd widened his eyes, his voice was fierce. And then, "You live your life, I'll live mine."

Rather than argue, DeMond acted on his plan that others called bizarre. He divided the house in half, drawing a line through the living room, using a piece of school chalk, across the floor, up the wall, bisecting the front door and the veranda. Each man had a bedroom at opposite sides of the one-story house. The kitchen, an open-sided shelter at the back, and the latrine—the *chimbudzi*—beyond a grove of trees—were all they shared. But Williams didn't cook, so DeMond jostled with Mahmoud at the woodburning stove, as the servant prepared Williams's meals.

"This for bwana," Mahmoud said one day, stirring a stew in a blackened pot.

"Why do you call him bwana?"

Mahmoud looked scolded and lowered his head, chewing his lips, then murmured, "He is my bwana."

At school the two Americans conversed—all business—but at home, in the divided house, they sat through the long evenings, each in his own portion of the living room, not speaking. Williams was served dinner by Mahmoud, who sidled through the front entrance with the dinner tray, observing the chalk line on the threshold and the floor as if it was a cliff edge, and it sometimes seemed to DeMond that the division of the house was a greater inconvenience to Mahmoud than to Williams. Mahmoud made Williams's half of the cement floor gleam with the paste of oxblood-colored polish. When Williams had visitors—was that giggling in the bedroom Djamila Malinki?—DeMond put up a curtain and talked about building a wall, and it disturbed him that Mahmoud did not seem shocked to glimpse Djamila in the house. One day he saw little Mahmoud pedaling Williams's bike, tall Djamila on the crossbar, bumping toward the forest.

This went on for an awkward month or more. Williams was bewildered and offended by the arrangement, but he said, "Being separated and singled out is nothing new to me."

In a chair in his half of the living room, DeMond fussily chafed a page of his book with his thumb and forefinger, then turned it, and stroked the beard he'd begun to grow; but he did not reply.

At last Williams surrendered, asking for a transfer to another school, and when he was picked up in the embassy Land Rover, the driver smiled at the divided house, lopsided, the two-tone floor, the mismatched chairs, the chalk lines. Mahmoud helped load the vehicle; no words were spoken, though Williams sighed loudly and cleared his throat disgustedly as he hoisted himself into the passenger seat.

"Bwana," Mahmoud said, after they'd driven away. "You want houseboy?"

"Don't call me bwana," DeMond said. "Don't call yourself *houseboy*."

"I cook for you, I polish floor." Still in his khaki uniform he looked eager. He snatched off his skullcap. "I make custard."

"No," DeMond said, "but good luck," and put his hand out.

Mahmoud extended his left hand, shook DeMond's right hand, his small child's face pinched and darkened, and in that moment, in the last of the light—an effect of his posture—he seemed to indicate a significance, that something was beginning or ending. The little man, so black and compact, looked like a punctuation mark.

DeMond repossessed the house. No one wanted to live with him on his severe terms, which suited him. He had asked to be alone, for the school to be his project, and now he had his wish. And Mahmoud was dismissed. The last DeMond saw of him he was headed downhill in his childlike shuffling gait, toward the shadowy entrance to the forest on the narrow road, carrying a bag of his possessions on his shoulder. Just before he entered the forest he looked back at DeMond. And then he stepped into the darkness, as the road tipped downhill, a kind of tunnel formed by the overhanging trees.

But not long after Williams left, and Mahmoud was gone, Djamila began drifting by, saying hello in a husky voice, asking for help with her homework, and laughing when DeMond said no and making his excuses in high stammering tones. She left oranges and bananas on his veranda. He let the monkeys steal them. One day she offered him a basket filled with dead mourning doves, their throats neatly slit.

"What am I going to do with them?" he said.

"You can eat them. Sah likes them."

She called Cully Williams *sir?*

Even on the veranda out of the sun Djamila's face glowed, perspiration beaded on her nose and soaking parts of her blouse, making it cling to her throat and her breasts.

DeMond said, "Don't come here again, Djamila. It's against school rules." And he shut the door on her lovely frowning face.

In the nights that followed he consoled himself by reflecting that he suffered more than she by refusing her advances. No one knew him; they summed him up as a crank because of the divided house, the arrangement with Cully Williams. But all DeMond had asked was to be left alone, in the bush, at his school, off the map.

It was a victory of sorts—DeMond had won his battle to be alone—but he didn't gloat; he'd gotten his wish. Yet Djamila still lingered, watched him from beneath her long eyelashes, still left fruit for him on his veranda, walked slowly past his house after school, gnawing a short stalk of sugarcane, kicking the red clay of the road and then entering the forest.

DeMond's solitude was a pleasure: the simplicity of his small house, his wood-fired boiler, the outdoor kitchen, his bicycle. His weekly bike ride, a sixteen-mile round trip to Kanyama to pick up his mail, was another pleasure. Friday was a half day at the school, the children let out at noon to help their parents, weeding in the cassava and bean and maize fields. DeMond mounted his bike after lunch and rode through the forest, down the dank hillside of dense trees, on the narrow road that was always in shadow. Pied crows followed him strutting, white breasted, and smaller birds flew down to peck at the insects his tires disturbed. If he left late or was delayed, returning at nightfall he might see the dusky flicker of a loping hyena, or an owl or a partridge squatting in the road, and often when there was rain a green fist-size land crab, rearing, raising its claws at his approach.

These wild creatures were a private satisfaction DeMond described in the journal he kept to record the progress of Kapeni School. Chinasala Village he needed to negotiate, because of the threatening dogs that came at him, bat-eared with big jaws and lolling tongues. He walked his bike past them, trying not to look afraid, and he used the bike to fend them off. He waved to the villagers for luck—shadowy men seated on stools under the broom-like thatch of protruding eaves—but they never waved back. Once, he thought he saw a white blouse and black skirt hanging from a clothesline and wondered if they belonged to Djamila, and his mind strayed—if that was so, what was she wearing now, the cloth wrap of a village girl, and might she be bare breasted, as many were?

Now and then, near Chinasala Village he encountered a flock of goats and was reminded of Cully Williams telling him how a man in a Land Rover had run over a goat and the villagers surrounded the vehicle and threatened the driver, preventing him from moving on until he paid a substantial sum of money. Another story: of a child knocked down and the driver dragged from the vehicle and beaten to death; another, of the pack of village dogs taking down a hyena.

It was hard to imagine such savagery in that small village of wattle and daub huts, the woodsmoke drifting past the conical roofs, some shafts of light filtering from the canopy of trees, a woman pounding maize in a mortar, a skinny girl yoked to a pair of buckets, the men on their stools—not drinking as other villagers did—and no longer calling out "Bwana!" as they had when he'd first arrived. Sometimes passing at sunset he heard a tumbling yammer, hurried contending voices, low to the ground, men praying. But the dogs scared him and he always passed the village as quickly as possible.

Farther on, nearer town, at the edge of the forest were fields of maize, the shucks and broken stalks littering the road, and now and then in the heat a snake as sleek as a length of garden hose sliding with a whisper and crackle through the dry maize shucks.

More fields and then the poor huts on the outskirts, the terraces of cement sheds set on trampled ground, the women gathered at standpipes, filling buckets of water; the Gymkhana Club, its paddocks and white fences, the Indian shops, the fish-and-chip shop, the Kanyama Trading Company, the post office, the Coconut Grove. That was the circuit.

The Kanyama Trading Company had a wire rack where new Penguin paperbacks appeared once a month. DeMond usually bought one and sometimes two. There was often mail in his postbox—letters from home, letters from old school friends, but never a letter from another teacher. He knew they regarded him as an eccentric after the business with Cully Williams, believing the dispute was racial. With his bundle of mail and the paperbacks in his basket he set off, up the hill, for Kapeni.

Passing the Coconut Grove at the edge of town, the girls on the veranda called out to him, making kissing sounds, the way you'd call a cat, and behind them, music from inside. "Bwana," they'd call out, or "Meesta," or they'd snap their fingers and yell, "Jig-jig."

What did it mean? It was so playful he smiled and tried to guess. DeMond always waved and, suspecting he was tempted, they'd perform an impromptu dance—they danced like his students, arms raised, knees up, high-stepping and laughing, or they might yodel, ululating, and call out, "Jig-jig" again, joyously.

He pedaled on, into the forest, bracing himself for the dogs of Chinasala Village, and when they rushed at him, barking wildly, nipping at his feet, he dismounted and protected himself with the bike. Away from the dogs, and the woodsmoke of cooking fires, and the odor of decay that clung to the village—the rotting maize stalks, the mildewed roof thatch, the human stink—he was nearer home, under dripping trees, owls on the road, the land crabs, his solitude, his school.

That was his first year. His habits and routines made his life orderly and kept him sane, but they were no cure for—what?—not loneliness but desire. Djamila had not abandoned her quest to tempt him. Though Djamila was not in his class she slipped him a note, in neat blue ballpoint on a torn-out copybook page, *I love you, mister.*

He was startled. Her persistence surprised him. Was it a feature of the simple village life—keeping to an idea, holding to a wish, the patience of an African peasant, a kind of endurance—that she could outlast him?

She still brought presents—bananas, green coconuts, more dead doves that looked like sacrifices. She had grown, and now in Form Four, her school uniform was snugger on her body. She seemed to know that he forced himself to look away. She was another reminder of Cully Williams, like Mahmoud, whom he sometimes saw staring into the road at Chinasala Village as the dogs barked. Djamila was not a coquette any longer but seemed haughty, sizing him up, guessing he was weakening.

And he was. He knew it was dangerous. A flirtation with a student, if found out, would get him transferred—banished from this lovely place, probably to share a house with another teacher. He had come to love his routines, the school, his house, his weekly ride into town. He had learned to cope with the dogs, he looked forward to the Trading Company and the market. As for the Coconut Grove—it had begun to amuse him, the blatting music, the cheerfulness of the girls, their hooting, the yodeling, the kissing noises.

One day, passing the bar, he got off his bike and pushed it to savor the attention. He kept walking, past the huts and the maize fields, but when he mounted the bike, he felt a tug on his arm—a young woman in a wraparound and a white blouse, smiling at him, like a market woman, as though she had something to sell, seeming to challenge him.

He had known for some time that villagers were alert to the smallest gesture. Maybe it was the effect of being uncorrupted by books. Were they watchful, like prey animals? No, they were hungry, and hunger inspired special skills. She could not read a printed page, but she could read him.

He said nothing, nor did she speak, but his silence was like encouragement. He heard her feet slapping the gummy clay of the red road, like a village wife following her husband at a decent distance. He had left later than usual, so night was falling as he passed Chinasala Village, the young woman behind him.

A dog approached, then another, whimpering, and soon three more, but though they growled softly and worked their jaws, none of them barked. The young woman muttered to them in a scolding tone, as though she knew their language. And that was when he turned in the failing light and smiled in relief at the young woman. Still, he did not mount his bike.

In the forest, under the trees, the woman drew nearer. He could not see her dress, he smelled her sweat, the odor of food on her, damp clothes, the sting of dirt.

He said in her language, "What is your name?"

"My name is Fatma," she said in English.

"Where are you going?"

"I am just footing."

They spoke in darkness, and the darkness made them insubstantial, like two blameless ghosts in the road. He did not feel obligated to say anything more, and he did not even say goodbye or thank you to her but got on his bike and rode onward, up the hill to his house.

That night, fatigued from the ride, and thirsty, too tired to cook, he sat in his living room by lantern light, drinking beer, smoking, glad that tomorrow was Saturday. When he rose to go to bed, lifting the candlestick, he saw like a sudden portrait a gleaming face at the window, Fatma, staring at him, her lips apart, showing her teeth, the more worrying that she seemed to be wildly smiling. He met her at the door.

"I need to make water," she said.

"The *chimbudzi*," he began.

"I am knowing," she said, and she walked behind the house to the latrine.

He was seated again, smoking, when she returned, barefoot in the living room, wiping her fingers on her wraparound.

"Give me one stick," she said and beckoned with her fingers.

He passed her a cigarette and lit it for her and in the match flare saw that she had initiation scars on her cheeks like claw marks that strangely matched some slashes on her torn blouse.

She sat apart from him on the sofa, smoking for a while. DeMond found a bottle still with some beer in it and showed her, but she wagged the cigarette, looking disapprovingly at the beer. Then she said, "You come here, mister."

He remained sitting until she spoke again, insisting, and then he joined her. She rested her hand on his leg. She said, "I know where is your sleeping room."

"You do?" he said. She was smiling, as she had from outside at the window. "Why?"

"Jig-jig."

Put that way, it seemed so simple, like play. In the bedroom she undressed him, clumsily, laughing softly, as though buttons and a belt and the rest were novelties. She shrugged, twisted out of her wraparound, and when it dropped stepped free of it. She was naked, in the overbright lantern light, a moving shadow on the wall. She lay back on the bed, her legs slightly parted, her arms behind her head. It was more play; DeMond found nothing sensual in it, nor was it sexual. She was offering comfort, and even her posture seemed to say, *Come to Mummy.*

He crept close to her. She embraced him and as she drew him down he knocked his head against the bedpost. She said, "Sorry," and pillowed him with the softness of her body.

For a moment, he was aware of her sour odor, a sharpness of sweat and dirt, and dust in the tangle of her hair, and another odor, as of old rags, the wraparound she'd discarded, the rank smell like a reminder of the wrongness of being with her. Yet as he stroked her, he seemed to be blinded, made senseless; her smell was not the soapy aroma of the students but the muddy smell of the country road, and though he made a feeble effort to resist, she guided him with her hard hands, laughing deep in her throat.

DeMond woke in the night and poured water into a basin and washed, then went back to bed, surprised by the risen odors. Fatma was asleep, snoring a little. The air charged with dirt kept him awake, and at first light he woke her and said, "Now you have to go."

"Give money."

While she dressed, DeMond went into the other room and waited, some bills folded in his hand.

"Here," he said, when she appeared, scratching at her wraparound; he gave her the money.

She pinched it, frowning, and said, "You no like me."

"I like you," he said and gave her more.

She laughed at the money and tucked it into a fold of her dress.

After she'd gone, he tidied the house—swept, mopped, changed the bed-clothes, and it was as though she'd never been there. Instead of thinking about what he'd done, he concentrated on what he had not done: he had not touched a student or any of the women teachers. He was not blameless, he knew that, but he had not disgraced himself or risked his job with Djamila or any other student. He had not played favorites, he'd made an adult decision, a village choice.

That was Saturday. DeMond was drowsy all day—he'd slept badly with the woman beside him. He'd been anxious, wakeful, eager for her to go. Sunday he spent grading papers, weeding his garden. Monday brought a visit from Djamila after school but a different Djamila, detached, softy smiling, as if she knew something and was trying to defy him; but he was brisk with her.

"I've told you before. I won't tell you again."

He had never been so certain; he was fortified, so whatever guilt or shame he felt was countered by the strength he'd been granted by the woman in the night. And he thought, *In a few months, if I'm tempted, I might take Fatma again*. The prospect offered some kind of consolation.

Tuesday was an ordinary workday; the woman was almost forgotten, the routine of the school dominated his thoughts, and a rightness in the world made him confident. But on Wednesday he woke with an obscure itch, and he found a stain, a drip, and knew something was wrong. He made it through the day, hoping for it to pass, but it was worse, more painful the next day. He dismissed his class and rode into town, to the clinic.

The doctor was Indian, his name *Radhia* stitched on the pocket of his lab coat. He examined DeMond solemnly, using rubber gloves. He snapped off the gloves, but he said nothing, merely stared at DeMond, as though evaluating him.

"Serious?" DeMond said.

"You have had contact with many women?"

"Just one."

"You are married man?"

"No."

"Gonorrheal infection," the doctor said, turning his back. "I will give you a jab to speed it up, then antibiotic tablets. You will notice change in symptoms in some few days. But finish the whole course of tablets. No alcohol."

DeMond was angry, ashamed, as the doctor injected him. He sneaked past the market and the Coconut Grove, he screamed at the dogs at Chinasala Village and they howled back at him and showed their scummy tongues, terrifying as always, as though they wanted to eat him. At home he sat, immobilized by his guilt, counting the hours until the next pills; but at school he was less the stern schoolmaster and more forgiving to the students. When, a week later, he swallowed the last of the pills, and he was cured, he said to himself, *I've had the clap*. It was foolishness, an experience of danger and risk, but he'd come through.

He was cured in every respect. He was restored to health—the itch, the drip were gone. His appetite returned. And his recovery from this medieval disease, a kind of survival, had given him firm resolve and made him a monk. What he'd done had been wrong, but the effect of it had made him straighter, more sober, better able to deal with his solitude, and more efficient as a teacher, shrewder as a headmaster. He did not scold the students for their lapses—their lateness, the incomplete homework assignment, the lost copybook, the slackening of attention. Now he understood wrong turnings.

Djamila had abandoned her pursuit of him, but she still lingered by his office door, inventing reasons to see him. He was more patient with her, too, and though it may have seemed to her like encouragement, he had never felt stronger, and his school was the better for his concentration. It seemed to him that his night with Fatma had made him a wiser teacher, in a better school.

His weekly trips to town he made with more resolve, too—he kicked at the attacking dogs at Chinasala Village, he made an efficient circuit of the market, the Trading Company, the shops, the post office, and when, inevitably, he passed the Coconut Grove and heard the catcalls from the veranda he gripped his handlebars and pedaled hard, away from the cries of "Meesta!"

The chief inspector of schools, unannounced, visited DeMond's class at Kapeni, sat in the back, plucked at the crease in his trousers, and took notes. Afterward in the office, he said, "Full marks to you, Mr. Larry," and showed DeMond the approving comments in his clipboard.

"Thank you," DeMond said.

"This is a model school. The bush schools don't perform well, usually, but in this one you pulled your socks up. For this reason I can approve a transfer to Zomba, to a new school in the town."

"I'm happy here," DeMond said.

But the inspector said, "If you turn down this transfer, we will not be able to effect another one for a year or more. And you will be alone still. Not with your people."

"What I mean by being happy here is that it's my school," DeMond said. "I improved it, and I believe I can make this school even better. I'm the headmaster."

"As you wish," the inspector said, and he left in his Land Rover, raising dust, gunning the engine and disappearing into the forest. Then the noise died away, and the dust settled, and DeMond was alone in the heat, and the slanting sun, still some dust from the vehicle sifting in its rays, as silence fell.

But he was thinking: *To be here is to be reminded of how I went wrong and it will make me stronger. My dedication will improve this bush school*—already the test results had risen. He did not see a time when it would cease to be his school, and that was another reason he rejoiced in his victory over Cully Williams.

All this in the three months since the words *jig-jig* and his error. But the trips to town did not become easier, the dogs were more vicious, the catcalls more strident, and he felt that he was cycling through an atmosphere of hostility. Once, at Chinasala, DeMond dismounted and waved, but the women turned away, and the man who saw him tossed his head. And DeMond continued on his way, past the owls and the land crabs and the hyenas that were never more than shadows in the twilight.

To do the right thing, to run the school well, meant that he was alone all the time—he had set himself apart. He had not minded being on his own, and his resolve had kept him from being lonely. Except for his students, DeMond saw no one these days. His school was his world, and in this mood he had some inkling of what the British had felt in colonizing the country—bringing order to the bush, building institutions, and claiming the colony as their own.

So he was surprised one evening on his return to his house to see someone sitting on his chair on the veranda—and nearer still he saw it was Fatma.

"You!" she said, and he was breathless for a moment.

She looked plumper, her hair was wild—tangled and dusty, and instead of a dress she wore a wraparound, multicolored, that fell to her ankles.

She smiled at him, her crocodile teeth. DeMond said, "You have to go."

She laughed, she stood up, she showed him her belly, plumping it in both her hands.

"It is yours."

"No," he said, and he tried to say more but his throat burned.

A bar girl from the Coconut Grove, who was always dallying with men—no, not possible. Instead of speaking in a voice he knew would sound panicky, he shook his head. But she was nodding, certain of it.

"How did you come here?"

"Footing, from my village, where I am living, Chinasala."

Her command of English appalled him. In her own language he could have argued, but the directness of English was a severer accusation, and it was as fluent as any of his students. That seemed proof that she consorted with other white men.

"You live there?"

"With my father. With my sister."

"Go home," he said.

"This is my home," she said and pointed to DeMond's bungalow. "Ask them, they will tell you."

Two figures approached, Mahmoud and Djamila. The little man in a skullcap had taken possession of DeMond's big black bike and seemed to be leering at him in triumph as he wheeled the bike through the red dust toward the house. Then Mahmoud turned, stuck his fingers into his mouth and whistled, and at that sound a pack of dogs came leaping from the forest.

NAVIGATIONAL HAZARD

One of the rituals, strictly observed by most of the expats at the University of Singapore when I taught there in the sixties, was to meet in the Staff Club after classes, drink beer at one of the long tables, and when any of the dozen or so drinkers left, disparage him, mocking what he had just said to the others. Willie Willetts took exception to this disloyalty. Willie was the curator of the university art museum, an expert in Chinese pottery and Khmer celadons. He described his recreations as, "Reading, thinking, and drinking."

"You know I'm not umbrageous, and I'm all for having a good grouse," Willetts used to say, "but this is distinctly unfair." He was only in his fifties, but I was twenty-six, so he seemed old to me. "You notice Harry Montvale never rubbishes anyone."

Montvale was Willie's friend and neighbor, older than he, a commanding presence when he visited the Staff Club. Among the pale, perspiring, chain-smoking, out-of-shape lecturers and professors gabbling in this daily sundowner, Montvale stood out: tall, sinewy, with an intimidating gaze, and placid in his silences. He was neat in the way he dressed, scrupulous in avoiding gossip, and with a stern sense of justice. Although he was diligent in paying for his round, he had—so Willie told me—nothing to live on except a small Royal Navy pension and was just scraping by, in a small house on upper Bukit Timah Road, a recent widower. I was to remember all this after I learned his story.

"Harry is a master navigator," Willetts said, as a form of introduction.

"Just a skipper," Montvale said, smiling in impatience, uncomfortable with Willetts's praise. "Mainly in the waters hereabouts—Straits Settlements. Charters, cruising, some fishing clients. I know the Borneo ports pretty well."

"I was thinking of getting a boat to Kota Kinabalu."

"I knew it as Jesselton—North Borneo. The MV *Keningau* sails there every fortnight. Let me know when you go. There's something I want you to verify for me."

A month or so later, after I booked my passage on the *Keningau*. I met Willetts and Montvale at the Staff Club. I suggested that we sit apart from the other expats, because I didn't want anyone to know my plans. They would mock me for taking a ship rather than a plane, they would speculate on what I'd do in Borneo, the futility of it, when I could be in the Staff Club drinking beer and denigrating a colleague who'd just left.

But Harry Montvale was encouraging. "You'll see some ports," he said. "Labuan Island, for certain. But it's in Jesselton that I want you to keep your eyes peeled. When you approach the harbor mouth, look for a tall pole indicating a navigational hazard. It will be in a place where there are no obvious rocks, where the water is deep—an odd place across from a rather grand Chinese godown. I'd be interested in knowing whether it's still there."

I took the trip and loved it. The *Keningau*'s skipper, Captain Meyrick, invited me to eat with him and his wife. I had a pleasant cabin. I read Naipaul's *A House for Mr. Biswas*. I played whist with a Malay rubber planter and a Chinese woman who lived in KK—as they called Kinabalu. The cards were always slammed down, the player calling out, "*Tumpang!*"—a colloquial Malay word meaning "pass it on." The night we spent at the dock in Labuan the monsoon rain was so loud, beating on the deck, I could not make out what the planter was saying. When the rain let up he told me that a baby boy had been born on the third-class deck. We climbed down the ladder and saw the infant, swaddled with its mother, among a sweating crowd of Tamil rubber tappers, en route to a plantation.

"Call him Kenny," the Malay planter said. "After this ship."

The next day, I went to the bridge as we approached KK.

"I'm looking for a navigational hazard," I said.

"That pole," Captain Meyrick said, pointing and seeming to wave it away, as he steered the ship around it. "Very inconvenient, especially in the dark, especially there."

The pole was, as Montvale had said, at the approach of the channel, in front of the Chinese warehouse he mentioned, the godown. The tall pole was black with age and, below the tidemark, thick with greenish barnacles, a metal plate attached to the top like a road sign, the paint peeled but the warning visible in three languages, *Danger*, *Bahaya*, and unexpectedly a waffle-like Chinese character meaning *perilous*.

"I'm glad it's still there," Montvale said to me in a grateful tone at the Staff Club when I returned, and with a sigh he attempted to disguise with the back of his hand he added, "Thank you. You've given me something."

"Tell him the story," Willetts said. "Paul's a writer. He'll appreciate it."

After some prodding, and insisting that we change our seats so that none of the expat drinkers could hear, Montvale said, "I was skipper of the *Selamat*. It was owned by a *towkay* here in Singapore, Chung Fatt Heng. He was ten years my junior but he made his first million in his twenties, just out of college, some kind of cigarette-smuggling scheme, avoiding taxes on them, and then selling cartons of them at a profit in a Malay state where they were heavily taxed."

"I've heard of that—lots of people do it," I said.

"Not to the extent that Fatt Heng did it. It was huge. He was moving shipping containers full of cigarette cartons. Think of the complexity."

"Just hustling," I said.

"What I mean is, think of all the people involved—all the trust needed. Fatt Heng was a man who somehow inspired loyalty."

"Why are you smiling?" I asked.

"Because loyalty is earned through righteousness."

As a yacht skipper, Montvale was impressed with such loyalty, since a vessel negotiating mangrove coasts and hidden reefs required the crew to follow orders and be watchful. Montvale said he'd done two tours in the Royal Navy, had been based in Singapore at the barracks in Sembawang named the HMS *Terror*. On his discharge, wishing to stay in the East, he'd interviewed to be master of the yacht *Selamat* and gotten the job. The pay was good, he could live on board, Fatt Heng seldom used the yacht. He took Fatt Heng's friends and clients on cruises, but mainly he sailed with guests who'd paid for the privilege. The *Selamat* was chartered by the week or, now and then, extensive monthlong cruises along the Malaysian coast. To live on this yacht, island hopping in the South China Sea, was to Montvale the life he'd dreamed of. These were the routes that Joseph Conrad had sailed, but he remembered how he laughed when he'd mentioned to his wife, Antoinette—Toni—how a Conrad run in these waters was often a voyage of betrayal. "And what do we have on board? Holidaymakers, bird-watchers, and sometimes gunny sacks of copra or bales of rubber. No betrayals!"

The *Selamat* was a ninety-four-foot yacht, ketch rigged—that is, double masted—with a seventeen-foot beam, a classic wooden boat, and "well bred," built in the Philippines of oak and teak and mahogany. At the center of the saloon, a carved teak dining table, with a sofa and chairs for six people. The yacht could sleep six, plus the crew, which included a gourmet chef—Toni. On the rare occasions when Fatt Heng was on board, Montvale and his wife slept in the stern cabin. But the rest of the time, which was most of the time, they occupied the owner's cabin in the bow—plenty of room, a head, a shower, a small galley.

The *Selamat* was their home, their luck, their world; and when a Singaporean businessmen, Bill Kelley—asked Montvale whether he would work for him, skippering his yacht the *Sláinte*, and named a high salary, Montvale was torn, to the extent that he shared the information with Fatt Heng.

"I made my fortune taking risks," Fatt Heng said. "So I understand your dilemma. I'd be tempted myself. I know the *Sláinte*—a nice boat."

Speaking slowly, Fatt Heng was seated cross-legged on a low bench that had once been an opium couch. Fleshy and inert, and with the facial moles that Chinese think of as lucky, and sometimes as a warning, he reminded Montvale of the figure the Chinese call Joss, a plump benign deity that is propitiated with incense and fruit. He seemed to be encouraging Montvale to take the job.

"I could use the extra money, sir," Montvale said. "Toni and I want to buy a boat of our own at some point and live on board as we do here."

"Think of what you're saving by living on board my *Selamat*," Fatt Heng said.

That was not the answer Montvale had been expecting. He had thought that Fatt Heng would offer him more money.

Fatt Heng said, "I like using the boat for guests, and there's some profit in it. But I'm a *towkay* at heart, happy in my godown. You probably notice that I become seasick. What use is a boat to a man who becomes seasick?"

"It pays its way," Montvale said. "It's a business."

"Water business," Fatt Heng said, dismissively, tugging his legs under him. "I'm a Sabah boy myself. I grew up on my father's coconut plantation in Sandakan. But I'm sentimental. Probably that's why I keep the boat. And you're a loyal employee."

"It's been a pleasure, sir."

"Glad to hear it. Now you say that Tuan Kelley offered you a job. But what if I made a counteroffer?"

Montvale named the amount that Kelley had mentioned.

Fatt Heng flicked his fat fingers, waving the number aside.

"Not money," he said. "Money is a simple thing. Look what I've made. I am offering you your freedom and your future." His moles folded into his smile as he peered closely at Montvale and went on, "I like letting my friends cruise with you. The charters are okay. I guess I'm breaking even. You know the cost of fuel, of repairing the sails, painting and upkeep. It adds up. But in eight or ten years I'll be moving on to something else. Need something new, lah!"

"I'll still be young," Montvale said.

"Yah. The timing's right. At that point I'll give you the boat."

"Give me the boat?" Montvale repeated. The offer surprised him, and in his momentary confusion he was unable to understand fully the implications. But Fatt Heng was still talking.

"I had a Saudi client," he was saying. "He wanted to invest in Penang, where I had some interests. He brought me to Saudi Arabia to finish the deal. One of the sheiks with him was fiddling with his worry beads. In this case they were made of emeralds. I knew that from across the room—bluish green, the way they shimmered. He was in white, looking like a priest, looking like all the others in the boardroom, the robes, the sandals, the thing on his head."

"It's called a kaffiyeh," Montvale said. "I sailed in the Gulf when I was in the Royal Navy. I bought one. It's secured by an agal."

"I am speaking of the worry beads. My partner, Jin Bee, was dazzled by them. After the meeting we gathered in the courtyard for tea, and smoking the hubble-bubble, just men together, Jin Bee says, 'Those beads are fantastic.'"

Fatt Heng swung his legs off the bench, rose from his seat, imitating the sheik, and gestured to Montvale, saying, "Take."

Montvale squinted at Fatt Heng's assertive gesture, though he remained rigid.

"That's what the sheik said. Without any hesitation, he handed the emerald beads to Jin Bee, and he insisted that he keep them. That was the custom. You praise something, they give it to you, no questions. And the sheik did it without flinching, though the beads must have cost in the tens of thousands."

"I've heard of that happening, though I've never seen it."

"It should have been an awkward moment, but it wasn't. It was a lesson to me." Fatt Heng returned to the bench and, nodding sagely, said, "I want to be that sheik. Not attached to what I own, so that my things possess me. But to be free of them, and fair."

The *towkay*'s smooth face conveyed certainty. In the constellation of tiny moles, Montvale saw luck and wealth.

"Stay with me for ten years and the *Selamat* will be yours. You can think about it."

"I don't need to think about it," Montvale said. "This is the answer to my prayers."

They shook hands on it. Montvale went back to the *Selamat* and told Toni the news. She said, "That's wonderful, but don't you think you should get it in writing?"

When Montvale mentioned a written agreement, Fatt Heng laughed. "You don't trust me!" and Montvale, embarrassed, backed off.

"In ten years I'll be fifty-eight," he told Toni. "We'll cruise around the world. Maybe do some charters for money."

So their future was assured.

Montvale was fastidious about maintenance, and in the past Fatt Heng had always paid. But Fatt Heng was not so prompt now, and sometimes he did not reply to a request to fund the repairs. With the confidence that the *Selamat* would be his in ten years, Montvale used his own money to refit and repair the yacht. He considered it his even now, years before the handover. Fatt Heng showed up less and less. One year he did not appear at all, and—claiming seasickness—he never sailed. The money from the charters went directly to his agent, who paid Montvale his monthly salary.

Every year, Montvale was offered a job skippering a yacht—bigger yachts, more money; he always declined, citing loyalty to Fatt Heng, though he never disclosed that he was remaining on the *Selamat* because in a few years it would be his.

And often, when the agent was slow to come up with his salary, or Montvale felt a task was urgent, he went on using his own money to replace a sail or a cleat, or to repair a spar or rigging. He bought a new tender in Malacca, a strip-built rowboat, painted red. When his urgent memo *Keel bolts need replacing* went unanswered by Fatt Heng, Montvale spent the last of his money that month on installing new ones. Looking around the yacht he could count the repairs he'd made, allowing him to conclude that by degrees he was making the yacht his own. In his fastidious way, he kept a file of receipts, documenting every repair.

When the *Selamat* was in dry dock for any length of time, as it had to be for refitting, Montvale and Toni rented a car and drove to Johor, or to Fraser's Hill or the Cameron Highlands, and sometimes to Penang. It was there, in George Town, that he learned that, having made conquests in land sales, manufacturing, and hotels, Fatt Heng had moved his office and residence from Batu Ferringhi to Jesselton in North Borneo. Montvale recalled Fatt Heng saying, "I'm a Sabah boy myself," and his mention of growing up on a coconut plantation. But Montvale suspected that removing himself to distant Jesselton was his way of keeping out of reach of the authorities in Kuala Lumpur.

Montvale had not needed to do much research to discover the latest of Fatt Heng's successes in business. His name was always in the *Straits Times*, the news of his latest deals in mining and oil exploration. Montvale marveled at how Fatt Heng had the loyalty of so many, and he thought of him as like a captain of the line, commanding a great schooner, that ventured across these seas, with a vast crew, one man in charge. He sometimes sailed to Jesselton and anchored where Fatt Heng's godown faced the channel.

Always, at the end of one of the holidays necessitated by repairs, Montvale was reminded of how little he owned ashore—nothing, really, no house, no car, not even much in the way of savings, because of his paying for the yacht's upkeep and repairs. But when they relaunched the *Selamat* and boarded it, they were able to say *We're home*. Trustworthy himself, he was trusting of others, and he had the reassurance that the yacht would soon be his.

Nine years into the agreement, after one of the seasonal refits, Montvale and Toni turned in their rental car and prepared to boat the yacht, at a mooring in Singapore. A stranger stood on deck at the top of the gangway—Chinese, unsmiling, his arms at his sides.

"You are?"

"I am Jin Bee."

Jin Bee of the emerald worry beads. He handed Montvale an envelope, saying, "For you."

Fatt Heng's distinctive dragon chop was on the envelope. The letter inside was brief, *I am selling the boat. New owner is Jin Bee. He will accompany you to Jesselton.*

Montvale felt sick, weak, empty, but all Jin Been said was, "You must talk to the *towkay*," and showed him a deed of ownership, and the papers proving the yacht was registered in his name.

The run to Jesselton was somber, but the winds were fair, and they arrived in the harbor after three days. Leaving Toni on board, Montvale rowed his tender into port and found Fatt Heng in his godown on the harbor, looking content behind a wide desk.

Before Montvale could speak, Fatt Heng raised his hand like a policeman stopping traffic, and said, "I changed my mind."

"But you promised."

"Show me the proof. Show me the paper I signed."

"I trusted your word," Montvale said. And he took the file of receipts from his briefcase. "Look. These are the dockets for all the repairs I've made."

Fatt Heng was unimpressed by the faded yellowed papers that had the look of old laundry chits.

"I used my own money," Montvale said, and when he saw Fatt Heng smile at his helplessness, he said, "I insist on being repaid."

"That's your pigeon," Fatt Heng said.

"If you don't compensate me, I'll undo them—shackles, spars, a new jib sail, new tender, bolts, everything."

"You can have them back. Jin Bee will replace them. He has money. The boat is his."

"I'll put that—that I can have them back—in writing," Montvale said.

It took the rest of the morning for Montvale to prepare the document, which he did with the help of a Malay solicitor in Jesselton, who was amused by Montvale defying the eminent *towkay*, Chung Fatt Heng, listing every can of paint, every screw, spar, sail, and bolt on the agreement, with the price of each, and the acknowledgment that Montvale was within his rights to repossess them.

"Not really much money," Fatt Heng said, signing the document, stamping his dragon chop beside his name. But as he did, bringing the chop down hard, his wide sleeve flapped and a bracelet of green stones dinged on the desk. Lifting his forearm, Fatt Heng made the emerald bracelet slip into his sleeve, and he frowned as the witnesses added their signatures. Dismissing Montvale, he said, "Jin Bee will supervise."

But it was days of work, and Jin Bee retired to the owner's cabin, while Montvale, assisted by Toni, removed the fittings, the jib sail, the spar, and a bucket of shackles. The yacht looked skeletal as Montvale steered it into the channel at the harbor entrance and dropped anchor, before Fatt Heng's godown.

"You might need this," he said to Jin Bee, handing him a life jacket.

Then he went below and began to remove the keel bolts he'd installed years ago. After two were loosened, water began to spurt into the hull. He managed to extract one of them, but the hull was filling fast. He was soon in the tender, rowing toward the mangroves, Jin Bee frantically splashing, behind him, as the *Selamat* sank in four fathoms of water, only seven feet of its tallest mast still visible when the yacht became stuck in the muddy bottom.

"True story," Willetts said. "You saw the hazard."

But Montvale was peering at the bar chit. He tapped it, saying, "Vimto Soybean Milk. We didn't order that. Must be some mistake," and called out to the waiter.

FATHER X

On the last of my monthly visits to him, my widowed father made a casual remark about his poor hearing. "The worst of deafness is not silence," he said. "I could bear that. It's that I can actually hear voices, noises that sound like words spoken in the next room. But I'll be damned if I can understand them." And he stared helplessly at me in bewilderment. He was in his late sixties but had a cherubic face, pink cheeks, and blue eyes and was balding in a way that gave him a tonsure. "Indistinct voices." And he smiled. "What is being said to us?"

I drove four hundred miles from Boston back to Baltimore where I was living with my fiancée and got the news the next day that my father had died soon after I left—without warning; he was not ill, and not very old, but his heart failed; and I was too far away to be of any use. I hated that he had died alone—he had buried my mother, to whom he was devoted, three years before—and in my grief I clung to that casual remark he'd once made to me about being deaf. Hearing distinct words but not understanding them.

That statement, characteristic of his honesty, helped me through the funeral arrangements, and I repeated the words to myself like a mantra. In the end it did not seem casual at all, but rather like an eternal truth, at least of my life, of being in the presence of a drama, aware of all its spoken details and taking it for meaningless mumbling, not realizing that a revelation was being offered that might change my view of myself, my family, the world—everything, including what I am about to reveal about my father here.

"But I have faith," he said. "With faith all things are possible. Maybe one day I'll get it."

He wanted so little; for as long as I knew him he was a housebound and unambitious man, content with his loving wife and his unusual writing career that was like a cottage industry, but of a spiritual kind.

I was alone at the wake, except for the few people who'd known him, the plumber and the electrician and the man who mowed the lawn after I left for college. Father had no close friends—he resisted intimacy with everyone except his wife, my mother, who was his whole world. When she died, my father helped me through that sadness, did all the paperwork, prepared the documents, and was resolute while I sobbed, bereft at the thought of losing my mother.

Father's patience gave him strength—goodness was his business, as I will explain in a moment; but goodness was his mode of being. My mother was such a part of him that I felt that when she died he was inconsolable and yearned to join her. I sometimes reflected that, though kindly toward me, my parents were so devoted to each other that in many respects they ignored me. Maybe this is a pattern with passionate couples who have kids? My folks were reserved toward everyone else, they had no room for friends, and they were disinclined to spend much time with me. I grew up in awe of them, intimi-dated by their closeness, while at the same time somewhat resenting the fact that for much of my early life I seemed to be in their way. The memory of this conflict made my grieving harder.

And then at the wake, alone with the funeral director, at the last hour, I got the shocking news.

"I thought the death certificate was in order, but it seems there's a prob-lem," he said, speaking much too slowly, because I wanted to know it all at once. His name was Ken Mortimer, of Mortimer Mortuary. "And it's not a misfiling," he added, as though to keep me in suspense.

We were standing so near the open casket I got a whiff of my father's body, the faint tang of chemicals, the perfumed hum of talcum and cosmetics that made his face puffy and doll-like.

"What is it?" I whispered, as though my father might hear. Proximity to a corpse awakens superstitions and provokes odd behavior. I was keenly aware of being within the orbit of his aura. The inert body of the man seemed to have powers, and it was no consolation to me that he was not wearing his bulky hearing aid.

Mortimer, the funeral director, wasn't fussed; he was soft-spoken and correct, which made what he was telling me much harder to take, because his tone gave it a certainty that was almost unbearable.

"The death certificate can't be authenticated," he said. "There is no record of your father anywhere."

"I don't understand. He has a birth certificate."

"Not a true one. It doesn't check out. There is no record of your father's birth that we can find."

"He was born here in Boston," I said.

By shaking his head slowly, as though in sorrow, the man made a tactful effort to refute this. "William Hope does not exist—at least on paper."

Hearing his name spoken, with this denial, so near to his lifeless body, cushioned in the silk-lined casket, I whinnied and became breathless and put my hands to my face.

"Date and place of birth," I said, protesting. "It's on record."

"No matches," Mortimer said. I began to resent his dark suit, his somber necktie, his highly polished shoes, his pinkie ring, the small gold lapel pin—all of it, for the authority it gave him; because I was rumpled and fatigued with grief and unsure of how to handle what he was telling me.

"What about my mother—her birth certificate? Her wake was held right here three years ago."

Mortimer was trying to be kind, to let me down gently. His considerate way of dealing with grief was a key element in his work. He was in a sense a professional mourner, the soul of sympathy, grieving with his customers, role-playing perhaps, because high emotion was the day-to-day with him. He remained compassionate yet unfazed, like a doctor delivering bad news.

"Your father supplied the documents then, which we didn't question," he said.

Each time he spoke I glanced at my father's powdered nose and rouged cheeks, his hair neatly combed, the trace of a smile on his lips, as though listening.

The man straightened and sniffed and faced me. "Forgeries."

"Their marriage certificate."

"No record of it."

"He was a pious Catholic. It would have been in a church somewhere in Boston."

Mortimer's saying nothing, his facing me without any expression, seemed the most severe way of refuting me.

"My father was an honest man. He would never involve himself in forgery."

"I'm not saying he did it." Then Mortimer sighed heavily, shaking his head. "But the papers were certainly forged. The seal, the notary, the dates, the signatures—all of it was false. None of it checked out. He is not William Hope. Your mother was not Frances Hope."

Dad always called her Frankie. He loved her, adored her, made her happy, while I watched from a little distance, admiring their love but feeling excluded.

"Who is he then?"

"No idea," Mortimer said.

My father was lying in the casket before me, within earshot of all this, and I was reminded again of how he'd spoken in his deafness of hearing words without understanding them.

"What will you do?"

"What we usually do. Keep some of his DNA. Maybe find a match. We took a sample, a mouth swab. And some of his hair."

"What about fingerprints?"

"The service is being held in half an hour. We'll have to secure the casket in the hearse. It's a good twenty minutes to the church. There isn't time."

But even as Mortimer was speaking I was calling the police on my cell phone, explaining the urgency, saying that fingerprints needed to be taken from a body immediately. "A set of remains?" the dispatcher said: a melancholy description of my father. And I had the sad duty of standing before the casket, keeping the fretting Ken Mortimer at bay, while a policewoman (name patch *Cruz*) held father's limp arm and rolled one finger after another onto the ink pad and then in the same motion onto the appropriate square of the document, taking his prints. Closing the lid of the casket Mortimer frowned at the sight of my father's inky fingers, as though we'd spoiled his work.

As a result of the fingerprinting, the service was held an hour late. The priest was annoyed, though the few mourners didn't seem to notice. But a large grieving family awaiting their own service, delayed by ours, stood in the parking lot, looking wounded, in sulky postures. I was struck by how many of them there were, their tears, their convoy of cars, each with a flag attached to an upright rod on a disk that was magnetized to the roof. Those mourners were a reproach to me as I entered the church for our small huddled service.

The ritual was familiar; still, I sat baffled, wondering who it was that lay in the casket. Puzzlement made me sadder, and for the first time since hearing the news of my father's death, I wept—sobbing until my throat ached. But I was sure I was weeping for myself, feeling abandoned, tricked by the man in the casket on wheels, watching the priest shaking holy water on the lid.

Who was he? Who, for that matter, was I?

He was a recluse. You might have suspected agoraphobia except that when my mother was alive they often went out in the evening for a drive. They took sandwiches. They parked near the harbor, facing the sea, and ate them. They left me at home, saying, *You must have schoolwork to do*, and I said yes, because I knew from experience that they did not want me along. I seem to be suggesting that they were cold to me, but they were so loving toward each other I had to admire them. They sometimes appeared to me like two people who shared an amazing secret that only they knew, that would never be revealed, that they marveled over in whispers in their parked car. *No mind is empty that considers the sea*, my father once said.

Their love radiated calm in the household. My mother glowed in his adoration. My father was humble, God-fearing, engaged in one of the more unusual professions—rewarding spiritually but not monetarily. He said he didn't mind. My parents lived frugally. They often spoke of the virtue of the Economy of Enough.

A pious Catholic, yet he seldom went to church, and when he did go to a holy mass he chose a service in a distant town, sneaked in by a side door, sat in a rear pew, his head down, more of his humility, reminding me of Christ's parable of the Pharisee and the publican—my father the publican who beat his breast because he felt unworthy and did not raise his eyes to heaven, as the boastful Pharisee did in the Gospel of Luke. Then he slipped out, by a different door.

His unusual profession? He wrote sermons for a living. He did not adver-
tise but his business was well enough known so that after a while priests found
him and solicited his help in composing the Sunday sermon, or the specific
homilies for weddings and funerals.

In the beginning it was done by mail order, letters addressed to Father X,
from priests requesting a thousand words on a particular topic or biblical
text, usually enclosing an envelope of dollar bills, never a check; the sort of
limp, faded dollar bills you might see in the collection basket or being inserted
in the poor box.

"A donation," the priest's note would say.

Father wrote in longhand, my mother typed the sermons, and it was she
who mailed the letters at the post office, while my father stayed home.

It had started as a column in a Boston newspaper, where my father worked
selling classified ads, at that time a profitable section of the paper, "small ads."
Father liked it because it was all done on the telephone, he had regular office
hours, he did not need to leave his desk; in his modesty, he seemed to enjoy
the obscurity of the job. A regular feature of the paper was "Thought for the
Day," by "Father X"—the name used by two journalists who wanted to conceal their identity. They took turns writing the "Thought," which appeared
beside the editorials, as a way of dignifying the page.

Overhearing the journalists complaining that they were behind in their
work and had to produce a "Thought," my father offered to help.

"You, William?"

His full name was William Lawrence Hope, he was then about forty-five,
and I would have been five. I was Larry.

"Think you can do it?"

My modest father said, "I'm willing to try. If you don't like what I write,
don't use it."

He wrote a column based on story in John about Jesus curing the blind
man. He made much of the Pharisees mocking Jesus, accusing him of being a
sinner, pretending to work a miracle on the Jewish Sabbath, the byplay with
the despised parents of the blind man, and the doubting onlookers.

"I like the dialogue in this story," he told me. "It has the flavor of true human speech. 'How can a sinner work miracles?' 'He is a prophet.' The parents

protesting, 'He was born blind.' And, 'I don't know if he's a sinner, but I was blind and now I see.' And 'I've told you already and you didn't hear.' You can see them all standing in a little group, with the confused parents, near the muddy earth Jesus used to rub on the blind man's eyes."

And my father's favorite line in it was from Jesus, when challenged, the odd seemingly ungrammatical protestation, "Before Abraham was, I am."

That column, on yellowed newsprint, was tacked to the wall of his study as his first effort, the one that earned him his job as Father X.

The two journalists were delighted, they ran the piece and asked for more, and soon my father had a new job at the paper. He still sold classified ads, but his "Thought for the Day" was so popular it was syndicated in the other newspapers owned by the company. To his relief, after his success he worked from home—the classifieds, the daily "Thought." He liked working in his pajamas, sitting in a wing chair, a clipboard on his knee.

It had all happened quickly. He said he was not surprised. He was modest about his column, but he insisted there was another factor.

"No one likes to write," he said to me more than once. "Writing is a chore for even an experienced journalist. For the average person it is awful to contemplate—the blank page, how do I fill it, what do I say? Even a letter. Ask someone to put something in writing—'write me a letter'—and you'll probably never receive it. Most people would rather do anything than write. Especially sermons."

Another day he told me why.

"They're happy to condemn sinners—just talking. But a reasoned sermon, with biblical authority, is another story. It's much easier to denounce someone out of hand than explain him in a well-written sermon. Remember, Jesus taught love and forgiveness."

"So you enjoy writing them?"

"I usually have something to say, which makes it easier. I believe in what I write. And I am inspired by the word of God."

The other journalists were writing the "Thought" as a job, having to meet a deadline. My father was doing it for pleasure and as a spiritual exercise.

"Maybe it's a form of prayer," he said.

Yet he still sold small ads and made a reasonable living, while my mother busied herself as his typist, as well as looking after wayward souls—unwed mothers, battered wives, counseling them and helping them find their way.

Father X's columns were quoted in churches, from the pulpit, and my father received many letters of thanks, as well as an additional income, writing sermons to order. *How does one console the parents of a dead child?* he was asked. He answered by writing a page of consolation, and he received some money in return. *This is the money the parents gave me, in gratitude. Please accept it as a donation.* That happened so many times he had a regular correspondence with priests, stuck for ideas for sermons, who implored Father X to help them out.

He gladly did so. He felt in this way that he was speaking to a congregation through this priest. He said that when he felt the fervor of devotion he could write a sermon in twenty minutes. "And that small effort might change lives." He had a thorough knowledge of scripture. "The human parts—people speaking. Those are real voices. 'Whether he is a sinner I do not know. There is one thing I do know. I was blind and now I see'—that's nice, that's real."

Most people who tried to write had nothing to say. "But this is the living word."

He did not regard this writing as a business. It was a mission, these were donations, not fees; but he realized that toward the end of any given week most priests were agonizing over the Sunday sermon.

One wrote to him, "I'd planned to play golf today. I thought I'd miss the tee time. Your help has allowed me to do this."

"Golf!" He laughed at the thought. Priests had boats, parties to attend, friends and families to visit. My father writing their sermons freed them to do as they wished and for those with a mission it gave meaning to their work.

"So you have the last word," I said.

"Not me," he said. He tapped his head and then pointed to the heavens.

Toward the end of the nineties, when the newspaper went digital, Father X's "Thought" appeared on its website. He posted sermons, he fielded questions, he accepted commissions to write for special occasions. Perhaps he realized how much power he had as a writer, that on a Sunday many priests would be standing before a congregation, reciting his words, always as he said, a message of forgiveness.

"Priests are like college professors," he said. "They give the same lessons every year. They repeat themselves. That's why, after a while, I seldom hear from them again. They have all they need from me."

He was never more passionate or persuasive than when he was writing of the sanctity of marriage, the word made flesh, God is Love. And that was the man I knew, the salesman in Classifieds who became a columnist, who ended up writing sermons for desperate priests—who were desperate perhaps because they had faltered in the faith.

But although he wrote under the name Father X, he was not William Hope. And if he was not William Hope, I was not Larry Hope.

When the funeral rituals ended I did not go back to Baltimore and my fiancée, Beth. I simply told her, "I need to stay a while, to sort out my father's papers." She accepted that explanation.

How could I tell her that I was not the man she thought I was? My identity was in doubt, my pious father had lied about his name, and so had my mother. Beth and I had talked about marrying soon. That had cheered my father. Once I had told him that his piety had inspired me to think of the priesthood—that I might have a vocation. "Think hard," he said. "It's a torment for many priests. Look how lost they are," and he showed me their letters, begging him to write for them.

My birth certificate was clearly as false as my father's. How could I get married if I did not know who I was? I looked again at my birth certificate, though I knew all the details, my name Lawrence Hope, my father William Hope, his profession given as *Journalist*, a modest way of describing someone writing spiritual texts for priests to uplift congregations; his date of birth; my mother was Frances, profession *Housewife*—more modesty, for as a social worker she eased the lives of many single mothers.

I looked for more paper, for any documents in my father's desk or around the house that might help explain who he was. There was nothing. He had not been in the army, he had not applied for a passport, he had never been in trouble with the law: more and more he seemed like a shadow.

"No hits," Mortimer, the funeral director, said when I called to ask about the DNA samples.

His call reminded me that I had the fingerprints. I took them to police headquarters and explained my problem, saying that I needed to establish my father's true identity to find out who I was.

"But I don't have much hope," I said. "I can't think of any occasion when my father would have been fingerprinted."

"You'd be surprised," the desk sergeant said, taking the envelope of prints.

That same week I got a call saying that they had a match, his fingerprints were on file in the federal database. I made an appointment to examine the relevant documents.

"These are the prints of Jeremiah Fagan," the officer said at my interview, pushing a piece of paper across the counter. "Here's his address and his details. They might be out of date—this was filed twenty-odd years ago."

"It's a firearms application," I said, with disbelief, and I saw that the date on it was the year I was born.

"And you can see it was approved. He had a license to carry a Class A firearm."

"My father carried a gun?"

"This is your father?"

To identify myself I had shown him my driver's license, where I was Lawrence Hope.

"I think my father changed his name."

"No, he didn't. That would have come up in the search. A name change would have invalidated the gun license."

"Why would he want to carry a gun?"

"There's his reason on the application," the sergeant said. "Line five. 'Personal protection.' If you want a copy, it's two dollars."

I sat in a coffee shop studying the application, trying to fit the new name to my father's face, reflecting on the date of the document, which was so near to my birthday; and at last I examined my father's home address, 600 Harrison Avenue.

Harrison Avenue is one of Boston's major thoroughfares—long and lined with important buildings, running south from Chinatown almost to Malcolm X Boulevard, which suggests the racial diversity of its residents. But where my father's house should have stood there was an imposing brick building that looked more like a school than an apartment house. Walking around it I saw, looming behind it, the granite steeples of the Cathedral of the Holy Cross.

The address I had was not a school at all, but rather the cathedral rectory. I knocked. A woman in an apron answered and said that the priests were either busy or away, and that if I wanted to talk to one I would need to make an appointment.

I said, "Tell me, who is the oldest priest here?"

"That would be Monsignor Bracken."

"Is he about sixty-five or seventy?"

"Could be."

"May I leave him a note?"

The woman agreed and helped me by offering me a piece of paper. I wrote that I hoped that I might meet Monsignor Bracken at his convenience the following Sunday, before he said Mass (as the schedule indicated) at one of the side altars of the cathedral.

Although I wrote my name and telephone number on the note, I did not receive a reply. After some days of speculation, I was eager to find out the truth. On Sunday, I stopped at the rectory at nine and was met by a young priest. I said that I was there to see Monsignor Bracken.

"Do you have an appointment?"

"I left a message for him."

"Just a moment."

He left me standing in the foyer, in the odor of candle wax and incense and starched linen and furniture polish. I heard what sounded like a complaint from a few rooms away, and then the young priest returned.

"You can go through," he said. "Second door on your left."

The old priest, Monsignor Bracken, was seated in an armchair, looking like a plump pink granny with tangled hair, a frilly blouse over his sloping stomach, and a shawl around his neck—vestments, of course, and his cassock like a gown.

He welcomed me—"Take a seat"—but was so abrupt I felt I had intruded upon him. And perhaps I had. In his lap, there was a sheet of paper, obviously something he was studying, with words in large letters, the sort of typeface that aids a public speaker.

"I'm sorry to bother you, Monsignor."

He looked troubled, as though I'd ambushed him and might have a serious problem to raise. But he cautioned me in a kindly way, "I don't have a great deal of time. I'm saying Mass at ten. Might we meet afterward in the sacristy?"

"Just a simple question."

"What is it, my son?"

"I am inquiring about a man named Jeremiah Fagan."

He made a disgusted face and at the same time gripped the arms of his chair with his plump hands, his fingers growing pale with the pressure of his grip, and for a moment from the sour way he twisted his lips I thought he was going to spit.

"What of him?"

"Am I right in thinking he once lived here?"

"Father Fagan was a disgrace, an immoral man, one of the priests who did violence to the reputation of the church. I don't want to hear about him. Now please leave me in peace."

"May I ask in what way immoral?"

Monsignor Bracken rose from his chair as a way of urging me to get up, and he directed me to the door using his big bumping belly, the skirts of his cassock whirling as he hurried forward, all this motion like an elaborate gesture of rejection.

"Yes, he was a priest here, but he sinned—grievously. And he tainted others with his immorality. It was a great scandal. But he will have to explain that to Almighty God."

"He died recently."

"Then he is in hell," the monsignor said and outstretched his arms to shoo me away, as you would a pestering child. "That's all you need to know. We will never forgive him for the damage he did. Now please go."

The young priest who had let me in must have heard some of this, because he looked fussed but said nothing, only snatched open the rectory door and shut it as soon as I stepped over the threshold, ejecting me.

This Father Fagan was my dad? I had to know more. I lingered, trying to make sense of it, and to calm myself I walked around the corner to the cathedral and entered, glad for a place to sit. It was so easy to see my father as a priest—he had the temperament, the piety, the humility—but what was the scandal? I hated to think that he had trifled with small boys, as many of the priests in Boston had done. But Monsignor Bracken had been so angry, damning him as immoral, it was possible that he'd been one of those predatory priests.

The tinkle of bells from a side altar distracted me from these confused thoughts, and I saw emerging from an adjacent door Monsignor Bracken, in a little procession, two women by his side, their eyes downcast. I crept toward them and took a seat at the back, near a pillar, where I could not easily be seen—nor could I see the action at the altar. Though my father seldom went to church, except in his furtive way, he had always encouraged me to attend Mass. But I had ceased to be a churchgoer. I was so out of touch, I was surprised to see women serving the water and wine, helping with the Communion hosts, where I had been used to seeing altar boys.

I heard the mass being said, Monsignor Bracken speaking in his liturgical singsong, and the serving women's responses, echoed by the muttering people in the pews.

And after a while the monsignor ascended the pulpit, he cleared his throat, and when he began to speak, at first slowly, glowing with confidence, as though inspired, I heard my father's voice, my father's wisdom, one of his sermons, with the human dialogue he loved, Peter asking Jesus, "What if my brother sins against me seven times?" and Jesus saying, "I do not say to you seven times, but seventy times seven." And Monsignor Bracken was emphatic in uttering the numbers, making it plain that there was no limit in forgiving someone.

It was as though my father was at that altar, in that pulpit, offering a message of compassion, speaking through that priest.

With his name I was able to find his story in the Boston newspapers, how Father Fagan had been surprised in a suburban motel with a nun, a Sister of Charity named Sister Constance; the investigation into their behavior, the violent threats against them, how they'd vanished together, and been denounced; how they had stayed in hiding, undetected, and ultimately their scandal was overtaken by the greater one of the pedophile priests.

But they had remained in the Boston area. I found their marriage certificate, on file in Boston City Hall, with their proper names on it—the marriage
had taken place six months before I was born—and at last more papers, a
house full of them, the sermons, the homilies, the compassionate words of love
and forgiveness my father had written under a pen name for the priests who
had condemned him.

HOME COOKING

I n my enforced first phase of catering, feeling humbled and needing to lift
my spirits, I made the whole business a performance—served the food as
well as cooked it. So I talked as I made my way around the table, ham-
pered by diners' shoulders and elbows, riffing off their conversation. Willard
is a college town, with a college town's talky dinner parties.

". . . sabbatical at Magdalene," I'd hear, and "Chuck's thinking of doing
some travel writing."

"The 'g' is silent," I'd say, presenting the tureen of chowder, "like the one
in bologna."

They'd stare, the table falling silent, while the first diner slopped the chowder into his bowl, splashing his thumb.

"Two main rules if you're a travel writer and married"—swinging the
tureen to the next diner. "Number one, don't whistle while you pack," and
I tried not to wince as they wagged the ladle instead of allowing it to sink.
"Number two, don't come back with a tan."

Or I'd bring the rolls in a particular basket on my arm. "Bread?" I'd say
but would not explain the basket until someone remarked on its bizarre
shape.

"We call this a buttock basket."

And I relished the vexed silence this produced among the flat-minded diners at the homes where I catered—the Murray Spectors, the Wellivers, the
Jiggs Alcorns, the Adamses, the Ratners, the Bud Huttys, the Knoxes, which
was most of the English Department. I used my vintage, big-combed, copper
tongs to dispense the rolls, as I shuffled around the table.

"Notice its amplitudes," I'd say. "You might know it as a gizzard basket? This one was passed down through my family. The story was that it was part of my great-grandmother's dowry. Locally made, like these tongs. Very popular in Willard in the 1880s. Ribbed, see. For fruit and eggs."

Then brisk and correct, I'd revert to being the silent caterer again, but just as I pushed open the kitchen door I'd lean back, canted on my heels, and listen hard, often hearing puzzled fragments of "What was that all about?" and "What's his name?"

Returning later to drift by the long table with wine, hunched in my pouring posture I tried to assess from the mutters and guarded glances whether I'd been recognized, or—from a kind of heat against the nape of my neck—whether anyone was staring at me behind my back.

At the end of the meal in those days, my clients insisted on a ritual I found embarrassing for its formality, singling me out in its glare. This was inviting the chef from the kitchen to take a bow, the diners snatching at their napkins and clapping. At first I resisted, because if I was recognized I'd be joshed into saying a few awkward words, and if I was not recognized I felt like a failure. But at that time, the Willard English Department was Anglophile—influenced by the authors they taught then—and this postprandial ritual was regarded as a British thing to be emulated. They prevailed on me, and so I presented myself and doffed my toque and took my bow. The host said my name. If it was Bud Hutty, he'd have to repeat it because he talked imprecisely owing to his boxed beard.

"Myles Gilbane," someone would reply. "That sounds familiar."

"Help us out here, Myles."

"If you enjoyed your meal, that's all I care about," I'd say, with the gusto you associate with obvious insincerity.

And often a small puzzled voice from the far end of the table: "Isn't there a writer with that name?"

"Myles is that man." The host then would say, as a kind of boast, that I was toiling in his or her very own kitchen.

And I'd have to utter the grim words, "I used to be a writer."

"So what happened, Myles?" This as a hearty challenge.

"I stopped."

In my defense, Murray Spector said one evening, "Emily Brontë stopped. Melville stopped. Salinger. Rimbaud. Harper Lee."

"Coleridge. The fatal visit of the person from Porlock."

"Who said the Porlock person should have knocked more often on the door of literature?"

"Did he knock on your door, Myles?"

"Robert Graves," someone down the table shouted. "Nice poem!"

As I said, this is a college town.

But I didn't stop writing, and neither did Melville. Like Melville, I stopped being published and so I took up another profession that had nothing to do with writing. Melville in his Customs House, me in my kitchen. Those diners in the early days, who knew my books, might get the titles wrong but would accurately recall that each of them in my "Willard Trilogy" contained recipes. They'd say, *Prom Night*—the title of the novel was actually *Senior Prom*—"that was full of food." Yes, the picnic, the tailgate party, Mrs. Macklin's muffins, the banquet's high point—the stoneware crock of salmon pea wiggle. *County Fair* had blue ribbon cakes, Boston cream pie, and thick stews; *Hayseeds* was potato heavy, with home cooking, family recipes, because my ancestors settled here when Willard was a small Episcopal school.

This religious institution, Willard Theological Seminary—muscular Christians—later expanded, became a land-grant agricultural college, and at last what it is today, a university of many thousands of students, some from distant countries, which has changed the culture of the town so radically my people would not recognize it. I hardly do.

But we Gilbanes had always lived off campus.

My novels were out of print, I sometimes said, but added, "You're immersed in them by tasting my recipes, I hope you like them." And, "Home cooking—that's always been my theme. I'm too busy now to write a word."

That was face-saving. But tasting my recipes, they were tasting my novels, more vividly than if they'd read them; and of course I kept writing—so did Melville, so did Rimbaud, so did Salinger, and like them I did not publish anything more. For reasons at first bewildering to me, no one wanted my books. At one time my work had been celebrated, and now it was dismissed in the most painful way, the letters of rejection beginning, "There are so many things I love about your book," and the things were listed, the praise continuing, until the inevitable, "But . . ."

It seemed as though my work was being suppressed, and my response was to talk all the more. Talk is less subtle and nuanced than formal prose, yet I persisted, and instead of chatting I began quoting my work.

"The mood of the mass of people is disappointment," I'd say, drizzling gravy over the mashed potatoes—it was Parson Eldritch's homily to his flock in my unpublished *Pioneers*. "Ask anyone in middle age if they have what they want and they'll say 'No—not yet. Not enough.' That is the American theme—having a great deal yet wishing for more, because there's always someone who has more, and America was founded on promises of more. But here we are heading into old age thinking, 'What happened to my life—to those plans I had as a youth?' It is unfulfillment, as tragedy, as farce. In the American heart—disappointment." And then, "Bit more gravy, ma'am?"

At a certain point in the after-dinner, applaud-the-chef ritual, the host would thank me, rising from his chair, as a way of signaling that it was time for me to put on my toque and go back into the kitchen. Later, as a result of my remarks, like the ones above, I got used to hearing, "Myles—I want a word with you." And yet I felt vindicated in my asides and my writing, because these people—the English profs—hired me as much for my home cooking as for the person—the writer—I used to be, the cachet of the recipes and meals in my novels served to them and devoured; gorging on my books, as I saw it, the very definition of the reader as omnivore.

After a few years, the applauding ritual began to diminish—perhaps the liberal-minded hosts became self-conscious about employing servants and scullery maids, or hearing my soup course remark, "Greasy Joan doth keel the pot." These days it hardly ever happens; and these days is the subject of this story.

In my second phase of catering, my wife, Priscilla, helped me serve. It came about this way.

"If we hire you again, I need you to stop talking to my guests." This was Professor Ratner, but I had been hearing variations of it for months.

Something in me wilted and went spiritless. It was like the rejection of my unpublished novel *Pioneers*, with recipes like the others, but only the recipes survived.

"I thought they'd be amused. One of them laughed."

"Maude Adams. She was being polite. She felt sorry for you."

I was kneading my toque in my hands.

"We appreciate your food. We'd like to see less of you. You need to stay in the kitchen."

"I don't have a server."

"Get one, Myles."

I felt sad and physically weak and unappreciated as you do when you're young and disparaged. But I was sixty-two years old.

With my wife, Priscilla, as server I kept to the kitchen. Cilla's family, the Tuckermans, goes way back in Willard, to its founding, her people being clergy, associated with Willard as a divinity school. She is thrifty, watchful, and feels no need to offer a comment. She's Willard, temperamentally speaking—unforthcoming, stubborn and a little chilly but efficient in serving, insincerely deferential, the Willard way, the equal of anyone. We are childless.

Like me, Cilla is a Willard graduate. She has often remarked on how Willard had changed as an institution, and the town with it. So many of the faculty members were the same but these days had a bounce they didn't have before; they were older, their manner younger—compliant, easily appeasable, not flat-minded anymore, hospitable to every literary variation and yet more resistant than ever to my work or anything like it. No more jackets and ties, their Anglophilia damped down, or nonexistent, but some of them had developed surprising habits.

One client—it was Jiggs Alcorn—greeted me with a hug, and when I went rigid in his arms, he asked me what was wrong.

"We don't do that in Willard," I said.

Or the kissing of women, at first on one cheek, then on both. Now you would have thought with this kind of hearty welcome you'd find greater humor, but in fact there was less. Here is an example. Another change in town: the mosque on Federal Street was once the Odd Fellows Hall. "So maybe it's still the odd fellows," was a remark among the old-timers, but my repeating it produced a hostile silence and again, "I want a word with you, Myles."

Similarly, my overhearing the mention of a gastric bypass—Welliver's—at one of the dinners.

"How appropriate in a stickler for punctuation," I said. "A semicolon."

Someone growled as I hurried away, wincing, knowing I'd hear once again, "I want a word with you, Myles."

As a result I was forbidden to leave the kitchen, and this was just as well. Cilla was exclusively my server. Cilla was the one who passed among the diners with a tureen of chowder, or the platter of chicken, the pot roast, the New England boiled dinner (corned beef, cabbage, parsnips), the homemade, molasses-soaked baked beans. All from my *County Fair* though no one would have known.

In this phase there were different sorts of people at the table, people I glimpsed but didn't speak to, who I imagine would never say, "Myles Gilbane—isn't there a writer with that name?" In fact, in the last year of the applauding the chef ritual, when the host announced, "Myles Gilbane," I became hyperalert; but there was seldom a flicker of recognition.

I'd always cooked. The meals in my books were meals I'd made, the recipes I'd tested, Willard dishes, family favorites, that I'd transferred to my Willard Trilogy. Knowing the ingredients, you'd know the culture, you'd see the fields—butter crunch lettuce and romaine in the spring, heirloom tomatoes and kale in the summer, sweet corn and eggplant later on, apples and peaches in September—I used whatever was in season, sprouts and turnips and squash in the fall, haunches of venison from deer I'd sourced from local hunters, chickens from my own coop, honey from my hives, maple syrup I'd boiled from my trees.

"Just dug them," I'd tell the host on a fall evening of the potatoes I was scrubbing the dirt off with my spud brush.

The Willard I'd grown up in was a town of brown gravy but not of sauces or spices, not much seasoning, except the herbs from my garden. But fresh fish, pot roast, casseroles; lobsters most of the summer—boiled, plain, anything but drawn butter destroys lobster meat. Nothing foreign or exotic.

The taste of my food was the taste of the earth, of Willard, where I was born and raised; where I wrote my books that celebrated the seasons and the landscape and the townsfolk I thinly disguised, books that were no longer in print, townsfolk who were no longer alive.

I boosted fresh-picked corn, beet greens, new potatoes, scrapple, sourdough bread, and the meat stews savored by the villagers on winter nights in *Hayseeds*. I went berrying. Strawberries in the spring, blueberries in early summer, and nasturtium blossoms in my salads. Maple syrup in the fall. Alewives, smelts, clams, and "quahogs," with the correct pronunciation. "Think of *Quo Vadis*."

"Here's Granny's fruit cobbler," I'd say, but I did not mention that Granny was my character in *County Fair*. The salmon pea wiggle I served them I had first served the doomed lovers at the banquet in *Senior Prom*.

No pizza, no noodles, no white rice—though I extolled the wild rice I cooked and explained how it had been harvested as grass seed for a thousand years by Native Americans not far from Willard. I stuck to what I knew, what had nourished me, the meals I'd included in my books—pies, flapjacks, cider donuts. Foreign cooking, I used to say, was always weirdly eye-blinding and multichromatic with disturbingly scorched flavors. I promoted the simple palette, the truth of home cooking, the primary colors of the ingredients—say, the purple saturation of beets, the downright green of fresh kale, the flesh of a slab of raw meat—the predictable flavor with a history, a culinary narrative. Taste as tradition.

"My meat and potatoes," I said to prospective clients, as a way of explaining the authenticity of my menu, "is meat and potatoes."

My early writing had been favorably reviewed and sold well. *Senior Prom* was praised by some critics as "superbly regional," though I rejected the description. An American novel either mattered or was beneath notice. "Innovative" was another compliment: it referred to the recipes. My work seemed to matter enough for the English Department at Willard to invite me to give a lunchtime talk to students. "Home Cooking" was my subject, but it referred to prose fiction. At the time I was finishing my second novel, *Hayseeds*—more recipes, a tighter plot, a critical success with modest sales. Completing the trilogy, and the set of meals, resolving the ambiguity of *Hayseeds*, I published *County Fair*, a failure in terms of reviews and sales, like nearly all the novels of Herman Melville.

My fourth was *Pioneers*, the settlers of Willard, the patriarch Pastor Eldritch, "praying Indians" and skirmishes with hostile tribes; and authentic recipes—succotash, squirrel stew, Indian pudding, and anadama bread—cornmeal and molasses, the cornmeal ground by the native Abenaki.

Pioneers was turned down and remained unpublished; I attempted another novel, without conviction, faltered after a few chapters, and did not finish the book.

It's the bookstores, people said. *It's the decline of newspapers. No one reads books anymore.* Yet novels were published all the time, as I knew from window displays in the campus bookstore—books I could not open without being gnawed by envy and rage for being out of sympathy with them, and so I stopped reading anything new.

I had no living, but my love for food was undiminished. I borrowed money and started a bakery, "Panis Angelicus," on Main Street, adjacent to the campus. Bakers' hours are a punishment, making dough long before dawn, the baking itself and the punitive store hours; and by the afternoon exhaustion, then early to bed until waking at three to mix the dough again, prep the starter for the sourdough, fill the pans, fire up the deep fryer for the doughnuts.

The revelation at the bakery, one of the most profound revelations of my life in this the first of my food endeavors, was that it was a business. It was not enough for me to produce crusty loaves and delicious donuts. I also had to sell them; I needed employees and a business plan. I should have known, because Willard as an educational institution was also a business. The Willard tuition was high, the football stadium was important, foreign students were courted, the logo shop was as big as the bookstore.

I had always thought that if I wrote a good book, it would be published and would sell well. It did not occur to me that good books might not sell, that they might be rejected not because they were poorly written but because there was no market for them, or the market was too small. Being in business myself now, I saw that you could have a great product and yet fail: prevailing taste was what mattered, with bread, with books.

And I reminded myself that I was not the first writer to have another profession. Melville became a customs inspector when his novels began to be ridiculed and rejected, and he was low on funds. Hawthorne made more money as the American consul in Liverpool than as a novelist, Wallace Stevens never relinquished his job as vice president of the Hartford Accident and Indemnity Company, William Carlos Williams was a greater financial success as a pediatrician than as a poet, and he kept doctoring until he died. I knew from living in Willard that many of the writers in residence were actually hard-up novelists, now drawing a good salary as college employees, with meetings to attend and papers to grade and heads of departments to please. That was not for me.

But Panis Angelicus failed.

"Where are the students?"

"They're down the street," Cilla said. "At the other place, where there's Wi-Fi."

I pointed out that this was a bakery, but it was no use. So I started Home Cooking, doing double duty: I cooked and served, talking to the diners at the table. Then it was, repeatedly, "Myles, I want a word with you."

That was the end of phase two.

Phase three was brief and shocking. Cilla was down with shingles—red welts on her body, as though she'd been flogged. But before then, while Cilla was still serving and I was confined to the kitchen—no idea who was at the table—I had been getting special requests, the most frequent one, "Myles, can you possibly vary the menu?"

That seemed odd to me—impertinent, in fact, if not perverse. You hire me for my cooking and now you want me to learn new recipes? It was like someone saying to me, *You need to write differently*. But one editor actually did suggest that, in just those terms. "America's changing, Myles. Give us something new."

"I like things the way they were," I replied, and I elaborated: as far as I knew I was the town's only novelist, I gave Willard a voice and a little fame—

the townsfolk of Willard were my people, with their characteristic accent, their crops, their livestock, their cooking, and their peculiar problems, one of which was that they were the sorts of people overlooked by other writers. They were, I said, natives of the place, with deep roots, as much a cohesive community, with an ingrained culture as any in a distant country.

"Imagine a Punjabi," I said, "or a Yoruba, or a Zapotec—and consider their attachments to the land, their sense of place—and you have a Willardian."

"This is America, Myles."

"This is Willard," I replied. "It's like those cultures."

"In what way?"

"Tenacious. But lacking in elasticity."

I was rewarded with that knowing smile you get in college towns, the pitying tilt of the head that means, *You're all wrong*.

Later, so disturbing to a writer's sensibility, I began to hear words I did not know. "We've invited a vegan." This was someone utterly new to me, a new word and a new being in Willard.

"Perhaps I should explain." It was Bud Hutty, who'd once taught Faulkner but now was teaching "magical realism" and frowned when I said, "You mean fairy tales?"

"No," he said, perfectly serious. "Harsh Ramanujan is teaching fairy tales."

I thought I had misheard, because as usual he talked imprecisely through his boxy beard. He explained that a vegan was something like a vegetarian.

"Easy. I'll make my Willard egg pie."

He smiled. "But no animal products or animal derivatives."

"Milk?"

"I'll have to check."

"Apple pandowdy will be safe."

"If there's lard in the crust it's a no-no."

This was a challenge, but with broccoli, kale, and stuffed cabbage I felt I had created a dish that did not compromise my home cooking or insult Willard tradition.

And serving—Cilla still suffering with shingles—I noticed something at that dinner that I saw more and more. Half were Willard teachers, the other half Willard students, and it was one of the students who was the vegan, a heavy man with wild hair, eating with gusto, not the pale slender woman toying with her clam chowder.

"Cruciferous vegetables," I said, arranging them on the vegan's plate. "And what do you suppose is the crux of it, you being, I suppose, a literary man?"

The table went silent.

"As Granny explains in the Willard novel *County Fair*"—and I did the nasal accent—"'It's their flowers, Seth. Always with four petals, forming a cross.'"

Then I made my exit, hearing that old familiar cry, "What was that all about?"

Another meal, another new word: This was at the Wellivers, as we were going through the menu. Fernanda Welliver said, "And one of the guests is transgender."

A writer since college, widely read, well-traveled, at that time in my mid-sixties, I had never come across this word before in my life. I could not come up with a distinct meaning, and I said so. Fernanda began to go into detail, until I was able to cut her off with, "I get it." I had a dim memory of a name I'd heard in my early youth in Willard, as well as an episode in *Hayseeds*.

I said, "Christine Jorgensen."

Another pitying smile, Fernanda smiling at me in triumphant pity. Thirty-something, born in Brazil, Fernanda said she'd had never heard of Christine Jorgensen (born George Jorgensen), though she mentioned some other trans-gender people. "We have many such in Brazil."

"Thanks for telling me."

"You look shocked."

"Far from it. I feel validated. You've just reminded me of something."

"And, Myles, please don't stare at Sandy."

I decided not even to look but rather, on the night of the dinner, to serve my meal with tact and discretion, bent backed, bowing as I ladled out the first course, the corn-and-lobster chowder, explaining that the ingredients were native to Willard—fresh-picked corn, local potatoes, and my garlic and scallions; and how the coastal waters teemed with lobsters.

"Funny thing about lobsters," I said, my head down. "Every year they squirm out of a small opening in their shell and are completely naked.

Ecdysis—molting. 'Shedders,' the lobstermen call them. You'd hardly know they were lobsters."

"Like soft-shell crabs," someone said.

"A periodic dysmorphia," I said. "Bodily ambiguity. It is not easy to tell, without the shell, whether a lobster is male or female."

This caused a hush. I was still serving the chowder, talking into the tureen. "In *Senior Prom*—out of print, but you might have heard of it, a novel set in Willard—a woman in a bar on Chamberlain Street picks up the main character, Lyle Gilbert, and says she'll drive him home. She's rather attractive, and flirtatious. Lyle is delighted, of course. She drives very fast, and with panache. When she arrives at his house there's only a small parking space in front. Lyle watches in amazement as she pulls forward, whips the car backward, and parallel parks with one turn of the steering wheel, zipping into the spot." I let this sink in. "'Uh-oh,' Lyle thinks, and then scoots out of the car and runs into his house."

I'd finished doling out the chowder, and in the silence that ensued I made for the kitchen, but before the door closed after me instead of laughter I heard, "Outrageous."

And later Ed Welliver said, "Myles, I want a word with you" and "We won't be needing you again."

"I know what you're thinking—about tolerance," I said. "But Willard is very tolerant, by Willard standards."

"Ever," he said, talking over me. "And Sandy agrees with me."

"Whatever blows your skirt up," I said, and I thought, *Just as well*. Cilla was still shingle-ridden, and I was having trouble handling the remaining clients, who had become more demanding, and new clients, too.

"We need something exotic," Jerry Wencus said to me about a week after the business at the Wellivers. Wencus was a new hire. Script writing, he told me. I widened my eyes. "Screenplays," he explained. And when I expressed surprise, he told me that the English Department was not called the English Department anymore. It specialized in gender studies, identity studies, global lit, graphic novels, and movies, too.

"Movies. It's such a funny word, like baby talk. Moo-vees," I said. "The old folk in Willard used to call them photoplays."

Wencus stared severely at me.

I said, "I don't do exotic. I do Willard."

And I explained that when I wrote my novels I felt I was returning my readers to their childhood—the schoolyard, the prom, the football season, the county fair and the harvest, to the Strand Theater where they showed—yes—photoplays. That was my aim in Home Cooking, too, because (as I had said in *Senior Prom*) a meal is not about appetite or hunger; a meal is an occasion, an event, people gathering and talking, exchanging ideas. My food I felt reminded people of their mother in the kitchen, the foundation of their lives.

Wencus wasn't listening. He said, "It's a dinner for some grantees and the next writer in residence." He named them—Sundar Chatterjee, Oddvar Hendrixen, Sarah Uppleby, Omo Wozi Obumselah. They were fabulous writers, he said. Oh, and their supervisor would be there, Bud Hutty.

"As I said, I've done some writing myself," I said.

"Do you publish under your own name?"

"I used to," I said.

"I'm thinking something spicy but not too spicy."

"Anything spicy is too spicy in Willard."

I said curry powder, turmeric, red pepper flakes, cayenne, and cumin are bamboozling spices—eye-blinding and multichromatic. The expedients of countries that need to mask the taste of the ingredients, or else preserve them by infusing them with a feverish tang. Cultures without refrigerators, or root cellars.

"It's a way of insulting good ingredients," I said. "Underneath colorful spices you usually find embalmed food—mummified meals," I said. "I always say, in home cooking taste is tradition."

Jerry Wencus said, "If you cook for us again, I'm going to need something different, more in line with what people are eating these days."

Others had made similar requests, sighing when I said my forte was home cooking. It was strange to me how the teachers at Willard, new and old, were eating differently. Another seismic shift in my lifetime, the things you couldn't say, the things you couldn't write. It was not the world I grew up in, the world I put into my books, the world of Willard.

When I said, *I like things the way they were before*, I was quoting myself, a line from the book I abandoned. And in *Pioneers*, which never got published, one of my settlers, newly arrived, says, "Sometimes in life, in a time of change, you think you've come to the end of something without realizing it is not an end at all but an enlargement, a continuing process of transformation. The trouble is that no one remembers how it all began, how without the testimony of witnesses it is irrecoverable."

"Don't think me disobliging," I said to all of them. "It's simply that I can only do Willard."

With reluctance, Wencus surrendered. I made allowances for the vegetarian, serving potato soup; yet he was the first to complain.

"This soup is cloudy," Mr. Chatterjee said. "Why is it so cloudy?"

"Its opacity?" I said. "Minute particulates."

"We have this in Norway," Oddvar said, spooning it into his mouth. Flecks of soup clung to his blond mustache. "It is *potetsuppe*."

"Granny's potato soup," I said and wanted to add, *County Fair*.

"Vichyssoise," Sarah Uppleby said. But put her delicate hand over her bowl. "I am lactose intolerant."

So I served her a bowl of succotash.

"That is *adalu*, beans and corn," Miss Obumselah said. The wrap on her head made her nodding emphatic. "We have it in Nigeria. It is porridge."

"It is not porridge," I said. And she winced. "It is pure Willard."

As I was setting out the main course, lobster meat prised from the shell, saying, "Lazy lobster—no tools necessary to crack them open," Oddvar spoke up again, "In Norway we have these."

I said, "You're referring to Norway lobster—narrow claws, sinewy claw meat. This is American lobster, found only in waters off the coast here."

"We have lobsters in Nigeria," Miss Obumselah said. "We put them in *adalu*."

"Crayfish," I said. "Cousin of a shrimp, spiny, a tail and not much else." I was still setting down the bowls. "These have meaty claws and a tail, bulkier, tastier. 'Bugs' the lobsterman call them. They exist nowhere else in the world." I took a breath. I said, "*Homarus americanus*."

I hurried to the kitchen (hearing "Did he say bugs?") and remained there, stewing. When I returned to pick up the plates, they were discussing *Huckleberry Finn*.

"The word is used more than two hundred times," Mr. Chatterjee was saying. "It is entirely unacceptable."

Sarah Uppleby said, "Guaranteed kerfuffle."

"*Heart of Darkness*," Miss Obumselah said.

Slipping her plate from under her gesturing hands, I said, "*Heart of Darkness*, like *Huckleberry Finn*, is a masterpiece. So is *Hayseeds* and *Senior Prom*."

"I hate this book," someone said.

"If I'd a knowed what a trouble it was to make a book I wouldn't a tackled it," I said. Tears pricked my eyes, and I felt a weepy constriction in my throat, like the taste of unfamiliar food. To prevent myself from bursting into tears, I continued in a lugubrious voice as I pushed into the kitchen, "I reckon I got to light out for the Territory ahead of the rest!"

Chewing his beard, Bud Hutty said indistinctly through its tangle, "That will do, Myles."

"You think he's okay?" I heard behind me.

A moment later Miriam Wencus entered the kitchen, clearing her throat, as people do when they're about to deliver bad news.

"I was just going to serve the next course," I said smartly, before she could speak. "In this stoneware crock is one of Willard's classic dishes. Do you mind grabbing that buttock basket—it's got the toast in it."

Miriam led the way, holding the kitchen door open for me, and I stepped to the table, where Jerry Wencus presided at the head of the table, Bud Hutty at the other end, the writers on both sides.

Holding the crock before them, ceremonially, I waited for silence, then said, triumphantly, "Salmon pea wiggle!"

After a long silence, Oddvar peered into his bowl as I served and said, "We don't have this in my country."

"Traditional in Willard," I said, "at the senior prom prep rally."

They smiled at the words, as though I had lapsed into another language.

"I know it's not bubble and squeak," Sarah Uppleby asked, winking at Miss Obumselah. "But I reckon we could absolutely pig out on it."

Flattening his hands over his bowl, Mr. Chatterjee said, "I am not taking fish."

That night, after Miriam Wencus lowered the boom on me, I stood at the sink, bent with suffering shoulders, doing the dishes. Stifled by my anger, I had a sense not just that I had lost, but that others were winning. Then Miss Obumselah nudged the kitchen door open. She stood in her finery that I had not noticed at dinner, not just the turban, but a gown, wide sleeves, gold anklets, silk slippers, queenly, angelic.

"Where do you come from?" she asked in a kindly voice.

"Here."

"What do you do here?"

"This."

She touched my shoulder and in a tone of great compassion said, "You need help."

I thought, *At last someone who understands that in some small corner of the culture there's still a call for home cooking.*

A COUPLE OF BOTTLES OF MOXIE

Stewing in the stillness of humid heat, a Wednesday morning in early June, I was sitting on the front piazza steps with Benny Koretsky, laughing a dirty joke into his ear. The joke was about a nasty priest named Father Inn, who had a sexy girlfriend. I was happy—no more school, the whole summer ahead! Benny was chewing his necktie, eager for the punch line, when my mother called out through the screen door.

"Jay—run across the street and buy some tonic, a couple of bottles of Moxie."

The screen door opened, out came Mother's arm tossing a coin that pankled onto the piazza, then the twang of a spring, and the smack of the door slamming shut.

That was my life at home when I was thirteen—nothing happened, then everything happened.

"What's wrong?" Benny said, taking the wet end of his tie out of his mouth and looking alarmed.

It was my face, tight with fear. I said, "I can't go to the library today."

"At least finish the joke."

"You know the rest."

He shivered a little and yanked at his tie in frustration. "But I like the way you tell them."

I was too rattled to appreciate the compliment. I picked up the quarter and started down the stairs. I couldn't explain how just a few words like *a couple of bottles of Moxie* would seem innocent and meaningless unless you were a child in the Justus family, in which case they were terrifying.

"You promised!" Benny called out.

But by then I was walking fast to the corner store, Sam's Variety (*Drinks, Candy, Sundries*) and Benny was heading to the Littleford Public Library. I couldn't explain that Moxie meant my uncle Frank Dittrick was going to visit, was probably on his way, and now it seemed like punishment for my dirty joke about Father Inn, because Uncle Frank Dittrick was a priest named Father Frank.

He had come to the house twice before, at short notice, with things on his mind. Each of those times I had been sent out for bottles of Moxie, and when he showed up, we gathered to greet him—Mother; my brothers, Fred and Floyd; and little sister, Franny. Uncle Frank sat in Dad's leather armchair in the parlor and I brought him a brown bottle of Moxie and a glass. He drank it, he smoked, he asked questions, he said Mass. Mother's youngest brother: she explained him by saying that he had entered the monastery when he was thirteen years old, and never left—"God called him."

The two swooping visits were sudden intrusions, surprising me—not just for the questions and the mass, but for his displacing Dad by sitting in Dad's leather chair. And the Moxie—something we never drank—and his smoking, which fouled the air. I was tongue-tied, baffled because of the limits of my small boy mind. I had never imagined a priest in our house, none had ever come, though I had seen Father Frank once before, propping up Mother at a family funeral. As a priest, Father Frank was not only powerful, he seemed to believe he was picturesque, as priests and policemen in Littleford often did.

His church, Mother said, was in Chicago—good, far away. I stopped thinking about his two visits. And then came that hot, humid Wednesday in June with Benny Koretsky.

Moxie was brown and bittersweet and medicinal, tasting of dead leaves— we'd all sneaked a sip. Father Frank was the only person we knew who drank it. When I'd bought it those first two times, he'd just flown in from Chicago. But the forbidding formula was the same: "A couple of bottles of Moxie" meant Father Frank was coming. Mother hurried to change from what she called her housecoat, which was like a smock, to the dress she wore to church and, surprisingly, lipstick.

He had shown up in the afternoon the first time while Dad was at work,

Mother alone with us, Fred practicing his trombone, Floyd writing an essay, me with a book, Franny dressing her doll.

"Put those things away," he'd said on that visit, and when we hesitated—where to put them?—Mother said, in a dark brown voice I hardly recognized, "You heard what Father Frank said."

After saying Holy Mass in the dining room, using the buffet as an altar, Father Frank turned, with the gold chalice glittering in his hand, and said, "The body and blood of Christ!" After Mass, settling into the armchair, perspiring a little, he'd sipped the glass of Moxie with one hand and made the sign of the cross over us, uttering the blessing in a tone of scolding benediction.

As Father Frank left, Floyd backed away and went to his room, slamming the door, and all I heard from Fred's room was his blowing into his trombone, not playing but instead working the spit valve, over and over.

Father Frank's questions the second time were fierce, he seemed greedy for attention, and was unsatisfied by the answers we gave him. Really, we had no answers. Fred said he didn't know why he'd chosen to play the trombone and not some other instrument—all he said was, "I'm in the school band." To Floyd, Father Frank said, "I've got a bone to pick with you," and Floyd seemed terrified, swallowing nervously; and to me, what did I want to be when I grew up? I was stumped for an answer.

Father Frank sniffed, making a face. "What's that smell?"

"Jay's got hamsters," Franny said.

"Did you clean their cage?" Mother said.

Before I could answer, Father Frank said, "Go get them."

They were in the back hallway, at the bottom of an old wire birdcage, crouched and blinking in a mass of wood shavings. They shrank into the shavings as I carried the cage to Father Frank.

"I swapped them with my friend Benny Koretsky for some of my comic books."

"Benny Koretsky," Father Frank said slowly, frowning, then poked the hamsters through the wire, and when they squirmed blew smoke at them. "Have you named these hamburgers?"

"Not yet."

Father Frank was still poking them with his finger as they squirmed beneath the wood shavings. He said, "Samson and Delilah."

"See?" Mother said, sounding pleased.

But I was angry. I wanted to give them my own names, and now with these names, Father Frank seemed to take possession of them.

"Let us pray," Father Frank said finally, and he prayed loudly, and blessed us afterward, slapping the air with his hands.

As Father Frank drove away, Floyd burst into tears and screamed at Franny, and Fred stopped practicing his trombone. That night, I lay in bed and prayed that we'd never see him again.

Then, that Wednesday, *A couple of bottles of Moxie.* By the time I got back from the corner store, Fred and Floyd had been summoned from upstairs, Fred holding his trombone upright against his body, like a shield, Floyd clutching a book to his chest, and Franny was pleading with Mother to let her pour the Moxie.

"You can get him the ashtray."

No one in our family smoked. The ashtray was just another curio on a shelf in the glass-fronted cabinet in the parlor with the souvenir dish of Niagara Falls, some dainty teacups and saucers we never used, and a plaster Infant of Prague wearing a red silk cape and a gold crown. We now knew that Father Frank's smoking would give the house a burnt-toast cigarette stink for a few days, which was like a ghostly presence of Father Frank himself, his smell lingering.

He smoked Fatima cigarettes, thinking perhaps, in a pious way they referred to Our Lady of Fatima, a story we knew from church. The Blessed Virgin appeared to three peasant children in the village of Fatima in Portugal in 1917, promising peace. The children spread the word and when people doubted it, the Virgin returned as an enormous fireball called the Miracle of the Sun, witnessed by thousands. But the woman on the yellow Fatima cigarette pack wore a turban and smiled and was Turkish—not the Blessed Virgin.

"I'm in charge of the ashtray," Franny said, holding it on her upright fingertips, as though awarding a prize.

We sat on the sofa in the parlor, waiting for the sound of the car, Fred blowing silently on his trombone while tugging the spit valve, Floyd nervously chafing at pages in his book, and I was holding my jackknife in my hand and flicking the blade open and shut with my thumb.

Mother said, "While we're all here waiting, let's say a prayer," and as we slid from the sofa to kneel on the floor, she added, "Three Hail Marys."

But on the third Hail Mary we heard car draw up in front of the house, the engine revving and quickly shut off, then the chewing and crunch of the yanked hand brake.

We heard footsteps on the piazza, Father Frank pulling open the screen door—the twanging spring again—and he entered the house, pointing his finger at us, a cigarette in his mouth, like an entertainer rushing onstage from the wings, calling attention to himself, saying, "You hamburgers!"

In a theatrical way, posturing, he kissed Mother and while he was still pointing to us, as we struggled to our feet to greet him, we four children lined up, as though for inspection. He walked past us saying to Franny, "Let's have a smile," to Fred, "Pull up your pants," to Floyd, "Let's see your fingernails— you're still biting them," to me, "Stand up straight, and quit playing with that knife."

This was worse than before, his sneering, his scolding. He took the ashtray from Franny and tapped cigarette ash into it, while clamping his teeth together and blowing smoke through them.

"Your clothes are like the French towns—Too loose and Too long"—to Fred.

He laughed hard, causing himself to cough, and I was reminded how the other times he laughed very hard at his own jokes, and not only his jokes, but laughed when he made a statement, laughter intended to make us small.

"You think you're a connoisseur but you're just a common sewer"—to Floyd, as he laughed again.

He had terrible teeth, big discolored ones, and he was still laughing in a chattering time-filling way, as he drew a photograph from his jacket pocket.

"Know who that is?"

It was a portrait of a smiling young man in a dark suit and tie, a large scrawled signature in black ink across the bottom. We didn't know and that made Father Frank lean over and peer into our faces, breathing tobacco.

"It's Julius La Rosa. He's on television."

We didn't have a television.

"Good friend of mine—famous singer."

Still holding the photograph, Father Frank marched back and forth, kicking to straighten his trousers, then sat in Dad's leather armchair, as he'd done the two previous times, puffing his cigarette, the ashtray on his lap.

"Very good Catholic. A daily communicant. He's got moxie."

"How well do you know him?" Mother asked.

"I hear his confession."

"In Chicago?"

"I'm in Boston at the Mother Church now," Father Frank said. "You're going to be seeing a lot more of me."

Mother said, "Jay, do you have something in the icebox for uncle?"

I went to the kitchen and got a bottle of Moxie and opened it, then brought it with a glass to the parlor, thinking, *He's in Boston*, and tried to smile when I handed him the Moxie.

The Moxie I associated with his bad teeth, which were speckled with brown dots I took to be decay, the same shade as the Moxie. He wore a black shiny gabardine suit and a white plastic dog collar—a Roman collar—yellowish on the upper edge and fixed with a stud in the back. When he hiked up his trousers we could see his thin black socks but never any flesh. The blackness of his clothes made it a peculiarly sinister outfit, and the thick lenses in his black-framed eyeglasses gave him mad oystery eyes.

He gulped his glass of Moxie, then put it down on the side table and said to Franny, "You, sugar, get me a piece of paper and a pencil."

Franny ran out of the room and came back with a pad in one hand and a pencil in the other.

"I would have done that," Fred said.

"But she's got moxie," Father Frank said, scribbling quickly on the pad. He tore off the piece of paper. He then folded it in quarters and smoothed it flat against his thigh, finally tucking it into his inside pocket.

"Floyd, name a color." He sat forward, snapping his fingers to hurry him. "Quick, any color."

"Red?" And saying it Floyd blushed, his cheeks reddening.

"Jay—name a flower."

I was startled by the question, but just out the window was a rosebush in bloom.

"Rose."

Father Frank turned to Fred, wagging his finger at him, saying, "Name a piece of furniture."

Stumped for a moment, silently working the slide of his trombone, Fred stammered and finally said, "Chair."

Father Frank took a sip of Moxie and swallowed it with satisfaction, smiling at us. He reached into his jacket pocket and withdrew the piece of paper, which he unfolded, smoothing it flat on his knee. He held it up.

"What does that say?"

Three words were printed on the paper: RED ROSE CHAIR.

"It's a miracle," Mother said, shaking her head.

Father Frank was fully in charge, he could read our minds. He showed his bad teeth in his triumphant laugh.

"It's a scientific fact—people are predictable!" He laughed again, then said to Fred, "You going to play that thing?"

Fred said, "I don't know."

"Trombones are for hamburgers—they never get the melody. You should learn the piano. Am I right?"

Mother said, "That's a good idea."

Fred said, "Okay," but still nervously worked the slide of his trombone.

"What's the book?" Father Frank said to Floyd.

"*Kon-Tiki*," Floyd said.

"Why are you reading it?"

Floyd struggled a little then said, "It's the name of their raft."

Now Father Frank turned to me, and asked, "Have you decided what you want to be when you grow up?"

"A doctor," I said.

"Think you can handle it?"

Father Frank smiled and took a sip of Moxie, and, swallowing, he shook his head. He said, "Listen, Jay. In an operation, when a person is cut open—this big"—he spread his hands wide—"you don't know this, not many people do, there's a horrible smell from the opening, all the guts in the body." He sipped his Moxie again and swallowed. "Wicked smell. Makes some doctors faint."

I saw the dark cut-open hole in the body he described, green fumes rising from it.

"Think about it."

Mother said, "More Moxie?"

"I won't say no."

When Mother was out of the room to get the Moxie, Father Frank said, "I'm going to the kitchen. I want each of you to come, one at a time."

He had done this on his second visit, seeing us individually, something I hated most, being alone with him, as he asked me to confess my sins to him. But how could I refuse? Never mind his cigarette smell and his bad teeth and his mocking laugh. He was Mother's brother, he was the man in black, he had been solemnly ordained, he'd taken Holy Orders, he was a priest who could give us absolution, he could purify our souls. It was as though God's trusted assistant was in the house, sitting in Dad's chair.

"You," he said to Floyd, as he left the room, and over his shoulder, "I've still got a bone to pick with you. But Fred's first."

Fred put down his trombone and walked slowly to the kitchen, as Mother joined us. We listened but at first only heard Father Frank's muffled talk, and after that Fred's whispers.

Soon, Fred was back in the parlor, clawing his hair, and passing me he said, "Your turn."

Seated at the kitchen table, Father Frank looked stern, the ashtray and the Moxie in front of him. I sat down, facing him, noticing as I had before how the lenses of his glasses made his eyes unreadable.

"I've been thinking about your friend, the Jewish kid."

"Which Jewish kid?"

"Lenny something."

"Benny Koretsky?" I said. "How do you know he's Jewish?"

"Am I ever wrong?" he said. He puffed his cigarette. "And you're not as smart as you think you are."

"I don't think I'm smart," I said, and I meant it, but saying it made me feel puny.

"How old are you?"

"Just turned thirteen."

He dug into his trouser pocket and fished out a handful of coins from which he pinched a quarter, handing it to me. "Happy Birthday."

"Thank you."

"Want to make a good confession?"

Though I knew this was coming, I panicked, and said, "I went to confession yesterday."

He looked at me with those eyes. "Is that true?"

"Yes."

He leaned closer and puffed his cigarette and his eyes widened and became aqueous in his thick lenses. I held my breath, staring back at him as though at a pair of oysters.

I was thrilled to think that he believed me—that it was possible to face a priest and tell a lie and convince him that it was the truth. It was the first time I had ever dared to lie to a priest. But just as suddenly I became remorseful, knowing that I would have to confess it as a sin, the next time I was in a confession box.

"Want to do your friend Benny a big favor?"

"Sure."

He dipped into his jacket pocket and took out a mass card, Jesus on the front, a prayer on the back. Handing it to me he said, "Learn that prayer by heart. Now send Floyd in."

"You're in for it," Fred said to Floyd, but Floyd knew it was his turn and had already started toward the kitchen. He'd put his book down, because Father Frank had questioned it, but without the book in his hand he seemed defenseless. He walked out of the room looking down at his shoes, his hands tightened to fists.

Although Mother was sitting with us, she stared straight ahead and didn't speak. All of us were listening to the sounds from the kitchen, not single words but gasps of accusation, a disturbance of air, Father Frank's voice, and now and then murmurs and grunts of agreement from Floyd.

Floyd remained in the kitchen when Father Frank walked into the parlor, saying, "Gotta go."

"More Moxie?" Mother said.

"Next time."

He stood in the doorway, saying, "Be good to your mother." And to me, "Learn that prayer."

But as he turned to go I said loudly, "Thanks for the quarter!"

He winced and staggered a little, as though I'd tripped him, then he mumbled something and hurried away.

Mother snatched at my arm and said, "Why did you say that? You embarrassed him."

It was just what I'd hoped, because all I could do with a quarter was buy a couple of bottles of Moxie, and it pleased me as much as having made him believe my lie about the confession. But I said, "Didn't you want me to thank him?"

We sat in silence after that, in the summer heat, in a strange blighted airlessness that had hollowed out the room, the smell of Father Frank's Fatima cigarettes lingering as his residue.

Finally Mother said, "Let's pray." And as we prayed I glanced aside at Mother and thought, *Mother Church*.

When Dad came home, Franny said, "Uncle Frank was here. I gave him an ashtray."

"You don't say," Dad said, sitting heavily into his armchair. It was hard to tell if he cared.

Fred said, "He thinks I should take up the piano."

"Is he going to buy you one?"

That night passing Floyd's room I saw him lying face down on his bed. I lingered by the door and said, "You okay?"

He rolled over, his hands clutching his face, and he wiped his eyes. I could see he had been crying. It shocked and saddened me, making me fearful, because Floyd seldom cried.

"Mum told him about my accident."

It was a subject we never mentioned, words we never said.

"What did he say?"

"That I'm a sissy." In Father Frank's growly tone, he said, "When you get married you're going to pee on your wife." Then he wiped his eyes again. "What did he tell you?"

"He's making me learn a prayer."

Father Frank visited again suddenly in July. I lied to him again about confession and felt both strengthened and burdened by another lie. Then he said, "Jay, how about the prayer? Let's hear it."

"Prayer for the conversion of the Jews," I said. "Let us pray for the prefidious—"

"Perfidious."

"Perfidious Jews. That Almighty God may remove the veil from their hearts. That they also may acknowledge our Lord Jesus Christ. Almighty and eternal God, who drives not away from his memory even the Jews—hear our prayers which we offer for the blindness of that people, that, um . . ."

"Acknowledging."

"Acknowledging the light of your truth, which is Christ, they may be delivered from their darkness. Through the same Jesus Christ our Lord, who liveth and reigneth with thee in the unity of the Holy Spirit, for ever and ever, Amen."

"Their blindness, their darkness," he said. "When you say that I want you to think of your friend."

Fred said, "What friend?"

"Benny."

Then Floyd lied, saying he had baseball practice at the park and couldn't stay. Father Frank said, "When Almighty God asks you about the state of your soul after you die, you can tell Him, 'I had baseball practice.'" Fred said he'd quit the band, and Father Frank seemed pleased.

"Let's pray," Mother said, as always, after Father Frank had driven away.

We prayed often that summer, we prayed before we ate, saying grace; we prayed before we went to bed—"If I die before I wake I pray the Lord my soul to take." We prayed for the repose of the souls of the dead members of our family, we prayed for sick people, for poor people, for those less fortunate, for our neighbors, for our friends, to forgive our enemies, and following orders, I prayed for the conversion of the Jews and felt sorry for Benny Koretsky.

Sitting, standing, often on our knees, muttering, murmuring, fingering rosary beads, nodding, bowing, intoning, and the hardest prayers we said were for Father Frank.

Once, when we finished, Floyd said, "He hates me."

"He loves you," Mother said. "He loves all of us."

"He makes fun of me."

"It's for your own good."

If we disagreed, Mother became agitated and angry and told us again how Father Frank devoted his life to Christ.

"He prays for you," she said to Floyd.

Walking away, Floyd said, "It's not working."

Mother didn't see that her brother was a bully, that his jokes weren't funny, that he was fierce. She took his ferocity for faith but when she repeated that he had gone into the seminary when he was thirteen, I thought, *Yes, he's still thirteen, like some of the boys in my class, the ones who mocked the smaller boys and teased the girls.* He was like the sneaks, the show-offs, the talkers, except that Father Frank was a thirteen-year-old with cigarettes and Moxie and bad teeth.

I was sitting under the tree in the backyard reading on another day when Mother called out, "Couple of bottles of Moxie."

Passing the back stairs I put my book on a step and took the quarter from her.

It was always midafternoon when he visited, and how did he know that the four of us children would be home, and that Dad would be at work? Franny was happy he was coming, Fred was bewildered, Floyd was terrified, and I was anxious, knowing that I didn't have the answers to the question, What do you want to be?

This time I could tell from the way he smoked, sucking at his cigarette, prowling rather than sitting, that Father Frank was more agitated than usual.

"Let's see those hands," he said to Floyd, and snatched at Floyd's fingers. "You're still biting your nails."

Challenged this way, Floyd was tongue-tied for a moment, then said, "I'm trying not to."

"Not trying hard enough!"

Franny said, "I saw him biting them."

"Good girl," Father Frank said. "What about the other thing?"

We knew this meant bed-wetting.

"It's okay," Floyd said, twisting his hands.

Striding toward Fred, Uncle Frank said, "Where's your trombone?"

"I'm taking up piano," Fred said. "Like you said."

We still didn't have a piano, though it was true that Fred had stopped practicing his trombone.

Father Frank tapped his cigarette ash into the ashtray Franny held up to him. He said, "I can't stay long."

"At least have some Moxie," Mother said.

Father Frank sat heavily into Dad's leather chair, and he smoked and sipped Moxie and finally pointed to the book I was holding. "What's that book?"

"*Tiger of the Snows.* About Mount Everest."

Smiling in pity, and blowing smoke through his teeth, Father Frank said, "Why don't you read a real book. Something wholesome. Get *Deliver Us from Evil*, by Dr. Tom Dooley. And what about your friend?"

"Which one?"

"The Jewish kid. You still hanging around with him?"

"No."

Another lie—Benny was my only real friend, who swapped comic books and always laughed at my jokes.

"He's doing it again!" Franny screeched, seeing Floyd with a finger in his mouth.

"I've got a loose tooth."

Father Frank snorted. He said, "Before I leave, anyone want to go to confession?"

We became silent, our heads down, to avoid his gaze.

"Okay, let's say a prayer."

We were still on our knees with our eyes closed when we heard him murmuring, meaning that he was making the sign of the cross over our heads, and when we opened our eyes he was gone.

As Floyd got to his feet and walked past Franny, he said, "Stay away from me, squealer."

Franny began to cry. She was the youngest, four years younger than me, the baby, the only girl, the funny one, the most playful, Mother's pet. But Floyd said he wouldn't talk to her anymore, he wouldn't play with her. And as Mother scolded Floyd for making Franny cry, he began to walk away.

"I want you to be more polite to each other," she said. "And to Father Frank. Why wouldn't you let him hear your confession?"

"Gave up biting my nails," Floyd called out, closing the door to his room.

"Anyway, I already confessed," Fred said.

"Me too," I said.

Three lies in three seconds.

The following Saturday I went to the library with Benny and found a copy of *Deliver Us from Evil*. While Benny rummaged through the stacks, I sat and began reading it. Dooley, the man telling the story, mentioned crying a lot, and Communists, and God, and pretty soon I slotted the book back on its shelf and looked for books about mountains and jungles and deserts.

On the way home, Benny said, "Jay, tell me a joke."

"I don't know any new ones."

"Father Inn . . ."

That dirty sinful joke about the wicked priest—telling it meant I had to describe sex, nakedness, Father Inn, and his crazy moaning girlfriend. But I remembered how much I disliked Father Frank, and how every time I said the prayer for the conversion of the Jews, I wanted to apologize to Benny.

"Okay, there was this horny old priest, Father Inn," I began, as we walked down the back streets of Littleford from the library. It was my gift to my friend Benny Koretsky, and I was cheered up hearing him giggle and gasp.

Father Frank came again, another Wednesday, and his first question to me was, "Did you find the Dooley book?"

"They didn't have it."

"Have you decided what you want to be?"

"Maybe a forest ranger."

He shook his head and sighed. "Jesus, Mary, and Joseph."

I realized I had a new problem, of trying to remember all the lies I'd told him, so that eventually, I could confess them to a priest who didn't know me, and who would forgive my sins.

After each of Father Frank's visits, Dad came home, he sniffed, he made a face, and said, "I know who dropped in."

From the way he said it, he sounded as though he disapproved, or was resentful, the priest always visiting when he was at work. But if he had criticisms he kept them to himself. Dad never raised his voice or quarreled with us, though sometimes his silences were long, and dark, and disturbing. It became a season of Dad's silences.

As the summer progressed, Mother welcomed Father Frank and did not seem to care that we boys dreaded his visits, that we'd become more secretive and evasive. Maybe Father Frank was telling us things that Mother wanted to tell us herself—things we'd done wrong, or to ask the impossible question, what we wanted to be. And we avoided little Franny, who'd become Father Frank's spy, making him scream into Floyd's face, "You're killing your mother!"

I had so much to confess I avoided confession; my soul was black, and so was Floyd's, so was Fred's. But they still went to church and prayed. Toward the end of the summer, my soul was so fat and sinful with lies, I stopped entering the church. I headed in that direction every Sunday but walked past it and hurried into the woods and walked on the paths until I guessed that the mass was over and then I went home, happier for having been alone in the woods.

Fred had quit the school band. He sat in his room staring out the window and now and then he drew cartoons—foolish faces, one ugly face with glasses, Father Frank.

In his bedroom, Floyd sat and fretted and bit his fingernails. He looked tearful and seldom replied when I tried to talk to him.

On one of his last visits, Father Frank was kinder to Floyd. He said, "I think you have a vocation. Know what that means?"

"Kinda."

"It means God wants you to serve him. He wants you to be a priest."

Lowering his gaze to examine his shoes, Floyd said, "You're probably right."

"Hear that?" Father Frank said to Mother. "He knows what he wants to be."

Afterward, when I saw Floyd, he rarely spoke, yet I knew he was lying, and he knew I was lying—too many lies to confess.

As always, on the days of Father Frank's visits, Dad returned home to a different house—he smelled it, he tasted it, he knew something was wrong. Because Father Frank was his brother-in-law, a priest who knew celebrities and lived at the Mother Church in Boston, Dad seemed helpless and puzzled in his silence.

And then a big shock: on Labor Day, Dad broke his silence to announce we were leaving Littleford and moving to Cape Cod—his company had transferred him. It was sudden, and within a week we were in a rented house in Centerville. We were too far from Boston for any sudden visits from Father Frank.

But it was too late. He'd corrupted us. Franny had become a sneak, and as for the rest of us, he taught us a life of concealment. We were liars now, we were cheats, and sneaks, and Floyd still wet the bed and would never be a priest. I hated Father Frank and blamed Mother for always welcoming him with a couple of bottles of Moxie.

Moving meant I'd lose my best friend, Benny Koretsky. Shortly before we left, Benny came over to say goodbye.

I risked the question I'd been meaning to ask, ever since (for Benny's sake) I stopped saying the awful prayer: "Do you ever think about giving up being Jewish?"

He laughed hard, with a confidence I envied. "My bar mitzvah's in a few months. How could I give up?"

"I mean all the praying."

"Nah." But the question seemed to give him an idea. He said, "Do you ever think about quitting the Catholics?"

I looked around to see if Mother was listening, then whispered, "Yeah."

Afterward, I remembered Benny saying, *I like the way you tell them*. It seemed an unexpected source of power. I was ashamed to think I was capable of telling convincing lies, yet I also saw it was a subversive strength. I'd lost my faith, but I'd gained something else, a reckless ability that would serve someone telling stories. *What do you what want to be?* Father Frank always asked. As a sinner, I could tell any story, even the wickedest one. I saw what I wanted to be.

Aide-Mémoires

CAMP ECHO

At the gateway to the camp, a man in khaki shorts and a white T-shirt and moccasins—a man dressed as a boy—was waiting at a shed that was like a sentry box. He raised his hand for us to stop and smiled at my father's open window. His hair was buzzed to a whiffle, he had pointy ears, and his face was sunburnt, his nose red and peeling. He held a clipboard in his hairy hands.

"Camper?" he asked, raising the clipboard.

"Right here," my father said. "Andy Parent."

"Welcome to Camp Echo."

"He's all yours," my father said, and to me, the last words I was to hear from him for three weeks, "Be good."

We had driven from home, my father and me, as usual without saying much. There was no radio in our old car, a 1938 Nash Lafayette with a thunderous muffler. My father's silences discouraged me from being a talker and made me watchful. Today he was taking me away to Boy Scout camp. The thought that I'd be alone there reminded me that I was small for my age, a skinny boy, with my hatchet on my lap and the foretaste of loneliness in my throat.

Past the close-together white clapboard houses on our street, we rolled down the hill to where the bungalows thinned out at the margin of the oak woods, no houses at all near Doleful Pond, nor any at the rezza—Spot Pond reservoir. A straight road beyond that into the low hills for an hour, and finally to the iron bridge across the Merrimack River, and along its north bank to the darker woods, where Camp Echo sat in a forest of fragrant pines at the edge of Echo Lake. Driving north from our crowded suburb, seeing fewer people, my mind eased; the landscape simplified and deepened with each mile on narrowing roads until we were on a dirt lane among log cabins in a forest so green and shadowy it was almost black beneath its boughs.

I pushed the heavy door open and slipped out of the car, then dragged my knapsack and sleeping bag from the back seat. My father reached from his window and patted my cheek in a tender gesture. He backed the car up, then jiggled and jammed the stick shift with a crunch into forward gear and drove away in his embarrassing car he called "the old bus," black and noisy and unreliable, with cracked whitewall tires, chrome strips curling from the front bumper, leaving exhaust fumes behind.

In a new setting, among strangers, my father used anxious jokes as exit lines. *He's all yours* was typical. But now he'd driven off, the dust was sifting onto the hot road, the blue fumes from the tailpipe drifting aside, swelling and separating; and when the car was past the last trees, I was standing in stillness, with the big man in shorts and moccasins scratching one pointy ear with a hairy finger. At the edge of the big field, the sun behind him, he loomed over me, his face in shadow.

"You can use this," he said, seeing me with the heavy pack and the sleeping bag.

A wheelbarrow was propped against the fence. He lowered it and righted it and threw my sleeping bag into it. I tipped in my knapsack. I tucked my hatchet handle inside my belt.

"It says Andre here," the man said, consulting his clipboard, tapping it with his pen.

"Andy," I said.

"I'm Butch Rankin—camp counselor. You're in Cabin Eight. Can't miss it. It's past the chow hall on the right."

So I took up the handles of the wheelbarrow and steered it through the gate and along the groove of one rut of the gravelly road toward a large log structure topped by a gray-stone chimney, the chow hall—then a field, and at the margin of the open field a row of about twenty cabins, their front doors facing the grass, a pole in the middle, holding a limp flag.

Dirt road, gravelly ruts, log cabins—with my piled-up wheelbarrow it seemed to me that I was wheeling my belongings into the distant past, a place entirely unfamiliar to me, simple and handmade, smelling of itchy dust and the aroma of recently sawed wood.

As I bumped the barrow along the wheel rut the rising breeze tightened my clothes against me and made me small. It occurred to me, I was on my own, headed to a log cabin in the forest where I would be living for three weeks, sleeping among strangers. This was new, and faintly worrying. I had spent a night or two away from my family at friends' houses—but never for so long, days and nights among boys I didn't know, none of them from my Boy Scout troop.

Camp Echo accepted boys from troops all over the Boston area, "The Minuteman Council"—my cabin was proof of that, because the five others were strangers to me. They had already arrived and chosen a bunk. Two were outside and said "Hi," while staring at me.

Inside, a boy folding a duffel bag said, "That top bunk is free."

A boy with wild hair lying on his stomach in the next bunk was looking at a magazine of photos he was half covering with his hand. He didn't say anything to me though he seemed to be muttering to the magazine, a page of white bodies.

Using the ladder on the side of the bunk I hoisted my sleeping bag and followed with my knapsack and hatchet. I had a sense of being new and not belonging, because I was the last to arrive, like an afterthought; and the others seemed self-possessed, confident with the authority of being already settled, their things put away. I tugged the laces of my sleeping bag and punched it to fluff it. I unstrapped my knapsack and dumped out my clothes. I was the tenderfoot, uninitiated, hot from the effort with the wheelbarrow and conspicuous in my unpacking, as some other boys entered the cabin.

At that moment I wanted to go home. I regretted that I'd come, and I felt foolish remembering how I'd eagerly looked forward to three weeks at Camp Echo, sharpening my hatchet with a whetstone, buying my sleeping bag and canteen at the army surplus store.

As I was sorting my clothes and hating the eyewatering mothball stink of my sleeping bag and the cabin's sharp smell of unpainted pine boards I heard a shout—another "Hi"—and saw Butch Rankin filling the doorway, still holding his clipboard. Now I noticed a hunting knife hanging from the belt of his khaki shorts and his sun-streaked whiffle.

"Roll call," he said, in a hearty voice. "Say 'here' when I call your name. Jerry Pinto."

"Here."

"Emmett Phelan."

"Here."

"Michael Plotnik."

"Here."

"Frankie Pagazzo."

"Here."

"Avery Pomroy."

"He's outside."

Butch Rankin turned and shouted, "Pomroy!"

"Coming," was the prompt but distant reply.

"Andy Parent."

"Here."

And as I spoke, I heard "Excuse me," as Butch Rankin stepped aside and a boy squeezed past him—a tall boy in a Boy Scout uniform, a bright red neckerchief with a carved eagle as a woggle holding it in place, a jackknife in a belt holder; he was wearing a wide-brimmed ranger's hat, and he was black.

"I'm Avery," he said and sat in the bunk that was under mine, at the back of the cabin.

"I guess you know why you're in this cabin," Butch Rankin said. "It's alphabetical—you're the *P*s—that's one thing you have in common. But you're Boy Scouts, you have that in common, too." He slapped his clipboard. "Stand up, guys. Ten-shun!"

I climbed down the ladder and others hopped off their bunks, and we lined up on the cabin floor, stamping on the boards.

"Close interval, dress right—dress," Rankin called out as we stuck out our elbows and aligned ourselves in a row. And then he pointed to a slouching boy with tangled hair. "What's your name?"

"Pagazzo," the boy said, in a mocking quack, his mouth open wide. One of his front teeth was cracked sideways, giving him a yellow fang.

"Stand up straight, Pagazzo, and fix those clodhoppers of yours. You're giving me ten minutes to two with your feet."

The boy took a breath so deep and loud his nose narrowed and grew pale and then he gargled, grinning with yellow teeth, as he exhaled and clicked his heels, and I knew at that moment we had a rebel in the cabin.

"You're here in Camp Echo to learn what we call life lessons. In a few weeks, you'll be tested at the Camporee, the shoot-out with Camp Metacomet across the lake—the Metacomet Challenge. Okay?"

Pagazzo said, "The Metacomet Challenge. Sounds wicked."

Butch Rankin frowned, then said, "Okay. The Boy Scout Oath. Let's hear it."

We raised our right hand, three fingers crooked, thumb pressing the pinky finger, and recited.

> *On my honor, I will do my best*
> *To do my duty, to God and my country*
> *And to obey the Scout law;*
> *To help other people at all times;*
> *To keep myself physically strong,*
> *Mentally awake, and morally straight.*

"At ease," Butch Rankin said and saluted us. "And you, Pagazzo. Drop and give me ten."

"For what?" Pagazzo said, frowning. His compressing his face made it yellower and his nose bigger.

Instead of replying to him, Butch Rankin leaned toward Pagazzo, hoicked phlegm in his noise in imitation, and said, "Make it fifteen for defying an order."

Pagazzo flopped to the cabin floor and with his bum in the air and working his skinny arms did fifteen laborious push-ups, finishing by gasping and flattening himself on the boards.

"As you were," Butch Rankin said, as an order. He left, pulling the cabin door shut with a thump.

"He had a conniption," Pagazzo said. He rolled over and, still lying on the floor, yawned with fatigue. "What a pisser."

"He's the marksmanship instructor," Phelan said.

"I'll clip him then. Give him two in the hat," Pagazzo said. "Then I'll say, 'As you were, dead-ass.'"

But Phelan had begun to talk to the others. "My father promised I could shoot his gun when I get back from camp. It's a Winchester thirty-thirty."

"What time is dinner supposed to be?" Plotnik asked.

"He keeps it on his boat."

"In about an hour," Pomroy said. "They ring a bell."

"His boat's in Osterville. It's a ketch."

"So I guess you can ketch it," Pagazzo said.

"Do you live down there?" Plotnik asked. "My folks took me swimming there once. The water was wicked cold. My father showed me some rescues."

"No, my dad's a doctor in Winchester."

Pagazzo said, "My old man's a waiter. At Perella's in the North End. Where the goombahs eat. They got guns like you wouldn't believe."

"I've already earned Civics," Plotnik said. "I want to pass Marksmanship and Lifesaving. The main thing my father says is don't let the drowning person grab hold of you or he can drag you down with him."

"What's that thing on your head?" Pagazzo asked.

A small woven disk was fastened by a hairpin to Plotnik's hair. I had never seen such an odd head covering and was glad Pagazzo had asked, because I wondered what Plotnik would reply.

"A yarmulke," he said.

"Looks like a Frisbee."

"The real name is kippah."

"Okay, Skippah," Pagazzo said, and at once Plotnik had a new name.

"A friend of my mother's has one of those, only a bigger one," Pinto said of Phelan's hunting knife.

Phelan unsheathed his knife and flourished it, wagging it before Pinto's face and said, "This is a genuine Bowie knife. You have to be eighteen to buy one. My uncle gave it to me. He was a US Marine."

"A leatherneck, big deal," Pagazzo said and drew a switchblade out of his pocket and flicked it open, swiping the air with it. "How do you like this guinea toothpick?"

"Be careful with that thing," Pinto said.

"You wish," Pagazzo said, and he swiped again. "I could deball you."

"I mean it," Pinto said with a screech in his voice.

"Sure. Every day and twice on Sunday."

Phelan was saying to Plotnik, "A guy came into my father's office. He had VD. He said he got it from a toilet. My father said, 'That's a hell of a place to take a girl.'"

"Hey, where's the moolie?" Pagazzo said.

Taking advantage of the confusion, I slipped out of the cabin, because I had nothing to say and it was too awkward to make conversation—most of the talk was in the form of boasts, or mockery. I was afraid of what they'd ask me. I had a hatchet: this was my boast, the hatchet buttoned into a leather hip holster to protect the blade I had carefully sharpened. I looped the hatchet holster to my belt, though its weight dragged my pants down, and the handle bumped my leg when I walked.

Avery Pomroy was standing away from the cabin looking at the sooty evening sky, his face upturned, his skin silvery in the dusk.

"What's up?" I said.

"That's the Big Dipper."

"I know that."

Still looking up, his voice slightly strangled from craning his neck, he said, "The two stars on the edge are Merak and Dubhe. I'm getting an astronomy merit badge. See how they're pointing?"

I could not see how they were pointing. I could just make out the corners of the container of the dipper. I said, "Yeah."

"To Polaris," he said.

"I was just going to say that."

"The North Star," he grunted, his face upturned.

"Right."

"And if it was a little darker we'd be able to see the Little Dipper." He swiveled his head to take in the rest of the sky. "Maybe later."

"How do you know this stuff?"

"My father's a teacher. He's got a telescope," Pomroy said. "We look at the moon sometimes. He can name most of the craters. No one knows how they got there. And no one's ever seen the other side of the moon. The dark side."

"I don't get it."

"Because the same side of the moon is always facing the earth," he said. "And that's Venus. It's always bright. Venus was the first one I learned."

He was walking unsteadily, leaning backward as he talked, because he was still scanning the sky, but he stopped talking and kept moving and soon was lost in the darkness.

Soon after that I heard a clanging of iron, not a bell but what I would later find out was a boy whacking a short length of train track with a piece of steel pipe.

The cabin door banged open and in the rectangle of light shining from the yellow pine boards inside I saw Frankie Pagazzo, followed by the others, Plotnik and Phelan and Pinto.

"Chow time," Pagazzo called out, running ahead.

We walked along the margin of the field in the moon shadow of the pines, boys from the farther cabins passing the flag-post, and we blinked entering the mess hall that was brightly lit and smelling of sawdust and beans and apple-sauce. Pomroy was the last to seat himself. A number eight on a card was stuck in a wire stand at our table, where six bowls had been set out with plastic cups, a glass pitcher at one end. The six bowls contained brown, soupy apple-sauce; the glass pitcher brimmed with purple liquid.

Plotnik pointed to the number eight at the table. He said, "That's a composite number."

"What language is that supposed to be?" Pinto said.

Wagging his pale finger at the seven on next table, Plotnik said, "That's a prime number."

"Primo," Pagazzo said. "That's wicked good."

"This year is not a prime number. But 1951 was."

"And your mother wears army boots," Pagazzo said, flicking the pitcher with his bitten fingers. "Bug juice. Anyone want some?"

He poured it out but did not take any himself, and instead put his hands behind his tangled hair and leaned back, tightening his yellowish face by squinting at us. He had a pale scar like a claw mark next to his right eye and when he smiled he made a chipmunk face and seemed to glory in showing us his broken front tooth.

"Know why I ain't drinking no bug juice?" He did not wait for a reply. He said, "They put saltpeter in it. Know why? So you won't get a boner."

Pagazzo lowered his voice on the word *boner* seeing Butch Rankin approaching our table.

"No suh!" Pinto said.

"Yes suh."

"I'm going to ask my father," Phelan said to Plotnik, seated next to him. "He knows chemistry."

Rankin said, "It's cafeteria-style, so pick up a tray, get in line, and help yourself."

We did as he said, filed with our tin trays past the metal tubs of fried Spam and mashed potato and baked beans, loading up, and then back at our table began eating, digging at the food with forks in our fists.

"The navy gets the gravy but the army gets the beans," Pagazzo said. "My uncle Mario says that."

Phelan was finishing telling Plotnik a story about his father in medical school, saying, "And before they tested their urine my father slipped in some gold leaf. His lab partner's a woman and she does the test and says, 'I have gold in my urine!' And my father says, 'What do you want me to do—sink a shaft?'"

Plotnik smiled nervously. He pushed a slab of Spam away from his potatoes and said, "Anyone want this?"

But no one replied, they went on chewing, and their faces seemed freakish to me. I was returned again to thinking of the strangeness of the camp, how it seemed unfriendly because of those faces, so different from the faces of my family, or anyone I knew, strangers' faces—and strangers seemed dangerous to me. Pagazzo's yellow face; Plotnik's pale freckled face; Phelan's receding chin and perfect teeth; Pinto's delicate features, his bat-like ears and pursed lips; Pomroy's gleaming black face and wide forehead, his cheeks bulging with food.

"Try the baloney instead," Phelan said.

"Baloney," Pagazzo said. "My old man calls it horse cock."

The way they ate, the way they looked, made me anxious—made me think I did not belong there, that I would never fit in.

They were animal faces. I knew them to be boys, but the features were so unfamiliar I saw them as masks, not ugly but so unusual as to be threatening, as though concealing a secret intention, they were conveying an expression that was meant to upset me. The sense I had was that they were half human and these masklike features were a way of protecting themselves.

I did not want to think much about it, but sitting there at the table with them, they seemed to me like dog faces, the snouts and wet eyes and tangled hair of mutts, made more doglike by the way they were eating—boys eating carelessly, hungrily, snapping their jaws, champing at their food, the teeth of twelve-year-olds having an animal largeness and bite. I knew boys like this at school, but these were boys I was living with in a log cabin.

Seeing strangers eat, flecks of food on their lips, the famished faces, that hunger, revealed more of their personalities than talking did and suggested the crudeness of their secrets. And so I hardly ate anything—I nibbled at the awful salty meat, poked at the dry potato and the beans, and what Pagazzo had said about the bug juice kept me from drinking more. The mushy apple-sauce had the sour fermented smell of wet fur.

At the end of the meal, still hungry, I made myself a peanut butter sandwich, and ate it feeling queasy, a kind of nausea knowing I had three more weeks of this.

Seeing me swirling some peanut butter out of a jar, Plotnik said, "Thirty days hath September, April, June, and no wonder. All the rest have peanut butter. Except Grandma who has a pail of blueberries."

The others stared at him, but I smiled: his little verse had made him seem human.

"You said 'bloobrees,'" Pagazzo said.

"Okay, let's do these dishes, guys," Butch Rankin said, walking among the tables. "I want this place shipshape."

We were given a big basin of soapy water and a small mop-shaped scrubber, and each of us was assigned a task, one boy scraping leftover food from the plates into a garbage can, other boys wiping the table, or washing the cups and plates in the basin, or drying them. I was drying with Pinto, who worked slowly and with great care, dabbing at the plate with the cloth wrapped around his finger, occasionally saying, "This one's still icky," and dropping it back into the basin.

When this was done, and the plates stacked, the basin of gray water emptied and put away with the scrubber and the wet cloths, we sat at the table again. A red-faced fat man in khaki shorts shushed us.

"Welcome to Camp Echo," he said. "I'm Camp Director Hempstone. Before I have my staff introduce themselves, I want to say one thing. Behave yourselves, do as you're told, and you'll have a great time. No bellyaching. No slacking. Get out of line and you will fail. Hygiene is very important, and so I say to you—two words. Be clean."

"That's about ten things," Pagazzo muttered.

"When you salute the flag, stand ramrod straight. I want snappy salutes and respect for the flag. My friend Arthur Schuck is chief Scout executive, and I want to quote him now," Hempstone said, glancing at a small piece of paper in his hand. "What is the main thrust of the Boy Scouts? Arthur Schuck tells us, 'To give to America a new generation of men of character, with ingrained qualities that make for good citizenship.'" He gestured with the piece of paper, saying, "Be glad you live in a free country where everyone is treated equally. Communists live in fear. If you waver"—here he paused and poked a fat finger at us—"the Communists are gonna cook your goose."

Hempstone then called upon the counselors, who introduced themselves, taking turns, strolling among the tables, the swimming instructor, the rowing coach, the volleyball coach, and Butch the rifle range director. An old bald bearded man in a neckerchief named Doc Leathers announced himself as the craft shop manager and twirled a length of plastic twine saying, "Anyone know what this is?"

Pagazzo called out, "Gimp!"

"Raise your hand next time," Leathers said sternly to Pagazzo.

But as soon as the man turned his back Pagazzo faced us and made himself briefly cross-eyed.

"I can teach you to make lanyards and key chains and boondoggles," Leathers. He tugged at the fixture on his neckerchief. "This here's a boondoggle."

As Pagazzo worked his lips in lunatic nibbling, mouthing the word *boondoggle*, Butch Rankin stepped behind him and twisted his ear, saying, "You again. That's enough of that."

A counselor had taken the floor in front of the tables. He said, "Let's have a song."

He sang it. We listened with embarrassment, while he sang full-throated and gesturing. When he finished, he said, "Okay, we'll take it one verse at a time."

> *Up in the air, junior birdman,*
> *Up in the air, upside-down,*
> *Up in the air, junior birdman*
> *Keep your noses off the ground . . .*

Walking back to the cabin, the six of us in the shadows, Pagazzo said, "Hey, how about Arthur Schuck? What a pisser name."

Plotnik said, "Know this one?" And he began to sing.

> *John Jakob Jinkleheimer Smith,*
> *His name is my name, too . . .*

Pagazzo interrupted, saying, "Quit it, Skipper. I know a better one," and snapped his fingers and sang,

> *My baby had a party the other night*
> *The party was getting dead*
> *I seen a piano in the corner*
> *And looked at my baby and said,*
>
> *Baby let me bang your box,*
> *Baby let me bang your box . . .*

"That's so dirty," Pinto said.

"It's as big as Fort Knox," Pagazzo said, and went on humming.

Pinto sang, "I'm on my way—to Apalachicola!"

Later, in the cabin, on my top bunk in my damp sleeping bag from the army surplus store I lay awake and heard the five other boys breathing, a fluttering sound, a scraping of air, softly snoring, and I thought, *This is the real world*.

I remembered their faces eating, how they'd reminded me of dogs, something rough and animal about them, and in the way they moved, not saying much, pushing along at a half trot, nodding as they walked, their mouths open, their tongues against their teeth, grunting as they sang, and the way they were sleeping now, doglike. But I also thought how their personalities were revealed in their eating, as when they were excited or angry—then I knew them better. How they ate was who they were.

My first night of sleeping in a room of strangers, their smells, their sounds— and I thought, *I have nothing to learn here except how to survive and get through these weeks*. I'm not good at anything, I have no stories, or songs, or sayings from my father; they were talkers, and all I could do was listen.

Then in the darkness, a ripping began, like cloth being torn, and the sound growing, swelling and becoming harmonious, a bugler playing the up and down of "Taps."

The cabin was like a living thing, it swelled and contracted with the breathing of the other boys. Somehow, I slept, but waking in the resinous smell of the cabin's pine boards, and the stink of sneakers, and five strangers, I wanted to go home. Then a blatting of the bugle, the *rat-tat-tat* of reveille, startled me out of bed.

The grass in the field was so thick with dew my sneakers were wet before I'd gone ten feet. I had followed the others out to the field, where eighty campers stood at attention before the flagpole, a boy beside it clutching a bunched-up flag in his arms.

Bent over his big belly, Hempstone ran toward him, shouting, "Don't do that, son! Do not let the flag touch the ground!"

Grasping at the loose corner of the flag that was drooping on the grass, the boy became red-faced and tearful.

"Kiss it!" Hempstone cried, and he lifted the flag's corner that was dampened by dew. He pressed it into the boy's face, and the boy seemed to gag, as he snatched it away and gathered the loose folds into a bundle, tugging the flag rope free.

Hempstone blew a whistle, then lifted a megaphone and yelled into it, his voice duck-like as it was amplified, "The Pledge of Allegiance."

We put our hands on our heart and as the flag rose, jumping on the ropes of the pole, as the boy yanked it, we recited,

> *I pledge allegiance to the flag*
> *Of the United States of America,*
> *And to the republic—*

Beside me, Pagazzo said, "For Richard stands" and "One nation invisible—"

> *With liberty and justice for all.*

"Play ball," Phelan said, under his breath.

"And one other thing," Hempstone yelled into his megaphone. "At Camp Echo the Scout Law is the law. I expect you to be physically strong, mentally awake, and morally straight. Otherwise"—his voice was a vibrating quack, as though he was speaking underwater—"there is no point being here. You will lose. You might as well go home, because that's where losers belong."

As he went on talking, I thought, *What am I doing here?*

"I'm a mentally asleep and morally crooked guinea bastard," Pagazzo was murmuring, and I envied him for being so reckless.

"We have a big competition coming up in a few weeks against Camp Metacomet—the Camporee, the shoot-out, the swim, the rope climb, the races. In the Boy Scout tradition, I say two words. *Be prepared*," Hempstone said, gargling into his megaphone. "Dis-missed."

We trooped with our ditty bags to the roofed washstands in the pine grove beyond the cabins, where the wooden privies stood, among the spigots and tin sinks. I brushed my teeth and splashed my face and followed the others to breakfast—more applesauce and bug juice, bowls of cornflakes, and sticky pastries. As we ate, Butch Rankin called out our assignments for the day, walking from table to table.

"Cabin Eight—swimming at eight thirty. Bring a pair of dungarees. Rope climbing after that. Then craft shop. Rifle range after lunch."

We washed the cereal bowls and the cups and spoons, then hurried to the cabin to change into our bathing trunks.

"Muggy," Phelan said.

Pinto said, "Today will be Muggy. Followed by Toogie, Weggy, and Thurgy."

"You wearing your Frisbee in the lake, Skipper?" Pagazzo said to Plotnik.

"It's not required for swimming or sleeping."

"What about when you're taking a dump?"

Pomroy turned, and leaning to face Pagazzo, who was a head shorter, said, "Can I ask you a question? Why don't you leave the kid alone?"

"You said 'axe you a question,'" Pagazzo said, clawing his tangled hair. "Hey, I'm joking around."

"You're making him cry. So quit it or else."

"I'm not crying," Plotnik said, but there were tears in his eyes and a sob in his throat as he spoke.

Pomroy was still staring at Pagazzo.

"You and whose army?" Pagazzo said, pushing open the cabin door.

"Don't forget we have to bring our dungarees," Pinto called out.

Beyond a boathouse and a launching ramp, two wooden docks extended from the lakeshore, about fifty feet apart, with swimming lanes divided by ropes attached to white floats that bobbed in the morning breeze.

The instructor was waiting for us on one dock. "I'm Blake," he said. "I want to see how good you can swim. So hop in and start swimming, three at a time."

Pagazzo, Phelan, and Pomroy squatted near the edge of the dock, each of them facing a lane. Then they sat, their legs dangling, Phelan and Pomroy flexing their arms, Pagazzo dipping his hand in the water and quickly blessing himself, looking anxious, making the sign of the cross over his body. Then they slipped into the water and began to swim toward the far dock.

I watched, wondering how I'd manage. I was a reasonably good swimmer but not strong, glad to be with the smaller boys—Pinto, who was delicate and skinny, and Plotnik, who was pigeon-toed and pale.

When the others thrashed back to the dock, Blake said to Pomroy, "Junkins beat you by ten whole seconds," and showed Pomroy his stopwatch.

"Who's Junkins?" Pomroy said, climbing up the wooden ladder and shaking water from his head.

"Him—he swam yesterday," Blake said and pointed to a slender black boy at the nearby boathouse who was tossing a paddle into a canoe and about to shove the canoe down the boat ramp. I knew Junkins from my high school but he was from the other side of town, in a different Boy Scout troop.

Pomroy looked at the black boy and then at Blake and shook his head and said, "Damn."

"What'd you say?"

"Nothing."

"I heard you say 'damn.'"

"Maybe I said 'dumb,'" Pomroy said.

Clicking his stopwatch in his agitated fingers, Blake said, "I don't stand for back talk."

Pomroy stared, looking furious, his face tightening, his eyes blazing. I was not sure what had just happened—a misunderstanding, possibly, but something new to me, and a mystery. It was obvious that Pomroy was frustrated and that Blake was angry, after a confusing interaction; and all this time I was watching the boy Junkins—maybe the only other black boy at Camp Echo, in the stern of his canoe, paddling away, gliding through the water on an arrowhead of ripples, his back turned, unaware that he was part of this confusion.

"What are you looking at?" Blake said to Pinto and me, standing on the dock. "Get in there and start swimming."

I heard Phelan laugh, as we slipped into the water and began to swim, and behind us Plotnik thrust himself off the dock and sat with screech in the water and began slashing his way forward with his white fists.

"Because, as Director Hempstone would say, you obviously have a problem," Blake was saying to Pomroy when I got back to the dock, still nagging Pomroy, who was leaning against a dock post, his arms tightly folded, looking at his feet.

As I climbed the ladder, Blake said, "What's your name, kid?"

"Andre," I said. "Andy."

"You're okay," he said, and then turned to Plotnik saying, "But you're a spaz. Any issue on a boat and you will definitely drown like a rat. If you represent us in the Camporee we'll lose. And Director Hempstone doesn't like to lose. We want winners at Camp Echo. You need to work on your stroke, pal."

"Yes, sir," Plotnik said, looking miserable, his skin bluish, his eyes wet and bloodshot from his swim.

"You'll never get a merit badge unless you improve."

"No shit, Sherlock," Pagazzo muttered to me. And loudly, "Maybe qualify for the drowning badge."

"Smart-ass," Blake said to Pagazzo. "Did you remember to bring your dungarees?"

"Oh yeah," Pagazzo said.

Blake eyed him, his head to the side, sizing him up, and said, "Good, because you're going to show us how to use them in case of an emergency." Then he pointed to Avery Pomroy. "You too."

The trick, he explained, was to pull your pants off in the water and make a knot at the end of each leg. By swinging them so the legs filled with air, they became a flotation device, each leg bulging and buoyant, supporting you.

Pagazzo and Pomroy thrashed in the water, slapping their pants and bobbing.

Pointing to Pagazzo, Blake said to us, "What's he doing wrong?"

"Bad knots," Phelan said.

"Atrocious knots," Blake said. "You need to seal the legs and make them airtight." He laughed and added, "Unless you want to drown."

"He looks like he's drowning," Plotnik said.

And it was true, Pagazzo was flailing with his sodden pants, and gulping water as he sank and struggled to keep his head up. As Blake watched, seeming to smile, Pomroy snatched him and held him up, Pagazzo clinging to the legs of Pomroy's big blue air-filled pants.

"That's his problem."

Now I saw that Pagazzo's dungarees were torn, the knees ripped; and the others saw it too: that he was poor, with ragged pants, and that was why he was going under.

That Blake did nothing to help Pagazzo scared me, and when it was my turn, I had trouble making knots in the legs of my pants. I swam for a while, then, treading water, I managed the knots and was relieved that I was able to support myself on my swollen dungarees. But Blake didn't take much notice. He seemed to be annoyed with Pomroy, who was crouched at the side of the dock, seeming to sulk.

Pagazzo's lips were blue and he was shivering. But he said, "I think I could have made it."

"You got holes in your pants," Phelan said.

"Same time tomorrow, fellas," Blake said. "We're doing surface dives. You're going to show me how to pick a heavy object off the bottom."

"I'll never be able to do that," Plotnik whispered in a tearful voice.

Consulting his clipboard, Blake said, "You're Cabin Eight. You've got rope climbing, then craft shop. Shake a leg."

"What about rifle range?" Phelan asked.

"After lunch. Now get lost."

I walked, hating it all, kicking at the thickness of pine needles under the trees. None of it was pleasant, all of it was like work, and Plotnik's fears and Pomroy's sulking made me gloomy. I felt lonely among so many other boys, their fears and humiliations like a sickness.

But I did not want to make myself obvious. I followed the little group to the dangling ropes, and stood in line, and when the counselor said, "You!" I climbed until my palms were raw. Pomroy climbed the rope to the top, and swung on the crossbar, doing a chin-up, his long legs scissoring.

The counselor said, "Look at that monkey climb."

When Pomroy descended the rope, he launched himself, leaping to the ground, turning his back on us and kept walking away.

Pomroy was waiting at the craft shop when we arrived. We sat in a circle on the porch of the shop and learned to weave lanyards with the plastic filament called gimp.

Doc Leathers, the bearded craft shop manager, said, "I want you to remember one piece of advice." He smacked his lips and recited,

As you go through life
Remember the goal
To look at the donut
And not at the hole.

"I've got stuff to do," he went on. "When I come back, I want to see some lanyards."

"Guy's sitting in a doctor's office. Doctor says, 'Hey, quit whacking off,'" Pagazzo said to Phelan, as soon as Ralph Leathers had gone. He spoke in a low voice, making Phelan giggle, and finally a bit louder said, "'Because I'm trying to examine you.'" But as he finished, he saw the bearded man, Leathers—he was still there, he had heard the whole thing—holding a handful of plastic gimp, staring at him.

Pinto said, "What's the quickest way to send a message. Telephone? Telegraph? Or tell a woman?"

Lunch was sandwiches, baloney and white bread and yellow mustard and bug juice, applesauce for dessert. I sat with Plotnik and Pinto, who had become the no-hopers. Plotnik avoided the baloney, Pinto carefully cut the crusts off his bread, and we listened to Pagazzo telling another joke, saying, "Pecker tracks. It was jizz!" and Phelan said, "Want to go to a cock and tail party?"

"You're a pisser," Pagazzo said.

"Got any Knickerbocker in your liquor locker?" Phelan said. He nodded in a dry chattering laugh. "My father always says that."

"Know what food is almost as bad as this stuff?" Pagazzo said. "Chocolate-covered fish."

We stared at them laughing. We couldn't compete. I felt more at ease among the weaker boys, the despised Plotnik, the timid Jerry Pinto, neither of whom had been able to make it up the rope. Pinto had woven a lanyard, though, but when he put it around his neck Pagazzo grabbed it and twisted it until Pinto screamed, "I can't breathe!"

At the far end of our table, Avery Pomroy sat, leaning on his elbows, chewing slowly, and his chewing was like the movement of his mind. He was probably ruminating on the morning, the business at the lake, the rope climb, "monkey." I wanted to talk to him, because he looked as though he was suffering, but I could not think of any words to begin.

Finally I said, "How's things?"

Without looking up he said, "Fabulous."

Dishes again, and we slapped the table with rags, and then we walked back to the cabin.

I climbed the ladder to my upper bunk and lay there on my back breathing hard. I was hot from the morning, from the strangeness of it all, tired from the effort of swimming and rope climbing, and what was most wearying was the anxiety of being among these boys—their moods, some of them hearty, others fearful, Pomroy compact in his silence, not revealing what was in his head. And I could not rid my mind of the thought that we were animals—animals in the way we walked, animals in the way we teased and pushed one another, in the way we thrashed in the water and dangled on the rope; in the aggressiveness of some, and the timidity of others, and most of all in the way we ate. Watching the tables of boys eating made me apprehensive, since in the very act of chewing they revealed so much of who they were, in their teeth, in the jaws and muscles in their neck, in the way they widened their eyes when they swallowed.

I fell asleep and woke to the sound of murmuring. It was Plotnik, crying softly, face down in his bunk. Feeling that I would embarrass him if I said anything, I lay there until the cabin door opened—Pagazzo, hooting—and Plotnik fell silent.

"Time to shoot some lead," Pagazzo said. "I'm supposed to wake up youse guys."

Plotnik rolled off his bunk and, putting on his yarmulke—a gesture that seemed to me sad, for the fastidious and furtive way he fastened it with a bobby pin—hurried away rubbing his eyes.

"Where's the banana man?" Pagazzo said, seeing me on my ladder.

There was no way to reply to that without conspiring with him in his rudeness, so I didn't say anything.

"I'll put a bullet in his moolie ass."

Just hearing him say these wicked words made me nervous. It was reckless and offensive; Pomroy might hear it and think I agreed, because I didn't object.

I was relieved to see Pomroy walking across the field past the flagpole, Pagazzo running toward him, calling out, "Hey, Pomroy, let's go shoot someone!"—and punching him in the upper arm with his knuckles, giving him a noogie. This made Pomroy laugh, and the fooling like friendship eased my mind.

The range was at the far end of the camp, a sectioned-off area facing a scooped-out hill of sand and a line of targets. Butch Rankin was waiting for us, holding a rifle in both hands. He wore a khaki shirt and aviator sunglasses and fatigue pants tucked into boots. Cradling the rifle he looked fierce and soldierly.

"Take a seat," he said and motioned us to a log that served as a bench.

"Bang, bang," Pagazzo said in a low voice, pointing a finger at the targets. "You're dead meat."

"Pipe down," Rankin said. Raising the rifle, he went on, "This is a twenty-two-caliber, bolt-action Mossberg."

"But twenty-three is a prime number," Plotnik said softly.

Rankin began pointing. "This is your barrel. Your tubular magazine. Your receiver. Your peep sight. Your cheek piece. Your bolt." He tapped the end of it. "Your buttstock."

Pinto had begun to shake, giggling, his hands against his face.

"I was expecting that," Rankin said and continued tapping the end of the rifle. "Your butt plate." He glared at Pinto. "You find this funny?"

"No, sir."

"I want to remind you this is a rifle range, and I am holding a lethal weapon." He lifted his sunglasses and stared at us. "No jokes. No horsing around. Any one of you shoot a gun before?"

Phelan said. "Yes, sir. My dad has a thirty-thirty. Also a twelve-gauge shot-gun."

"Must be a hunter," Rankin said. "Anyone else?"

"In Perella's, this restaurant, where my father's a waiter," Pagazzo said, looking eager, "there's a guy who comes in with a gun that he keeps in his pocket. One of the goombahs. He showed it to my father."

"Big deal," Rankin said. "Okay, what I want to emphasize is that this is a dangerous weapon. It is not a toy. It is deadly. In the wrong hands or inexperienced hands it can cause death or injury. I will show you how to handle it safely, how to load and fire it. If any one of you mishandles it, or poses a risk, you will be given serious demerits and banned from the range. I hope that's clear."

He went through the parts of the rifle again, then slipped out a narrow cylinder from the tube and demonstrated how to load it, dropping bullets into the tube.

"Always keep the muzzle pointed to the ground or downrange," he said. "Now choose a rifle from the rack. Remove the bolt until I tell you to replace it. We'll shoot three at a time. Squeeze the trigger slowly, don't jerk it."

Pomroy, Phelan, and Pagazzo were first up, Rankin supervising the loading. The boys lay on their stomachs, holding the rifles while propped on their elbows, facing the paper targets thirty feet away.

"Fire at will."

Clapping his hand to his mouth, Pagazzo said in a muffled voice, "Where's will?"

"I heard that!" Rankin shouted at Pagazzo, as the rifles cracked.

Each of the boys fired seven bullets, then removed the bolts and returned the rifles to the racks. "I want to shoot some Commies," Pagazzo said, as he walked past me.

"This is a practice session," Rankin said. "Next session we keep score. If you follow orders and learn the rules, and if you manage to hit the target, you might qualify for a badge. You heard what Director Hempstone said about the shoot-out at the Camporee with Camp Metacomet. Hey, I want some sharpshooters." He turned to where I sat with Pinto and Plotnik on the log. "Okay, you three. Select a rifle. Load it and assume the position."

We did as we were told, but when we knelt and flopped onto our stomachs, Pinto bobbled his rifle, then snatched it, squawking a little in fear, his bat-like ears making him seem more frightened.

"Do not point the rifle that way!" Rankin shouted. "Steady your weapon. Fire at will."

My palm was damp, my trigger finger slippery, and with sweaty eyes I saw the target through a blur. But when I fired I experienced a jolt of pleasure with the bang of each bullet, joy in the explosion, the crack of the bullet like a wordless statement I was making that came from somewhere within me, and for the first time since arriving at camp I was happy.

Peering through his binoculars Rankin said, "You're a wicked good shot. You got the eye, kid. You're Andre, right?"

"Andy."

"Keep it up, kid. You might come in handy when we compete against Metacomet."

I had almost failed at swimming and rope climbing—I was so skinny and small. But at the rifle range I realized I was good at something—I, who had never been good at anything.

So, in the late afternoon, watching the softball game with Pinto and Plotnik—none of us made the team ("You throw like a girl," the coach said to Pinto)—I summoned the memory of the rifle range, and Rankin saying, *You got the eye, kid.*

I could tell from their posture and their sighs that Pinto and Plotnik were miserable. Pinto had stopped singing "Rose, Rose, I love you . . ." But Plotnik murmured a dirge in a low voice that began,

Who'll dig the grave for the last man that dies . . .

Some boys smelled of failure. This made me feel superior, but also sympathetic, for their being weaker than me. I had the strength to feel sorry for them, as I did with Pomroy. I had never pitied anyone before.

Time passed more quickly than I had expected. Every hour was accounted for on the schedule, there were no slack periods; the day was eaten up in routine— something new to me, because I was known at home as a dreamer—not a compliment, but a fault. My mother said of me, *Andy's mooning around again.*

The counselors kept us busy, and bossed us, but I could see that they were bossed by Director Hempstone. We feared Hempstone, but it surprised me that these big confident men—as they seemed to me—feared him too. Blake, the swimming instructor, was standing by the chow hall door one lunchtime as we were leaving. Hempstone passed him, saying, "See me in my office after lunch," and Blake—so hard on us—looked terrified.

Hempstone was not tall but he was bulky, with a thick neck and plastered-down hair, and fat fingers—he snatched at the air with them as he gave an order. When he spoke, his tone was usually one of complaint or dissatisfaction, a few tremors short of anger. His natural expression was a scowl, his mouth turned down, and the only time I saw him smile was when a boy tripped and fell forward onto his tin dinner tray, bashing his face and lying there before us, whinnying in pain and humiliation.

"See?" Hempstone said. And his smile was toothy, with hunger in it. "What did I say about running indoors?"

The counselors' obedience to Hempstone confused me, because they could be so cruel to us, especially cruel to the weaker boys like Pinto or Plotnik, or to a rule breaker like Pagazzo, or to Pomroy for no reason at all. Except for Doc Leathers, who called himself a woodsman and wore a plaid flannel shirt, the counselors were big and muscular, usually wearing T-shirts and shorts.

I began to see that a loud heavy man like Hempstone was a natural authority figure, that he was powerful in his shouting and his bulk and the way he parted his lips to show his teeth. Hempstone could not be questioned, he had to be obeyed, and that he had power over these younger muscular men made him someone to be feared, whose every word was an order. I wanted to find him foolish, but I kept this thought to myself, because if Hempstone found out, I would be punished. I secretly wanted Hempstone to fail, but I had no idea how this might happen—and if it did happen maybe we would all be blamed.

In the days that followed, Pagazzo took to calling Plotnik a spaz, because Blake the swimming instructor had used the word, and he referred to Pinto as a "fanook." Emmett Phelan treated Pagazzo as his sidekick and encouraged him in his jokes, and they swapped copies of their nudist magazines, *Sunshine & Health*, but refused to let us look. Avery Pomroy kept apart from us, like a foreigner who spoke a different language. He was usually seen with the only other black Scout at the camp, Roy Junkins, the skinny boy from the canoe that first day, who walked with a bounce on the balls of his feet, often filling a silence in conversation by singing the snatches of hymns.

CAMP ECHO   •   237

He lifted me up from the deep muddy clay
And he planted my feet on the king's highway!

How could I tell them that I saw that they were suffering, that I was sharing their misery? I did not have the words for it, so I was storing it within me, not knowing what to do with it, or how to rid myself of it. I had my own miseries, too, and my own satisfactions—marksmanship was the main one. Just holding a rifle was a pleasure; but all this was inside me. And so with no way of telling it, with no one to tell, I began to live another simultaneous life—secret feelings, secret pleasures, secret fantasies. I dreamed of being far away, out west or in a forest, with a gun, taller in cowboy boots.

My secrets strengthened me. I became a better climber, a faster runner. I spent my spare time sharpening my hatchet, and when we chopped branches into firewood I hacked madly with it, crowding the other boys. I learned to make surface dives and go deep enough to retrieve a horseshoe from the bottom of the first swimming lane, about seven feet down and lying in the mud. Phelan also managed it, so did Pomroy, but none of the others.

Instead of praising us for bringing up the horseshoe, Blake, the instructor, said, "That's what's expected of you. It's only the beginning—there's harder stuff ahead. The rest of you are feebs."

And Pagazzo giggled, hearing a new word.

Learning to paddle a canoe was not hard, nor was rowing a boat—and we were taught how to feather our oars in a high wind. Part of canoeing involved tipping over the canoe and swamping it, so that it floated filled with water just below the surface. The trick was to turn it upside down with your paddling partner, then swim under it, pushing it up and sideways to empty it, righting it, and when it was refloated, climbing in, as a self-rescue technique. Pagazzo, my partner in this, hooted when we succeeded and called out, "Your turn, you feebs!"

Pinto and Plotnik managed to tip over their canoe but they could not refloat it and ended up clinging to it, softly quarrelling.

"Homo and Shlomo," Pagazzo said from the bank, his arms folded, watching them pushing the submerged thing to shore.

Phelan said, "Like my father says, you should be on a stage. There's one leaving in ten minutes."

Pagazzo smiled and showed his broken tooth and started toward the woods, saying, "So there was this guy and his girlfriend in a cabin playing strip poker. And the guy says, 'I got three aces . . .'"

Phelan followed him eagerly, laughing, as Pinto and Plotnik begged to be helped. Pomroy shrugged, seeing their predicament, and without saying anything, tugged the canoe onto the sand and tipped the water out of it, while we watched. As Pomroy walked away, Pinto called out, "Thanks!" but Pomroy kept walking.

That night, after dinner and the dishes, Butch Rankin blew a whistle and said, "Pipe down!" and made way for Director Hempstone, who stood in his loose brown shorts and knee socks and wide-brimmed hat and waited for silence.

"No songs tonight," he said, when we were still. He went on in a spooky whisper, "Follow me into the moon field, for the ceremonial powwow. Be silent—obey your *netop*, and follow."

"I am your *netop*," Butch Rankin said to our table. "You heard the sachem. Follow me."

Pagazzo had begun to mumble and mock, as he did whenever he heard an unfamiliar word, but as soon as he did, Rankin whipped around and said, "One more word out of you and I'll report you to the sachem."

But this strange threat made Pagazzo choke with laughter.

In the milky light of the full moon I could see the other boys headed toward the flagpole in the middle of the big field, where a fire was blazing. Director Hempstone stood in front of it, gesturing for the boys to sit. Soon we were all seated cross-legged on the grass, watching him with flickering firelit faces.

"As your sachem I say, *wuh-nee-kee-suck*! Greetings! Welcome to the sacred powwow and where the *squitta* rises from the sacred fire to the gleaming *appause*"—and here he pointed to the full moon. "The *appause* and the *cone*—the moon and the sun—are our *nitka* and *noeshow*, our mother and father. And we meet on the night the maple leaf is the size of a mouse's ear, with the blessings of the *Kiehtan*—Our Great Spirit."

This was too much for Pagazzo, who put his face in his hands and moaned with pleasure. Director Hempstone began pacing back and forth.

"Your *netop* is your friend, and you must obey your *netop*, because the *abamocho* walks by night. This is why we *ponesanto*—make a fire. The fire illuminates the *abamocho*. I say to your *netop*, that the *abamocho* is our enemy. He comes from a foreign land where there is no freedom. He has the cunning of a *wawk-sis*, whom you call the fox. He can conceal himself like the *mo-tuck-was*, whom you know as the rabbit. And what is his plan?"

Here, Director Hempstone took a chunk of wood and tossed it into the fire, which sent up a gust of sparks.

"His plan is to destroy your wigwam. To break the lodge pole of your *wetu*!"

He threw another piece of wood into the fire and the force of this one knocked some other burning pieces aside. The stream of dancing sparks and the flames of the fallen logs raked Director Hempstone with shadows and made him look crazed and dangerous.

But he raised a cautioning hand and said, "You must fight the *abamocho* with everything in your power. You must swim faster, row with skill, climb with strength, and most of all you must shoot straight. Or else the *abamocho* will destroy everything we hold dear. If you agree, call out in your proudest voice, *wuh-nee-kee-suck*!"

"*Wuh-nee-kee-suck!*" we screamed, because all this time we had been listening impatiently and it was a relief to shout.

"Your *netop* will bring you the ritual succotash," Hempstone said. "By the eating of it you will abide by the traditions of your sacred *wetu*, in the protection of your people, your *nitka* and your *noeshow*, against the godless *abamocho*."

Butch Rankin stepped in front of our cabin group and held out a bowl. He handed each of us a plastic spoon and said, "One at a time. Eat of the succotash."

When it was my turn I dipped my spoon in and tasted. It was mushy corn, the kind we had some evenings slopped next to the mashed potatoes.

Director Hempstone was not done. He lifted a basket and said, "The powwow is ended. Now I want you to come up here, single file, one cabin at a time, and take your badge. This can be sewn to your uniform as a proud reminder of our powwow."

The badge was an American flag and a coiled snake, with the message *Don't Tread on Me*.

"Creamed corn," Plotnik said, as we walked back to the cabin.

Later that week we went through the shower ritual. This required lining up naked, holding a towel and an envelope with a letter home inside it, the envelope addressed to our parents. One shower a week, one letter: that was the routine. Director Hempstone collected the envelopes as we filed into one side of a shower stall, soaped ourselves, washed off, and hurried out the other side where we were handed the towel we'd brought.

"Your shower bath," Hempstone called it. "Let's see those letters."

I handed mine over. I had written, *Dear Dad and Mum, Camp is fun. I passed the swimming test. We get to shoot guns. I might get some merit badges. We had a big powwow with a bonfire. The food is pretty good. I'm in Cabin Eight. I'm trying not to be homesick. Your loving son, Andy.*

I was standing on the grass, drying myself off, when I heard Hempstone say, "Who's Frank Pagazzo?"

"Over here," Pagazzo said, wrapped in his towel, awaiting his shower. "I'm Frankie."

Hempstone was holding an envelope up to the sun and twitching it. "There's nothing in here," he said. "You were supposed to write a letter."

"I did. It's inside."

Hempstone slapped the envelope into Pagazzo's hand. "Go ahead. Open it, son."

Pagazzo then did an amazing thing. He crumpled the envelope and stuffed it into his mouth, and as he did his towel fell free. Standing naked, he mumbled through the wad of paper, "Quit looking at my peepee."

"Get him out of here," Hempstone said to Butch Rankin, but Pagazzo had already begun walking away. Hempstone said, "Go write a letter and come back here for your shower bath or you'll get demerits."

Pagazzo turned and made a face at us, a broken-tooth smile, to show he wasn't intimidated.

"Hey, maybe I wrote it in invisible ink," he said at dinner, stabbing a slice of Spam with his fork.

I had written to my parents that the food was pretty good, because I had been taught not to complain or criticize, to accept whatever I was offered and to obey. But the food was disgusting—soggy cornflakes for breakfast, baloney sandwiches for lunch, french fries and Spam and boiled vegetables for dinner, purple bug juice and applesauce at every meal. Some evenings we had hot dogs instead of Spam.

We were usually so hungry we ate whatever we were given, though Pagazzo still mocked the bug juice and Plotnik avoided the meat.

"It's against his religion," Pagazzo said.

Plotnik winced and I guessed what Pagazzo had said was true.

"You guys killed Jesus," Pagazzo said. "That's a fact." And he wagged his finger at Plotnik. "Christ killers. You think your shit's ice cream."

Instead of replying to his insults, or getting angry, Plotnik seemed to soften and get sad. He had a beaten look and looked small when he was insulted, the hurt showing in his reddened eyes. He was a reader—the only boy in our cabin who studied the thin red-and-white merit badge pamphlets, *Marksmanship* and *Lifesaving*. He knew all the requirements of shooting, but he was a poor shot at the range; he knew the details of the best strokes, the rescues and carries of a swimmer in trouble, but he thrashed in the water and sometimes needed to be rescued himself. He took refuge in his bunk, doodling—not pictures but numbers, making a series of calculations on a page that looked like a private language.

Although Jerry Pinto was poor at swimming, too, and rope climbing, and timid in the canoe and rowboat, he was deft at weaving lanyards from gimp filaments. Each boy, quietly, asked him to make a lanyard, with a whistle on the end, to be worn around the neck. Agreeing to this meant that Pinto (sitting near the craft shop, twisting gimp) was no longer persecuted by us, though the boys in Cabin Seven went on teasing him.

Pinto was also a good singer and knew the words to "Up in the Air, Junior Birdmen" before anyone else. Plotnik was a math whizz, noticing prime numbers everywhere, and he and Pinto were expert at tying knots—the bowline was Plotnik's favorite, the sheepshank was Pinto's. Phelan was envious of their knot tying, but he had mastered rowing and sailing. He knew the names of the parts of a boat—the gunwales, the thwarts, the rope he called the painter. Phelan had traveled to New York City with his parents and had sailed with his father to Nantucket: those were stories he told to us, who hadn't been anywhere.

Frankie Pagazzo excelled at softball, at stealing bases and hitting, and he seemed to know more about the world than we did—about gangsters and wise guys. He impressed us one night describing how he had sneaked into the Old Howard, a burlesque theater in Scollay Square. "They were bollocky, but they were old women, and some of them were fat."

Pomroy could look at the sky and point, naming stars, and he was the fastest runner in camp. He said, "They won't never catch me," but when I asked "Who won't?" he just shook his head.

I wanted to be good at something—anything, better than anyone else; and so at the rifle range when Rankin said, *You got the eye, kid*, I realized I could shoot; that I might get a Marksmanship badge. And I liked handing in my target after a session, and Rankin saying to the others, "This is what we want—a tight cluster."

With a gun, a loud lethal weapon, I felt powerful. I knew I wasn't strong, but now I had another arm—an arm of iron, an explosive arm. I didn't want to shoot anyone, but I liked the thought that I could frighten any enemy that came my way: stick the muzzle of my Mossberg into the face of a tormentor, to terrify him and watch him plead for his life.

We were Boy Scouts, we were all the same age, and about the same size, and in the same cabin, but we were mismatched, and few of us were friends. We had been thrown together because our names began with P, and we'd all arrived at Camp Echo on the same day. Phelan laughed at Pagazzo's jokes but in a superior snotty way. Pagazzo was clever in dealing with Phelan's boasts; instead of competing with him he joked about himself or his family. When Phelan talked about his father's Oldsmobile, or his mother's roses, Pagazzo said, "My father's got this shit-box of a car—it scares people," or "My mother grows moulinyan—the kind you eat, ha! She got a green thumb, and I got a green peepee."

• • •

One night after dinner and after songs, Butch Rankin stepped forward and announced, "Big tug-of-war tomorrow. Look at the bulletin board and see which cabin you're competing against."

We went separately to the bulletin board, to look at the brackets, and then walked back to the cabin. After lights out, and "Taps" died away, the cabin lay in silence. Then someone spoke in the darkness—it might have been Pagazzo—"Cabin Seven."

"I hate them," Pinto said.

"Me too." That had to be Plotnik.

After some murmurs, finally Pomroy spoke up. "We can take them."

"Yeah," someone said. And someone else, "Yeah."

The following morning, standing at attention, saluting the flag, we heard catcalls from the boys in Cabin Seven, and Pagazzo said, "Candy asses," and we all laughed, a wonderful sound, our laughing together.

And later, in the middle of the morning, when the tug-of-war took place on the ball field, Butch Rankin officiating, we held our end of the thick rope, and the rope seemed to bind us together. The boys from Cabin Seven watched us from their end, beyond the rag tied in the middle of the rope that had to be pulled across the marker, the dividing line, which was in the middle of a mud puddle.

Phelan cupped his hands to his mouth and said in a low voice, "The main thing is to start strong—jerk them off-balance."

"Get a good grip," Pomroy said. "We need an anchor man."

"You be anchor man," Pagazzo said. And to me, "Andy—you get behind Emmett. I'll go behind you. And these two guys in front."

"If we stand in a straight line we'll be able to exert the most pulling power," Plotnik said. "It's basic physics. Horizontal force."

Pinto giggled at being first man, facing the enemy, with Plotnik chattering behind him. I looked back and saw Pomroy winding the rope around his waist, and Phelan whispering, "As soon as we get the signal, just heave."

"Straight line," Plotnik said, glancing behind, and flapping his hand.

Then I heard Butch Rankin call out "Ready," and the shrill whistle, and at once we pulled hard—so hard the rope slid toward us, and Phelan shouted, "Heave!" We pulled hard, as one, as I saw the smaller boys at the front of Cabin Seven's side, stumble, and when they did we pulled again, dragging them and the boys behind them into the mud puddle.

Another whistle and the cry, "It's Cabin Eight!"

We fell on the grass, hugging and laughing, delighted with our win, as Pagazzo shrieked, "Pig pile!"

It was the happiest moment I'd experienced at Camp Echo. We were a team, we were winners, and in our victory we'd become friends. We watched the next tug-of-war with more interest, wondering which cabin our next opponent would be, sitting close together on the grass, laughing at the muddy clothes of the losers from Cabin Seven.

"Second heat," Butch Rankin said. "Cabin Eight pulls against Cabin Two."

"Same strategy," Phelan said, and we took our places on the rope, as before.

But the boys from Cabin Two were bigger than us, and soon after the whistle blew, and Phelan cried, "Heave!" we were dragged so hard the rope burned through my fingers, and in the next moment I fell forward and saw Pinto and Plotnik in the mud puddle. We let go of the rope, and dispersed, and were separate as before, and did not mention the tug-of-war again, not even the victory, when we'd rolled on the grass, hugging and happy.

Avery Pomroy kept to himself, or chatted with Roy Junkins, sitting apart, whispering with their heads down, sometimes nodding together. At night Pomroy lingered outside the cabin in the dark until "Taps," stargazing, and it sometimes seemed to me that standing, his head back, staring at the sky, was his way of avoiding looking at any of us.

Although Pomroy was fast on the track, a strong swimmer, and one of the best paddlers, a reliable hitter on the softball team, and a nimble rope climber, he got no praise. His being a good athlete seemed to be resented.

"You're doing what you're supposed to do," the counselors said. Or "You can do better. There's always room for improvement." And they still compared him to Junkins, who was faster on the track.

Pomroy stopped speaking to any of us. He still participated in sports and showed up for classes, but kept silent, making an effort—to swim, to climb, to paddle—then standing aside and staring, saying nothing, or hovering with Junkins, talking softly.

So it was a surprise to me one day in the second week, when I heard him shouting outside the mess hall. I ran to the sound of his voice. I had never heard him raise his voice before. There was pain and indignation in his shout, and something else—the sound of someone different, someone I did not know and had not realized was in him. I saw him being forcibly restrained, held by the arms by one of the counselors.

"He called me a nigger," he shouted, trying to break free, while a frightened-looking red-faced boy backed away. The red on his cheek was a handprint.

Director Hempstone, hearing the commotion, hurried from his office and approached Pomroy, who was still being held back by the counselor but with less force, because the red-faced boy had slipped away.

"That kid," Pomroy said. "He says to me, 'You're a nigger.'"

As Pomroy pushed the counselor's hands away from him and made a hand gesture that meant *Keep off me*, Hempstone said, "Now you're being a troublemaker."

"Some of these guys heard him," Pomroy said, standing straight. Narrowing his eyes in appeal, he peered at the boys gathered near him. I was among them, but we said nothing, only shrugged in a sheepish and unhelpful way.

"Who heard it?" Hempstone said. "Who heard that word?"

We shuffled our feet in the dust and looked down and said nothing. When I glanced up, I saw Pomroy's furious face and staring eyes, looking trapped and terrible, his shirt torn, dust in the coils of his hair.

"No one's backing up your story, son," Hempstone said. He then reached to grasp Pomroy's arm, but Pomroy slapped Hempstone's hand away, and Hempstone howled, "You are expelled!" And to the counselors who'd heard the fuss, "Did you see what this boy did to me?"

Pomroy was escorted by two counselors to the cabin to pack his things. I stood outside, trying to think of something to say, and when he came out, carrying his bag, looking fierce, I said, "Hi."

He glared at me and said, "I ain't forgetting this."

In the darkness, after the bugler blew "Taps," Pinto said, "He was a wicked good runner."

"He knew the names of a lot of stars," Plotnik said.

"Bob Hope. Jerry Lewis," Pagazzo said. "I know the names of stars."

"Rock Hudson," Phelan said.

Pagazzo said, "See what I mean?"

But I thought, *I ain't forgetting this*.

At the end of that week half the campers went on a daylong canoe trip to a cove at the far end of the lake. Pinto and I, assigned to the same canoe, soon fell behind the others—Pinto in the bow paddling casually, just dipping his blade into the water and trailing it, while I thrust hard with my paddle, trying to keep up. Then he poked his finger into the water and twirled it and sang.

> *Rose, Rose, I love you*
> *With an aching heart . . .*

"Paddle harder," I said. "Push the water, Jerry!"

"I'm trying." But he hardly paddled and we dropped far to the rear, so that when we got to the cove the counselors called Pickerel Rock—the other boys were already in the water, splashing and shrieking, or taking turns swinging and leaping into the water from a rubber tire that was suspended on a rope tied to an overhanging tree branch. All the boys were swimming naked. We were late, and fully clothed, so we were conspicuous.

I began kicking off my shorts and hopping out of them.

Pinto said, "I don't think I'll go in," and instead sat under a tree, weaving a lanyard.

"Who's that kid?" someone said.

A soft giggle: "It's the fairy."

Four boys crept up the bank past me—I recognized them as the boys from Cabin Seven. They pounced on Pinto, shouting, "Depants him!" and began pulling down his shorts and then dragging him over the roots of the big tree and down the embankment to the water's edge. Pinto shrieked, "No! You're hurting my arm!" as they kicked water into his face.

It was not until he was crying loudly—sobbing into his hands—and twisting to get free of the boys that Blake, the counselor, spoke. He had been watching the whole time, and because I saw that he said nothing, only stared at the struggle, I did not intervene to help Pinto.

"That's enough of that," he said, and the boys laughed, and released him, one of them as a last insult stinging Pinto's ear by flicking it with his finger. Being naked, they seemed more wicked than if they had been clothed. They turned their white buttocks on him and swam away.

Pinto was in tears when I knelt and handed him his tangled shorts.

"I think I broke my wrist," he said, sobbing.

His knees were scraped and reddened from bumping the roots, and his shirt was torn. He hiked up his shorts and sat hiccuping as he wept and wiping his face with his hand, dirtying it further.

Blake ignored him at first, but then he walked over—I thought, to console him or examine his bruised knees.

But he stood a few feet away and made a disgusted face and said, "You've got to learn to take it, sonny."

Pinto stopped crying and looked briefly surprised and disappointed, and when Blake walked back to the shore to watch the boys swimming, Pinto took a deep breath and began again to whimper.

"Did you see what they did to me?"

"I was going to help."

"Why didn't you?"

"I thought the counselor was going to stop them," I said. "I didn't know what to do."

That was the truth. Four boys had jumped him. There was no way I could have defended Pinto against the four boys from Cabin Seven we'd beaten in the tug-of-war, and now I saw that if I had tried I would have been defying the counselor—Blake, who did nothing.

What was worse, after the canoe trip to Pickerel Rock, the other boys teased Pinto all the more, crowding him, saying, "Let's depants him again," and mocking him, putting a hand over their mouth and, in a muffled cough-like shout, saying "homo."

It got so that I was fearful of staying near Pinto, because I guessed they'd pick on me next. I was sorry to see boys walking past him and flicking his ear, or boasting, "Did you see me goose him?"

Goosing was something new to me; so was depantsing and towel-snapping at the sink in the morning, and the especially hard noogies—boys' knuckles, usually Pagazzo's, jammed against my arm—that hurt. And swearing, the simple dirty words, spoken or spat out casually, that made me wince and feel that just hearing them I had done something wrong.

"She's a prime number! I could nail her," Pagazzo said, tapping the photo of a naked girl on a page of *Sunshine & Health*.

"You wish," Phelan said.

It was the first photograph of a naked girl about my age I had ever seen. She wore a sunhat and a pair of sandals but was otherwise bare. She was smooth and slim, with soft pale flesh, and a small tuft between her legs, and tiny breasts with swollen nipples. On other pages the naked men and woman were slack and ugly, like white hairless monkeys, some of them playing volleyball, all of them smiling horribly.

"Give her Spanish fly," Pagazzo said. "Turn her into a nympho."

A dose of Spanish fly made a girl beg for sex, he said. It seemed to me a miracle drug but I had no idea what it was, and when Plotnik asked what it looked like ("My uncle's a pharmacist"), they goosed him.

Plotnik was often goosed but was otherwise ignored or pushed aside, except by Pagazzo, who pestered him. "Where's your beanie?" "You lost your Frisbee?"

"Why don't you leave him alone?" I said one day, because I could tell that Plotnik was frightened by Pagazzo and, glassy-eyed, was about to cry. But it seemed to me that Pagazzo was more a clown than a threat.

"He's a sheeny," Pagazzo said. "The sheenies killed Jesus."

"Pants pressers, my father calls them," Emmett Phelan said, laughing. "Canada geese! New Yorkers!"

Phelan's laughter encouraged Pagazzo, who kept after Plotnik, now with two more names to call him. And whenever he saw me alone, Pagazzo said, "Where's your sheeny friend?"

Late one afternoon Pagazzo and Phelan asked Plotnik if he could show them how to tie some knots. Pagazzo was carrying a rope. Plotnik, who was always looking for friends, said, "Sure." They went into the woods and tied him to a tree. I heard Plotnik's sad pleadings, while they were tying him up. I waited until they left him, then I followed the sound of his shouts for help and untied him. He was so upset he didn't thank me. He sobbed and ran away and hid and missed dinner.

At night, in the dark, there was usually silence, or snoring, or someone saying, "Rifle range tomorrow."

Shooting the Mossberg rifle was the activity I liked most. Rankin put me down for the shoot-out with Camp Metacomet. I had discovered something I could do well—hit bull's-eyes, a tight cluster of bullet holes that impressed Butch Rankin, who praised me to the others sitting on the log at the range. I was determined to get a merit badge, I wanted a patch lettered *Marksman* on my shirt pocket. My swimming improved to the point where I might get a Lifesaving badge, though I was not strong enough to win any races. Shooting was not about physical strength, but rather about accuracy and a steady hand. I wanted them to call me Hawkeye.

Rowing, too, was enjoyable, because unlike paddling a canoe I could do it alone. Launching the rowboat, shoving it down the wooden ramp, and climbing in, setting the oars in the locks and pulling hard into the middle of Echo Lake, was a pleasure for the solitude it gave me, sliding across the dark water, easing myself away when anyone came close. Being in a boat was like being on an island, a space that was all mine. As I rowed I talked to myself, or sang, often the song that Jerry Pinto sang in a high voice, "Rose, Rose, I love you, with an aching heart . . ."

At the beginning of the third week, the boys from Cabin Seven who had tormented Pinto at Pickerel Rock began to tease him again, chasing him, threatening to depants him. One evening at dusk, being chased by the boys in the woods, Pinto tripped and fell hard. Returning from rowing, I had seen him run into the woods, and heard the thump of his fall, and just then his wailing. I hurried toward the screeching and saw him clutching his wrist.

"I really broke it this time!"

The boys who had chased him lingered, as Pinto went on sobbing. I helped him up, but he slumped, still crying, and so one of the boys supported him and we took him to the infirmary.

The nurse was Hempstone's wife. She said, "How did this happen?"

"I was running in the woods," Pinto said.

"Serves you right. You should know better. What's wrong with you?"

I said, "It wasn't him. These boys were chasing him."

"What boys?" Mrs. Hempstone asked.

"Them, from Cabin Seven."

"It wasn't us!" one boy said. "We didn't do nothing."

"You chased him, you teased him, you depantsed him, you know you did," I said.

"It's a lie!" the other boy said.

"Stop shouting," Mrs. Hempstone said. "Now get out here, all of you."

Outside, the bigger boy from Cabin Seven said, "Know something?" and stood in front of me, blocking my way, so I couldn't get past him. "You're a squealer." What I didn't realize was that the other boy had crept low behind my legs, so that when the big boy pushed me I fell backward, toppling over the crouching boy.

"You're a fairy, like him."

After dinner, Pinto's father and mother arrived to take him home. I helped, carrying one of Pinto's duffel bags, and was fascinated by his close resemblance to his mother, the same soft eyes and narrow face, and she looked tearful too. Pinto's father, who had big bat ears like his son, stood to the side, his hands in his pockets, jingling coins.

"Some boys chased him," I said.

"I'm okay, Ma," Pinto said, protesting.

"So this is how you kids behave," his mother said to me. "You should be ashamed."

There were four of us in the cabin now, and by this time a routine was established—reveille, saluting the flag, washing up, breakfast, swimming, boating, then lunch and more KP. In the afternoon, rope climbing, the rifle range, the craft shop. After dinner the sing-along, and on Wednesday the letter home and the shower bath, all of us in line, naked, a towel in one hand, an envelope in the other.

It was part of the routine that Pagazzo teased Plotnik—"Sheeny," "Christ killer"—but Plotnik didn't reply. Phelan always laughed, as though hearing it for the first time. No one else seemed to care, not even Plotnik. But he trusted me enough to cry in front of me when he was complaining about them,

Walking to the chow hall one evening, behind Pagazzo and Phelan, Plotnik said, "It's a wicked good thing I don't have a hunting knife."

"Why?" I asked.

"Because I'd stab him in the nuts," he said in a low voice.

At the rifle range, beside me, shooting in the next lane, Plotnik moaned, his glasses slipped down his nose, and in a small piteous voice, he said, "I can't even hit the darn target."

His saying *darn* made me feel sorry for him. I whispered to him, "Watch."

I squirmed sideways and fixed my sight on his target and fired, then slid the bolt and fired again. Plotnik said in a new voice, "Wicked."

Three more rounds, and Plotnik was on his belly, smiling, and when it came time to show our targets, Rankin smacked Plotnik on the head and said, "At last, you're learning."

It annoyed Phelan that I was the better shot. But he had another talent. He made friends with the camp counselors, talking to them confidently, almost as though he was their equal, usually mentioning his father's sailboat in Osterville. I disliked him, yet I was impressed by his poise, and I felt strongly that he would succeed in life—good things would happen to him, and he craved good things. As for myself, I often reasoned that my lack of ambition would guarantee that I'd be a failure. Pagazzo would be a failure, too, but he would rejoice in it, laughing.

Phelan was unusual in another way: he talked to boys in other cabins, something I couldn't bring myself to do. I saw Phelan as a man of the world, like his father, whom he always quoted. He wasn't smarter than the rest of us, but he was confident and a bit bigger. It interested me that he did not defend Plotnik against Pagazzo's teasing, that the tormenting made him quote his father.

"New Yorkers!"

But because Phelan's shooting at the range was poor, Rankin did not put him on the roster for the shoot-off at the Camporee. And these days all Rankin and Hempstone talked about was the upcoming competition with Camp Metacomet.

"We are winners," Director Hempstone said. "I want you to show me that we will go on winning. You are Boy Scouts, you are young Americans, you are the future. You will have many challenges but you have much to prove—you must not fail."

He went on like this for so long, going red-faced, often mentioning Communists, I stopped listening and thought about myself. I was relieved I could shoot a rifle and hit a target, but being at Camp Echo showed me how insignificant and weak I was, and in my heart I believed I did not know anything. I missed Pomroy, because his being sent home was unfair, and he represented an injustice; and I felt sorry about Pinto because he was so small and innocent. I remembered him singing, "Rose, Rose, I love you"—and got sad, remembering his pinched face, and—sitting behind him in the canoe—his small skinny neck as he paddled, kneeling in the bow. I had watched these boys being mocked, and had listened to the abuse, and I had done nothing to help them. I wished they'd come back to camp, so that I could stick up for them.

Pagazzo soon got himself into a fix. He had somehow found a lanyard that Pinto had made, and he began to wear it. One of the counselors, Huggins, the softball coach, admired it and said, "Is that your work?"

"Sure," Pagazzo said in his cocky way. "I'm an expert."

"Great. Then make me one," Huggins said and took Pagazzo to the craft shop where he bought a bag of gimp.

In the cabin, Pagazzo sat on his bunk fretting over the loops of plastic. He said to me, "Hey, you were Pinto's friend. Give me a hand. You must know how to do this."

Telling him I had no idea, I took pleasure in his helplessness.

"I'll take the pipe, I'll be in Dutch," he said. Then he screamed, "You Communists!"

None of us was adept at braiding and knotting the gimp, as Pinto had been. With a thin smile, Plotnik said, "You'll have to do it yourself."

Phelan, who felt superior to Pagazzo, said, "Tough luck."

The next day Pagazzo went to Huggins and handed him the ragged lanyard he'd made.

Huggins held it up and squinted at it and made a face. He said, "This is a blivet."

Pagazzo said, "What's a blivet?"

"It's two pounds of shit in a one-pound bag."

"So I guess it's pretty good, huh?" Pagazzo said and began to laugh.

"That's a demerit, son."

Pagazzo got more demerits for towel snapping and laughing during the Pledge of Allegiance, and when his copy of the nudist magazine *Sunshine & Health* was found under his bunk during a cabin inspection—"What's this?"—he was sent home.

That left Phelan, Plotnik, and me in the half-empty cabin. And because there were so few of us we always struggled in the games against other cabins. One after-dinner competition was called the Snipe Hunt. It required cabins to grope around the darkness of the woods and locate various objects—a five-pound rock, six red berries, a stick exactly twelve inches long, and so forth—and these were brought to the mess hall to be measured and weighed, to see which cabin won.

We lost, of course, and Phelan swore and blamed us, because he had wanted to win. And as a consequence of rushing around in the dark woods Plotnik got blistery patches of poison ivy on his hands and legs. The night before his parents picked him up, he packed his knapsack and lay on his bunk fully clothed, not saying anything, and in the morning walked out of the cabin and slammed the door.

With his arms folded behind his head, Phelan said, "There's no Jews in Baldwin, my father's country club."

It was now just Phelan and me in Cabin Eight; Emmett was a tall, toothy boy with an Irish smile and reddish hair that flopped over his eyes, and I was skinny and shorter, and evasive. We were a mismatched twosome at reveille, and an odd couple at the big table at mealtime, but with very few dishes to wash. For a brief period—a day perhaps—I thought we might be friends. I longed to see his hidden copy of *Sunshine & Health*.

One afternoon when he was leafing through the magazine, I said, to start a conversation, "I sort of miss Pinto."

"Percy Pinto," Phelan said. "I don't. He was a homo." He turned a page and peered closely. "They're dangerous."

"But Pagazzo was a bully," I said.

"He was funny. I liked how he called himself a guinea wop."

At night, after "Taps," we went to bed, sleeping at opposite ends of the cabin, saying nothing. Nor did Phelan speak to me during the day. He talked often to the camp counselors, and to Hempstone, telling them about his father, and vacations they'd taken in Florida in the winter, and how his mother grew tea roses.

But at the rifle range, in the lane next to me, I could hear Phelan grunting with frustration when he shot and missed, then watched with a furious face as I hit the bull's-eye with all my shots.

"Good grouping," Rankin said, poking his finger at my target. "You're going to be our guy at the shoot-out."

One afternoon I saw Phelan with the swimming instructor, Blake—Blake sitting, Phelan standing, telling a story, and I was impressed as always by his confidence, his posture, the way he gestured to the much older man. And I approached them, not knowing what to do or say, but did not go close. I was too awkward to go nearer, too embarrassed to walk away.

Phelan broke off in the middle of his talk and glanced at me. He lost his smile and said gruffly, "What are you looking at?"

Blake laughed at this, and I used the rejection of his laughter as an opportunity to walk away. My blushing made my face feel hot.

That night, in the darkness of the cabin at taps, Phelan said, "Rifle range tomorrow."

To spite him for humiliating me in front of Blake I said, "I learned to shoot in Texas."

Texas was the wildest, farthest, most exotic place I could think of—desert, cactus, tumbleweeds, six guns, big hats, horses.

"My uncle lives there," I said. "He has a six-shooter." Phelan said nothing. "And boots." I wanted a pair of those boots. "I'm going to Texas again." Phelan was awake, still breathing. I said, "Mustangs."

Then I lay there in the odor of pine boards that seemed sharper in the dark, thinking how I would like to point a rifle at him, to frighten him—what pleasure it would give me to see him stammer and plead. But it also pleased me that he believed my lies about Texas.

And while I was at it I imagined doing the same with Pagazzo, for teasing Jerry Pinto and Michael Plotnik. I saw myself raising the muzzle of the gun while they pleaded for mercy. I worked the bolt and loaded a round and aimed it at Phelan's eyes and Pagazzo's nose, and as I poked it I watched them backing up and begging. And then, defiantly, I called up the image of Hempstone and imagined pointing the gun at him—just a Boy Scout, but one with a loaded gun—and I saw him cowering.

At the range the next day I mentally put Phelan's and Pagazzo's and Hempstone's faces over the targets, and I shot round after round, becoming sweaty and breathless as I fired, hollowing out the bull's-eyes with a cluster of punctures.

"Wicked good," Rankin said. "What's wrong?"

He saw that I was crying, that my cheeks were wet with tears, and that my nose was snotty.

I said—I don't know why—"Someone died in my family."

"Sorry to hear it. Hey, you've earned yourself a merit badge. And you're representing us in the shoot-off."

"Cabin Eight?"

"The whole camp. You're representing Echo."

I was so shocked by the lie I'd told about someone dying in my family, I racked the rifle and went quickly away, leaving Phelan still shooting. And that night I did not go into the cabin at "Taps." I went to the latrine and walked in the shadows of the pines around the back of the chow hall.

Hearing laughter and loud talking from the counselors' staff room I sidled near a lighted window and listened. I could not understand what they were saying, but each time one of them spoke the others hooted very loudly, with a chattering laugh, their mouths wide open and toothy, their red faces shining with sweat, looking like monkeys. I had the impression they were laughing at us, monkey men laughing at monkey boys.

The last days at camp were predictable—swimming, rope climbing, songs after dinner, the cold shower bath in the wooden stall on the lawn, the final letter home. Phelan had stopped talking to me, yet against my will, I still admired him for having the strength and concentration to ignore me when we were alone in the cabin—cleaning it for inspection, or getting ready for bed. But I also thought how much I would enjoy having him turn to me and make one of his rude remarks, and how I would say, "Did you say something to me?" and point the gun at him and threaten to shoot him in the face.

This thought eased my mind for long moments, and then troubled me, because I realized that I hated the song, "I'm Happy When I'm Hiking," and I was fearful of the boys from Cabin Seven who had teased Plotnik and Pinto, and listening to dirty jokes worried me, because what if Hempstone saw me, laughing at those wicked words?

All the boys seemed to me like monkeys, or doglike and awful in their bullying and noise, and the counselors seemed like conspirators, the food smelled like rotten apples, the cabin of damp boards and pine sap. I was a good swimmer now, and I could climb to the fat knot at the top of the rope and could cut notches in logs with my hatchet, and I could run through the paths in the pinewoods in the half dark of a Snipe Hunt. I felt like a monkey myself.

And I could shoot. I liked hearing Butch Rankin's warning, "The range is hot. Fire at will," and pulling the trigger and hearing the crack of the bullet. It gave me a thrill in my guts to fire a gun.

And my target got Phelan's attention. When I saw him glancing at it, I said, "Texas!"

"Camporee tomorrow," Director Hempstone said after dinner on the last Friday. "I want everyone in dress uniforms. If you have sashes with badges, I want to see you wearing them. I want to see medals. I want to see neckerchiefs with toggles and shined shoes. The runners can bring sneakers and put them on over there."

"Over there" was across Echo Lake, at Camp Metacomet, where we sometimes heard squawks and shouts ringing on the water. Most of our campers went in a yellow school bus, but Director Hempstone invited three of us to go with him in his wood-paneled station wagon—Roy Junkins, who would be running, Phelan the rower, and me, in the shoot-off.

"I'm counting on you, son," Hempstone said to Junkins, who was in the back seat with me.

"Avery was a lot faster than me," Junkins said.

"Who's Avery?" Hempstone said.

Junkins turned to me and widened his eyes. Phelan, in the front seat with Hempstone, said, "I'll do my best, sir."

"Win, Emmett. Make us proud," Hempstone said. "Beat Metacomet! Win!"

Driving through the woods around Echo Lake to Camp Metacomet, Phelan began chatting with Hempstone, beginning each sentence with, "My father says . . ." And I listened intently, both impressed and resentful, as Phelan was quoting his father, because I could not imagine talking to Hempstone, or anyone at Camp Echo and mentioning my father—nothing he said, nothing he believed. And Phelan was still talking.

Then Hempstone said, "Damned Harry Truman."

"My father's got this story about Truman giving a talk to a whole bunch of Indians at an Indian reservation," Phelan said. "Truman says, 'The government will help you.' The Indians call out 'Oomlah!' Truman says, 'I am on your side.' The Indians yell 'Oomlah!' Truman keeps talking and always gets this big cry 'Oomlah,' and he's really happy. Afterward, the chief says, 'We have a feast for you across the field in the wigwam. Be careful—there was a herd of cows in this field. Don't step in any *oomlah*.'"

Hempstone said, "Your dad's a card."

"Thank you, sir, I'll tell him you said so."

Roy Junkins widened his eyes again, but said nothing.

Pretending to welcome us, the campers at Metacomet gathered at the entrance, on either side of the dirt road, and shouted. But it was not a welcome—they were simply yelling—and it was as though we were passing through a gauntlet of man-faced boys yelling, "Oomlah!"

Metacomet was a messy camp, unlike our neat and well-tended one. Metacomet's grass needed cutting, the piers at the swimming area on their side of the lake were unpainted, and some of the ropes were left uncoiled on the dock. They didn't have Butch Rankin to say, *I want this place shipshape*. It surprised me that they were stronger swimmers than us—we only won two of the six swimming races. Phelan came second in the rowing. When we trooped to the field for the running, Hempstone said, "I'm counting on you, son," to Junkins, but Junkins looked away, and shrugged, and loped in last. Hempstone threw up his hands.

"What's your name, son?" Hempstone asked me.

"Andy," I said.

"Listen to me," he said. "Our guys lost—no gumption. Do you have gumption?"

"I think so, sir."

"It's up to you, Andy. You gotta help, you gotta do your best. We need a big win here."

For the first time at Camp Echo, Hempstone was speaking directly to me, appealing to me, and I almost smiled at this fat man with the crazy hair asking me to help—Hempstone, who'd send Pomroy home; who'd let Plotnik and Pinto get bullied; who'd mocked Pagazzo; who'd made friends with Phelan; who'd concocted the Indian ritual and served us creamed corn in the moonlight, by the bonfire. Hempstone was asking me to forget everything I'd seen and heard and to believe in Camp Echo.

"You're in the head-to-head in the shoot-off," he said. "You're a smart kid. And you know we are winners at Camp Echo."

"Yes, sir." But I thought, *You don't know me.*

"That's the spirit," and he patted my head. "Now go get 'em."

The Metacomet rifle range was in the woods, barely visible among the crowds of Boy Scouts gathered behind the barrier, Echo on one side, Metacomet on the other, all of them shouting. Rankin walked beside me, holding the Mossberg, his free hand on my shoulder and, when the Scouts saw me, one side howled and the other side cheered.

"Stay behind the firing line!" their range master shouted and lifted his binoculars. "Safety first!"

We fired in heats, four at a time, the boy from Metacomet and me. But I had looked closely at the target from Metacomet, and none of the shooter's bullets had hit the red bull's-eye—one nicked it, the others were in the black or dotting the outer circles.

On the last heat, we lay side by side, and when I heard "Fire at will," I did not shoot at once. I looked at my opponent's target and saw that his first two shots were in the black. I shot at my target and then squirmed sideways and fired again and heard a shout of triumph from behind me—probably the man with the binoculars. I liked that shout. I moved my rifle and fired again as my opponent fired, and I put another bull's-eye in his target. And again I heard it, a full-throated cry, echoed by the boys from Camp Metacomet. I loved the silence from the Camp Echo Scouts. It was as though a giant had come to the rifle range and sat on them, and the giant was me.

As the targets were held up—Metacomet's with a tight grouping in the bull's-eye, mine with a scattering of wide-apart holes—Director Hempstone walked away. Rankin wouldn't speak to me. Later I found Hempstone sitting in his station wagon with Emmett Phelan, but when I opened the back door, he said, without looking at me, "Take the bus, son."

The bus was full, with many boys standing, but the seat next to Roy Junkins was empty. When I sat there, Junkins didn't say anything; then he elbowed me in a brotherly way and smiled, as though we'd won.

"I ain't never coming back here again," Junkins said.

"Me neither," I said, surprising myself by saying it, and realizing I meant it.

On the last day, it rained. Emmett Phelan's father picked him up in a blue Oldsmobile—a big hearty man in a golf cap who hugged Emmett and who waved at Director Hempstone. He glanced at me waiting under a tree in the rain near the gate, as Emmett whispered to him—probably saying something like, *He's a pisser. He lost the shoot-out.*

But I was glad only Butch Rankin was there to see my father pick me up in his embarrassing old car—no one else, none of the other boys or parents. My father was late and I was the last to leave, Rankin in a rubber poncho saying, "I've got to sign you out."

My father scribbled his signature on the clipboard and smiled at Rankin, who said, "He's got a great eye. I don't know why he lost."

"Be good," my father said. He hadn't heard. On the road he said, "You got some color in your cheeks," and when I did not reply, he said, "So what's the verdict?"

"Wicked," I said, and I thought as I had with Director Hempstone, *You don't know me. Nobody knows me. Good.*

STOP & SHOP

Follow me, kid," Ray Mammola said, pushing through the basement door, untying his long white apron with one hand and using the broken nail of his dirty thumb to slide an inch of blade out of his box cutter knife. "You tell anyone where I am and I'll use this on you." His low, snarly voice was worse than a shout. "Think I don't know how? Ask anyone. I was in Korea. I seen action."

He slipped his apron over his head and heaved a wide carton labeled *Bathroom Tissue* from a stack, placing it end to end with another carton the same size, all the while swinging the box cutter and talking, his voice seeming to come out of his big broken nose.

"Them crates behind me—it's all jerkins in jars, so heads up when you stack them on the deck."

His back was turned to me, and now with wicked swipes of his knife he began slicing off the top of one of the wide cartons, in a sequence of thrusts, each like a beheading, zipping off, first the long side, then the ends, leaning and slashing the cardboard until he'd freed it, lifting it open like a lid. His recklessness excited me, but I was thinking, *Jerkins?*

"You were supposed to do this yesterday."

"I had soccer practice."

For the first time he turned around to face me, still holding his box cutter. "You any good?"

"No."

He laughed, not in a mocking way, but a surprised appreciative laugh. My answer surprised me, too.

"All this stuff needs to be priced. You got your stamp?"

"Right here." I tugged open the roomy front pocket of my apron and showed him the upright chrome contraption, with numbers on adjustable wheels that printed the price on the jar cap or box top in purple ink.

"Twenty-nine cents each," he said, turning away and starting on the second carton, knifing the top open with what seemed savagery calculated to intimidate me. But his efficiency with the box cutter thrilled me. "After that, there's more cases for the pickle aisle, them quart jars of kosher dills and the sweet ones, them bread and butters. Start loading the dolly." Still running the blade through the top edge of the cardboard carton he said, "By the way, what's your name?"

"Andy Parent."

"You a Canuck?"

"I'm an American."

"Okay"—he leaned over the open carton and began to claw out rolls of toilet paper, creating a long trough through the middle in each carton and then cutting a section of cardboard where the boxes met. Concentrating on this he didn't say anything more, and now he was digging out loose toilet rolls, putting some on the basement floor and rearranging others in the end-to-end cartons.

"And the jars of mustard," he said. "Same aisle. Price them, stack them on the dolly. Stock all them shelves, and look alive."

I tried not to seem shocked as he climbed into the bed-like trough he'd made in the two cartons of toilet paper. He knelt and then lay down and sank into the softness, yawning, extending his legs, folding his arms across his chest like a corpse in a coffin, still holding his box cutter in his fist.

"Remember what I said, Andy." He wagged the box cutter at me, then closed his eyes and seemed to gargle luxuriously and go to sleep.

Upstairs, I was stocking the shelves in the pickle aisle, when Mr. Crotty, the store manager, approached me, looking fussed, pinch-faced, his thin cheeks glowing with exertion. His blue smock was a sign of his seniority, his name *Kevin Crotty* embroidered on the pocket.

"There's a black kid up front by the registers looking for you, Andrew. Keep it short." Saying *shawt* in the blunt Boston way was his being fierce. "This is a supermarket, not a social club."

I slipped the crate of gherkins that I'd held jammed between my chest and the shelf to the floor.

"And where's Ray Mammola?"

"I haven't seen him."

"You sure?" He peered at me, the eyes and teeth of a small nibbling animal. His confident authority made me evasive and I found it easy to lie.

"Yes, sir."

He glared at me and in my lie I felt older, like a conspirator, an outlaw, doing whatever I wanted.

Roy Junkins was waiting behind one of the registers. He looked uncomfortable among the shoppers, dancing from one foot to the other as though controlling a soccer ball. He widened his eyes and said, "Coach Ferretti sent me. I'm supposed to tell you we got an extra practice tomorrow for the Governor Dummer game."

"That's not for two weeks. Anyway, I'll be on the bench."

"Everyone plays. He'll put you in."

"For five seconds. Third string. First string wins the game. Roy, come on."

"We're unbeaten!"

"No thanks to me. Anyway I might have to work. I got promoted."

With a note of sorrow in his pleading voice, he said, "It's a team, Andre."

A blue figure twitched at the far end of the aisle, Mr. Crotty glaring at me. "Cheese it, Roy, I can't talk. Okay, I'll see you at practice on Monday."

That I got promoted was not an exaggeration. I had started in the summer rounding up shopping carts in the parking lot and hating it, especially on rainy days. I still attended soccer practice regularly and was on the verge of quitting the Stop & Shop when a new boy, Felix Perez, was hired and I was moved inside, bagging groceries, while Felix did the shopping carts. A month of that—and soccer games at Newton High and Philips Academy—and the grouchiness of customers saying, *Careful with my eggs* and *Don't put the Ajax in with my chicken*. I was a servant, at a buck an hour, and ready to quit when I was moved up again to help Ray Mammola, stocking shelves, and Felix was promoted to bagging.

Lying about Ray should have made me feel bad—Ferretti, the soccer coach, had an honesty policy ("Hands up if you fouled someone"); but lying to Crotty had the opposite effect. It made me smile inside, it suggested that Ray trusted me. Roy Junkins was my friend, and he believed in the team, but he was a starter, and starters were gung ho. I was not gung ho about anything, not even the Stop & Shop.

I had just raised the crate of gherkins to my chest again—the technique was to use both hands—when Mr. Crotty approached me again.

"I don't want your friends coming around. Understood?"

I wondered if he was saying that because Roy was Black, but I said, "Yes, sir."

"And what about Ray?"

"I still haven't seen him." It now gave me pleasure to defy him.

"He was supposed to tell you to take a break. You can go at four." It was another fierce Boston pronunciation, *foh-wah*. "I want you back here in twenty minutes." He hesitated, then said, "Another thing, Andrew. Mr. Hackler, the area supervisor, is making a surprise inspection."

"When would that be, sir?"

"Did you hear me? A surprise inspection. We don't know. That's why it's called a surprise."

"Right. I see what you mean."

"Everyone on their toes, like a fire drill." And he walked away, narrow shoulders, narrow head, blue floppy smock. *Fy-ah drill.*

The United Food and Commercial Workers Union, of which I was a fifteen-year-old card-carrying member, specified that we workers were to be given a twenty-minute break for every three hours on the job. The break room was in the back, next to the employee toilets. On my way through the stockroom I stole a jelly donut out of a box, and a carton of chocolate milk out of the dairy case. The break room was clouded with cigarette smoke and chatter, three men at the card table, Omar from Produce, Vinny the head of the deli section, and Sal the butcher talking together. Sal's bloodstained apron over his knees gave him a kind of brutal majesty. Felix, the bag boy, sat eating something from a paper plate he held close to his face.

"What's that supposed to be?" Sal asked Felix.

Still eating, Felix said, "My mother tamale."

"I want a taste of your mother's tamale," Sal said, and the others laughed, though Felix went on eating.

"Where's Ray?" Vinny said. When I stammered, he said, "You can tell us! Never mind—we know he's sleeping."

"Right," I said, and saying that made me feel conspiratorial again.

"We need a fourth here—you'll do," Vinny said to me and began to deal cards for whist, the usual break-time game. As he snapped the cards down he pointed to my jelly donut and said, "If you'd eat that, you'd eat anything."

We played whist quickly, gathering and piling tricks. We were in the middle of one hand when Ray flung the door open, yawning. He took the cards from me, tapped my shoulder. I got up and gave him my chair.

"Did he ask?"

"Two times."

"What did you tell him?"

"What you told me," I said. "And there's going to be a surprise inspection from Mr. Hackler."

"Hitler," Ray said. "The mystery man."

"I'll give him a hit on the head," Vinny said.

Sal said, "Ray was in the service. He never leaves his buddies behind." He nudged Felix, "Get it?" Then he said to Ray, "That's his mother's tamale he's eating."

Staring at his cards, Ray said, "Who dealt this mess?"

Soccer practice the following Monday started with a prayer, and then Coach Ferretti read from his notes the order we'd be playing. I was third string, so I sat on the bench, between Fesjian and Brodie, waiting for my turn. Mr. Ferretti came over and sat heavily next to me, bumping my shoulder as a rough companionable greeting.

"Missed you on Saturday, Andrew."

"I had to work."

"Work is a good character builder, but so is teamwork. The Governor Dummer game is coming up. We have a good chance to stay unbeaten."

Roy Junkins had drifted over and heard what the coach had said. "We'll win, no sweat."

"We'll win if we work together as a team," the coach said in a reprimanding voice.

"Bunch of percies," Roy said.

"I don't want to hear that word," Mr. Ferretti said.

The belief at our public high school was that only wealthy, overdressed, fairly stupid boys went to private school, their parents buying them an education; and poorer, tougher, more athletic, highly motivated boys attended public schools. I was a sophomore, a wing on the soccer team, skinny and not particularly strong, but fast enough and accurate when I had an opening in the box, which was seldom. Because so few high schools had soccer teams, we played the Tufts freshmen and the Harvard freshmen and the prep schools, and we had not lost a game.

"This is a team," the coach said at the end of the Monday practice. "Everyone plays. No heroes, no glory boys."

But I knew that when the game was on the line, only the first string mattered, and the scorer would be a hero, and it wouldn't be me. Still, I ran, I kicked, I headed the ball, Coach Ferretti praised me, and afterward we went to Brigham's for ice cream.

We crowded into a booth and talked, the usual hot whispers about the names for different parts of girls' bodies. I glanced at the soda jerk, Joe Slubsky, digging his scoop into the tubs of ice cream; his apron, his high-crowned paper hat, saying nothing. His English was poor, his face was averted, but he was listening and I knew what he was thinking. We were sweaty, and dirty from practice, talking about what girls looked like naked, and he half envied us and half hated us.

School, and more soccer practice the rest of the week, Friday evening at the Stop & Shop; Friday night at my grandmother's house because her home was walking distance from the store—I got out of work too late to take the bus home. Sunday church, Monday school, and more soccer, then the weekend, Stop & Shop.

Work, school, and soccer seemed like a whole life but it was a life I barely inhabited. I was somewhere else, helplessly yearning, yet constantly reminded—by Crotty, my teachers, by the coach—of their importance.

Think of your future, they said. But my future was a blank. How do you get from here to there?

My dilemma was easy to explain, if anyone cared to hear it, though no one did. I was not adrift, I was stuck. Being fifteen years old was like being on the lower floor of my grandmother's three-decker house where, on the floor above, a man was speaking to a woman out of earshot in a different room, who couldn't hear him, but was talking back to him, though he couldn't hear her. To a shout, which might be tedious or revealing, or shocking, or life-altering or wise, each yelled, "What did you say?" Other people, too, calling to each other on the floor above them, each deaf to the other.

Though I could hear every word, they didn't know I was listening, or even that I existed. But that was not my dilemma. My dilemma was: What do I do with all the things I am hearing?

It was an intimation, not that I would be a writer in any important way, but that writing this down might help ease my mind.

My secret dreams were of success, of good fortune, of heroism, and I could not understand how work or school or soccer mattered. *No heroes, no glory boys*, the coach had said, Yet I longed to be a hero—not a scorer on the field, or a brain at school, but big and dangerous. Heroism was like a blessing. It came unbidden: you were chosen, you were someone reckless, like Ray Mammola and some of the other men at the Stop & Shop, Vinny saying "I'll give him a hit on the head," Sal with his bloody apron, and "Who dealt this mess!" and Omar in Produce who could juggle oranges, and Felix who brought me a tamale to try. The Stop & Shop was a team, too, but a more complicated one, old guys and young guys.

I loved the heartlessness of their talk. I remembered Ray's gusto with the box cutter, swiping open the cartons of toilet paper and making himself a nest for a nap. He was a full-time employee, in charge of inventory, but he also broke the rules and got away with it. Mr. Crotty needed him, which was why he was always looking for him.

"Kevin Crotty," Ray said. "He doesn't know whether to scratch his watch or wind his ass." Ray was the talker, the smoker, the winner at whist. Seeing Felix and me coming out of the toilet he said, "You guys comparing tools?"

"Stop & Shop's merging with the A&P," he said one day. "They're going to call it the Stop & Pee."

Sal said, "What's with this surprise visit of the supervisor?"

"Hackler," Vinny said.

"Hitler," Ray said. "No one knows what he looks like. He sneaks in and rats on us. If I ever find out who he is, I'll pinch his head off."

Except for Felix and me, they were all older men. They smoked, they swore, they teased one another; Ray talked about Korea.

"Best feeling in the world?" Ray said. "It's not sex. It's after a long march, all day. You sit down and take your combat boots and socks off. And you feel the breeze on your toes and you wiggle them a little."

They jokingly complained about their wives. "My wife says to me—"

"My day off tomorrow," Vinny said.

"Doing anything special?"

"Stay home. Make babies."

I tried not to smile, but it excited me to hear it.

Sal said, "It's not how long you make it, it's how you make it long."

"I live in a duplex," Ray said, studying his cards. "You know, those places attract some strange people. Last year I was sleeping in my room and three naked woman were pounding on my door. They just would not stop."

"So what did you do?" Omar asked.

"I got up and let them out." Then Ray pitched a card. "Trumps!"

"Union meeting on Sunday," Sal said.

This was news. The men conferred about going there, who would ride with whom. Ray nudged me. "You can go with us, kid. You, too, Felix the Cat."

On that Sunday I went to church with my grandmother. I sat, I stood, I knelt. Even the flowers and the candles on the altar seemed meaningless, but I went through the motions, I prayed, feeling that no one was listening. My old unanswered question: how do you get from here to there. "Have faith," the priest said in his sermon. Back at her house, my grandmother said, "Andre, *qui sont ces hommes?*"

They were in the car, beeping the horn.

"*Les gars—mes amis*. Gram, I got a union meeting."

Ray and Vinny in the front, me and Felix in the back seat. Ray was ending a story he was telling Vinny about Korea. "I'm drunk, I'm bollocky, I tip her over and she screams . . ." Then to me and Felix, "Hey, the union men!"

I had no idea where we were going and was surprised when, after half an hour, we were in open country—narrow roads, a pond, woods in leafless November.

"They hold these things in the sticks," Ray said. "They can get a bigger function room that way, more parking, cheaper rental."

The hall was a high school gym, filled with Stop & Shop workers, all older men, sitting on folding chairs, talking among themselves, until a man on a platform called them to order. A banner over his head was lettered *United Food and Commercial Workers 595*.

"We want more money," someone called out.

"Keep your shirt on," the man said.

It was not a team, it was more like an army—I thought of them as soldiers, and many of them like Ray had probably been soldiers, either in World War Two or Korea. They had the heavy faces and the look of exhaustion and the tattoos and the toughness. One man near me was saying to another, "I've gotta put food on the table." This wasn't soccer or school; it was serious, their livelihood. They were all sorts, mainly white guys, and some women—I saw Veronica and Lucy from the cash registers talking with other workers—but also some Black men conferring in a group, and Omar, who had found some Arabs to joke with, and Felix, relieved to be in a secure corner of Puerto Ricans.

"Maybe they'll vote you a buck ten," Ray said.

Men called out from the floor, some stood and made short speeches that provoked arguing and interruption, and all of it happened in the air above my head, the talk, like the smoke, until a vote was taken and hands were raised and the men roared.

"Know what I like about this?" Ray said, leaning back, relaxed, his hands behind his head. "Guys like Hitler aren't allowed in. He's management. We're the workers."

"If he tried to get in, I'd give him a hit on the head," Vinny said.

"If we knew what he looked like," Ray said.

Darkness had fallen by the time the union meeting ended. In the car, driving away, Ray murmured to Vinny, "Why not?" and farther down the road suddenly slowed the car and drove into a field at the far end of which was a tent decorated in strings of Christmas lights.

"Where are we?" I asked.

"Little surprise," Ray said. "It's a carnival."

He parked and we walked across the shadowy field of wet grass to the tent, where we slipped through a thick canvas flap. A man just inside asked us for fifty cents and gave us a ticket. Inside, men in heavy coats pressed against a bare, brightly lit stage. Some of them I recognized from the union meeting, all of us standing on grass. Behind me, Felix muttered, "*Qué pasa?*" After a while, a few of the men began calling out in impatience.

Then an old man in a derby hat and bow tie and a striped vest walked onstage and said, "Welcome, gentlemen. Welcome! Let me present Miss Lana Lane!"

A woman wearing a red two-piece bathing suit and a beret appeared from the curtains, did a few dance steps, and then paced back and forth, wiggling a little and laughing and waving. The men hooted at her. One called out, "Take it off!" She teased with her fingers and then reached behind her, unhooked her top, and held it carelessly against her breasts, teasing some more, while the men shouted. I was shoved on both sides by the much bigger men, and then pushed nearer the stage, separated from Felix. The woman quickly revealed her bare dog-nosed white breasts, then laughed and skipped offstage.

"Gentlemen!" It was the man in the bow tie, returning. He fanned his face with his derby. He was white-haired, with yellow teeth in a wicked grin. He said, "If you want to see more, it'll cost you more."

He shook his derby hat and handed it into the crowd of men. They passed it around, putting money into it, mostly coins, and some dollar bills, like a collection in a church.

And that was when it struck me that this tent and this gathering was like a church—the attentive men, the flickering lights, the stage like an altar, the old man like an evil priest, taking the money, the painted pictures on the tent walls adding to the effect of a ritual or a mass.

"Once again, Miss Lana Lane!"

The woman walked onstage from the side curtains. She was entirely naked, except for her black beret, the first live naked woman I had seen in my life. Without her high heels she was flat-footed and walked like a soldier, her yellow feet slapping the stage. Her breasts were small, her legs heavy. She lifted her arms and laughed, then walked in a circle, smiling, not looking vulnerable in her nakedness, but defiant in the glare of lights and the raw upturned faces of the men.

The tent became more church-like, the men very quiet, concentrating, leaning and looking closely. When the woman walked near the edge of the stage I could see her flesh move, the nod of her breasts, the shake of her fattish thighs.

The silence of the men seemed to embolden her. She laughed out loud and snatched off her beret and rubbed it against her belly and the hair between her legs, seeming to exult. She held the beret on her secret spot, clutching herself, then flung it.

The beret sailed like a Frisbee toward me. I reached to smack it away and when it snagged on my fingers, a shout went up from the men.

"The kid caught it!"

By then the naked woman had walked offstage. Ray said, "Show's over," then "Put it on, kid."

I tugged the beret onto my head.

"On you it looks good." Ray led the way back to the car and slammed the door and sighed. "Work tomorrow."

"I got school."

"Good. Get an education, kid," he said. He squirmed in the front seat and faced Felix and me. "Or you'll end up like us."

Monday: soccer practice. I wore the beret ("What's that supposed to be?" Coach Ferretti said) but I did not tell anyone where I'd gotten it or what I'd seen, even afterward at Brigham's, when they were talking about girls' bodies and sex and how to buy Trojans at a drugstore.

"Big game Saturday," Roy said.

We practiced twice that week, doing sprints, exercises, headers, Ferretti saying, "This is a team. Never mind that it's Governor Dummer. We can win if we all work together."

That Friday afternoon, Roy said, "See you tomorrow on the bus"—he meant the game, the trip to Governor Dummer.

And I thought, *Maybe—my last game. I'll ask Crotty for Saturday off.* But going with the team, I knew I wouldn't play any serious time, I wouldn't score, I'd be on the bench; yet it also meant that I would not make myself conspicuous by staying away.

"We're collecting for the March of Dimes," Mr. Crotty said, before I could ask for Saturday off. He handed me a large can with a slot cut in the top. "I want you at the front door."

A cold dark early evening in raw mid-November, I wore my winter coat over my apron, and my beret pulled over my ears; and I shook my collecting can, "March of Dimes!" ambushing the shoppers leaving the store pushing their carts, wagging the can at them, making it jingle. I wanted it heavy with coins to present it to Mr. Crotty: *Look—it's full*, as a way of getting the day off on Saturday to go with the team to Governor Dummer.

By seven thirty, the can was weightier, the coins slewing and clanking. I obstructed the departing shoppers and surprised them with the can. The store closed at nine, then empty shelves to be restocked; and the walk to my grandmother's; and the game tomorrow. I did as I was told, I obeyed and behaved; yet I did not see where, in any of this, I belonged.

As I shook the can I imagined the soccer game and saw myself on the bench. *Shake, shake.* Shelves to stock. *Shake, shake.* Schoolwork, *shake, shake.* The can like the derby hat at the carnival show, filling with money. I didn't know what to do. Shaking the can was like shaking dice, trying to discern my fate, yet my belief was that I was no one, I was nowhere.

Absorbed in this I did not see the man approach me. I looked up and there he was, standing before me, too near, as though he knew me. He wore an overcoat and a wool scarf, and a green Tyrolean hat, a feather in the band. Carrying a briefcase, he peered at me through his gold-rimmed glasses, closing in, taking charge, as though he had chosen me and had an answer for me.

I held him at bay with my collecting can, tipping it toward him.

"March of Dimes, sir."

He leaned over the can and put his face near mine, but he was not looking me in the eye.

"I don't think I like your hat."

He had a well-fed face, smooth cheeks reddened in the cold, his green velour hat tipped to the side, with the jaunty feather. He was too close to me— ridiculously so for a customer; nor did he have a coin for the can.

I said in his voice, "I don't think I like *your* hat."

Instead of laughing, as I'd expected, he panted and became fierce. "You don't get it." He panted some more. "I don't like your hat."

"Right." It seemed a game, a contest in which it was a mistake to back down. "And I don't like yours." It seemed when I said it that his hat did seem much sillier than mine with that feather.

"Don't talk to me that way," he said, one of his front teeth snagging on his lower lip.

"You just said that to me!"

It seemed unfair—perverse. He could criticize my hat, but I couldn't say the same to him? And all this time I was darting at the customers, calling out, "March of Dimes," so they could put a coin in my can.

"I like my hat," I said, though until he had spoken to me I had barely been aware that I had it on. His mention of it provoked the memory of the carnival tent, and the naked woman, her flinging the beret at me, and Ray saying, *Put it on, kid*.

"Just who do you think you are?" the man said, his cheeks tightening with anger. He began to shout at me, then, gagging on his words and seeing that he was attracting attention, he seemed to think better of it. He rushed back into the store. I sneaked a look inside and saw that he was talking to Mr. Crotty, chopping the air with his hand. When he was done, he rushed toward me, red-faced, his arms working, swinging his briefcase, and for a moment I thought he was going to hit me. But he hurried past, into the parking lot, and the darkness.

Mr. Crotty was beckoning. I went inside.

"What happened out there?" *Out thay-ah.*

"The man said, 'I don't like your hat.'"

"And?"

"I said, 'I don't like *your* hat.'"

Mr. Crotty winced, then said, "What else?"

"He kept saying it. So did I. I thought he was joking."

Mr. Crotty did not look angry. He wanted detail, and the detail did not distress him—it seemed to fascinate him, as though he was hearing something reckless and bold, a kind of daring, and that he had found out something new and interesting about me. He did not want to betray his fascination yet I could see it a little like mirth, in his eyes, and in his nibbling lips.

"Do you know who that man is?"

"No, sir."

"He's Mr. Merrick Hackler, the area supervisor. He's very important. He doesn't joke. It was his surprise inspection." Mr. Crotty did not seem angry, and yet I fully believed I was going to be fired. But that did not dismay me. Being fired was something final—it was a direction, like knowing I was no good at soccer. "You upset him."

I said, "What should I do?"

"Don't do it again, ever." *Evah.* Was he smiling?

Now and then I'd had a glimpse of what it meant to be an adult, like seeing Ray at the carnival, or hearing *Making babies*, or *I've gotta to put food on the table*. Now I saw for the first time that Mr. Crotty had suffered, and hated Hackler, and that I had been an instrument of his revenge. But he could not reveal it to me. He looked sad and beaten, like a servant, in his blue smock-like coat with his odd name stitched on the pocket. I had thought of him as powerful, yet he was like the rest of us, Ray and Omar and Sal and Vinny and Felix—perhaps more punished.

By the next coffee break everyone knew—proof that Mr. Crotty had approved, probably told the assistant manager, who spread the word. The others were laughing when I entered the room.

Ray put his arm around me. "Andy, tell us exactly what you said to Hitler."

I told it haltingly. In this telling I was older and stronger, and the story more orderly; I was defiant and satirical, a wise guy.

"Know where the kid got that hat?" Ray said, and described the carnival, the naked woman, using the dirty words that came naturally to him.

As though coaching me, he said, "Sit down, kid. I want to hear it again. This is beautiful." He quieted the room with a shout. "Listen!"

I told the story again, more slowly, and in this version I was a hero, standing my ground, and Hackler was red as beet and had spittle on his lips.

"I don't like your hat!" Vinny shouted.

"I thought Crotty was going to fire me."

"They can't fire you. You're union! We're all union. We'd go on strike!"

Early the next day, Saturday, Roy Junkins appeared in the aisle I was stocking with jars of grape jelly, standing on a stepladder. He was carrying his gym bag. "The bus is leaving at noon." And in his sorrowing voice, "Andy."

I kept putting the jars on the shelf, sliding them back, lining them up.

"The team needs you."

I kept the crate propped against my chest. I didn't think of how I'd mastered this, pricing them and then using both hands. I thought of the break in about an hour, and a donut, and a hurried game of whist, and Vinny and Ray and Sal and Omar and Felix, and *Who dealt this mess?* I'd listen to their talk, and maybe they'd ask me to tell the story again.

"I'm working," I said.

Roy shrugged and scuffed the floor with his foot to show me he was disappointed. He looked small from where I stood on my ladder, as I watched him walk away, burdened by his gym bag bumping his leg, down the aisle, past Ray, past Mr. Crotty, out the door to the game. Then I resumed stocking the shelf, and whistling.

FIRST LOVE

Say good night to Grandpa," Jack said.

The boy murmured, "Good night," in a shy breathy singsong.

"Good night *what*?"

"Good night, Grandpa." Corrected, the boy looked miserable, mounting the stairs slowly, as though slightly lame, while I watched his small scuffing feet in sympathy, helpless to ease his awkwardness.

I was surprised a moment later when Jack said, "We need to talk, Dad," sounding severe in his demand, because I was thinking of the boy.

"Lovely kid," I said.

"He's got a lot on his mind."

"I was eleven once." I wanted to say more when Jack interrupted.

"He doesn't need to be told he's grown a lot since you last saw him."

"It was meant as a compliment. And that was not exactly what I said." I was about to say *I hate to be misquoted*, when Jack spoke again.

"You make these disownable assertions and you always avoid the point."

I knew I was being scolded, yet I couldn't help admiring Jack's precision, especially that neat smack with the back of his hand, *disownable*.

"He has no control over his height," Jack was saying. "It's not a compliment. He's the smallest boy in his class, and in case you're interested he's having a tough time at his new school."

"I could sense that," I said, beginning to rise from my chair, gripping the arms, thinking how, in old age, just getting up from a damn chair required a plan in advance for a sequence of moves.

"I'm not through, Dad."

Feeling scolded again, I sat heavily in protest and held my knees, noticing in my resentful scrutiny that my son's hair was going gray just above his ears, and that seemed to add to his air of severity.

"It's your absurd church story."

I said nothing but found more to criticize in my son's appearance—the uncombed hair, the sweater pulled out of shape, his expensive but unpolished shoes. Surely such negligence was unacceptable in (as Jack once described himself) a customer care coordinator, who needed to be a convincing authority figure and communicator. Or was he scruffy because his wife was away?

"Absurd how?"

"That you went to church with your old granny as a five-year-old. The long walk through the woods—miles apparently. And then you came to the river . . ."

"I know the story," I said. "Why are you rehashing it?"

"To emphasize how preposterous it is," Jack said. "How, at the river your old granny . . ."

"Please." I raised my hand and wagged my finger like a wiper blade before him, but he persisted.

". . . put you on her shoulder and waded across the river, until the water brimmed chest high."

Now I smiled, seeing it clearly—the old granny, the brown river, the small boy braced on her shoulder borne forth in the swift current to the far bank of tall reeds, the church steeple in the distance, like a pepper mill upright in torn clouds, the boy bright-eyed in the purple dawn, clinging to the white frizz on the old woman's head.

"I was trying to inspire him. It's about piety. Filial piety and spiritual piety."

"But it never happened," Jack said coldly.

"It most certainly happened." Then I smiled again. "Just not to me."

"He's not one of your readers, Dad. He's a small boy. He's struggling at school. And he's impressionable."

I said, "I never scolded you as you are doing to me now." I expected Jack to admit this, but instead he shook his head peevishly, looking more aged and careworn, while I sat and twinkled, as though defying him to reply.

"Maybe I never gave you cause to scold me." Jack had been standing all this time, and now he folded his arms and looked down at me, seated, still defiantly twinkling. "One more thing, Dad. Imagine how much richer your life would be if you listened."

"I have spent my whole life listening." And I folded my arms, in mimicry of my son, as though to signal I was about to change the subject. "Some grandparents sell their house and relocate. So that they can be near their grandchildren."

I saw the eager, futile, clumsy oldies, hovering, babysitting, twitching at the margins of the marriage, cheering the grandchildren's sports events, reading to them, taking them for ice cream, panting and stumbling to keep up with them, foolishly looking for praise.

"At least I've spared you that."

"Oh, yes, I just remembered. 'I loathe great acting.' 'I hate vacations.' 'Politics is choosing the tallest dwarf.'"

I had reddened as my son spoke, mimicking my voice. I said, "He told you, did he?"

"Look, I'm glad you're here, Dad, even if it's only a week. Obviously Ben looks up to you. He found you on the internet. He says he wants to read your books."

"I told him not to. That would spoil things," I said. Softening my tone, I said, "Does this mean I can't take him to school anymore?"

"No. I need you to. Laura won't be back for days. I have to go to work. You came at a good time. Just"—he raised his hand and lowered it like a hatchet to mean *Enough. No more.*

"I thought we had an understanding," I said the next day as we walked to school, the boy's short legs scissoring beside my loping legs. I remembered what Jack had said about Ben being the smallest boy in the class. But he was a beautiful boy, his hair silken, gray-blue eyes, long lashes, pale cheeks; his thin legs, his trousers stylishly tight. Yet even with his quickened stride he could not keep up with me.

Feeling the necessity to explain, but hating having to, I said, "My story about going to church, being carried across the river on my granny's shoulder—that was supposed to be our secret."

"Dad asked," the boy said, his voice hoarse with reluctance.

"Asked what?"

"If you were telling me stories."

"You could have said, 'I don't know.'"

"That wouldn't be true."

I saw that the boy was scrupulously honest—how awkward and inconvenient: he will never understand the irony and impressionism in my fiction.

"Right. So if I asked you, 'Do they talk about me?' would you tell me?"

"I guess so."

"What do they say?"

The child's face tightened, his eyes narrowing, as though looking at something in the distance. He's trying to remember, I thought at first. But something in the boy's posture, seeming to duck, making himself small, told me the boy was trying to forget.

"'He goes on and on about his new book.'" In that believable sentence the boy lapsed into a new voice, which I took to be not Jack's but Laura's.

"Heigh-ho," I said, with a wave of my hand, as though undoing a curse. Then, softly, "Maybe I shouldn't tell you any more stories."

The boy was silent but his face contorted for a second with a noticeable twitch, as though an insect had hit his cheek.

"Unless you want me to."

From the way Ben slowed and trudged I could tell he was pondering this, thinking hard, each footstep like a sudden shifting thought, and I remembered, *He's got a lot on his mind*, so I didn't press him.

At the school gate, he said, "Are you coming to the soccer game this afternoon?" and added, "You don't have to if you don't want to."

"I wouldn't miss it for anything."

"Dad never comes—he's always working."

"He's a customer care coordinator," I said, trying not to sound satirical. But the boy hadn't heard. He'd sprinted into the schoolyard, in the direction of a dark girl in a blue beret, bigger than he, who smiled when she saw him.

I spent the rest of the day recopying a story I'd written in longhand, thinking, *I must remember to tell the boy this*. My method was to write a draft in ballpoint, but instead of correcting it line by line I set the pages before me and copied them, correcting as I went, and always the story was enlarged, the dialogue crisper, the descriptions denser. But the light was bad, the chair was wrong, I missed my own desk, and at last I left the house, walking by a longer route to the delicatessen, disliking the idea that I was killing time, and hating the useless hours afterward on a park bench, looking like a futile old man, waiting for the school day to end.

The game had started by the time I got to it. I watched with the mothers, surprised by their youth, admiring how lovely they looked in their enthusiasm. I caught Ben's eye and waved to him, but I lost interest in the game and turned to the people in the stands, the mothers near me, the students sitting apart—girls and boys together, all races, confident, casually dressed, and I saw among the other spectators the dark girl in the blue beret, her chin in her hands, and now I saw her eager eyes, her pretty lips, her face brightened by her glee watching the game. She stood out from all the others, but she was too young to know how lovely she was, and that her life would be both blessed and cursed by her beauty.

Then, distracted, I grew sad seeing a boy in a necktie and long-sleeved shirt, with spiky hair, sitting apart from the others—the boy I had been, even to the chewed tie; tense, unathletic, puny, hoping not to be noticed. I spent the rest of the game glancing at the dark girl, grieving for the geeky loner.

"When I was eleven," I said on the walk home, "that was a big year. I fell in love."

I saw Ben look away, and he began to walk faster.

"She was the new girl in the class, from Holland, amazingly enough. 'Our Dutch girl' the teacher called her. She was a bit bigger than me and she had a beautiful face. Marta van de Velde. It was my first experience of love."

I looked at the boy for a reaction. Still silent, Ben shifted his gym bag from one shoulder to the other. He said, "Did you see my header? Did you see us score that goal at the end?"

"Of course—that was outstanding."

But I hadn't seen. I had been thinking of Marta van der Velde, her smooth face and blue eyes, her small prim lips, the way she sat, her twitching lashes when she looked down, her hands clasped on the desktop. What was it that attracted me? Her beauty, certainly, but something else—a suggestion of humor in her watchfulness, and a gentle manner. And her flesh. She was someone I wanted to touch, someone I wished to hold. That was it—to hold her, and be held. I was, at that age, innocent of anything more.

She sat across the aisle, the new girl Marta, in her white blouse with the lace collar and the bunchy skirt and black buckled shoes. And I stared, twisting my chewed tie in my bitten fingers and wishing to hold her—somehow, to lie next to her, as I imagined later, my eyes shut tight, before I went to sleep.

"Why did you like her?"

"Good question!" I said, "It was her smile, her smooth cheeks, her eyes, her pretty fingers. She was sweet. She wasn't a tease."

"Is that all?"

"She didn't look like any of the other girls. And she was nicer than me."

"In what way?"

"I love these questions, Ben. She was happier. She was better in most ways. She had unusual handwriting—upright and strong. I liked seeing her holding the thick pen in her delicate fingers."

"There's a girl in my class, Brady—she's like that."

I had been thinking of Marta. I said, "I didn't know what to say to her."

"Brady smiles a lot, but she never talks to me. She's bigger than me. She plays volleyball." Seeing that I was not responding, he narrowed his eyes and went silent.

But the boy's silence provoked me, and in some small corner of my brain I recaptured the boy's words as a whispered echo, the name of the girl.

"Her first name is Brady?"

The boy nodded and said, "But she has her own friends."

"All I wanted to do was look at her, stare endlessly at her, as you would a work of art. What would you say to a work of art? You'd just stand there like a goofball and admire it and feel small, lost in your fascination."

Ben said, "We've got another game on Friday," and quickly, "You don't have to go if you don't want to."

"I'll be there," I said. "Maybe Brady will be there."

The boy shrugged, hunching his shoulders, looking smaller.

"I followed her home," I said.

The boy was trudging again, each slapping footfall like an arrested thought.

"I loved her," I said. "I didn't know what to do." The memory possessed me, induced a reverie, and in my concentration I forgot where I was until I got to the walkway of my son's house. I said, "This is between us."

"What is?"

"What I just told you."

"I didn't understand what you were saying."

I patted the boy's smooth cheek, my hand lingering on its warmth.

I counted on seeing Ben: by concentrating on him I understood myself at that age. I had not realized how small I'd been at eleven, and—though I'd also played on the soccer team and competed with the rest of the boys in the gym in phys ed—how puny.

So I grieved for my younger self, but I knew that boy better—the boy I'd been—and I marveled that I'd been so bold as to declare my love for Marta van der Velde. I remembered it: the small brown paper bag of fresh fudge, and the note inside, *I love you.* I'd covertly raised the lid on her desk before school and left it inside, next to her fat pen, and her pencils and ruler.

Had she known it was from me? I hoped so.

"Do you want to impress Brady?" I asked Ben after school the day before the game. "By playing well? Maybe scoring a goal?"

"I'm a wing," Ben said. "I pass the ball to the striker."

"But are you happy to see Brady in the stands?"

"I don't think about it."

I nodded—it was just what I would have said, and I was glad once again to be reminded of the habitual evasions of my younger self.

"Of course not, why should you? You've got other things to think about," I said. "Tell me about your English teacher."

"Mr. Bowlus. He has hairy ears."

I laughed out loud and began to cough and staggered a little.

"Are you all right, Grandpa?"

Too moved to answer, I hugged the boy and then realized that he was trying to twist free.

• • •

I was at first puzzled by the smell of bacon the next morning, the clank of a kettle, the bubbling of eggs frying in fat—odors and sounds from the kitchen that seemed intrusive because I was unused to them. Laura, busy at the stove, kept her back turned when I greeted her, saying I was glad to see her. But I was dismayed, because her showing up meant an interruption of my routine with Ben.

Laura said, "Hi!" calling out to me over her shoulder, while shoveling in the skillet with her spatula and whacking it once.

Seeing Jack opening his car door, I hurried to the driveway and said, "I had no idea Laura was coming back so soon."

"She lives here, Dad. She's my wife."

"Maybe I should go."

I wanted him to protest: *No, stay. It's great having you here.*

But he said, "It's up to you."

That left me without a reply, and after Jack had gone to work, hearing Laura in the kitchen, talking on the phone as she chopped—What? Onions, carrots—on the butcher block, holding the phone in the crook of her shoulder and ear as she worked, slashing (it seemed to me) harder than necessary, I felt excluded, and superfluous, the chopping sounds like a severe warning.

I had apologized to them for this visit as an interruption, yet I knew they did not allow themselves to be interrupted. They were in motion when I arrived, and they stayed in motion. They did not break their stride. They worked, they went out. *We're seeing friends*—wasn't I a friend?—*You have a chance to bond with Ben.*

I'd saved them the cost of a babysitter, yet being with Ben was what I wanted. And there was the game.

Searching the stands for the girl I'd seen smiling at Ben that first day in the schoolyard, and at the previous game, I spotted her easily, the blue beret, the cheeks the shade of milky coffee, and bright eyes, the glint of green, dark eyebrows, full lips—a beauty. Her loose tracksuit bulked on her but her hands and wrists were slender. She was smallish, the size of Marta van der Velde—

but bigger than Ben; not a woman yet but a girl, unformed, a luminous child, concentrating on the game that had just begun.

I followed the game through Brady's gestures and expressions, the way she clapped when the ball was kicked, her hands over her face, peering through her parted fingers at tense moments, clawing at her beret at the sound of a whistle. She sat with other girls but she seemed oblivious of them, until one of them tapped her arm and pointed behind her. A tall smiling boy dropped beside her and, using his elbow, rocked her sideways, her whole body swaying, as he laughed.

She didn't object, neither did she speak to him. Her fingers laced together, she averted her eyes, as—I saw—Ben labored to keep the ball between his feet, dancing around it, causing the opposing player to lurch and stumble. But Brady didn't see Ben's nimble move. She was distracted, looking down, her hands over her ears. With the tall boy beside her, she'd lost her smile and had stiffened.

Marta in her strange upright handwriting had eventually thanked me for the fudge, but she had never mentioned the note, the words of which now embarrassed me again, more acutely than the first time when, waiting to follow her home, she was nowhere to be seen.

Preoccupied with this memory, my back to the stands, I did not see Brady leave, and the tall boy was gone, too, though I had no way of telling whether they'd left together.

"That's our first loss," Ben said afterward.

Had there been a scoreboard? I hadn't noticed.

"I was sitting near Brady," I said. "She was watching you."

"Okay," the boy said without emphasis.

"Isn't that what you want?"

He was silent, his gym bag bumping his leg. After five steps he said, "I don't know."

I was sorry we were nearing the house, where I couldn't speak to him as I wished. But passing the park bench where I'd killed time two days ago I suggested we sit for a while.

"Marta van der Velde had a friend," I said, as I sat. "One of the bigger boys. A seventh grader."

"Did you know him?"

"We didn't know any of the older boys—not their names. They never spoke to us. Seventh graders were thirteen."

"We're all on the playground together," Ben said.

"I don't even think he was in our school."

"Did she like him?"

"I think she was afraid of him. He was big. He made me feel small."

Saying that I seized the boy's attention. And I remembered Jack saying, *He's small for his age*.

"He met her after school," I said. "When we came out to the street he was there, waiting. She walked quickly over to him, being obedient, and she seemed afraid of him. He took charge of her, standing so close to her that when I walked by I could barely see her. His arms were around her, as though he was folded over her."

"Did you say anything?"

"At first I didn't know what to say." I was looking closely at Ben. "Then the next day in class I said, 'I'm going to California. I'm not sure when I'll be back.'"

The boy squinted and looked doubtful, unprepared for "California."

"It was a sunny, far-off place—palm trees, and heat, and the Pacific Ocean."

"It was a lie."

"It was a hope, Benny. It was a wish."

I remembered more, another dream, of Africa: I wanted to know what no one else knew. I wanted to go where no one had ever gone. I did not want to be told anything; I wanted to be the teller.

"I felt small," I said. "I wanted to impress her."

The boy looked doubtful again, shaking his head slightly, with uncertain eyes.

"I loved her," I said. "That was my way of telling her."

And my belief was that if I am prevented from doing what I want to do, I will be unhappy. I knew I needed to be original in order to exist; to distinguish myself in some way to Marta and everyone else, to defend myself in doing this thing, whatever it might be, in art, or writing, or travel, and I knew nothing of any of those things, but if I dared and took a risk I might find out.

"Did you tell anyone?" Ben asked—he was thinking of *I loved her*.

"I couldn't," I said, and I now realized why: because I wanted to keep the secret in my heart. No one knew what it was. If I told anyone they'd tease me and tell me it was a weakness, and try to thwart me, because in the past whenever I revealed something I felt deeply about I was mocked.

"You could have told the girl."

"Marta van der Velde," I said. "I wanted her so badly." I resisted saying that I hated that seventh grader who'd put his arms around her. "For a long time I didn't want to think about it. I'm thinking about it now in a new way, and it's very awkward. Do you understand?"

"You're thinking about it now," the boy stated plainly, and it seemed in his repeating it that it was proof of his understanding.

"It's like this," I said. "You receive something special in a big box. It's very well packed—a painting, a lamp, a vase—and you unpack it carefully, saving all the wrapping. And when the object is unpacked and looking very small and delicate, you put it aside and take all the tissue, the padding and the Bubble Wrap, the straw and Styrofoam beads and put them all back in the box. But it won't fit. A third of the stuff lies at your feet." I found myself giggling sadly. "It just will not fit."

The boy drew back, looking alarmed, and lifted his gym bag to his thighs as though to protect himself.

"How is it that you can take more out of a box than you can fit back in?" I said, my voice rising.

Clutching his gym bag, the boy looked as though he was going to cry.

"Memories are like that," I said. "You've taken too much out. And you're stuck with it." Seeing that the boy seemed frightened and tearful, I said, "But I'm lucky. I became a writer. A writer can always dispose of those extra memories."

"Where have you been?" Jack said, greeting us at the door, when we got to the house.

"We lost the game," Ben said.

"Remember when I asked you what your parents said about me?" I asked Ben the next day on the way to school. I had stewed miserably in the night, and slept badly, recalling Marta van der Velde and *I'm going to California*.

The boy nodded, his face tightening, looking accused.

"'He goes on and on about his new books,' you said."

"*They* said it," the boy was swift in his rebuttal.

"It's true—and you know why?"

He made a face, twisting it, to indicate he didn't know or didn't want to venture a guess.

"Because no one else does, Benny," I said. "I need to keep the thought of my work alive in my mind, and sometimes talk about it, because I'm not sure it's alive in anyone else's mind."

We continued to walk, Ben beside me, trudging again, as always his bewilderment evident in the way his feet moved.

"What else did they say?"

In a reciting voice, the boy said, "'Writers are never satisfied with their books. But Andre is.'"

I was stung, but I laughed, admiring my son again. So it seemed I had fathered a wit, even if the wit was used against me.

"'He's arrogant'; I suppose they say that."

Ben said, "No—they don't."

"But people do. It's not arrogance—it's a survival skill." I thought again of Marta van der Velde. I said, "Do people say to you, 'I know what you want, little boy!'"

"Sometimes."

"But they never do. They never know. They used to say that to me. They thought they knew. But they had no idea, because they didn't know me." I lowered my head and looked at the boy. "You're wondering what I wanted."

The question startled him. He said, "I guess so."

"I wanted to go where no one else went," I said. "I wanted to know what no one else knew. I wanted to do what no one else did."

"How do you do that?"

"By becoming a hero," I said. "That's what Marta van der Velde gave me. A wish to be bold. A determination to excel."

"Action hero," Ben said.

"I didn't know that expression." Then I covered my face. "Oh god, I've talked too much. Are you going to tell them? Promise me you won't."

"I promise," he said, looking terrified.

That evening, Jack said, "We've got a dinner tonight. Some friends."

Saying that always sounded to me as though my son was hinting that I was not a friend.

"I'm glad to babysit."

"No. They're coming here. They're expecting you to be here."

I relaxed at the thought of meeting new people—they might be readers. They were the Strawsons, Jack said: he in marketing, she a teacher. Their son was in Ben's class.

"I'll need to get ready," I said and went up to my room and poured myself a large whiskey. Hearing the doorbell ring I waited until I heard greetings, then drank the last of my whiskey and joined my son and his friends.

"This is my father," Jack said.

"Andre Parent," I said and looked closely for any sign of recognition.

We ate, I listened, no questions were directed my way, I smiled and responded at the right moments, and toward the end of the meal Jack said across the table, "I've been meaning to ask you guys about your trip."

"India." And the man turned to me. "Have you been to India?"

"Many times. All over," I said. "Wrote about it."

But the man was still talking, describing his impressions of India, the poor people, the noise, the food, his wife chipping in with, "The crowds, the dust, the heat—you wouldn't believe the squalor."

"I just remembered," I said. "I promised to tell Ben a story."

"We'll save you some dessert."

The boy was too sleepy to listen. I sat by the bed, seeing myself in the boy, conjuring up the image of Marta van der Velde, whom I had not thought of for sixty-five years. Yet it was she who had aroused the desire in me that I took to be love—and it must have been love, because it had inspired my chivalrous wish to be a hero. The inspiration not a book, not a great historical figure, not a rousing speech by a teacher; but a shy pretty Dutch girl, newly arrived, with a smooth face and gray-blue eyes, a compact figure at the desk beside me, who had been claimed by an older boy. She had given me something else to love and long for.

I dozed, and when I woke, Jack was beside me, his hand on my shoulder.

"I must have nodded off."

I tottered to my room yawning, but, having been abruptly awakened, could not get to sleep for a while. I remembered that Marta van der Velde had the beginnings of a figure—and I smiled in the dark. It was the purest love; nothing had preceded it, nor had I told anyone in my life. *But my life is my response to that first love.*

I woke late, Ben had gone to school. I regretted that I had missed him, the morning walk, the conversation with the boy that provoked memories.

They had finished breakfast. Laura was tidying. Fussing, putting things in order seemed to be her way of ignoring me, because in the act of tidying she could always blamelessly turn her back to me.

"Did you tell him?" she said.

Jack cleared his throat. "Laura has some friends coming later today. We'll need your room."

"Later today" meant I'd have to leave soon. But this sort of rudeness had the effect of making me excessively polite and accommodating, to remove the curse. I became hearty, I said I understood. I went upstairs to my room and gathered my clothes and my whiskey bottle and packed my bag. Then I sat in the parlor with my hands in my lap. I didn't want to face them. What was there to say? I was being expelled.

"I got your car out of the garage," Jack said. "It's a tricky driveway."

"That was thoughtful."

"Benny will be sorry he missed you," Laura called from the next room. I could see she was sorting magazines, flipping them, kneeling, facing away.

"Tell him something for me," I said. "Tell him I'm going to California. I'm not sure when I'll be back."

THE SILENT WOMAN

After a wretched, wakeful night, my hot head buzzing with annoyance, I sat squirming in my study waiting for Ollie to arrive. At nine he put his head in, smiling with his usual greeting, "How are we doing, Andy?"

I said (as I'd rehearsed, tossing in bed), "I'd rather you didn't call me *Andy*."

This was a week or so into our arrangement, his acting as my research assistant.

"But it's your name, dude."

I stiffened and said, "I'm Andre to my readers. Andy to my friends, Mr. Parent to everyone else."

"Like, aren't we friends?"

Looking puzzled, Ollie slouched into the room and sat on the sofa. And that was another thing. I had not invited him into my study, I had not given him permission to sit, and, maddening to me, he began, head down, to pick at a magazine on the coffee table, which I found boorish and intrusive.

Nor had he removed his bulgy black wool hat, which enclosed his head like a toque and gave contrast to his pale face, pinkish in spots from exertion, or maybe affront. He sat forward, teetering slightly at the edge of a cushion, knees together, plucking at the magazine with slender fussy fingers, paging past the story I'd published in it, my admittedly egotistical reason for it lying on top of the stack.

I believed that everything about Ollie Pirkle could be explained by his being twenty-two years old and just out of college. Audacious—a word he liked—he might have replied that everything about me could be explained by my being seventy-six. But never mind my years; I was then and still am a reasonably productive writer, most of my books in print, and I was contemplating a new book, an unusual one for me, for which I needed help. I was planning a novel based on the early working life of George Orwell, when he was still unpublished and gauche Eric Blair, employed as a policeman in Burma, five years doing a job he later admitted he "thoroughly disapproved of."

I advertised for a research assistant at the local college and asked each applicant the reason for their wanting it. Ollie's answer was the best.

"One of your novels was withdrawn from a course I was taking," he said.

"Really—why?"

"Curriculum-based trauma. Trigger issues. Objectifying women." Ollie had a lovely ironical smile. "It made me want to read it."

"Sixty years ago that's why I wanted to read Henry Miller." The name meant nothing to him, so I said, "What do you think of my book?"

"I downloaded it. I'll let you know when I've read it.""

Ollie wanted to be a writer, he said—a wish that made me wary—but what worried me more was his answer to my saying, "I'd need you to do some intensive research."

He said, "Sure—as long as I don't have to go to a library."

I was too shocked to laugh. I said, "A library is where books are found."

"I can find stuff online."

"All of it?"

"Why not?"

He did not know that George Orwell was a pen name. He had not read *1984*, though he was aware that it was a novel about the future—which he found hilarious ("Like, *1984* was almost forty years ago!"). But he used the word *Orwellian* with confidence, to describe oppression and despotic government control.

I explained my book. This was the man no one paid much attention to, the almost unrecognizable Eric Blair, the young embarrassing policeman—embarrassing in later years to Orwell himself—like an antihero out of Kipling, a rogue in uniform, flourishing a swagger stick, drilling his native inspectors, and ordering beatings and arrests. Blair the colonial, the womanizer others called a poodle-faker, and—though secretly, silently doubtful—a servant of the 1920s British Raj. It was an experience so intense and shameful he resigned and, atoning, became a dishwasher in Paris and a tramp in London. Ultimately, with a name change he was the ascetic left-wing anticolonial pamphleteer and prescient novelist who called himself George Orwell.

I put Ollie on probation and challenged him with an assignment. "I need you to assist me in finding details of his life as a policeman."

"I can do that."

"He wrote an essay called 'A Hanging.' I suspect it took place while he was posted for four months to a prison, a place called Insein, not far from Rangoon. See what you can scare up."

Ollie busied himself in the upper story of my garage—so-called carriage house—where I'd set up a desk and a printer, working at his laptop, while I continued my narrative, writing as usual in longhand in my study. Within an hour he'd downloaded *Finding George Orwell in Burma*, which of course I'd read—the physical book in my study.

"Good on the present woes in Burma. Excellent on topography. Thin on the past. Nothing about Orwell that isn't in the biographies. Also, a bit tendentious."

"Meaning?"

"Look it up."

But he dug deeper; he brought me pages from a colonial officer who'd worked at the prison, some anecdotes of a High Court judge who'd visited prisoners there, including some men in the condemned cell, and, last, his triumph, an aerial view of Insein Prison as it looked in 1925, a great mandala wheel, corridors as spokes, the cells ranged along the periphery of the rim.

Smoothing it on my desk he said, "Says here it's a panopticon, whatever that means."

"'All-seeing'—Greek."

None of the biographies mentioned that the prison in Burma was a panopticon, nor its connection with Jeremy Bentham and Foucault, nor—importantly—its relation to the Orwellian concept of surveillance.

"That makes sense. The watchtower in the middle of the thing—all the cells are visible."

"Like *1984*. One person can see everything. Big Brother. Orwellian."

"Bingo."

He impressed me by adding that before looking for the Insein material he read "A Hanging" and remarked, "What I really liked was the prisoner sees a puddle and steps aside, so he doesn't get his feet wet. And he's, like, going to his death."

"That's the hammer stroke," I said. "You're hired, Ollie."

"Cool."

The radical transformation seemed to fascinate Ollie greatly, especially Blair the old Etonian bullying the Burmese and boozing in the Gymkhana Club, the "Shooting an Elephant" years, the shortest and least-detailed chapter in any Orwell biography, usually based on misleading descriptions in his novel *Burmese Days.* That tall skinny callow youth, just about Ollie's age, had power and responsibility and a gun and a whip, a pukka sahib, while Ollie was— what?—inexperienced, still living with Mummy, with all the presumption of someone who knows nothing of the world. *Aren't we friends* was a perfect example of that.

"I've known you, I guess, a week?"

"Ten days," he said, looking down, still flicking at the magazine. "I started on the fifteenth."

Hating the fact that he was avoiding eye contact—but it was his way—I said, speaking to his wool hat, "Friendship takes a little longer than that to ripen. It is earned through trust. You're my employee, Ollie. And I'm many years your senior. Perhaps a little formality is in order."

He closed the magazine he'd been slashing at as I gave this sententious speech. Then he looked at me, with a slight smirk. "I can't get past your name."

I resisted reminding him that his name was Ollie Pirkle. I said, "*Parent* is French. Properly 'Poronh.' It's Quebecois, shortened way back from *Parenteau.*"

"What do you want me to call you?"

"Have you heard of a writer called Robert Frost?"

"Yes, but I haven't read any of his stuff."

"A wonderful poet," I said. "When I was about your age I saw him walking down the street in Amherst, where I was a student. I ran into a nearby bookstore and bought his latest collection of poems, *In the Clearing*, then followed him into the Jones Library and asked him to sign it."

"And, like, did he freak out?"

"No, he signed it. But my point is I said, 'Thank you, Mr. Frost.' He was in his eighties. I was twenty-one. He seemed to me a shaman, an enchanter, shaggy-haired Tiresias in an overcoat, squinting into the distance. 'Thank you, Mr. Frost.'"

Ollie went silent as he shrugged; it seemed to me his generation didn't know how to apologize, because they could always download reasons to believe they were right.

My life, my work, was ruled by routine. But Ollie had no routine—he was often late, he was sometimes early, he squatted like a monkey on his chair before his computer and would have missed lunch most days had I not signaled to him that it was time to leave for the café in town. He had poor table manners, he sat askew, he picked at his food with his fingers, he never took off his wool hat, he played with his phone as he ate, he was like a small child. But there was a sweetness in his disposition, a vulnerability obvious in his pallor that gave me concern. His intelligence had never been seriously tested. The fingers he used to eat with were delicate and graceful—South Indians ate like that off a palm leaf; and with the softness of a small child he seemed somehow oddly edible.

One day, out shopping, I bumped into a prof from Willard who said, "I see you at Grumpy's these days in the company of an epicene young man."

"A good kid—really smart," I said, insulted by the description. "My research assistant."

But the recondite word nagged at me and led me out of curiosity that evening to look for my copy of Jonson's plays and reread *Epicene*. I had it in my study the next day when Ollie came in to deliver some notes.

Seeing the fat old book open before me he said, "Any good Blair stuff in it?"

He couldn't imagine that, embarked on my writing project, I'd be reading about anything except Blair or Orwell.

"No—it's a Jonson play. *Epicene*."

"Like, Doctor Johnson?"

"Ben Jonson, the playwright."

"Two Johnsons—cool."

"You majored in English, Ollie, and you didn't know that?"

"I majored in Creative Writing at Willard—a great program. And I guess there's a ton of things I don't know." He was not chastened, he was a Gen Z nonapologist, delivering news. He tapped his phone. "But I can always find out."

And later that day he said he'd found the whole play on the internet, and read it—"But I skipped some of the boring speeches"—and was thrilled by its invention and its jokes, especially the charade of the marriage, the substitution of the character Epicene in the marriage. "Like a kind of transgressive rom-com."

With that he started out of the room, but remembering, turned and added, "That amazing subtitle, 'The Silent Woman.' And the word *epicene* is awesome, not effeminate but both genders at once."

"I think it means effeminate."

"You're wrong. It means both male and female. Except in some cases the woman is silent."

You're wrong was an impudent expression I naturally resented in any context. But I checked the definition—it, too, was Greek—and it meant possessing both male and female characteristics. Ollie was right. And I admired his curiosity and diligence, how he'd taken the time to read the play and respond, as he had with Orwell's "A Hanging."

I have mentioned that he was like a small child, and in many ways he was—impulsive, clumsy, innocent of the world. That made me protective toward him, but I was also protective because he was so resourceful, so helpful to me in my project. He found diaries and letters of old Burma hands, he introduced me to books of Burmese fauna and flora, he unearthed a memoir of an opium addict Blair had known in Mandalay, one Captain Robinson, also a policeman, who'd become a Buddhist monk to kick the drug, and when that failed, he'd attempted suicide. But his pistol slipped and instead of blowing his brains out he'd blinded himself. George Orwell had favorably reviewed the memoir in 1944.

"Crazy family."

He meant Blair's French grandmother, Madame Limouzin, who had lived most of her life in Moulmein, and Blair's louche uncles, one married to an Indian, another to a Burmese, and Blair's half-caste cousins, despised by the British, one for being a chee-chee, the other a Chutney Mary, belittling words that Ollie found online and taught me.

"Check this out."

It was a photograph of tall smiling Eric Blair the policeman in a group photograph of his fellow policemen in Mandalay.

"And compare it with this."

Another photograph, this one of George Orwell, the combatant in the Spanish Civil War, fierce, unsmiling, Trotskyite, anticolonial.

"It's like two different people."

"Yes, Ollie. That's what interests me. His experience in Burma as a sahib with servants turned him into his opposite, initially a dishwasher and a tramp, and for the rest of his life being free. He said something like, 'Freedom of speech is the right to tell people what they don't want to hear.'"

"That blows me away," Ollie said, and he faltered, covering his face with his pale hands and murmuring beneath his fingers in a prayerful way. Taking a deep breath, he recovered, dropping his hands. "Like, how did he explain it in his autobiography?"

"He didn't write one. And he tried to prevent a biography from being written about him. Needless to say, he didn't succeed. There's a dozen of them."

"What about you? When are you going to write one?"

"Someone once said that Malraux's books were messy and conventional. But his life as an adventurer and cultural celebrity and poseur was a masterpiece. My life is not a masterpiece."

"What is it?"

"Messy and conventional in part. Episodic and reckless and filled with bad decisions. I once wrote a story, 'Two of Everything,' how I had two lovers, two houses, two countries. Now I can hardly claim one. Henry James said, 'Live all you can.' Foolishly, I took his advice. I overdid it, owing to my ardent and irrational esurience."

Ollie stared at the word *esurience* leaving my lips.

"Look it up," I said. "And you?"

He said, "My life, like, hasn't really started."

Ollie left me with that melancholy thought. I resisted telling him that when I was his age I was in Central Africa, living all I could, and along with its excesses it gave me something to write about. And later my marriages, my son, my failures, the wreckage, and, as Borges said, my supreme solitude in old age.

I was immersed in the past, he was peering into the future. He talked about living; I thought constantly of dying. It was a pleasure to be with someone who didn't complain about ailments and ill-health, someone so casually life-affirming.

He reminded me that I was out of touch with the present, that the world I'd known had moved on. But he was ignorant of the past, the names of recent presidents rang no bells, Vietnam was a name he knew, but a blur. Speaking of Orwell and religious fanaticism I once alluded to 9/11.

"I was born that year."

Apart from my books, which he'd begun to read, he'd read almost nothing. He'd never traveled, he couldn't drive, and it was only after working for me for a month that he'd moved out of his mother's house into an attic room in town. "I need it for my sanity—my family's a serious obstacle to my mental health. Kind of like Blair's, I guess. Or yours."

He mentioned the books of mine that had addressed the subject of dysfunctional families. And I was reminded again of why I'd hired him—because he held my work in high regard, and I was vain enough to be grateful to him for that.

Still, he unearthed helpful material, details of the sort of uniform Blair the policeman would have worn, information about the Burmese nationalist movements, the street entertainments known as "pwe," the food, the weather, and what timber company had probably owned the elephant Blair had shot in Moulmein in 1926.

Ollie lived online. It was his mode of being. For meals, for shopping, for games. His friends, he said, were online. As a nondriver he found his rides online. The internet was a conduit to his brain and his being. He lived with that odd presumption you might mistake for asceticism, without physical books, without paper, sharing but always presuming he'd find what he needed—food, rides, information, and I suppose love. It was not asceticism, it was an effortless—a privileged—existence. Princes lived like that. His computer was his tool for writing: he said he wrote every day.

"Want to show me something you've written?"

"I finished a piece, about ten pages, but I'm not happy with it. It seems tendentious."

"Here's what to do. Get a pen and some lined paper and copy it out, long-hand. I guarantee that after you recopy it slowly you'll find it improved."

He laughed and said, "Write the whole thing like this?" making a silly scribbling gesture, helplessly wagging his hand. "That's too much work."

"Writing is work, Ollie. I order you to do it."

He did, he struggled, he had poor penmanship, he wrote mainly in block letters, like a first grader. I didn't read what he wrote but I glanced at a page and it looked to me like a long, semiliterate ransom note. That was a surprise, that he'd never learned to write properly in longhand, but apart from that he was without any surprises. That was what it meant to be young—to be unsurprising, to live in that princely way online, tapping out commands. While for me, at my age, nothing was new. My fingers were ink-stained, I was weighed down by experience, some I'd never off-loaded, as I told him.

"Like what?"

"Like the most beautiful woman I'd ever seen I found in a bar called the White Rose in Vientiane. I walked in and saw her surrounded by about eight other women. I walked up to her and she took my hand and led me to her room."

"Just like that?"

"It was during the Vietnam War."

"That again. So what happened."

"I must draw a veil over what followed with the Silent Woman."

"Ha!"

"But that was in another country, and besides the wench is dead."

"You're full of these great quotes!"

"What's that about votes?" I said and turned my good ear to him.

"I think you're going deaf, Mr. Parent."

Stating the obvious was another of his traits, characteristic of the presumptuous young, as a child will say, *You have a big nose*.

"I'm not deaf—deafness is silence. I hear a hum, a buzz, I hear you speaking in your particular voice, but I don't always understand. You say, 'My suitcase,' and I hear 'Buy toothpaste.' But that's the least of my infirmities. Please go find some more Blair, Ollie."

Even given his pallor and occasional languor, it was shaming to have a young robust man around. His good health intimidated me and sometimes depressed me, like an obscure and indigent writer being in the presence of a bestselling author, outshined and envious and resentful, and reminded of their failure.

It is also in the nature of being twenty-two to be self-absorbed, but this was exaggerated by his online life, always facing a screen, which made him supremely inattentive to me when I was anywhere near him.

To get his attention I'd say, "I've been told I have the face of an apostle." When he didn't glance my way, I'd add, "I have rarely made a rational decision in my life." Then I'd give up.

Over lunch, I told him that I sometimes drove to New York City to see my editor. I knew the location of every rest stop men's room for two hundred and fifty miles. I woke twice a night for a bathroom break. I often stumbled, I had trouble hoisting myself out of the bath. Cataract surgery had left me with "floaters," and so out of the corner of my eye I might see a rabbit or a rodent or a blown leaf, which was in fact a floater in my aqueous humor. I'd lost most of my hair, many of my teeth, my arm strength, my mojo. I was cursed with anomia, my memory for names impaired. "He was in that movie"—and of course Ollie didn't know the movie, but he'd find it on his phone. Certain words eluded me. "It's a French word, it's often used with hieroglyphics, it means a sort of oblong frame."

Ollie tapped his phone. "Cartouche."

After almost two months, I realized that he'd found all the essential Blair material and knew Blair well enough to say that, as a single man in Rangoon, Blair had been at times esurient. But I'd embarked on my book; I didn't need Ollie. Actually I did need him, but it was tedious to have such a young man around all the time—his bad posture annoyed me, his awkwardness made me impatient, I hated his silly hat. Long ago, when I'd been a teacher, I kept my job because I felt I was learning from my students; and when I stopped learning, I knew it was time to resign. I had never looked back.

What did I want now? I wanted more—not sex, not two of everything, but a nurturing friendship, an awakening to something new, an adventure, a revelation, a thing I'd never known before, truly life-affirming and surprising, relieving my loneliness and offering me hope, something that I could believe in, that would make me as happy, as writing always did, to stop me thinking about death—to be more than entranced. I craved to be exhilarated.

Ollie was useful as a researcher, but it was the first time in my life I'd spent with an employee so young. I began to regret that I'd admitted him to my life. I had learned quite a bit from his searches but personally, he held no surprises. He was a drudge, the humming unstoppable circuit of the internet passing through his body. It pleased me that this circuit allowed him to discover details of Blair's Burma. He said it was all a revelation. He'd never been lacking in presumption but he said he was more confident now.

"Empowering," he said, which made me smile. "I feel I've grown. I live on my own now. I'm my own person. Thank you, Eric Blair, for becoming George Orwell. Thank you, Mr. Andre Parent."

Yet I could not detect a difference. He looked the same as when he'd said to me that he'd be my research assistant, *As long as I don't have to go to the library*—a sentence I still found astonishing.

One lunchtime at Grumpy's I steeled myself and said, "Friday will be your last day."

Ollie nodded his thickly hatted head but hardly looked up from his phone. That seemed another trait, his manner of acceptance—that he was naïve and yet unshockable, from years of soft landings and safety nets. He knew he'd find another job in this era of labor shortages.

Friday came, I'd had another bad night before, wakeful, hotheaded, wondering if I'd made the right decision, resenting the thought that I'd be alone, writing my book, solitary meals at the café, probably bumping into the Willard prof who'd ask, "What's become of your epicene friend?" But it was the life I'd chosen, and I'd been reminded many times of what a selfish beast I was, locking myself in my study. But a writer was a selfish beast, or else there was no writing. And the writing life was compatible with, of course—nothing.

I heard the car in the driveway and knew it was a taxi from the sounds of its impatience, the peculiar swerve-crunch of driveway gravel, the loudness of the door slam, the hurried departure.

And here I was squirming again, as on that early day of *I'd rather you didn't call me Andy*. I took a deep breath, knowing that he'd put his head in to say goodbye, before going to his cubicle in the carriage house and working his last day head down at his computer.

I'd left my study door ajar and was facing it when it creaked open wider and a person leaned in—not Ollie, but a pretty, young woman, with dark shoulder-length hair, reddened lips, and hoop earrings. She wore a short linen jacket over her white blouse, stylish jeans, and yellow sneakers.

I was startled for a moment, then I saw my mistake.

"Ollie."

The long lustrous hair swished with the head shake, the earrings danced.

"Come in."

A graceful movement, a dance step to the sofa but not a word. Silent but smiling.

"Sit down—please call me Andy," and I struggled to my feet to welcome her, exhilarated.

GHOST FEST

Great graphics, and a catchy name," Olivia, my research assistant, said, showing me her phone, the garish invitation to the event. "Ghost Fest."

Not catchy enough, I thought. My usual reaction to such invitations was *Find another monkey*, but Olivia was young enough and keen enough as a budding writer to take pleasure in literary weekends. She added it was to be sponsored by Willard College but held at a venue in Norbury. My former lawyer, Bill Tully, was living near there. I hadn't spoken to him since before his retirement, but we could stop in to see him on the way. Still, after a lengthy absence you're never sure you're going to find the same person. And it would be helpful to see him—as I saw many things these days—with Olivia's eyes. So I agreed to Ghost Fest.

In the car, on the day we left, Olivia said, "Did you tell him I'm transgender?"

"I didn't tell him anything. And he doesn't reply to my emails."

I couldn't read her silence; she spent the hour-long trip tapping her phone, then at last she looked up, "Take the next left. A hundred and twenty feet."

At the end of the country lane, behind a tall chain-link fence (*This Property Protected by Video Surveillance*), the low one-story building was dimmed by drifting sea mist, making it seem insubstantial if not haunted. A sign beside the locked door in the chilly foyer read, ALL VISITORS MUST IDENTIFY THEM-SELVES, and near a small framed window in the steel door, an arrow pointed to a perforated metal disk resembling the cover of a plughole in an industrial sink.

"We're here to see Mr. Tully—William Tully."

"You family?" came a voice.

"Friends."

Then a face filled the window—pale, jowly, with narrow inquisitive eyes flicking from me to Olivia. I could not tell whether it was a man or woman.

A sudden buzz rattled the door. I pushed and we entered, but blocking our way was a stout middle-aged woman—of the pale jowly face—mannish but bosomy, in a gray uniform, knock-kneed the way heavy people often are, giving her an apparently unbudgeable posture. Her shirt had epaulets and was tightened over her paunch, her wide black belt holding what might have been a phone in a leather holster, though it was bulky enough to be a weapon of some sort. Her hair was drawn back tight against her scalp, exposing her prominent pink ears, veiny from being lit by an overbright light behind her. She raised a fistful of keys on a chunky chain and beckoned us forward.

"You need to sign in."

She led us to a visitors' book that lay open on a lectern. I went first, entering my name, address, phone number, my car's license plate, Tully's name under *Destination*, and the time, which was just after ten o'clock on a dark late-autumn morning.

As I turned away to allow Olivia to sign in, I saw that the woman in uniform was holding a plastic tray at the level of her belt.

"Empty your pockets, please. And what's in that paper bag?"

"A book. I wrote it, as a matter of fact."

She didn't inquire, she raised her tray, on which I placed my wallet, phone, keys, some loose change, a ticket stub, and a small notebook. She trawled through them with scrabbling fingers, and after I'd scooped them up, she called to Olivia, "Ma'am?"

Olivia tipped her handbag onto the tray, a clatter of keys, a lipstick cartridge, a pink powder puff in a foil pouch, a comb, a wallet, a yellow plastic pill container, a tangle of hair fasteners, her new phone.

I said, "Is this necessary?"

The woman didn't answer at once; she poked at the keys, she fingered the label on the pill container, and then squinted at Olivia, who smiled back at her.

"We screen for sharps."

Olivia gathered her belongings and tucked them into her bag, as the woman slipped the empty tray onto a shelf.

"I'll take you through."

What pricked my eyes and made me wince as we walked was a sourness in the air of boiled vegetables, and a hum of soapiness, too, with the unmistakable odor of human bodies—the pong of mortality. But there was no sign of food, nor of any other people. As for the odd ambient sound, I might have been imagining it in the moan of old age in my ears.

"Okay?" I said to Olivia.

"Cool," she said, still smiling. "I've never been in a place like this."

Ahead, the stout woman was unlocking a set of double doors that gave on to a long corridor at the end of which was another set of doors. Walking toward them we passed rooms, some of them with their doors open or ajar, giving us glimpses of narrow beds, and now and then shadowy people motionless in chairs, or standing slightly stooped, staring at the bare floor, in what seemed attitudes of grieving.

Past the second set of doors, the woman marched ahead and paused, folding her arms at an alcove, a plate on the door, *Tully*.

She rapped twice, calling out, "You've got visitors," and from inside came the screech of chair legs being scraped on a hard floor. As the door opened, she said, "When you're ready to leave, notify the floor superintendent and she'll escort you out."

Meanwhile Tully was gasping, a bit breathless from hurrying to the door, open-mouthed, blinking, white-faced, like a mouse surprised from sleep in a cage.

"Andy," he said. "Is that you? What a nice surprise." He glanced at Olivia, seeming bewildered, seemed to sniff, his nose upturned, swallowed whatever he was going to say to her, and then murmured, "Come right in."

"This is my research assistant, Olivia."

Tully glanced at her—her dark velvet jacket, her plaid skirt, her lustrous hair tied behind—but didn't respond. He shuffled to his bed and sat on the edge, motioning us to the two chairs—the wooden straight-backed chair he'd been sitting in, which I'd heard shoved back, and an armchair. I took the wooden one, Olivia seated herself in the armchair, crossing her legs, with her phone in her lap.

The room was warm, and close, with the same sourness of the corridor, and except for a stack of books on a table, and more on shelves, the room was bare. No mirror, no calendar, no clock. The window gave on to a thin leafless tree, its broken branches making it look like a stark hat rack.

"This is happy valley," Tully said, arms outspread, and as he spoke with gusto, I sensed a mirthful chirp from Olivia.

"They frisked us," I said. "We had to empty our pockets."

"There was an incident," Tully said, shaking his head.

"Someone got shanked?"

Olivia laughed, but Tully continued in a concerned voice, "Poor old fellow with dementia. Got hold of a jackknife somehow. You can't be too careful."

"And the forbidding fence."

"Now and then a guy tries to wander off."

"How's the food?"

"Meatloaf tonight," and seeing me smile, he added, "I love meatloaf."

This was a new Tully, uncomplaining, serene if a bit puzzled, seeming to avoid eye contact with Olivia.

"I tried to call," I said.

"I don't have a phone," he said, and then severely, this time with a glance at Olivia, who seemed to be recording him, "I don't need a phone. No young upstart law partners telling me what I know already. I have everything I want. No car—great. It's kind of a blessing. Hey, there's a TV in the lounge but why would I watch the depressing news?" He grunted. "Or listen to the awful music." He patted his bed. "Heaven."

"You're still a reader, though," I said, indicating the books.

"I see you brought me one."

I handed it over. "My new novel."

"You're still working, Andy," and for the first time, he smiled a baffled smile.

"It's not work, it's how I live, it's what I do, and I want to keep doing it. It's not that I'm a lawyer or a dentist. Think of it as my late period. In the nature of a farewell, as I've been telling Olivia."

This did not provoke him to look at her. He said, "I imagine lots of writers retire."

"The great writers never stopped writing—name one that retired."

Tully started to speak, but Olivia cleared her throat and said—her first offering, poised and sweet—"Like, didn't you say that Shakespeare retired when he was, like, in his late forties?"

"I told you that because he was unique among literary geniuses in doing so. Dickens, Tolstoy, Twain, all the greats, kept at their desk till the end. Henry James was dictating deliriously on his deathbed."

Olivia said, "Jan Morris was still writing when she was ninety-four."

"Never heard of her," Tully said.

"Transgender," Olivia said. "She had gender reassignment."

"Imagine that." Tully yawned into his hand.

But Olivia persevered and quickly found Jan Morris on her phone. "Travel books. History books. Mr. Parent once met her."

"Mr. Parent," Tully said, in Olivia's voice, and sniggered. "Retirement suits me, Andy. And here—no grass to cut. All my meals. Free laundry. Like a hotel."

I wanted to say: *I enjoy mowing for the sweetness of freshly cut grass and the wide satisfying stripes on the lawn, I like cooking, I prefer my house to any hotel.* Instead, I asked, "What's it cost here?"

Tully was hard of hearing, and when he asked me to repeat myself I realized how banal my questions were, pointless really, and hearing myself saying them I was bored and wanted to leave, and I thought how, if I'd ever found myself in a place like this, I'd escape. The guy he mentioned who braved the fence: I would be that man.

"It's expensive." He told me the amount and it seemed like a boast. "It's a lot more in the medical wing."

I didn't ask him how long he'd be there. I knew the melancholy answer.

Now he looked at Olivia, narrowing his eyes as though in resentment. He tapped his head. He said, "I've got so much in here. Years of experience as a trial lawyer, my beautiful late wife, my son, my cases." Still tapping, he added, "All here."

"That's cool," Olivia said.

But Tully didn't hear her. He said, "Experience doesn't stop just because you're retired. People come here visiting and see a lot of old folks and think of them as all done, living a kind of monotony. But even when you're old, there's drama every single day—physical changes, little accidents and big ones, a kind of suspense most of all. You remember things from long ago—great memories." He tapped his head again. "In here."

"So you don't go out at all?" I asked and had to repeat this banal question.

Tully looked grim and squirmed at the edge of the bed.

"My idiot son took me to the mall. He thought I needed some fresh air. Imagine—among insolent kids hanging out on benches. Nearly got run down by a lout on a skateboard on the way in. 'Watch out,' he says. I said, 'You watch out!' My son drags me from store to store, all selling things I don't need. I saw an old guy looking at a fancy suit. I felt sorry for him."

"Because of the suit?"

"Because he's old, he's invisible. No one helping him. Doesn't know he's lost."

"Were you tempted to buy a suit?" I asked twice.

"No one needs a suit here, or a safari jacket like yours." Making a disapproving sound, sucking his teeth. "That's another great thing. I've got plenty of clothes" He gestured to a closet, bulging with clothes on hangers, its door ajar. "They'll see me out."

That thought hung in the air, that he'd be buried in one of those suits.

Olivia cleared her throat and then spoke up. "Mr. Tully, um, can I ask you a question?"

"What's on your mind, young lady?" he said gruffly.

"Have you ever, like, seen a real ghost?" And tapped her phone—yes, she was recording him.

He hummed and from his hum and the way he stared at her I thought he was going to insult her, but at last he said, "In a place like this ghosts are very common, so the nurses say. They see them all the time, walking the corridors at night, out on the lawn—they're part of the scene here, and I guess pretty content. But outside—that man in the clothing store. He was a ghost. All those old people drifting around—seniors, you might say." Now he stared at me and nodded. "To other people they're ghosts." He turned to Olivia. "I suppose you think I'm senile like that old guy in the store."

Interrupted in peering at her phone, Olivia seemed too shocked to reply.

"He doesn't know he's invisible. That he's ghostly and superfluous. Except for Big Pharma, no one advertises to old people. We don't buy cars, we don't buy clothes." Tully frowned at Olivia, who'd resumed tapping her phone. "We don't waste money on high-tech gadgets that are no different from toys."

Tully seemed so agitated I felt I should intervene, so I made a business of snatching at my sleeve and peering closely at my watch and saying, "Look at the time. We're going to be late."

Tully slid off the bed, looking relieved that we were going. "I'll call the nurse. You need an escort," and he went to the table beside the bed and pressed a button on a plastic panel.

At the door, the escort just outside, he said, "Thanks for coming, Andy."

As Olivia began to speak, Tully raised one hand as though to repel anything she might say.

"I hate your generation," he said and shut the door.

Slumped, head bent, in that prayerful meditative posture people have when studying their phone, Olivia was silent as I drove toward Norbury. Finally I said, "Sorry Tully was so rude to you."

"Being harsh is wicked bad for your health. I feel sorry for him."

"What he said about changes—it's true. Older people lose interest in personal relationships, maybe have less empathy, and value their solitude more than ever. The news isn't news to them. I now understand my father better. Tully's become kind of an ascetic."

"Kind of a ghost." She raised her phone. "It's just ahead. Eight hundred feet."

"Norbury?"

"The Pavilion."

Norbury Pavilion, outside the town, was a high-domed structure that could have passed for a temple or a mother church of some sort, glass and steel, brightly lit, with a shelf upraised over its entrance, a marquee lettered GHOST FEST in winking lights, and under that, WELCOME WILLARDITES!

"Willard's cohosting, with Norbury Community College," Olivia said, as I parked.

Once upon a time I'd spoken about my work at Harvard and Stanford, but this rueful thought was tempered by a warm greeting in the lobby of the Norbury Pavilion, a young man and woman at a table on which tags had been neatly arranged, set out like cards in an oversize game of solitaire.

"Name?" the young woman asked, smiling at Olivia.

"Olivia Pirkle," and scanned the QR code with her phone.

"Olivia—great to see you!" The woman reached and put her finger on a tag and handed it to Olivia, saying, "That red dot indicates you're on a panel. I'm looking forward to hearing you."

Meanwhile the young man was looking past me with an inquisitive smile, so I stepped closer and said, "Andre Parent."

"Sorry, I didn't see you." He leaned over the tags, his hands wide apart and hovering, with tremulous conjuring fingers.

"No tag by that name, sir. I'll make you one."

"Andre Parent," I repeated, then spelled it slowly, as he wrote it with a Sharpie on the blank tag. Spelling my name to a stranger was always an important moment of growing clarity, like a swelling of light and warmth, as I got to the last letter, the completion of my uttering a formula, the listener's bewilderment deliquescing to recognition, and finally, *You must be the writer*.

But he said nothing and I saw his torpid smile was for the fidgeting boy behind me.

"He's the plus-one," the young woman at the table said.

"You'll need this, sir," the young man said, handing me a lanyard, and adding, as though to a child, exaggerating his gestures, "You clip it on then slip it over your head. There you go!"

On the way to the café, brooding over *He's the plus-one*, I said, "I don't get it. Wasn't I invited to speak?"

"Like I showed you, the invitation was sent to me," Olivia said. "I thought you'd be interested."

"Those people seemed to know you."

"Social media. Lots of chat."

"And you're on a panel?"

"Yes, about uncanny stories. Our theme is 'Don't Open That Door.'"

"Bit of a chestnut, actually. The forbidden door. Horrors on the other side."

"Whatever."

While Olivia circulated, talking to people who recognized her name on her tag, I stood apart, eating a sandwich, drinking coffee, reflecting that I had spent a lot of my writing life at literary events such as this. But I had not been to any for years, and this one seemed unusual for being so crowded, all the attendees very multiethnic, colorfully dressed, here a turban, there a skullcap, over there a group of women in hijabs, listening to Olivia. The glorious light from the dome glowed on each person's head, giving them a sort of halo. They were young, they were children—no, they were grandchildren. I was less a grandpa than a different species altogether, an earlier life-form, crooked and slow and balding, feeling the impulse to hide at the far side of the room where I saw tall potted plants.

When I walked through the crowd, nodding and smiling, an odd thing happened, or rather didn't happen: no one returned my nod, no one smiled back. Rather than being inconspicuous, I was invisible, slipping past them.

Seeing me hurrying away, Olivia caught up with me, a young woman by her side. Olivia said, "They had some really cool morning sessions, and there's a workshop later." Turning to the young woman, Olivia introduced me, "This is Andre Parent."

"Hi," the young woman—girl, in fact—said.

"The writer," Olivia said.

"Hi again," the young woman said, though she did not turn, keeping her fascinated eyes on Olivia, raising and fluttering her fingers, in the manner of a perfunctory farewell, and to Olivia, "Are you stoked to be on the panel?"

"Superstoked—it's after this one. 'Global Ghosts.'"

A warning bell rang soon after and we entered the auditorium, which filled quickly with excited whispering youths. When the houselights dimmed and the participants took their seats—six of them, with a moderator—the audience cheered and whistled. The panelists were a racially diverse group, three men, three woman, dressed in exotic clothes—turban, gown, hijab, though one of the young men looked like a surfer, in a T-shirt, board shorts, and sandals.

They took turns describing ghosts in their various cultures, and the common theme was that, wherever one went in the world, one would find that the dead are present—the dead do not die, but rather coexist with the living, as restless and sometimes intrusive or informative spirits: the old woman met on a jungle path who delivers a warning and it turns out she's been dead for twenty years, the cadaverous wife who turns up at the wedding of her husband and accuses him of murder—the Banquo theme; the room haunted by the ghost of the person who committed suicide there.

When it was over—great applause, whistling, waves—Olivia asked me what I thought.

I didn't say it wasn't news to me, none of it frightening. The traditional ghost story with all its tedious conventions and its inevitable and predictable payoff is either grotesquely comic or monumentally silly.

"Pretty cool," I said, and she seemed pleased.

"There's a workshop on folktales and fantasy."

"I'll sit that out and wait for your panel."

I was sorry I'd come, I wanted to be home, I longed to be at my desk, I wished to be away from this crowd, I yearned for solitude. Yet I was fascinated by Olivia and her friends, their youth, their newness, their apparent rapture in being there, their credulous attention, the way they were bathed in light from the dome. I had memories of such joy.

I found a corner of the lobby and sat. A large screen on a television set was showing news. I saw it, and the activity in the lobby, with Tully's eyes, and I was reminded of his disdain—his hatred of TV news and world events. I knew what he'd been thinking: the prospect of war, of mob violence, of bad government—we'd seen that and more, another crook, another tyrant, another catastrophe, the eternal return, and so similar you're sick of hearing about them; they're more tiresome than wicked, exhausting rather than tragic. Tully knew that outrage is a waste of time. You have so little time.

No one saw me sitting. This in itself was a revelation. I seldom got out of the house these days, except for a weekly chess game with my friend Murray Spector. I had not felt old at Tully's but I felt old here, being scarcely visible, that I have ceased to matter and it's an impertinence for me to believe that I might—and shocking to people when I spoke up, their thinking, *Who can that possibly be? Oh, yes, the plus-one.*

"There you are!" It was Olivia, her cheeks flushed with excitement and pleasure. "I'm on in ten minutes."

The panel on the theme "Do Not Open That Door" was like the earlier one, composed of six people—handsomely dressed, silks, one with a cape, a boy in a black cowboy hat, Olivia the most soberly attired of the lot in her velvet jacket and plaid skirt.

The first speaker, a robed girl, child-size, with a topknot and slender motioning hands, began to describe the forbidden door. "The hinges were rusted on the heavy wooden planks, it seemed as though sealed by time and weather. But I heard a strange mewing from within . . ."

The audience was vibrant with expectation and eagerness, an impatience to listen, but I thought not half so impatient as the old ghostly person in their midst, so near to death, half wishing to know the day, half fearing the moment of oblivion—not morbid but restless, as though wanting to get it over with, perhaps standing before such a weathered door himself and reaching to shove it open.

I was bored—disenthralled—with the tales of what was found behind the forbidden door—spooks, ghouls, bats, horrors, cobwebs. I stopped listening. Consider the old man, I thought, half wishing for a fatal accident, yearning for the end, escape-minded, flinging himself into the darkness.

Then I recognized Olivia's solemn smoky voice. I looked up and saw she was reading from the screen of her phone, her version of "Do Not Open That Door." She didn't speak much about its forbidding appearance, though she mentioned it seemed creepy. What she emphasized were all the warnings, her parents, her relatives, people she knew—hovering, intrusive—cautioning, saying that she could have anything she wanted in the magical house, but that she must not open that particular door.

"I was a frightened boy," Olivia said. "My hand trembled on the doorknob. I twisted it and quickly realized the door wasn't locked. It seemed loose, somewhat ajar. I eased it open . . ."

The audience grew silent, many of them held their hands to their face.

A shuffling of feet, a kind of vacancy and a buzz of apprehension. I admired Olivia's poise, her waiting, the way she became watchful.

"When the door swung fully open, it was not darkness that I saw, but golden light and to my surprise a woman I recognized as myself—standing there, staring at me, motioning for me to enter. I was hidden behind that door."

Olivia clasped her hands and bowed, and the audience applauded, as she smiled beautifully, acknowledging it, and took her seat, rising once more briefly, her words of thanks drowned out by the clapping.

It was new to them, it was clever of her, a nice twist on the old theme, and more personal than anyone might have guessed. I was glad for her, glad they were all young, glad they didn't know the old world, glad they didn't see me, a relic from that world, of everything they didn't know. I listened to these stories but, really, like people newly born, they did not have the slightest idea.

"You were great," I said, on the way home.

"You don't think I hammed it up?"

"Not at all. Good story—you behind the door. The scariest creatures are ourselves."

Rain had begun to crackle on the windshield, and I drove carefully, eager to be home at my desk, sipping a drink, relishing the clutter in my study, the fragments shoring up my ruins that Tully lacked, a story half-written to return to, my books, the artifacts from my travels, the framed photographs of previous lives, wives and Jack and his son, and long-lost pets and dead friends. It was the tomblike bareness of Tully's room that had appalled me. Or was it the tedium of being—old age like a form of sleepwalking, longevity like insomnia? The abiding fear that the old are not whole but rather damaged and reduced and at risk.

"No one listens," I suddenly said, woken from my reverie. I was aware that Olivia had put her phone down, that the screen had gone dark. "And old people mumble, they fall silent, we know so little of their thoughts, or we get it second- or thirdhand. They may go on writing but so few of them publish their fearful innermost thoughts past a certain age, and never near the end. You always get them secondhand."

"Maybe true."

"I've begun to think of writing as a bad habit. I'm too old to break bad habits."

"Like, you were always the great traveler. You're still traveling, in time—you're so far ahead of me—of most people. Like, in some distant country, writing about it."

"Sending dispatches back, telling people what it's like, a traveler in a little-known land, going deeper."

I expected her to pick up her phone, but she didn't, she was listening.

Just ahead, drifting sea mist reminded me of Tully's place, and thinking out loud I said, "It must be near here."

Olivia was saying, "What is?" as, peering into the mist, I saw the outline of a figure standing by the side of the road, framed by the archway of an overpass, spectral, hawk-nosed, as though summoning the will to cross. I remembered how Tully explained the severe fence by mentioning how residents sometimes slipped out and wandered away. This man looked familiar, in the cowering posture I associated with fear or grief.

"Why are you stopping?"

"That guy."

"What guy?"

The man stiffened as he saw me, bumping onto the hard shoulder of the road, drawing near him. Fearing he'd be scared if I shouted, I said softly, "Can I help you?"

He didn't reply. At first, I thought he looked like Tully—white-faced, glassy-eyed, rumpled—but when I went closer I saw that he resembled me, the same unruly hair, thick eyebrows, a similar safari jacket.

"I have a feeling you're a resident of the care home."

He seemed to shudder, as though reflecting my anxiety, being old and exposed on a road at night, cars and trucks loudly passing. But though he slowly backed away, I understood his fear. He didn't want to spend another night in that forbidding fenced-in place, the floor superintendents like prison guards. He reacted as I would have done, raising his hands to fend me off, to avoid capture. He had a home somewhere, he was escaping, as I would have done.

I reached and grasped empty air, as he twisted sideways, eluding me, determined to save himself, knowing that for his safety I'd be driving him back to the room he hated. Suddenly his face was fixed, illuminated by a flash that gave him a horror-stricken mask.

I turned to see Olivia goggling out of my car window, holding her phone. *Good*, I thought, *we can identify him*.

But the flash had spooked him; he grunted and vanished in the drifting mist, eclipsed by shadows.

"What was that all about?" Olivia asked, when I climbed behind the wheel and started away.

"Old guy, probably wandered off. Got away from me."

In the confident, correcting tone of a youngster, Olivia said, "Mr. Parent, no one was there."

"Yes. You got a picture of him."

"Of you. To light you up. I was afraid you were going to stumble."

She tapped her phone open and showed me an overbright photo of an old pop-eyed guy in a safari jacket by the roadside.

"That's him."

"That's you. Alone. You were talking to yourself."

I was sure she was wrong, but there was no point arguing with a young person on a wet road at night. Then I thought again, and in a small voice said, "I'm lost."

Olivia brightened, flourishing the glowing map on her phone. Then she scowled with terror, as I began to laugh, hideously, just as a ghost would laugh.

FINITUDE

I'd seen the sinister-looking thing the previous year, the cluttered table beyond our booth at the Luna Llena ("Comida Oaxaqueña"), like a flea market stall piled with misshapen ceramics, scattered flowers, bowls of withered fruit, obscure tokens, cookies stacked like coins, plastic toys, a scowling mask, and more, all a jumble, lit by fat candles cupping small flames. A chess game I played at the Luna on Mondays with Murray Spector was our weekly battle of wits, in which we engaged as old friends. Often during a game, the Luna's owner, Wilfredo Rocio, drew up a chair and with a lordly gesture signaled to the waitress to serve us tamales. "*Para nosotros los viejos*," he'd say, "For us oldies," since he was about our age, seeming to regard the game with sleepy eyes, but watchful in his way.

"*Mi ofrenda*," he said.

"His altar," Spector said without looking up, shrugging in his tweed jacket, elbows on the table, his gaze fixed on the board. It was one of Spector's boasts that he'd spent a winter in Oaxaca, "like D. H. Lawrence."

Gruff, fatalistic, mustached, monosyllabic, Wilfredo that year had stood round-shouldered in thought before the trinket-strewn table—altar—sometimes appearing to pray, his head bowed, a squat somewhat pear-shaped figure like a chess piece himself, muttering in oddly digestive gulps of grief.

"*Dia de los Muertos*," he said simply.

"Veneration near the chile verde, grace with guacamole," Spector offered in a whisper, but then—he'd glanced up—he checked himself, ashamed.

He'd seen among the ambiguities, the scattered trinkets and flowers, a small framed photograph of a sadly smiling woman standing on a flagstone patio, like another chess piece on a board. And that was how we learned Wilfredo's wife, Guadalupe, had recently died.

I was moved by Wilfredo's public display of unembarrassed sorrow before the altar, something valiant about it, and now I took in the rest, chocolate monkeys, marigolds, ribbons, dishes of red peppers resembling firecrackers, and the misshapen ceramics were small human skulls, near a faded snapshot of a bride and groom.

"Lupita," Wilfredo said.

Grief is holy but grief is also exhausting, for the grief-stricken and for anyone nearby, an unshareable weight. Wilfredo's tears and tragic face that year had me thinking I'd avoid it if the altar surfaced again. I sympathized with the poor man depleted by sorrow, but there's something suffocating about mourning, and, except for the photos, the altar was unreadable. The whole lugubrious yard sale installation cast a pall over the restaurant and a shadow over our chess game.

But in the year that had passed, absorbed by my determination to be on time for the weekly appointment with Spector, I'd forgotten the altar.

That chess day was important to me, because—because, you grow old, friends fall away, they diminish and disappear, they're tipped over or are swept from the board, and like any chess game there are fewer and fewer pieces in play, the endgame beckoning. The ticktock of time grows louder, and for that unstoppable sound, any routine is reassuring, giving the impression of continuity. Our weekly chess game assumed a greater importance, as something constant and immutable, not just a life extender but an almost esoteric strategy to defeat age and death. Every Monday mattered, and a game with delays seemed at times a secular form of prayer, a ritual in aid of everlastingness, if not an immortality gambit. It had taken me years, but I now understood old folks at checkerboards or card tables or conferring over coffee; their passionate punctuality, resisting intrusions, their need to gather, for warmth.

Because I'd forgotten, the following year—a year during which Wilfredo never once alluded to the death of his wife—I'd entered the Luna and seen the table, the skulls, the flowers, the photos, and only then remembered. Standing before the clutter, Wilfredo was startled in his meditations, but acknowledged me with his sleepy eyes. I couldn't leave, though I'd wanted to. I didn't find the table colorful. It was macabre, the more macabre for being improvisational and disordered, and a chaotic distraction to our chess game.

It wasn't Wilfredo's grief that disturbed me, rather something odder and unexpected this year: his passivity, his acceptance, the way in which he was standing watch, his very posture, keeping a vigil, a chess piece waiting to be pinched into action and played.

I wanted to go home. Instead, out of respect I nodded solemnly, excused myself, and crept to the booth beyond, where Spector had set up the chessboard. Wilfredo mumbled something in Spanish, not taking his eyes from Lupita's photograph.

Even without understanding what he said, what struck me was his tone of conviction, a sort of half-amused wonderment of resignation, and once again I was sorry that I had not remembered the day, the altar, the funereal atmosphere, the Luna Llena empty this Monday afternoon—airless gloom and the jumble on the table, overhung with the smell of scorched pig fat, of futility and fried tamales.

"He's doing fine, given the circumstances," Spector said in a low voice.

"Day of the Dead?"

Spector made a fish mouth of denial, then shook his head no and whispered, "His anniversary." And he leaned closer as he said, "You don't know about the anniversary effect?"

I glanced at Wilfredo before I replied—he was compact, rook-like, seeming to hum—but really I had no proper reply, except to wince in bafflement and finger a pawn.

"Anniversary effect?"

"It was a year ago exactly that he lost his wife. It kicks in on the anniversary—anxiety, depression, mood swings, grief."

"He doesn't look sad."

"That's my point, Andre," Spector murmured across the board. "He's processing it. I think he's taken a lot of comfort being with us, as fellow seniors. Some solace for losing his wife—you know she was from Argentina? He was very proud of that, her narrow escape in that terrible time. Her family was in the crosshairs, well-educated people of some standing in the community.

But it's a consolation that he seemed glad to see me today." Spector covertly extended a finger to induce me to look at Wilfredo. "Like us, he hears the drowsy buzz of old age."

It was true, Wilfredo seemed thoughtful, not bereft but composed, almost serene, as though on a key square of the board, strangely exalted, rigid with conviction. I kept my gaze on him, and as I studied him my impression faded. He seemed stunned, motionless, and again—it was his shape—as inert as a chess piece, the embodiment of patience.

Keeping his head down, Spector breathed, "Death is the ultimate inconvenience—but he's doing well, better than me."

"How so?"

"I often hear a sad song and think, hey, that's another one that would be appropriate, played at my funeral." He snorted then said, "White to move."

I nudged a pawn forward saying, "I hadn't given it much thought since last year at this time," and glanced again at the altar.

"I think of it every day," Spector said. "The hooded figure waiting in the wings." He plucked a pawn, set it down, held to it a moment, then let go. "You have only one true detestation in your life."

"And that would be?"

"Finitude. Human finitude."

I smiled at the word, and guessed he might be right, and wondered how I could use this precise word myself somehow.

"Who said, 'A train has to stop eventually. I only wish it wasn't at such a lonely station'—was it me?"

But he was talking over me, saying, "You work, then you retire, and the next event is where do you end up? Not death but just before it. Death row."

He was still speaking in a guarded whisper, glancing at Wilfredo, as I moved my knight.

"We're coasting toward it, delaying the inevitable—but, see? He's got a plan"—and he indicated Wilfredo—"a ritual. That altar's a great solace."

"Writing's my consolation. What I do these days I think of as aide-mémoires."

"You lived by your pen. Me, I never quite achieved that."

Because he craved respectability and needed security, until his retirement

Spector headed the Willard College creative writing program, a rather grand
position that provided him with a large office, a secretary, helpful grad students, and a good salary. Spector looked like a writer, with a massive head,
heavy brows, a virile nose, a sculpted beard, and even on these chess days at
the Luna, a tweed jacket, sometimes a cravat, while I wore a shapeless safari
jacket and looked like a deliveryman.

Spector's books had been well-reviewed but had modest sales, yet his salary had saved him from the sort of literary hackwork I'd accepted—book
reviews and travel assignments, and between novels, "How about five hundred words on your favorite piece of luggage?" Like many academics I knew,
accustomed to a captive audience, Spector talked too much, and worse—fatal
for any writer—he seldom listened.

Spector countered my knight with one of his own. He'd stopped glancing
at Wilfredo.

"I want to go out on a high note," he said. "I'm into a new book. I don't
know what to call it—my working title is *The Last Word*. It's much the best
thing I've done."

His need to praise himself I found a bit sad, and mentioning a work in
progress was something I superstitiously avoided doing, usually denying I was
writing anything. *Woolgathering*, I'd say, which had the merit of being half
true.

"The great thing is that I've been writing it quite apart from my duties at
Willard," Spector went on. "It's untainted by the creative writing program. A
little taste of how you've lived your writing life."

That was presumptuous—he had no idea of the drudgery I'd endured;
but I was struck by *I want to go out on a high note*—this sense that, whatever we were talking about, as old men we were never far from talking about
death. And as we spoke, Wilfredo had been keening softly in his sinuses, like
a dreamy child grieving, as he faced the framed photograph of Lupita, still
standing slightly hunched, his neck shortened, his arms to his sides, his stubby
fingers clutching empty air, in the posture of a man on a parapet contemplating a jump.

I moved a bishop and at once regretted it—another instance of Wilfredo
and his altar casting an inconvenient shadow.

"I've always been making up stories," Spector said, smiling at my blunder. "I resisted writing about my personal life. I always thought of it as spending my capital."

Odd that, a writer describing life experiences in terms of money, though I knew what he meant, and it had the ring of truth: but money had kept him confined at Willard College.

He moved another pawn, saying, "Now it's time. I'm putting everything of my life into it and when I'm done I'll have nothing left, I'll be empty. But this will be my big book."

I faced Wilfredo, while Spector kept his gaze on the board, not seeming to hear the gulps and grunts of the old gray man standing before his altar. If there was any truth in the so-called anniversary effect, I could see no evidence of it.

"Retirement is terrible," Spector said. "At best you're ignored. But you know you're superfluous. You don't matter. You're often ghosted and some-times disparaged."

"Isn't a career of having your books reviewed pretty good preparation for that?"

"You put yourself in a precarious position, Andre."

He meant my moving my bishop, nothing metaphysical.

"Not at all," he said, answering my question. "Being ignored or dispar-aged while you're alive is an indication of how you'll be treated after your death. That's shocking. You realize that your work won't matter. You won't matter. It's a grotesque foretaste of what people will say about you when you're dead."

"But you're going out on a high note."

"That's the idea. *The Last Word*, a prizewinner"—as he moved a bishop and plucked one of my pawns—"or another arresting title that will cause the browser's hand to leap to the shelf."

My turn: I protected my king with my knight, as Spector raised himself in the booth.

"*Venga!*" he called out to Wilfredo, and again, "*Venga!*"

As he said it, Wilfredo bowed his head and touched his heart, then turned away from the altar and dragged a chair over to the open end of our booth.

He sat down and sighed, not sadly but with a grunt of relief. Though he said nothing, he seemed utterly composed.

I was glad to have him near. It meant this talk of retirement and death would have to stop, in deference to his mourning. Wilfredo usually watched our games, but impassively; it was never clear to me whether he understood chess, but his stillness and his gaze seemed to indicate he took an interest, his elbows on his knees, his hands under his chin making a pedestal for his head, his mustache compressed, his thick gray hair combed straight back.

"We're talking about old age," Spector said.

"*La vejez*," Wilfredo said, scarcely moving his lips.

"Let's stick to the game, Murray."

"Of course we never voluntarily retire," Spector said, talking over me. "We face a different fate—something worse. We fall out of fashion. Our work ceases to find favor. No one cares. If we continue to write it's strictly for ourselves. We work in utter obscurity."

Wilfredo seemed to become grave as he listened, his face tightening with concern, his eyes narrowing.

"We work in the dark—we do what we can, we give what we have. Madness of art, and so forth," I said. "Now, please make your move."

But Spector was leaning across the board, with an underbite of resentful indignation. "And not a single writing student at Willard has ever read that, because Henry James is not welcome in the curriculum." Then he looked up and smiled. "Checkmate. 'Mate,' you know, means *dead*, Andre."

Wilfredo reacted to this by turning away and raising one hand, flicking his fingers, signaling to a young waitress who, a moment later, crossed the square tiles from the kitchen, tittupping on each tile, to bring a platter of snacks and a cup of tea for him. I found the waitress disturbingly lovely, queenly in her floral-embroidered blouse and stylishly ripped blue jeans.

"The young," I said. "They determine fashion. To dress up is so hopeful." I was thinking of the waitress in her gorgeous Mexican blouse, her youth, the glow she bestowed on the restaurant by moving through it, tripping from tile to tile. But also the complex fate of her being so lovely and obviously so poor, the thought of men pestering her, yet seeming so reliable here. She'd begun work sometime after Lupita died and was necessary to the running of the place, Wilfredo's mainstay. *La reina pequeña*, Wilfredo called her. The little queen.

"Most things are simple for the young," Spector said. "Because they have no memory."

"Memory can be a burden," I said. "The past is much more real to me than the present. Maybe they have an advantage, the young. Seeing things afresh."

Spector sighed and said, "I've been dealing with the young all my life."

"Teachers tell me it keeps them young."

"It kept me old. What Frenchman said 'I want to drown them all in my vomit'?"

In our next game, Spector swept a rook forward and Wilfredo frowned at the move while blowing on his cup of tea, sinking the tea leaves.

"It's their contempt, devising bizarre novelties they think will baffle us," Spector said. "It's their way of disposing of us. They resent us."

"Isn't it we who resent them, for their hopes?"

"We've a perfect right to. We take precedence."

But I was thinking, *bizarre novelties*. I'd lived long enough to know that bizarre novelties are seldom new, or even bizarre.

Meanwhile, Wilfredo had drunk most of his tea, quietly sipping. He wagged his cup, sloshing the thickened leaves—Mexican tea, *epazote* on the Luna Llena menu. He called to the young woman to refill his cup with hot water, which she did with a blackened kettle, and then Wilfredo gazed into the cup as though assessing it or else looking at his reflection.

"*La vejez*," he said with a soft smile. "*Mira*."

Adding water to the sodden tea leaves had produced a cup of weaker tea, his visual metaphor for the diluted power in growing old.

There followed one of those episodes in a chess match in which time has no meaning, an interval of suspense and shallow breathing, punctuated by a slow series of moves and long delays, advances and captures, something circular about it, and satisfying for its silences. It was a reprieve I needed, from the oppression of deathwatch, of finitude, the dread I carried with me, weighing me down. I seldom cared who won, all I hoped for was that the match would continue—would swallow the day and give me peace.

And it was a comfort that Wilfredo sat in that silence without stirring, seeming to be part of the drama of the game, his chin on his fists, or content-edly sipping his tea. For that interval resembling eternity he was one of us.

The only indication that time had passed was that dusk had fallen, the win-dows had darkened, shadows shrinking the room, and some diners had taken seats in other booths, not many, but noticeably placing themselves at a distance from Wilfredo's cluttered altar.

"A prize," Spector said at last. "I feel confident my book will win one. But what is the moment that matters?"

I was not sure this was a question for me, but in any case I said, "Winning a prize is a big deal."

"No," he said. "Not the prize. It's the acceptance speech. I think of it all the time. At this stage of my life it would represent a summing up. My book would be the occasion for it, but the speech itself would resonate."

"You're practicing the speech?"

He didn't hesitate, though he looked directly at Wilfredo, saying, "There was a word that was often used in Latin America decades ago—*desaparecer*. It was used in a special way, as a transitive verb. 'They disappeared the man,'" and he smiled at Wilfredo.

Wilfredo lifted his head from his fists. "*Desaparecieron el hombre.*"

"Exactly. Mine will start, 'The young disappear the old.'"

"*Los jóvenes desaparecen los viejos.*" But instead of smiling back, Wilfredo winced and looked saddened.

"I'll then pause and say, 'You disappear words you don't like.'"

Swallowing hard, Wilfredo said, "*Ustedes desaparacen las palabras que no les gustan.*"

"You disappear many books."

"*Ustedes desaparecen muchos libros.*"

"You often disappear the truth."

"*Ustedes con frecuencia desaparacen la verdad.*"

Wilfredo was engrossed but had stiffened with fear, like a child submitting to a bleak lesson, and he'd lost the serenity he seemed to have when he'd stood, head bowed at his altar, or earlier in our chess match, contentedly watching the back-and-forth of our combat, capture and evasion. He gripped his knees, waiting for more, as Spector paused in his acceptance speech.

It was a strange conceit, Spector's dream of going out on a high note, accepting the prize for his book, then taking the floor and seizing everyone's attention by delivering a lengthy address, not of thanks but of denunciation, an old man's rant, having the last word before leaving the stage and—as he was describing now—slamming the door behind him.

But in his peroration, he'd lost his grasp of the match and the stalemate I'd managed, which I now exploited with panache.

"*Final de ajedrez*," Wilfredo said, getting up from his chair, rising with conviction.

"Endgame," Spector said. "That's my title! The word *ajedrez* is from Arabic, of course."

But Wilfredo had quietly stepped away, unhesitating, shuffling slantwise across the tiled floor, from square to square, to the kitchen door and vanishing behind it.

And then, Spector, having exhausted himself with his thumping acceptance speech, sat with me in silence, as we continued the cat-and-mouse routine of the endgame, each of us hoping for the other to blunder. This, too, was like a way of extending the game, thwarting each other's moves, dodging, retreating, shuttling, procrastinating, the repetition producing a sort of anxiety filled with self-delusion, in a feeble attempt to avoid the inevitable that was still indistinct at the vanishing point.

I remembered that spell of movement and futility, the way it seemed suddenly, as I played my last knight, to provoke a sudden clatter and crash from the kitchen, the young woman in the Mexican blouse bursting from the door, not pretty anymore, her face ugly with fear, clawing her hair and shrieking.

"*Venga! Venga! Venga!*"

Note

The story "The Vanishing Point" appeared on *The New Yorker* website; "*Dietrologia*" was published in *The New Yorker*; "Navigational Hazard" in the collection *Conradology*; "Stop & Shop" in the anthology *It Occurs to Me That I Am America*; "Hawaii Sugar" in *Subtropics*; "Love Doll" in the collection *Anonymous Sex*; "Adobo" in *The New Abject*; and "Camp Echo" on the Scribd website.

"Father X" appeared in the collection *Tales from a Master's Notebook*, edited by the Henry James scholar Philip Horne, and was based on an idea that James sketched in one of his notebooks, as follows:

"*Jan. 28th 1900.* Note at leisure the subject of the parson & *bought* sermon situation suggested to me by something mentioned by A.C.B. My notion of the unfrocked, disgraced cleric, living in a hole &c, & writing, for an agent, sermons that the latter sells, type-written, & for which there is a demand."